# DAUGHTER
# FROM THE
# DARK

ALSO BY MARINA AND SERGEY DYACHENKO

*Vita Nostra*

# DAUGHTER FROM THE DARK

*A Novel*

## MARINA AND SERGEY DYACHENKO

*Translated by Julia Meitov Hersey*

HARPER Voyager

*An Imprint of HarperCollins Publishers*

DAUGHTER FROM THE DARK. Copyright © 2020 by Sergey Dyachenko and Marina Shyrshova-Dyachenko. Translation © 2020 by Julia Meitov Hersey. All rights reserved. Printed in the United States of America. No part of this book may be used or reproduced in any manner whatsoever without written permission except in the case of brief quotations embodied in critical articles and reviews. For information, address Harper-Collins Publishers, 195 Broadway, New York, NY 10007.

HarperCollins books may be purchased for educational, business, or sales promotional use. For information, please email the Special Markets Department at SPsales@harpercollins.com.

Harper Voyager and design are trademarks of HarperCollins Publishers LLC.

FIRST EDITION

Designed by Paula Russell Szafranski

Library of Congress Cataloging-in-Publication Data has been applied for.

ISBN 978-0-06-291621-1

20 21 22 23 24   LSC   10 9 8 7 6 5 4 3 2 1

# CONTENTS

# PART I

# SUNDAY

A shard of glass crunched under his heel.

The streetlights had been out in the entire district, so Aspirin walked home in the company of stars.

He could have picked a long and reasonably safe route along the main street, but Aspirin was a strapping young man and had no fear of nocturnal thugs. And while the shortcut led him through foul-smelling alleys, Aspirin had developed a rather philosophical attitude toward the environment. In a matter of minutes the heavy iron door of his building would shut behind him, and all this would be closed out. Vasya the concierge knew that on Sundays Aspirin came back around one thirty—not three or four in the morning as usual—and there was even a chance Vasya would open the door for him.

Aspirin switched on a pocket flashlight before turning into a dark walkway; almost immediately he saw the girl and froze on the spot.

At first he thought the girl was drawn on the wall, so still and two-dimensional she appeared on the background of red, black, and blue graffiti. As soon as his flashlight fell on her face, though, she shut her eyes, put a hand up as a shield from the beam, and clutched her toy closer to her chest.

"What are you doing here?" Aspirin asked on impulse.

He moved his flashlight from side to side. The walkway was empty. He turned back to the girl and shifted the light away from her face and onto her arms that clutched the yet-unseen plush creature.

"What are you doing here?" he repeated, this time with more conviction.

The girl said nothing.

About ten years old, she certainly did not look like a tramp or a beggar, or an unhappy child forgotten by her drunken parents. She didn't even seem scared. The way she held her toy showed reserve rather than fear. Yet that was perhaps even stranger, because self-assured young girls standing in darkened alleys after midnight wasn't what most people would consider normal.

Aspirin definitely didn't think it was normal.

"Did you have a fight with your folks?" he suggested, immediately feeling like a complete idiot, although he couldn't place why. But as the girl remained silent, he felt that was certainly adding to his disquiet.

"Are you just going to stand here like this?" Aspirin was growing more annoyed by the minute. "Waiting for the boogeyman to come and stick a knife into your heart? Where are your parents?"

The girl looked surprised at that. It was unclear what had sparked her interest—the perspective of meeting a boogeyman, or Aspirin's interest in her lineage. At least he had her attention.

"Fine, let's go," Aspirin said, stifling his impulse to smack the girl upside the head. "Let's go—I'll take you to the police station, let them deal with you and your folks. Idiots, can't watch their own kids."

Aspirin was afraid the girl would start crying, shifting the situation from ridiculous to critical. If that did happen, though, it would only be for a few moments, because in reality he was planning to hand the child to his concierge and be done with it. Vasya was a kind man who occupied his free time with finding homes for stray puppies and kittens; last winter he'd even found an arrangement for some street waif. He would be the perfect person to call the police.

The girl watched Aspirin with clear, intent—and perfectly *adult*—eyes.

"Are you frightened?" she asked finally.

"*Me?*"

He was initially incredulous, but at that very moment he realized the girl was right. He was frightened—perhaps of the responsibility that fell on him from out of nowhere, perhaps of something else. It may have been the girl's shadow over the ugly graffiti.

"What are you doing here all alone?" he asked, his voice a touch calmer.

"I am not alone. I am here with Mishutka." She finally loosened her grip and Aspirin saw a light brown teddy bear with plastic eyes.

"Well, if you are with Mishutka, that's a totally different matter," Aspirin allowed. "Where do you live?"

The girl shrugged.

"Children should not be out on the street at such a late hour." The little girl looked at him skeptically, and he didn't blame her. Even to himself, Aspirin sounded like an old bore. "It's too dangerous."

"Yes," the girl agreed. "He's looking for me. He came for me."

"Who?"

The girl did not respond.

Aspirin quickly scrolled through a few possible scenarios. Parents in a fight, possibly divorced. Or the mother is an alcoholic, and the father got custody. Not a common situation, but it was a possibility. In any case, the father came for her, and she didn't want to go with him. The usual scenario. Domestic squabbles. Preteen issues.

The reasons didn't concern him.

"All right," he said firmly. "Either you come with me, or . . . you can stay here. So, what'll it be?"

The girl watched him silently, her eyes round and blue, like those of a child on a greeting card.

"I am going," Aspirin said with relief. "Family problems are not my forte."

He pointed his flashlight onto the cracked pavement and moved toward the street. Stars glimmered above his head. *How wonderful that I don't have children*, Aspirin thought, looking up at the clear summer sky. *How wonderful that I didn't marry Lucy back then*, he thought, turning into a courtyard. *How wonderful that I—*

His reverie was cut short. A group of teenagers, drunk or high—or both—sat underneath a dying linden tree in the corner of a playground. Of course it was a playground, a perfect place for them to congregate.

He actually wasn't sure they were high. He wasn't even sure they were teenagers. It was hard to see in the dark, hard to count the glowing ends of their cigarettes, hard to ask for their IDs.

It wasn't hard to know he wanted nothing to do with them.

"Hey, you! Come here!"

It was a young voice, but insistent. It sounded like it was used to getting what it wanted, despite having nothing to back up that bravado. Aspirin moved his flashlight over the group. About half a dozen kids, one girl. And what's worse, one pit bull.

"Drop your flashlight, shithead!"

Aspirin heard a low growl.

He switched off the flashlight and stepped back into the street. Couldn't they just leave him alone?

No such luck. He was destined to be accosted by the young this evening.

"Come here! Better for you if you do!"

"What do you need, children?" Aspirin inquired in a business-like tone. "I am DJ Aspirin."

The group sniggered. Either these kids didn't believe him, or they never listened to the radio.

"Aspirin, Oxycontin—got a light?" the only girl in the group asked cheerfully.

He took a few steps back, watching the dog. One of his buddies had a dog like that. That dog once bit off his owner's finger.

"Keep your dog on the leash," he suggested coolly.

They laughed, the girl louder than the rest. Such an unpleasant combination, Aspirin thought, that broad and her dog.

"Abel, get 'im! Get his balls!"

That was all he needed to hear.

Aspirin turned and ran. *A stick, please, a metal bar, an iron one, or a shiv. There's not enough time to find a brick, it's too dark . . .*

And as he sprinted away, he cursed the fact that the pepper spray he normally kept in his bag was now safely tucked away in the trunk of his car back in the garage.

A streetlight came to life by the entrance to the courtyard. Its dim glow was just enough for Aspirin to avoid crashing into a trash barrel. He sidestepped at the last moment and glanced back to see the pit bull that resembled a pale stuffed sausage fly across the courtyard, followed by eight legs stomping, eight arms flapping in the air, four mouths shrieking something unintelligible . . .

Only now did Aspirin think of the girl who was likely to still be standing there, in that very archway, clutching her teddy bear to her chest.

He picked up a broken brick and threw it at the dog, almost hitting it. The animal slowed down, but only for a brief moment.

"What are you doing, you asshole?" the broad screamed. "Abel, get him!"

*Wasn't he already trying to get me?*

Aspirin dived into a concrete archway illuminated by the streetlight. Despite Aspirin's hopes, the girl had not run away; she pressed herself against the wall, listening to the screaming, stomping, and growling.

Aspirin grabbed her hand and dragged her out of the courtyard. Considering that even without such ballast Aspirin ran more slowly than a short-legged dog, it was probably a mistake.

The archway ended. The girl pulled her hand out of Aspirin's, turned around, and tossed her teddy bear back into the archway, toward the shadows dancing on the walls.

He cursed, thinking she'd ask him to go back for the bear, but instead she just stood there, waiting. He was going to ask her what her problem was when he heard the scream—nothing like the wild, raucous yells of teens having a lark. No, this was a shriek, a wail.

It sounded like the kind of scream that ripped apart someone's vocal cords.

A second later he saw an enormous shadow growing on the concrete wall over the graffiti.

The dog groaned. There was a sound of flesh slapping the wall—a horrible, viscous noise—and then everything was quiet except for the sound of stomping feet, which died down in the distance.

Lights came on in the windows of the neighboring buildings.

"We're leaving," Aspirin said, not thinking clearly, led solely by instinct.

"One minute," the girl said, "I need to get Mishutka."

"We don't have time—"

But she had already entered the archway, picked something off the pavement, patted it clean, and pressed it against her chest. Aspirin glanced over her head: the immediate courtyard was empty. However, in the opposite far corner of the courtyard, the dead body of the pit bull lay on the ground.

At least, one half.

"Let's go," the girl said.

"Yes . . . let's. Um. Go."

He grabbed her hand and pulled her away, trying to stay in the shadows and avoid the eyes of the sleepy residents, whose heads were now popping up in the windows and balconies all over the street.

"Weird night tonight," Vasya the concierge said when they got to his building. "Did you hear all these dogs barking like crazy? I heard someone shriek—scary stuff. Any trouble on your way home?"

"No trouble," Aspirin lied. "But I met this—this kid here."

The girl watched the concierge with polite interest.

"In the middle of the night?" Vasya marveled. "Were you all by yourself?"

"I was with Mishutka," the girl clarified.

"Ah," the man said, humoring the little girl.

Aspirin didn't see how anything was funny about it.

The elevator arrived. Luckily, Aspirin caught a glimpse of Vasya's face through the narrow gap in the shutting doors; he stepped forward, preventing the doors from closing.

"The child is lost," he explained to Vasya. "Tomorrow morning I will call the police—need to find her parents. But I couldn't leave her on the street, could I? Not with wild dogs and whatnot."

The concierge's eyes softened. "Yeah. These . . . these people leaving kids all over the place. If it were up to me, I'd execute people like that in the public square."

Being reminded of executions in the streets, Aspirin took a deep breath, stepped back, and pressed 5. The girl said nothing; she simply gazed up at him, stroking her bear's head.

The elevator made a grinding sound and stopped at the fifth floor. Aspirin had to take a few more deep breaths before his hands stopped shaking and the jumping key found its way into the keyhole.

"Come in."

The lights switched on. The girl just stood in the middle of a spacious entrance hall, squinting—just like back in the courtyard. Aspirin shuddered.

Without taking off his shoes, he went to the kitchen, opened a drawer, and found a bottle of brandy. He poured a splash into a teacup and downed it. If he felt any better, the effect was marginal.

The girl remained standing in the middle of the hallway, but now her shoes were off. Aspirin was surprised by her perfectly clean socks, new, white with narrow red stripes.

"What is your name?" he asked, breaking the silence.

She gave him a reproachful look. "What is yours?"

"As—" he started, but then bit his tongue because "Aspirin" was not exactly an appropriate introduction. From what he'd gleaned of her attitude, he was pretty sure she wouldn't be impressed by his alter ego. "I'm Alexey." He walked over to the hall closet, rummaged around, and pulled out something. "Here, put these on."

She stuffed her feet into a pair of women's slippers, about five sizes bigger than her own.

"Are you hungry?" he asked coolly and nearly howled from frustration with this situation. It was just so unnatural, so false—all this nonsense: slippers, kitchen, pelmeni, tea . . .

Where the hell did this girl come from?

And what was he supposed to do with her?

"I am not hungry, but Mishutka is," the girl said solemnly. "Do you have any honey?"

"I guess . . ." The request—to feed her stuffed animal—seemed the most normal thing this little girl had done all night.

In the kitchen she sat on a stool, put her bear on the edge of the table, and folded her hands in her lap. Mishutka sat leaning to the side, staring ahead with button eyes, plush paws limp by his sides.

A shard of glass protruded from one of the paws.

Shuddering inside, Aspirin removed the glass with a napkin and tossed it into the trash.

"Mishutka says thank you very much. So how about that honey?" the girl asked.

"One moment. Should I put it into a saucer, or can he eat out of the jar?"

"Either way," the girl said.

"Buckwheat, linden, or wildflower?" Aspirin inquired.

The girl glanced at her toy.

"Flower would be best. But it's not crucial."

"Of course," he said hoarsely. "And does he need a spoon?"

The girl smirked. "Where did you see bears eating with a spoon? In cartoons?"

"Mmm," Aspirin said noncommittally. He placed a jar of flower honey in front of the bear, struggling with the tight lid. Finally getting it open, he stepped over to the sink, crossed his arms over his chest, and stared, as if expecting the button eyes to blink, and the bear to reach for the jar with its overstuffed paw, scooping out honey and aiming it at the mouth embroidered on the plush face . . .

The toy remained still. Because of course it did. Aspirin needed to get some sleep.

The girl took the bear's paw, sniffing and wrinkling her nose in delight. "Mishutka likes it a lot. Thank you."

"You're welcome," Aspirin sighed. "And now that he's eaten . . ."

"What do you mean 'now that he's eaten'? He's barely started."

Aspirin looked at his watch. It was half past two. By the time they ran from the scene of the crime, by the time they made it home by back alleys, by the time Aspirin figured out what to do . . .

"Do you have a home phone number?" he asked without much hope.

"No," the girl said, pretending to scoop out the honey with the bear's paw, smacking her lips with pretend pleasure.

"Are you planning on returning home?"

The girl picked up a napkin and wiped the bear's face clean. She had short pink nails and clean untanned arms. Her freshly washed T-shirt was adorned with two flying dragons and the words KRAKOW. LEARNING TO FLY.

"Have you ever been to Krakow?"

She didn't respond.

Aspirin poured himself more brandy. His hands had almost ceased shaking.

"What was it, exactly?" he asked, staring at the girl's striped socks.

"Where?"

"There, in the alley. What exactly happened last night?"

The girl sighed.

"He came for me. And I don't want to go with him."

"Who is he? Your father?"

"No, he's not my father."

"A stepfather?"

"It's just Him."

"'Him'? Him who?"

The girl sighed again. It was unnerving seeing a young girl so exasperated. Especially one who was also so calm after the night's events. Aspirin rubbed his palms together nervously.

"Who killed the dog?"

Without hesitation, the girl nodded in the direction of the toy bear. Aspirin thought of the pale pit bull torn in half.

"Actually," the girl said thoughtfully, "they killed it. A while ago. When it chased you, it was already dead."

That made no sense. None of this made sense. The dog looked like it had been blown apart. "But there was no explosion," Aspirin mused. "Maybe . . . maybe they had something like . . . something fell in the dog's path and blew up." But again, he hadn't heard anything.

Nothing but that incredible shriek.

"A mouse ran by and flicked its tail," the girl said without a smile. "The egg fell down and exploded. Are you sleepy?"

More nonsense. And yet, it made the conversation seem more natural—as if they were talking about numerous different things at each other, and not with each other—and so he responded in kind. "I was just on air for six hours, telling jokes and other nonsense," Aspirin admitted. "I talked to some idiots who called the station. I put on stupid songs they requested. Then a bunch of underage delinquents set their pit bull on me. And that pit bull goes ahead and dies. And not just dies, it explodes. So maybe I'm tired. Maybe I'm just going crazy."

"Don't worry about it," the girl said, her tone just a touch patronizing. "You can have another drink and go to bed."

"And when I wake up, you won't be here," Aspirin suggested dreamingly, already reaching for the brandy.

"Don't count on it," the girl said and hugged her teddy.

# MONDAY

**M**iracles don't exist, so when Aspirin limped into the kitchen at nine in the morning, the girl was sitting on a stool in front of a perfectly clean table, legs crossed, staring out the window and humming softly to herself. Aspirin's passport lay opened on a metal tray in front of her.

"What the . . . ?"

Incensed, Aspirin swore as no one should swear in front of children; he immediately felt guilty . . . and that angered him further.

The girl turned to face him. Her brown teddy bear sat in her lap, or rather between her crossed legs, watching Aspirin with its button eyes. An empty honey jar stood on the floor by the chair leg.

*No wonder the girl is up, going through my things,* he thought. *She's hopped up on all that sugar.*

"So you're Grimalsky, Alexey Igorevich, and you are thirty-four years old," the girl said in the voice of a public prosecutor.

"Listen," Aspirin managed through gritted teeth. "Take your bear and go. I don't want you here, and I don't want to see you ever again. I am counting to ten."

"Or what?" the girl inquired. "What happens at 'ten'?"

"That's what I get for trying to be a good Samaritan," Aspirin murmured bitterly. "For letting a lost child spend the night."

His legs and back ached after last night's chase. His mouth felt dry and gross. A miniature hammer banged slowly and triumphantly in his right temple, either from the situation, the brandy from last night, or a combination of the two.

"Or," he said, passing his guest, picking up his passport, and feeling marginally more confident, "or I will call the police."

"And what are you going to tell them about me spending the night at your apartment?"

Aspirin finally allowed his mushy knees to buckle, lowering himself onto a stool. The girl watched him with interest.

"What do you mean?"

"I'm just curious—what does a grown man say to the police about letting little girls stay with him overnight?"

God . . .

"Listen," Aspirin said thickly. "I don't know who taught you this filth, but—there is such a thing as forensic evidence, medical expertise, you know? I don't want any of this, but . . . everyone will know that you are nothing but a dirty little blackmailing shit, do you understand?"

The girl moved her bear from her lap to the table and folded his paws in a more relaxed manner.

"Then it's true," she said indifferently.

"What?" Aspirin tried not to shout, though he wasn't quite sure why he had such restraint at the moment.

"He said . . . he always tells the truth." The girl looked pensive, her blond eyebrows forming an unfinished sign for eternity.

"Listen, my dear," he said with disgust, "why don't you get the hell out of here. Otherwise, I promise not to conduct a single good deed in my entire life. I won't even share a can of tuna with a hungry kitten."

"Oh, I am terrified—you are soooo scary. As they say, don't try to scare a porcupine with a naked ass, right?" she smirked. "You make it sound as if you're the king of good deeds. A bona fide Santa Claus."

Aspirin got up. He wanted to grab the little bitch by her ponytail and drag her over to the door and beyond. Instead, he waited a second—then burst out laughing.

Really, this was utterly comical. He was arguing with a preteen. Why would he need to worry about what an underage delinquent says?

Still giggling, he went back to his room and picked up his phone.

**"I don't get it,"** Victor Somov, nicknamed Whiskas, asked Aspirin. "You brought an underage girl into your apartment?"

"She's just a kid. I thought—"

"You brought her into your *apartment*?" Whiskas repeated.

"Well, yeah, kind of."

A pause.

"I don't get it," Whiskas said again. "What for?"

"I wasn't myself," Aspirin admitted. "She was by herself after midnight. And then there was this pit bull coming at us, and then . . ."

He stopped, not sure how to tell the rational Whiskas about the irrational terror that overtook him in that courtyard.

"Were you sober?" Whiskas asked.

"Yes—I drove home. I don't drink when I am behind the wheel."

"Good for you," Whiskas commended him with mock sincerity. "Did you enter your home alarm code in front of the girl?"

"I didn't set the alarm yesterday."

"Why?"

"I don't know. I forgot."

"Pure genius," Whiskas said, his voice full of wonder at the idiots born on this earth. "Aspirin, one of these days I am going to send a couple of thugs over just to teach you a lesson."

"Please don't," Aspirin said, then cocked an ear—in the living room the nasty child had opened the piano and was now hitting random keys. "Listen. I think she's crazy."

"Not as crazy as you," Whiskas assured him testily. "See if there is anything missing in your apartment. I'll be there in twenty minutes."

"Sounds good," Aspirin said with relief.

In the living room the girl continued to press random piano keys like someone who'd never seen a piano before. Aspirin glanced at his watch wondering whether twenty minutes was enough time for the strange little creature to destroy the instrument. He hoped Whiskas would hurry.

Victor Somov managed the security detail at the nightclub Kuklabuck where Aspirin lit up the crowd on Tuesdays and Fridays. Victor had once helped Aspirin out of a sticky situation that involved the accidentally crushed bumper of a fancy car. Whiskas was considered an intellectual—he forced every bouncer on his team to read Murakami—but that was not what Aspirin valued the most about him. Victor Somov was a good friend because he was the perfect listener. He was attentive and a little slow, with an air of deliberateness that felt like attentiveness. He also had an aura of confidence and serenity, and that was exactly what Aspirin usually needed after his long, stress-filled days.

Or crazy, dog-and-girl-and-bear-filled nights.

Enlisting a professional to help with a child was overkill. Aspirin was showing weakness, and he knew it; he felt awkward now about calling Somov. But he also had no choice. If the girl refused to leave on her own, he would have to—what, grab her arms? Shoulders? Grab her by the throat or hair? He would have to seize her and drag her out, and she would most certainly scream, and the neighbors would hear her screaming and then he'd probably be screaming his way to prison. And that wasn't in his plans. No, in a few years Aspirin was going to make some decent dough, buy a house in the country, erect a tall fence, and get a dog. Just not a pit bull. A German shepherd. He would live without a telephone, without a television set; a stereo and a laptop would be enough.

And he wasn't going to let an act of charity turn his dream into a nightmare.

He listened again: a melody replaced the erratic sounds in the next room. An uninitiated listener would think that the girl continued to press random keys, but Aspirin heard a ragged, unschooled, strangely captivating song emerging from the instrument. A few measures—stop—repeated now, with more conviction.

A new measure . . .

He peeked into the living room. The girl stood in front of the instrument, finding the melody by ear, but not in the usual way of children trying to pick out a song. She didn't hit the keys with one finger; instead, she passed her left hand over the octaves, while the right barely touched the keys, like a blind person reading Braille.

Her teddy bear sat on the piano between an antique clock and a china doll Aspirin had brought from Germany, seemingly watching her and keeping a glass eye on him at the same time.

"Right," the girl murmured to herself. She placed both hands on the keys now. Her left hand played a chord, the right hand led a melody, and for a second Aspirin felt dizzy. He saw his future, and it was so serene and so joyful, as if he were a schoolboy at the start of an endless vacation. He took a step toward the piano, about to embrace and kiss this marvelous girl who came to teach him how to live his life for real, without depression and fear, without small upsets, without Mishutkas, to live and listen to music, to live and rejoice in living. He placed his hands on her shoulders and at that moment the china doll, securely attached to its stand, stepped forward, lost its balance, and toppled over onto the keys.

The melody died. Shards of porcelain lay on the carpet. Aspirin jerked his hands back; the doll's head, curly-haired and indifferent, lay between E and F of the second octave.

"It wasn't me," the girl said with a guilty look. "I didn't do it."

Aspirin rubbed his temples. He still felt a little dizzy.

"No . . . it's okay," he said, but he wasn't sure if anything was ever going to be okay. "Do you know how to play?"

"Well, no," the girl admitted. "I just try to pick the right notes . . . and the keys are in order, so it's not that difficult."

He tried to work his mind around that, but things were still a bit blurry after the song. "What were you playing?"

The girl crouched down and started collecting the shards of porcelain. He saw the back of her neck under the blond ponytail, her spine, and her scrawny shoulder blades.

"It's his song," the girl said, addressing the floor. "If it's played correctly, it leads you away forever. But you can only play it properly on his pipe. Or maybe if you get a big orchestra . . . maybe. If you gather virtuosi from the entire world, a few thousand of them, then maybe you can make it work. Maybe." She looked up at him. "Do you get it?"

She stood up. The remains of the doll lay in her hands.

"I am sorry," she said, looking into Aspirin's eyes. "Have I upset you?"

"Goes in the trash," Aspirin said, still not sure what he was being told.

Obediently, she went to the kitchen, and he heard the shards of porcelain hit the bottom of the empty trash pail. She came back holding the doll's blue dress gently with the tips of her fingers.

"May I have it?"

"You may," Aspirin said. "Who are you?"

"You should have asked me right away." The girl gave him a shy smile.

"What do you mean?"

"Well, I kept waiting for you to ask who I was, and in the meantime you figured I was a beggar, a gold digger, or something worse."

Aspirin plopped down on the sofa and crossed his legs.

"But I did ask you your name."

"But a name isn't who someone is, right?"

He didn't know how to respond to that. After a beat, he asked again, "Who are you?"

"I—"

She opened her mouth as if about to recite a memorized, well-prepared lesson—then suddenly she paused and stopped smiling.

"What is that?" she asked nervously.

"Where?"

"That sound."

A mere second earlier the neighbors upstairs had switched on their audio system, heavy bass making the walls vibrate.

"Neighbors," he said, shrugging. "They are music lovers . . . of a sort."

"Are they deaf?" the girl asked after a pause.

"They love their bass." She was distracting him with these inter-ruptions. "Tell me where you ran away from."

"I didn't exactly run away," the girl said, scrunching her eye-brows again. "I just left."

"Escaped from a music school in a prison facility?"

"No," she said, scornfully. "From this . . . from a very nice place."

"A very nice place?"

"Yes. I'd like to return there someday."

"Return now!"

The girl sighed. "I can't. Mishutka and I have something impor-tant to do."

She picked up her teddy bear and pressed her cheek to the short, light brown fur. A horrifying moment later, Aspirin realized she was crying.

"What's wrong?"

"It's scary here," the girl said. "Back there, last night—I was so scared."

"That's not surprising," Aspirin said, though he didn't remem-ber her seeming all that scared in the alley. After a pause, he added, "Me too. But we are doing just fine now, aren't we?"

"No." The girl shook her head, still hiding her face behind the bear. "We're not fine. You're afraid of me."

"Nonsense." Aspirin came over and crouched down next to her, quelling the terror from seeping into his voice or through his eyes. "Hey. Don't cry. Do you want a cup of tea? I have cookies."

She nodded, still not looking at him. Aspirin went to the kitchen and filled a teakettle with fresh water. If nothing else, he would feel much better if his unwanted guest had enough to eat and drink be-fore she left.

At least no one will accuse me of being a bad host.

They waited in silence until the teakettle purred, growled, and switched off with a loud click. Aspirin took out a box of tea bags and put one in each mug, filling the mugs with the boiling water. He put a plate of stale cookies in the middle of the table.

"What about Mishutka?" The girl's voice was weak from crying.

After a moment of hesitation, Aspirin reached for the third cup. The girl placed the bear at the table. Aspirin sighed and filled the bear's mug with hot water and a tea bag.

"Actually," he said, moving the sugar bowl closer to the girl, "I am not afraid of you. Why in the world would I be afraid of you? Drink your tea. I just got angry when you took my passport." He was almost convincing himself of what he was saying.

"It was on the table in the hallway."

Now Aspirin remembered having to bring his passport to the post office and then tossing it on the hallway table. Which meant she hadn't been rooting around in his apartment. Still . . .

"This is not a good reason," he said firmly. "You cannot just pick up someone else's documents, especially a stranger's, in their apartment . . ."

"I needed to know who you were."

Aspirin shook his head at her naiveté. "I told you my name. What exactly have you learned from looking at my passport that I didn't already tell you? My age? Why would that matter?"

The girl hung her head.

"Don't take it personally, but there are rules, after all," Aspirin said, enjoying his small victory. "You must have parents . . . or some guardians or something. And you must live with them—those are the rules. So where are they?"

"My guardians are very, very far away." The girl smiled. It was a strange smile, more fitting for a wrinkly, experienced old woman. It made Aspirin wary for some reason.

"Where is that?"

The girl touched the paper tag and lifted the wet brown tea bag above the amber liquid in her mug.

"Wow."

She dipped it into the mug and pulled it out again.

"You've never had tea from a tea bag, have you?" Aspirin asked softly. "What sort of boondocks are you from?"

"Alexey." The girl's eyelashes stuck together like icicles. "Don't kick me out."

Aspirin almost choked on his tea. Although it was exactly what he wanted to do, it galled him to have her voice it aloud. Spluttering, he exclaimed, "I am not kicking you out! Finish your tea in peace. Have a cookie. But we don't live in a forest, for god's sake. You must have some sort of identification. A passport of your own. Or a birth certificate. And . . . I have to leave—a business trip!" He made that up on the fly and became very enthusiastic. "Yes. I must be leaving shortly for a business trip. And it's a long one. My train leaves in one hour. So you see, I'm not kicking you out. But you can't stay here. We both belong in other places, you know?"

As he spoke, though, the girl seemed to have suddenly lost interest. She was staring at a toy silver bell, a simple knickknack sitting on one of the kitchen shelves.

"What is that?" she asked. And without asking for permission, she reached for the bell and picked it up.

"Put it down," Aspirin said and frowned. "Haven't you been taught to ask first? It doesn't belong to you. Come on!"

The girl didn't put it down, though. Rather, she shook the bell. A sound flew around the kitchen, weak but clear.

"The note A," the girl said.

And immediately the doorbell rang, squawking like a deranged chicken.

"Here we go." Aspirin got up, any guilt for getting rid of the girl fading once more. "This guy is here to help you."

Walking to the door, he had a fleeting idea of giving her the bell. Especially if it got her to leave sooner. He opened the door.

"Hello," Whiskas said, stepping over the threshold.

"Hello." Aspirin tried not to fidget. "Want a cup of tea?"

"A cup of tea? Seriously?" Whiskas gave him a suspicious, side-long glance. "Let's deal with your problem first."

They entered the kitchen as the girl poured her tea into the saucer to cool it, her sharp elbow up in the air.

Whiskas stopped abruptly, making Aspirin collide with him.

"A tea party?" Whiskas inquired.

"She was hungry," Aspirin mumbled apologetically.

"Not at all," the girl said softly. "We are just having a cup of tea. With Mishutka."

21

She petted the bear, nearly making the toy's heavy head dip into the scalding liquid.

Whiskas looked at Aspirin. Aspirin looked away, his expression signaling yes, he was an idiot, and he knew it.

"What is your name?" Whiskas asked the girl.

She hunched over the saucer; a single blond hair fell from behind her ear and snaked along the surface of the tea.

"What is her name?" Whiskas addressed Aspirin. Aspirin shrugged. "What, haven't you learned her name?"

"I haven't had a chance."

Whiskas looked incredulous. "Not enough time?"

"Not quite . . ." Not sure how to answer, Aspirin picked a cookie from the platter and devoured it with abandon.

"All right, finish your tea," Whiskas said to the girl. "We're going to the juvie."

"Where?"

"If you don't tell me immediately who your parents are and where you live, I will take you to the juvenile detention center, and you will have to speak to the specialists." Whiskas smiled unpleasantly as he said this.

"I don't live here," the girl said softly.

"Toto, I've a feeling we're not in Kansas anymore," Whiskas said in a high, reedy voice. "Then you will be sent home. If you have any money. Come on, bottoms up."

"If you need money for a ticket, I can give you money," Aspirin offered. Whiskas groaned and glanced at him without a hint of respect.

"What the hell is wrong with you? She'll happily leech off you, and all you need right now is someone pestering you."

"I won't," the girl said, even more softly. "I don't need anything from him. I just want him to admit he's my father."

Aspirin choked on his cookie and bent over in a violent fit of coughing.

Whiskas straddled a chair. For a while he watched the girl sip her tea. Eventually his eyes moved toward Aspirin. Aspirin still couldn't talk—the cookie stuck in his throat.

No one tried to help him.

"What was that again?" Whiskas said, eyes steady on the girl's face.

"I am his daughter." The girl sat up proudly. "He and my mom— they broke up. I wasn't born yet. Ask him—he remembers Luba from Pervomaysk, he must remember her . . ."

"What Luba?" Aspirin coughed out, finally regaining the gift of speech. "What do you mean, Pervomaysk?"

"Luba Kalchenko. You vacationed together in Crimea."

"Crimea? Victor, this is a nightmare, she's lying, it's all lies . . ." Whiskas's professionally steely eyes grew colder.

"Alexey Igorevich." The girl's voice sounded thin and pitiful. "I don't need anything from you. We are going to make it. Mom has disability benefits, because of that hazardous industry job she had, and she has diabetes. And Grandma has her pension . . . I don't need any money! I just wanted to come and see . . ."

"Victor, she's lying," Aspirin said, laughing nervously. "It's simply ludicrous. A real circus, that's what this is."

But it was clear his friend wasn't buying the girl's words anyway. Whiskas's wide face twisted in disgust.

"Anyone can come and claim whatever they want," he informed the girl through gritted teeth. "Maybe you are my daughter. Or the pope's."

Tears rolled down the girl's face. She reached for her back pocket, pulled out a small black-and-white photo, and slapped it down on the table like a trump card. Whiskas and Aspirin bent over the photo in unison. At one time glossy, but now frayed and faded, the snapshot showed a couple embracing. The woman's face was clearly seen in the image; she was a brunette of about twenty, not quite beautiful, but pleasant-looking. The man's face was blurry—he must have turned his head when the camera clicked. The sea frothed in the background.

"That's him," the girl said, licking a huge tear from the corner of her mouth.

"It's completely impossible to tell who that is!" Aspirin yelled. "Plus," he said a tad less aggressively, "people hug each other all the time. That's not proof."

Whiskas studied the photo. His steely eyes bore no expression whatsoever.

"What do you want from me?" Aspirin took a step back to the window. "Money? How much can I give you to make you leave?"

"I don't want any money," the girl said firmly.

"Alexey," Whiskas rose. "May I speak with you for a moment?"

"What—"

"*Now.*"

Aspirin followed him into the hallway, confused when it seemed like they were just about to make headway with the girl.

"What the hell?" Whiskas inquired.

"What do you mean, 'What the hell?' She's lying," Aspirin whispered. "I swear. There was no Luba from Pervomaysk. I'm not sure I even know where that is, let alone gone there."

"As if you would remember them all," Whiskas murmured. "How did she get into your apartment?"

"I told you—I brought her in."

"Well, if you brought her in, you can take her out," Whiskas said, turning to leave. "Your family problems are your own responsibility. See you."

Before Aspirin could even protest, the door was shutting behind him.

"What the *hell*," he said.

In the kitchen the silver bell rang—the note A, as the girl pointed out.

Aspirin shuffled into the living room and stretched out on the sofa.

How had he managed to get himself into this idiotic situation?

His mother always said that one's personality defines one's fate. All it takes is to show a sign of weakness once; all sorts of disasters flow into that crack. All his life Aspirin would avoid old women begging on the street; he simply excluded them from his line of vision. Perfectly undisturbed, Aspirin would eat his lunch in full view of a hungry runaway. So why now? How could this happen to him after decades of casual disregard? How did he manage to bring someone else's child into his home, his fortress, which no strangers were ever allowed to enter?

And what did he do when his friend took the word of this random little girl over his?

He had asked Victor for help, but—somehow—it had made things worse. Because Victor didn't believe him, and now he was stuck with this child. Somebody else's child. Insolent. Ill-mannered. Hungry. Dirty. Well, clean at this point, but that was temporary.

Aspirin lay for a few minutes, then got up. A boil must be lacerated while it's fresh, as unpleasant as it might be—he knew that much. The problem must be solved without delay. And he, Alexey Igorevich Grimalsky, was perfectly capable of taking care of himself.

Especially when there was no one else he could ask for help.

He went back to the kitchen. The girl sat on the same chair, cuddling her teddy bear and staring out of the window. Aspirin took a closer look and realized that the blurry young man in the photo had nothing in common with Aspirin himself—whatever familiar features brought out by Whiskas's probing eyes had been nothing but an illusion, a hypnosis perhaps, or—who knows—it was quite possible that the confident voice of that little witch brought out a false sense of guilt in Aspirin.

"It's not that bad, you know," the girl said, still staring out of the window.

"Let's go," Aspirin said, taking her elbow. He felt her thin arm, so warm, so smooth, tense slightly under his fingers.

"I am staying here." She turned her head, but remained seated. "There is a law. If you spend the first night under someone's roof, that's where you stay. We are connected now. And neither you nor I can break that connection."

What nonsense. "We'll see about that." He pulled her by the arm, about to jerk her up and drag her into the hallway. And then he let go because a deep, throaty snarl filled the kitchen. Aspirin's fingers slackened before he remembered where he'd heard that sound before.

"Quiet, sh-hhhh." The girl hugged the toy closer to her chest, caressing its fur. "Do not be afraid, Mishutka. It's going to be all right."

Aspirin backed away, convinced the girl was mad—and that he was going quite mad himself. He watched them for a few minutes, then picked up the bottle of brandy from the shelf and an unfinished cup of tea from the table, and retired to the living room.

**A clap of thunder woke him up.**

In his dream he heard snarling, piercing shrieks of people being torn in half, saw shadows dancing on a dirty wall covered with graffiti . . .

He woke up and knew it was nothing but a thunderstorm. Outside the air was gray and rain battered the glass; the curtain stayed still—someone had thoughtfully shut the window. A lamp glowed softly.

Aspirin lay on the sofa, heavy and doughy, like a dying jellyfish. A tray was placed on the coffee table. Aspirin smelled food and sat up.

Steam rose from a thick chicken cutlet. Three fat slices of tomato stared back at him. A large mug was filled with coffee.

"Eat," a disembodied voice said from the darkness. "You skipped breakfast."

"What time is it?" Aspirin asked hoarsely.

"Almost five."

"How long was I asleep for?"

There was no answer. Aspirin sat up, wincing. An empty bottle of brandy leaned timidly against the side of the sofa.

He picked up the knife and fork. The chicken cutlet was tender, with just the right amount of salt and pepper, crispy on the outside and perfectly lovely.

"I see you're a fully baked housewife," he said chewing with gusto. "Can you sew? How about knitting? How old are you?"

His questions were met with silence. The girl sat on the floor, legs crossed, Mishutka pressed against her chest.

"And what is your name, by the way?" He thought about something else. "And where did you get the chicken? I know I didn't have any in the refrigerator."

26

"You didn't have any vegetables either," the girl said. "Or pota-toes. I bought it. At the market near the subway."

"Right," Aspirin said and reached for the coffee. "Did you also stop to pick up a roofie, by any chance?"

"Stop to pick up a roofie," the girl repeated, as if fully appreci-ating the scope of his joke. "Why would I bother? You slept all day without any help. Is that your way of avoiding problems?"

Aspirin swallowed the insult along with a huge gulp of coffee. It must be noted that Aspirin's favorite beverage was beyond all compliments—Aspirin definitely couldn't make coffee as excellent as this.

Lightning flashed, followed by a bark of thunder, and spooked automobiles howled in different voices. Aspirin put the mug back on the tray.

"And what else have you been doing?"

"I read. I found all sorts of magazines here."

Aspirin looked down and saw two issues of *Macho* and three issues of *Lolly-Lady,* pages spread widely and most indecently. Had she really been looking at those pictures?

"Doctor Aspirin—that's your byline, isn't it?" the girl asked sol-emnly.

Aspirin groaned—this was much worse than he thought. He switched positions and fluffed the pillow under his head.

"I figured it out," the girl said sunnily. "'One hundred recipes for healthy intercourse.' 'How to meet a blonde.' 'How to break up with a blonde without heartache.'"

He groaned again. "Who sent you?"

"No one. I came on my own. You found me, remember? But . . . I need you."

"Why?"

"I can't do anything by myself. I don't know anything. I am scared of everything."

"I noticed," Aspirin murmured through gritted teeth.

"It's true," the girl sighed. "I have no one. Except for Mishutka."

The girl approached, and Aspirin flinched, thinking she was

bringing the bear closer to him, but she just picked up the tray with the dirty dishes and moved toward the kitchen.

"Hold on!" Aspirin yelled to her back. "What is your name, anyway?"

Another clap of thunder followed a flash of lightning that illuminated the dark room: a Japanese calendar on the wall, book spines on the shelves, and the girl's pale face.

"Alyona," she said gingerly, like someone who had just come up with a name and was not sure it actually fit.

"Liar," Aspirin said.

The girl shrugged and walked out of the room.

Aspirin shook his head. The hallucination continues, then, he thought. Gusts of wind made the windowpanes tremble. In the kitchen the dishes clinked delicately.

How could he have fallen asleep? He just dropped everything and got himself wasted. She could have brought people into his apartment—her masters, or whoever sent her here.

"Hey," Aspirin yelled hoarsely, hoping to be heard in the kitchen. "Where did you get the keys?"

"In the pocket of your jacket," the girl answered serenely. "In the hallway."

He rose, fighting off nausea.

"And now where are my keys?"

"Same place. I put them back."

The sound of running water, the sound of a fork dropped into the metal sink.

"For your information," Aspirin said, "I am changing the locks—tomorrow. Both of them. And the alarm will be on, and you don't know the code. And the money? Where did you get the money?"

"Forty-five."

"'Forty-five' what?"

"Your code is forty-five. You left it punched in, and never put it back to zeroes. And the money—I took it from your jacket and put the change back in your pocket. But since it was to buy you food, it's not really stealing, is it?"

The logic was irrefutable—and infuriating.

The sound of running water stopped. Aspirin forced himself off the couch and went into the kitchen. The girl stood in front of an empty, sparkling sink, drying her hands with a towel.

"A different concierge was on duty today—her name is Sveta," she said. "I told her I was your daughter from Pervomaysk. She looked very surprised."

"I have no doubt." Aspirin's voice was low and hard. "And now you're going to leave."

"Where? In the rain? In the thunderstorm? Don't be silly."

"Don't call me silly! Stop condescending to me! *I'm* the adult here, and I don't care if there is a monsoon outside: you're still going."

Alyona smiled. "You have a nice large apartment. Some people stay in communal apartments all their lives, four people per room. Yet you're too greedy to let an orphaned child stay with you. Even though you live alone and have plenty of space."

"Who took you in last night? Gave you a place to stay? Who protected you from those thugs and their dog?"

"Mishutka protected me," she said, almost as if she was confused by the question.

"That's it. I am calling the police." Aspirin turned to leave.

"Go ahead, call them," Alyona said to his back, her voice icy. "It will be interesting when they come. I will tell them you made me walk around naked. And that you made me stand in different poses. And you wouldn't feed me unless I complied. And also—"

He slapped her face, so hard that the little bitch flew off, slamming her back into the sink. It had been gutting, hearing her words. Hearing how easily those accusations could be thrown out, and knowing how easily they would work against him. Victor hadn't believed him; the police wouldn't believe him. No longer able to comprehend words—his or hers or anyone's—and no longer seeing anything with clarity, Aspirin ran into the bathroom and turned the hot water to the maximum, trying to wash off the feeling of her face on the palm of his hand.

He wondered if he could get it hot enough to wash her completely out of his life.

To wash off the stain that was spreading on his soul.

Hands red and raw, he turned off the faucet. With the noise of rushing water and faulty plumbing no longer filling his ears, silence was everywhere. Not a single sound came from the kitchen. Outside, the rain banged on the metal awnings. Aspirin grabbed a towel from the hook.

"You . . . you deserved it," he said, knowing it was a lie. Knowing that more lies were coming. "And if you don't leave this minute, there is plenty more where that came from!"

He reached the kitchen, and the girl remained in the same spot. Large drops of blood from her nose fell onto the T-shirt with the inscription KRAKOW. LEARNING TO FLY, followed by nearly invisible tears.

*And that's how they catch us idiots*, Aspirin mused. *They sit in subway stations holding their babies. They send over innocent-looking little girls, and you, allegedly so damn clever, find yourself to be a complete and utter and* despicable *moron . . .*

Another thunderclap forced the cars parked outside to shriek in unison.

"What do you want from me?" Aspirin barked, trying to replace all his various emotions with a single one—extreme anger. "A daughter of mine, are you? From Luba in Pervomaysk? How dare you! You're an evil, nasty bitch! Get the hell out of my apartment!"

"Fine." The girl's voice was hoarse from crying. "If *you* say so. I am going to tell Sveta that you got drunk, beat me up, and kicked me out. Maybe she'll let me sleep in her room tonight."

The floor swayed under Aspirin's feet. For a few seconds he watched her pale blood-and-tear-stained face, and then he went into the bedroom and picked up his phone.

Could he call someone? But whom? What would he say?

The apartment was dark, as if it were very late at night. Just as Aspirin gathered enough courage to call the police, yet another clash of thunder was followed by the doorbell.

Did Whiskas decide to come back?

And of course, Alyona was in the kitchen, crying, her nose bleeding onto her shirt . . .

What if this wasn't Whiskas, but the girl's owners, the ones who'd sent her over?

Aspirin darted to the door and pushed the dead bolt into place. Even if they had a drill, or a copy of his keys, or a welding tool—he'd have time to dial the police and reach for the gun. Let them come.

The doorbell rang again. Aspirin stood on tiptoes rummaging on the top shelf of the closet. Where was it? Here it was, the dusty handle of his gun . . . Aspirin hadn't touched it in a long time, had never had a chance to practice. Not to mention he was kind of scared—the gun *was* illegal, a compulsive purchase . . .

Or not so compulsive after all?

"Don't open it," the girl said to Aspirin's back. He suddenly realized that the girl stood right behind him, watching his fumbling around for the weapon, which meant she could easily tell the cops at the first opportunity:

"Mister policeman, sir, he's hiding a gun in his closet!"

He jerked his hand away and wiped it on his pants. The girl was obviously street-smart—she must have figured it out by now.

"Mister policeman, look at the top shelf!"

Those words, unspoken, scared the hell out of him.

The doorbell rang for the third time, and this time it was long and insistent. *What happened to me in the last twenty-four hours?* Aspirin wondered. *I have totally lost it. Maybe it is a postman. Or Sveta the concierge. What is it about this girl that makes me so dumb in her presence? Instead of digging myself out of this situation, I keep burying myself further and further.*

He lifted the steel tongue covering the spyhole and immediately imagined himself staring into the barrel of a gun. He blinked; he saw the distorted corridor and the figure of a man standing in front of his door. At least the spyhole was not covered from the outside, and the lightbulb was not removed—that much was good.

The man at his door was a stranger, though. That was about all Aspirin could determine.

"Who is it?" Aspirin said, trying to sound like someone who was bothered for no reason whatsoever.

"I am here for your guest," the man said. "Are you sick of her yet?"

Aspirin looked behind him.

**"Don't open the door!" The girl stood by the kitchen door, clutching** her teddy bear to her chest, looking up at Aspirin. She was not scared of dark corners, or street gangs, or Whiskas with his threats, and she definitely was not afraid of Aspirin.

Now, though, her blue eyes brimmed with terror.

"I am here to pick up Alyona," the man said from behind the door. "She's being completely ridiculous, and I apologize for her behavior."

"Don't open the door." The girl hunched over by the kitchen door. "It's *him*. He found me."

That's it, Aspirin thought with grim relief. Whoever this visitor was, whatever sort of relationship he had with the girl—this adventure has finally come to its end, and tomorrow I will convince myself that this Alyona had never even happened.

He pushed the dead bolt aside.

"Alexey," the girl said thickly, "please don't open the door. Not just for my sake. Please—he can't come in unless you ask him to."

Aspirin undid the top lock. He was worried that the girl would cling to him, weeping and begging, but she remained, still, by the kitchen door; gradually, she bent farther and farther down, as if in pain.

*Could it be a trick?* he wondered. *They could be in cahoots. They could be lying in wait until I opened the door.*

"Who are you?" he asked in the most authoritative voice he could muster.

"You want to see my passport?" the man chuckled.

"Sure," Aspirin said. "I want to know who you are, who are you in relation to this girl, and why you haven't been watching your child. Are you her father?"

"Alexey Igorevich, do you really care about that?"

Aspirin took another look through the spyhole. The man grinned at him.

"Don't open the door," Alyona whispered, sliding down the door frame. "Please."

She looked terrible, blood-covered nose and lips on a pale face, dark circles under her eyes, panic-filled gaze. No one could be that good at pretending.

"How do you know me?" Aspirin asked. "Never mind—it does not matter. The girl does not want to come with you. I am calling the police."

"Aren't you tired of your own nonsense?" the man asked, sounding weary himself. "If you thought it would help, you would have called them a long time ago."

He was right, and Aspirin felt guilty.

*I am the man of my own house,* he said to himself and stood up straighter. *Why the hell should I feel guilty, scared, embarrassed, or whatever else I am feeling right now? I am a man, and I have rights. My neighbors are on this floor, the concierge is right downstairs, and the police are just a call away.*

But he was sure he wasn't about to involve any of them, and the frustration boiled over.

"What are you so worried about?" he barked at the girl. "If you don't want to go with him, you don't have to. Just tell me who he is."

She shook her head.

"So are we going to continue chatting through the closed door?" the man asked.

Aspirin ground his teeth and unlocked the bottom lock. He opened the door—jerked it open, really, in an attempt to demonstrate his complete and utter lack of fear.

The man stood by the door. If he was impressed by Aspirin's display, he didn't show it. He was tall, taller than Aspirin, and was clad in a gray hand-knit sweater and camouflage pants. A second later, when the guest stepped over the threshold, Aspirin saw that he was not wearing shoes. His narrow bare feet left wet prints on the tile.

"Peace to this home," the guest said casually, looking around and pretending not to notice either Aspirin or the girl crouching on the floor.

In support of his greeting, another sharp, loud crack of thunder followed another bright flash outside. Aspirin flinched.

His guest turned his head, finally acknowledging Aspirin's existence. *Federal Security Service,* Aspirin thought. *Or some sort of mafia dude.* The uninvited guest had eyes of greenish-blue, cold, indifferent and yet piercing. Nineteenth-century vivisectionists must have had eyes like his. *I am not giving him the girl,* Aspirin thought, and his abdominal muscles contracted involuntarily. *I would rather give her to the police, or leave her at the train station to fend for herself. But I am not letting him take her.* Having made the decision, Aspirin suddenly realized that the pool of excrement he'd been swimming in for the past day was rising way over his head.

Meanwhile, his guest gazed at the girl. Alyona sat on the floor, and her glassy eyes resembled the guest's own stare. *They* are *related,* Aspirin realized. *Good God almighty.*

Alyona spoke. Staring into the face of the barefoot stranger, she spoke in a harsh, fierce voice full of threat. Aspirin did not understand a single word. Moreover, he could have sworn he'd never heard this language before in his life.

Yet whatever she said was clear to their guest; the man listened. Aspirin observed him some more, and was surprised to see the man's sweater looked perfectly dry, while his camouflage pants were wet up to the knee, and his feet were clean and wet, as if he'd driven right up to Aspirin's door with his legs resting in a basin of water.

The girl spoke louder. When she started shouting, the guest snapped at her in the same language. She took a deep breath and continued speaking, now in a softer, calmer voice, her lips a thin line.

They are not Gypsies, Aspirin mused. Not Arabs, either. Central Asia? No way . . . but what was that language? Who are they? More important, what are they doing in my apartment?

"Just a minute," he began, but no one paid him any attention. The girl went on speaking, burning the stranger with her eyes, or rather, freezing him on the spot, because her eyes now looked like two icicles. The guest listened. Aspirin felt the hallway growing cold, as if a very powerful air conditioner had suddenly switched on—sixty-four degrees . . . sixty-two . . . sixty . . .

The stranger then said something curt and imperative. He took a step forward, clearly intending to grab the collar of the girl's dirty T-shirt. The girl recoiled and looked at Aspirin. He looked back at her.

"Hold on," Aspirin said (by then the temperature in the apartment had plunged down to just above freezing). "You have yet to explain to me who you are to her, and where you are taking her. And I haven't seen your passport. And . . ."

His guest turned to face him, and the yet unsaid words froze in Aspirin's throat.

"He beat you up," the stranger said.

"He brought me here! I spent the night here!"

"He made a mistake." The stranger continued to stare at Aspirin, and Aspirin felt a strong desire to turn into a cockroach and hide under the molding. "Wouldn't you say you made a mistake, Alexey Igorevich?"

"I . . ." Aspirin managed.

The girl spoke again in the same language. The guest took his eyes off Aspirin (much relieved, Aspirin took a step back into the dark living room) and moved closer to the mirror. Aspirin thought he saw ice crystals forming on the surface of the mirror.

The guest adjusted a cord on his neck—a red and yellow cord under his collar. An outline of an elongated object larger than a cell phone was noticeable under his sweater.

"Turn on the light, Alexey Igorevich."

"What?"

"I said, turn on the light in the living room. Since we're going to have a talk after all."

The light was switched on. A crumpled throw, an empty bottle of brandy, and random magazines and CDs strewn on the floor came into view, and Aspirin cringed at the state of his apartment, only to be upset—it wasn't like I invited these guests!—only to then feel fear once more.

The antique clock made one last sound and stopped. Its pendulum slowed down, the shorter amplitude coming as no surprise to Aspirin.

"May I sit down on the sofa?" the barefoot guest said with a smirk, already moving toward the couch. He clearly never bothered to ask for permission. Aspirin made a feeble attempt to fold the throw, but the guest took control by tossing the plaid fabric into the corner of the sofa. He sat down, crossing his legs.

The girl did not come into the living room, but instead lowered herself on the floor by the door.

"Did she really spend the night here?"

"What are you trying to say?" Aspirin scowled.

"I am trying to say that the morning came, and the girl was still here, under this roof. Nothing else was implied, so don't look at me like that. Alexey Igorevich, why did you do this?"

"What exactly have I done?"

"Why would you bring someone else's child into your house in the middle of the night?"

"Because there were druggies out there!" Aspirin snapped. "And alcos! And all sorts of hoodlums! Is that not clear to you?"

"It is not clear to me," the stranger confirmed ruefully.

Aspirin noticed that the stranger spoke without a trace of an accent. Just like Alyona.

"Helping a child is a normal human reaction," he said, cringing inside and wondering if the blood had dried on her shirt.

The stranger sighed, pursed his lips, then asked something of the girl. She responded curtly, almost rudely.

"My dear friend." The stranger moved his bare foot, glancing first at Aspirin, then at Alyona in the corner. "Do you realize how many children are shaking in the freezing rain just about now? Some of them are beaten up. Or raped. Does that bother you at all?"

"Of course it does! But why does it matter—who are you to moralize and preach to me?" Aspirin desperately wanted to reach for the blanket. Or at least to wrap his arms around himself—the room was freezing cold now. However, he restrained himself, unwilling to show his weakness. "I didn't invite you here tonight. Either you tell me who you are and then take the girl, or . . ."

"Don't let him take me!" Alyona shouted.

"Or?" the stranger asked curiously.

"Or just leave," Aspirin finished softly.

Deep in thought, the guest reached for the empty bottle with his bare foot. For one crazy second, Aspirin expected him to use his toes to unscrew the top; instead, the stranger pushed the bottle over like a bowling pin.

"This is getting rather complicated," the stranger said. "Fine, I will tell you. I am the director of an orphanage, and this little brat ran away from us without any warning. And now I have come to bring her back. Do you have any questions?"

"I have many, but they are irrelevant—you're lying," Aspirin said. "You are not a director of an orphanage."

"Then who am I?"

*I would love to know that,* Aspirin thought.

"Grimalsky, you don't care about her," the stranger said. "Where I would take her, whether it would be good or bad for her . . . she would never bother you or make you do things you do not want to do. Doesn't that sound good?"

Aspirin said nothing.

"Weren't you going to kick her out just before I showed up? Hmm?"

"I will deal with her myself," Aspirin said softly. "Wherever I am going to take her, whether it would be good or bad for her . . ."

"He said it!" The girl jumped. "Did you hear that?"

Another clap of thunder outside.

"Grimalsky, you are so screwed," the man on the sofa said sadly. "I really wanted to help you, but even good intentions in your execution end up in . . . ahem. Here, take this." He reached inside his shirt and pulled out a leather cord with a document holder and an elongated leather case attached. He took out a laminated stamped document and dropped it on the sofa.

"Birth certificate of Grimalsky, Alyona Alexeyevna, born in 1995, mother—Kalchenko, Luba, father—Grimalsky, Alexey. I am not offering you money, since you're well off, and Alyona is a modest, unspoiled little girl."

"How . . ." Aspirin exhaled.

His guest rose from the sofa, putting away the document holder along with the leather case.

"It's simple, Alexey Igorevich. I gave you an out, but you refused. So you are very, very much in it now. And so good-bye, hopefully, for a while."

"This is a fake!" Aspirin flung himself to the sofa and grabbed the document. The names and dates were not written in longhand, like on Aspirin's own birth certificate, but typed on what appeared to be a defective typewriter. Only the signature of the head of the Office of Vital Records was in longhand. In his opinion it was such a poor forgery, Aspirin had to laugh.

"This is a fake. It's ridiculous."

"It's not ridiculous." His guest stopped in front of the opened piano, with the head of a porcelain doll still resting on the keys. "Because the document is real—at least, it matches the appropriate entry in the Registry of Vital Records of the town of Pervomaysk."

"I haven't . . ." Aspirin choked with indignation. "I have never been to Pervomaysk."

"You certainly have been to Crimea. With Luba."

"It's a lie! It's a trick! I have not . . ." Aspirin turned his head in search of the girl, but she'd already left the room. "I don't want her—take her! Get out of here, both of you!"

"I am certainly leaving," his guest said, placing his hands on the keys. A chord hung in the air. Aspirin flinched. The guest's fingers, long and tan, with white knuckles, flew over the keys, and Aspirin stopped speaking because those random sounds made his skin crawl.

"I did warn you," his guest said softly. "She's not exactly God's gift to mankind. However, if you ever upset the newly born Alyona Alexeyevna . . . 'Tis a vile thing to die, my gracious lord.'"

He touched the keys again. Another chord. The antique clock's pendulum twitched and moved faster than usual, as if trying to show off its efforts.

"You can't leave her here!" Aspirin shouted. "Do you understand? I am going to leave this apartment to a . . . children's fund! In my will! You can't have it!"

"Shut up," the barefoot man said tiredly, stepping away from the piano, out the door, and into the hallway.

The girl stood with her back to the mirror, still deathly pale, still wearing the blood-spattered T-shirt. Her lips moved, but Aspirin could not understand the words.

"Yes," the barefoot man said. "Here you go."

Again he reached under his shirt and took out a small clear package. He gave it to the girl. A long pause hung in the air. Aspirin saw a set of strings through the plastic. He saw that the girl wanted the strings, but was for some reason afraid of approaching the man and taking the package out of his hand.

The barefoot man opened his hand. The package slowly (or so it seemed to Aspirin) floated onto the tiled floor.

"See you later, kid," the barefoot man said. "Have fun crashing your dreams."

He left, closing the door behind him; the temperature inside the apartment went up a few degrees.

Even if it hadn't, Aspirin was sure he'd be sweating anyway.

"I had to wash everything," Alyona said. "My T-shirt . . . and my pants. I hung them up to dry—do you mind?"

She stood in front of Aspirin, wrapped in a white towel, looking a lot younger than her real age.

"That's fine," Aspirin said with no particular interest. He sat on the floor sorting out his CDs. The stereo system waited patiently, its empty tongue at the ready.

"I can sleep in the chair, like last night," Alyona mumbled.

"There is no need for that," Aspirin said just as indifferently. "Go ahead, choose the best bed in the house. It's all yours, no need to be shy." He waved his hand around the room. "The apartment is yours. Well, rather, it belongs to your masters. You will probably be sent to your next assignment soon."

"You didn't understand anything at all," Alyona whispered.

He looked at her. The girl wrapped the towel tighter around her body.

"I am a little hungry," she said softly. "May I take some bread and butter? There is some in the kitchen, I bought it today."

"Alyona." Aspirin dropped the CDs and reached for the girl; he almost touched her shoulder, but at the last minute stopped himself. "Let's play nice."

"I'd like that," she said and smiled, as if she had been waiting for those words.

"I am sorry I hit you," Aspirin managed.

"No worries." The girl nodded. "I understand. You were frightened."

"*Frightened?*"

"You are scared all the time. But it's understandable. It's pretty terrible here. Even Mishutka can feel it—he seems so sad all the time. May I take a little honey for him?"

"You may," Aspirin said neutrally. "Tell me something, Alyona . . . They must have really scared you. No wonder you're practically shaking at the mere sight of that."

"Please don't talk about him," Alyona asked softly. "Not now."

"Then you are scared."

"I am," the girl admitted sadly.

"What sort of an organization do they have? A cult?" Aspirin asked with a great deal of caution. "Hypnosis, perhaps? Demon worshippers?"

Alyona curled up in an easy chair, covering her knees with a towel, looking like a little terry cloth snow pile.

"Are you afraid of demons?" she asked staring into Aspirin's eyes.

"What is there to fear?" Aspirin giggled. "It's people I am afraid of. Like your buddy there."

"He's not human."

"Is he a demon?" Aspirin giggled again. "And you spoke with him in demon language?"

Silently, the girl studied her left hand with a hangnail on the index finger.

"Do you have manicure scissors?"

"In the bathroom," Aspirin responded automatically. "Just admit it, you and he are in cahoots, aren't you? You've played a nice trick on me, haven't you? He wouldn't have taken you anyway, right?"

The girl climbed off the chair and turned toward the bathroom, the end of the towel trailing after her.

"He would have taken me," she said without looking at Aspirin. "You are a coward and a traitor—without a doubt. But you helped me once again.

"And that matters."

The bathroom door locked behind her.

# TUESDAY

And so, my darlings, Tuesday morning is a Tuesday morning, and it is always quite sad, because here we are facing a new working day, but there is a tiny little circumstance that should comfort both you and me—and the said circumstance is that it is not a Monday morning, hence we're one baby step closer to our Holy Grail, also known as the weekend . . ."

This sort of rubbish came out of him naturally; he was quite capable of producing this string of words in his sleep or under anesthesia. One of his buddies once pointed out—not without a hint of envy—that Aspirin's verbal ejaculation had nothing to do with the higher function of his nervous system, but was rather a purely physiological act, like sneezing or defecation, and the joy it brought his listeners was of a purely physiological nature.

That buddy of his wasn't entirely wrong.

"And here we have our first caller on the line. Let's see—who do we have here? Inna is on the line, hello, Inna. Are you home or at work? You're home? See here, Inna, the entire country is envious of you, because the rest of the country is at work at this moment. We're going to play a game, you know the rules, but let me remind the rest of our listeners—I am going to think of a word, and Inna has to figure out which word I am thinking about. Inna, you have one minute, you can ask me questions, and I will answer. And—go."

Today was Tuesday, and he was supposed to be at Kuklabuck at eight in the evening. Aspirin hadn't expected to get any rest the night before, but by half past midnight he was gone—and didn't wake up until six in the morning.

Alyona was asleep in the chair when he left his bedroom, wrapped in the towel, the chestnut brown teddy bear with the plastic eyes pressed against her chest. A small T-shirt, jeans, striped socks, and white panties were drying on the radiator. Aspirin stood in the bathroom for a long time, staring at the clothes, trying to understand what to do, where to run, and whom to call.

At eight in the morning he was live on the air. Half an hour before that he managed to get hold of Whiskas.

"You should have told me the truth from the start." Whiskas did not hide his annoyance. "What the hell was all this nonsense about some random girl, and you picking her up out of pity?"

"She's not my daughter! I am telling you—I was set up. Her documents are fake. They speak some sort of weird language. Albanian, or something like that. They are going to murder me, and because of her they will inherit my apartment!"

"That's paranoia," Whiskas snorted into the phone. "You are not exactly feeble, you are a public figure of sorts, so why would they want to take a risk like that?"

"When you see my cold body in the morgue . . ."

"Take your Prozac and let me sleep. I worked all night, you know."

Whiskas hung up.

Aspirin wasn't feeling all that well, so he decided not to drive and instead called a cab; he had twenty minutes before the start of his show. The girl in the towel woke up and raised her head.

"I am leaving," Aspirin said. "Get dressed and get out of here. I am not leaving you alone in the apartment."

"Where should I go?" she asked, still not quite awake.

"I don't care where you go. To the playground. All children need fresh air. Quickly, my cab is waiting."

"Can I come with you?" The girl was already in the bathroom, which he would have given her credit for, if he was feeling generous.

He wasn't.

"No. I am going to work."

"My jeans are still wet."

"They will dry on you. Or go without pants, your choice."

"May I please stay?"

"No."

"May I sit in your office? I will be very quiet."

"I said no!" Aspirin barked. "You will sit outside!"

The girl came out of the bathroom. The dark spots weren't completely gone from her T-shirt—on a closer look, one could trace where the blood had dripped from her nose. Aspirin winced.

"Move it."

He pushed her out of the apartment and emitted a mental sigh of relief—here was a hint of progress. The girl was out of his home and her questionable birth certificate was in Aspirin's bag. That left very little in terms of possible pressure on him. Almost none.

"Wait! I forgot Mishutka."

"He can wait." Aspirin pushed the elevator button.

Twelve minutes remained until the live broadcast. The car was waiting by the entrance.

"Sit here." He pushed the girl toward the bench.

"May I please come with you?" she asked once more.

"You may not."

He slammed the car door. The cabbie drove confidently, passing on the right, crossing the solid line—Aspirin would never be brave enough to drive like that. At the studio he was met with reproach, but he ignored it; he slammed the soundproof door, slipped into his place in front of the microphone, pulled on headphones, and began, "And good morning to you, my darlings! DJ Aspirin is with you this morning, and that means that your boring hours at the office, in front of the monitor, behind the wheel, behind the desk, or any other place you consider your working space just became a little bit less gray, a little more colorful because with you, right here, right now, is *Radio Sweetheart*! *Radio Sweetheart* reaches out with its soft paw, touches your ears, and here you are—at the top of the hour, our next artist assures you that everything will be just peachy."

He turned off his mic and received a stream of invectives from his producer. He asked for a cup of coffee. To the producer he said, unnecessarily, "Oh, Julia, if you only knew what happened to me."

To Julia's rather logical inquiry about what exactly happened, he only sighed heavily and said nothing.

Some time had passed. Pop music played. Young'uns called and asked for more pop music. Aspirin ate sandwiches, drank coffee, and thought about pop music taking over, even the young people, and that tonight Kuklabuck was hosting an interesting band that was riding the hip-hop wave and doing it well. Those guys had recorded two videos, but had no chance of making it on television, because pop music had taken over . . . and his thoughts went around and around like this.

By the end of the fourth hour, he'd forgotten about the girl and about his own problems. He no longer thought of anything at all. Words poured out of him like sweetened water.

"Inna, your first question!"

"Is it a male or a female?"

"Bravo! You must have a degree in linguistics! It is neuter."

"Does it exist at home or outside?"

"Both—it can be found at home or outside. Anything else?"

"Is it soft or hard?"

"Hmm . . . that depends. It can be hard. But not too hard. It can be cut with a knife."

"Is it animate or inanimate?"

"Oooh, Inna! How would you cut something animate with a knife? Let's say it used to be animate, but now it is not. What else?"

"Is it standing or lying down?"

"Usually it's lying down."

A pause filled with heavy breathing.

"Inna, your time is almost up, and all of us are waiting for your answer. If you guess right, you will be going to the movies tonight—two tickets are waiting for you. Only a few seconds left . . . Here comes the signal! Time's up! So what is it that I was thinking about?"

"A bench?" the invisible Inna suggested.

Even his ever-patient producer rolled her eyes.

"Well," Aspirin said. "Inna, I do believe you've earned those tickets. We care about the effort, not the results. Besides, you know the word 'inanimate,' and that's impressive all on its own. I was thinking of bacon, bacon was my word, simple, oh so simple. Stay on the line, so we can tell you how to claim your prize!"

It was time for the weather report. It promised thunderstorms and torrential downpours. After the weather report there would be a five-minute ad block, which meant Aspirin had time for a quick cigarette with his coffee.

In his shirt pocket, his cell phone twitched and played the theme from *Star Wars*.

"Aspirin, for God's sake! Is your phone not on mute?"

"Julia, easy, we're not on air right now," he murmured, pulling out the phone. He didn't recognize the number. "Hello?"

"Alexey." It took Aspirin a few seconds to recognize the voice of Vasya the concierge. "Your place . . . well, there is this situation in your apartment, and we need you to come home."

"What happened?" Aspirin felt cold.

"I think you've been robbed."

Aspirin realized he'd forgotten to activate his alarm—again.

"If you think I am being robbed, you should call the police."

"But it's the screaming . . ."

"Who is screaming? The robbers?"

"Yes . . . I thought . . . you haven't left anyone in the apartment, have you?"

Alyona's sad face flashed in front of Aspirin's eyes; he thought of the way she stared at the cab pulling away.

"The girl . . . ," he murmured.

"Your girl is here, I took her into my room. So, should I call the police?"

"Call them!" Aspirin yelled. "You should have done that right away!"

The line went dead.

**A police car and an ambulance were parked by the entrance, sur-**rounded by the curious neighbors—because how could anyone stay away? Voices caught his ear:

"Alexey, is that your apartment?"

"What happened?"

"Did you hear the screams?"

A stretcher covered with a sheet was being carried out at that very moment. For a second Aspirin thought it was a dead body. A moment later he saw a jaundiced, blood-covered face. "The dead body," he moaned and swore under his breath.

**"Is your apartment number fifty-four?" an officer asked him. He nod-**ded numbly. "This way, please."

The door to his place was ajar; Alyona stood at the threshold, and she did not seem frightened in the least. On the contrary, she smiled as soon as she saw Aspirin. "You cannot imagine what happened here!"

The rug in front of the door was covered with some kind of wood chips or shavings. Did they drill around the lock?

The door opened fully. A round-cheeked policeman peeked out. "Are you the owner?"

"I am. What happened?"

"Come in."

Aspirin stepped inside and nearly passed out. The hallway was covered in blood. Not in that there was a lot of blood (which there was), but blood was everywhere—the mirror, the floor, the walls, the furniture. His apartment had been turned into an abattoir.

Alyona stood nearby, seemingly unphased.

"You should take the child out of here," the cop said. "It is a crime scene after all."

"Go sit outside," Aspirin managed through rubbery lips.

"I sat outside all day," Alyona snapped. "And what's so bad in here? So there is some blood, big deal."

Aspirin caught the cop's eyes. "Children these days," he croaked. "Movies, games . . . blood everywhere."

"Your identification," the cop demanded coldly.

Aspirin dug up his driver's license. The cop studied the document thoroughly and skeptically, as if not quite believing its authenticity.

"The child's identification?"

Aspirin barely contained a howl. Glancing at Alyona (she was smiling), he found the laminated birth certificate in his bag. The cop studied Alyona's identification just as thoroughly.

"Proof of residency?"

"What happened here?" Aspirin said, tired of the questions already, his voice slightly higher and thinner than he wanted. "What happened to my apartment?"

Men in light blue scrubs came out of the living room carrying another stretcher. The stretcher was turned sideways, pushing Aspirin into the blood-splattered wall. He saw a young face with marks of degradation; the man on the stretcher was unconscious. Three deep scratches crossed his cheek and one ear dangled on a thin strip of skin.

"We're off, all right?" one of the men in scrubs said, holding the door with his foot.

"Go ahead," the cop allowed.

The door closed behind them.

Aspirin wished he could have gone with them, and never returned.

**"Could they have been mentally disturbed?"** Aspirin asked hopefully, taking in the scene, and not seeing how anything else might be possible. Or, at least—as Alyona stood next to him—not *wanting* to imagine anything else.

The senior police officer screwed up his face with distaste. The junior officer asked, "What about the weapon?"

Aspirin took yet another look around the apartment. Shelves where he kept his CDs had been turned over as if someone had clutched them trying to get up. There was blood on the sofa, and brown spots covered the rug. Everything else seemed undisturbed—his books, paintings, a souvenir candlestick from Venice. Nothing was broken or moved from its place.

"Don't touch anything until the forensic examination is completed," the junior police officer said for the umpteenth time.

"Of course I'm not going to touch anything," he said in disgust. "But how am I supposed to sleep in here?"

"Sleep in the bedroom. It's clean."

"Thanks a lot," Aspirin sighed.

Obviously, he wasn't going to make it to Kuklabuck tonight. Aspirin called Kostya Foma, his colleague cum adversary, and begged him to take his place, come up with an alternative plan, and figure something out. He described the events of the day in such vivid colors that even Foma seemed to have believed him. At least he promised to help.

"Just think about it," the officer said after Aspirin hung up. "We arrive, the locks are broken, the apartment is knee-deep in blood, and these two people are screaming, blood-curdling screams—'Help us!' 'Let us out!'—that sort of thing. Your door is nice, solid oak—heavy lock and all that. And when we finally managed to open it . . . well, it was shocking. Each man had multiple wounds made with sharp objects—like someone was trying to shred them."

"Who?"

"Exactly—who?"

"Well, it wasn't me! I was on the air," Aspirin said quickly.

The cop looked at him in surprise.

"I'm on the radio. DJ Aspirin."

The cop now gazed at him with a look of puzzlement. Trying to smooth over the awkward moment, Aspirin asked, "So what does this all mean? What do you think happened?"

The officer shrugged. "One is still unconscious. The other one says that yes, they targeted your apartment—broke the lock, entered, started ransacking it. And then they were attacked by a monster. That's exactly what he said—a monster. With fangs and claws. A furry one. Standing on its hind legs—the size of a man."

Aspirin thought about the pit bull. "It's delirium tremens, clearly."

He didn't think it was clear, at all.

**The police didn't seem to think so either. "What about the weapon?"** the younger police officer asked again.

"I have no idea. Did they attack each other?" Aspirin said.

"Why would they do that?"

"How else do you explain all this . . . mess!"

"Don't worry," Alyona said cheerfully, standing at the threshold, as usual. "I will wash up everything, it'll be like new."

She pressed her teddy bear closer to her chest.

"Brave kid," the senior officer murmured. "You're lucky she was outside."

"Yes," Aspirin said. "Quite lucky."

"Is your apartment equipped with a security system?" the younger officer asked.

"Yes. But I forgot to turn it on."

"That's a shame." The senior officer sounded judgmental. "It's because of forgetful people such as yourself—"

"What? I *asked* for this?"

The officer shrugged. "You might as well have left the door open."

"And that explains all the blood?" Aspirin was starting to get angry.

Another shrug. "Just saying." The senior officer looked down at his notes. "By the way, where is your dog?"

"I've never had dogs. Or cats, or birds, or hamsters," Aspirin stated.

"You don't like animals, do you?"

"I am a busy man. I feel compassion for living creatures, and I don't want to lock anyone in an empty apartment." Aspirin rubbed his hands over his face. "I don't understand this, though—I pay monthly dues for the concierge . . . why wasn't he watching? How'd these guys get into the building?"

"Could have posed as delivery guys. Just buzzed at random until someone let them in. Happens enough. But that's why you use a personal security system," the senior officer said, reproach in his voice.

"This one guy put a security system on his car," the younger officer said, reminiscing, "and if there was an unauthorized start of the engine, a four-inch steel spike popped out of the driver's seat. And this one time, this kid broke the lock, got into the car, started the engine—"

"Why are you telling me this? You caught the men, so why don't you look for their 'monster,'" Aspirin snarled. "Fur flying all over the place. Paw prints. Maybe my neighbors saw something, or the concierge noticed a beast running around. Damn it, I have this disaster on my hands—my apartment was broken into, I feel violated—and you're blaming *me*?"

"No one is blaming you," the senior officer mumbled.

The younger one looked away.

**"I refuse to believe it."**

"Why?"

"Because the moment I allow for the possibility of a toy teddy bear killing a dog on a street corner, and then slicing up a couple of thugs, then I might as well believe anything. Witches, psychics, Harry Potter, Father Frost . . ."

"No one is asking you to believe in Father Frost," Alyona said. "That's just silly. May I have something to eat? I only had two chocolates from the concierge since this morning."

Aspirin dug up a package of pelmeni from the freezer and put a pot of water on the stove. He noticed how clean the table was. It was sparkling. Aspirin himself never cleaned that thoroughly.

"May I have some more honey?" Alyona asked shyly.

"For Mishutka?" Aspirin said. "To help him disembowel people?"

"Don't encourage him," Alyona looked down. "If they hadn't locked themselves up in the bedroom, he would have disemboweled them for sure. He's got an instinct."

"It's a miracle that he didn't attack the police." Aspirin tossed the pelmeni into the boiling water. "Does he have that much respect for the authorities?"

"I was there when they entered the apartment," Alyona said. "And I yelled for him not to be afraid."

"For *him* not to be afraid?"

"I know he looks big and scary, but he really is a gentle bear." Aspirin couldn't help but laugh at the idea of this animal being afraid.

She sniffed. "I know it's funny to you . . ."

"Funny? This whole thing is absurd!"

"Not what happened today," she said with disdain. "That's just a bear acting like a bear, yet you have trouble believing in an incident as common as this was. Meanwhile, the real miracle that had happened right in front of your eyes—that you didn't even notice. And it didn't surprise you in the least. It didn't surprise you that *he* didn't take me back with him. *He* let me go. *He* let me stay here. And *he* gave me strings! It is a miracle. And it's a miracle of kindness."

Both of them fell silent.

It was late. An hour ago the door had closed behind the policemen, who had taken their sweet time with the investigation (doing what, exactly, Aspirin couldn't fathom, other than preventing him from cleaning up). Finally Aspirin signed the report and was allowed to get the blood off his floors—which, of course, had dried and set. Alyona volunteered to help; she handled the broom and mop (and, eventually, a sponge on her hands and knees) silently and efficiently. The hallway and the living room eventually stopped resembling a butcher shop. Aspirin rolled up the rug and carried it into the hall. He had no idea what to do with the sofa, but Alyona managed to pull off the cushion covers and stuff them into the washing machine. Set to heavy duty, the washing machine chewed the red fabric viciously, rinsed, and chewed it again. *It's ruined anyway*, Aspirin thought, listening to the muffled squelching of the wet material.

"I am so tired I can't even enjoy it," Alyona murmured, and Aspirin found himself agreeing with her.

He fished the pelmeni out of the boiling water, found the butter in the fridge, and dropped a yellow slice over the steaming globs of dough: "Eat."

"Thank you." Her nostrils trembled—she must have been starving. "What about you?"

"I'd rather vomit," he said.

Alyona chose not to ask any questions, for which he was grateful. She leaned over the bowl and blew vigorously. A dozen of the pelmeni disappeared before they had a chance to cool.

"Aren't you in the least bit afraid of blood?" Aspirin asked her softly.

The girl shook her head.

"Why not?" Aspirin planted his elbows on the table.

"Because I am not in the least bit afraid of death," Alyona said calmly. "What did you think?"

Aspirin was silent for a few minutes. Alyona had enough time to get a slice of bread and wipe the plate clean.

The way she answered made him feel that there was something she knew that he didn't—and wasn't sure if he *wanted* to. He wasn't even sure how she could possibly know what was inside him, but in this moment, it was clear she possessed that knowledge as surely as she had devoured the pelmeni. And he was compelled to hear the answer anyway.

"Am *I* afraid of death?" he asked in a mere whisper.

"Of course." Alyona leaned back on her chair and sighed contentedly. "You are afraid of it. Here, everyone is afraid of death. Almost everyone. The ones who know they're going to die, at least."

"And you?"

"I am not going to die," Alyona said with a smile. "I know that everyone is alive. Everything is alive. And there is no death. There is no death anywhere."

Aspirin's mind was whirling, and his words came out in a jumble. "Who told you that? Tell me more. What do you mean when you say 'here'? Are you—and your buddies—waiting for the end of the world? And are you waiting for some sort of passage to a different world?

"How can you be so sure about death?"

Alyona was no longer smiling. She picked up her bowl, carried it to the sink, then wiped the crumbs off the table.

"You've got lots of CDs," she said, turning on the hot water faucet. "I saw them when I was cleaning. Do you listen to music a lot?"

"It is considered polite to answer when grown-ups are asking you a question," Aspirin advised. "Don't change the subject. Who is that 'not human' of yours? Is he your sensei? Your teacher? A spiritual leader? He's clearly not your father. So what right does he have to take you or to let you go in the first place? And what language—damn you to hell—what language were you speaking?"

Alyona washed her bowl. She picked up a jar of honey and placed it on the table. "I am going to get Mishutka."

"Don't you dare," Aspirin blurted out.

Alyona stopped in the doorway: "What?"

"He's . . . he's all bloody." It sounded lame to Aspirin even as he said it.

"He's clean. Not a spot on him. You saw it yourself."

"Fine! I'm scared of him. Happy? And I don't want to see him ever again," Aspirin said. "Make sure he never gets in my line of vision. Ever. Otherwise, I am going to toss him straight into the trash compactor."

Alyona did not respond. She picked up the jar of honey, found a spoon in the drawer, threw a reproachful glance at Aspirin, and left the kitchen.

Feeling powerless from one of her wordless looks once more, Aspirin turned on the television set. The news anchor was talking rubbish; Aspirin switched to the music channel, turned up the sound, and felt better immediately.

The band playing on the music channel at this hour was very familiar to Aspirin. They had a tough time breaking through, because their leader went for the alternative angle and looked for inspiration in the most unusual places. But that's one of the reasons Aspirin respected them. They played ethnic tunes on a clay whistle while the heavy metal background gave them nearly symphonic depth. It was a strange combination, but the energy pouring from the stage into the mosh pit drowned the audience in ecstasy. The band did well at Kuklabuck, but only once. They said the owner, after having a grand old time that night, decided the next morning they were more suited for marginal audiences. Aspirin disagreed, but disagreeing with the owner didn't pay the bills.

Obviously, then, they were not suited for prime time. It was past midnight, though, a perfect time for marginal audiences.

The neighbors knocked on the wall. Aspirin counted to ten and turned down the sound. He lowered his head into his hands, feeling the physical weight of everything that had happened to him the last couple of days pushing down on the base of his spine.

Forty-eight hours had passed since he'd brought Alyona into his home. The newly born Alyona Alexeyevna, the moniker bestowed upon her by her barefoot mentor.

(One of the police officers had asked him where his child's room was. Aspirin explained that the girl lived with her mother and came for a short visit; the officer admitted he was surprised by the lack of toys, children's books, clothes, or anything at all. Aspirin responded by saying maybe the monster took them.)

Aspirin had to admit—he was his own worst enemy. He'd brought it on himself: the first time when he did not leave the girl alone where she was, and the second time when he refused to give her back to his camo-clad guest.

That guest whose stare made the mirrors frost over.

All of a sudden, the living room filled with music. The sounds of Carmina Burana made the neighbors bang on the wall with renewed abandon.

"Turn it off," Aspirin yelled, but got no reaction. Grunting, he went to the living room (he was very proud of his audio system—even at this insane volume it projected a clear, clean sound) and pressed Stop.

Alyona sat in the chair feeding her bear honey from the jar.

The neighbors continued to bang on the wall. Aspirin wondered if they were going to ring the doorbell. Then the phone rang.

"Pick up the phone," Aspirin said to Alyona.

Alyona reached for the receiver: "Hello? No, this is the right number. It's his daughter. What? Yes, I turned on the music. Yes, he's home. No, he was not asleep. That's fine. I will tell him. Good night."

She hung up.

"Angry, aren't they," she mumbled to herself.

"Do you realize what time it is?"

"You turned on the television, didn't you?"

She always had a smart answer. He wanted to be angry, but she sat there with Mishutka.

The bear lay in her lap, so small, so fluffy, soft and sweet.

Aspirin went to bed.

# WEDNESDAY

Aspirin was woken up by a garbage truck that roared, growled, toppled over the barrels, and missed the target as usual. The sounds of grinding metal and the howling of the engine brought to mind a battlefield. Aspirin glanced at the clock: 5:45. He groaned.

Last morning gave him a gift of ten happy seconds when he believed the girl was merely a dream. This morning he was not so lucky; as he opened his eyes, he knew everything and understood everything and liked nothing.

The truck drove away, leaving a trail of fumes in its wake. Aspirin stayed in bed, listening to the wind, distant barking, the sounds of a house waking up. He heard movement in the living room, sounds of breathing, and soft steps on the laminate. Aspirin peeked through the crack.

Clad only in a T-shirt and underwear, a set of headphones on her head, Alyona walked around the room, moving in a rhythm Aspirin could not detect. She lowered herself onto the floor, then stretched to the ceiling, then started dancing silently, her feet flying up above her head. Aspirin thought she must have taken gymnastics. Eventually Alyona sat down on her heels, pressed her forehead to the floor and froze.

Aspirin waited a minute or two, then walked into the living room, looking askance at the teddy bear nestled in the chair among a handful of CDs. He turned off the audio.

Alyona remained still.

A pile of CDs lay on the floor: Grieg and Wagner, Prokofiev and Mozart. The CD Alyona had chosen was Tchaikovsky's Sixth Symphony.

"Hey," Aspirin said.

The girl sat up and pulled off her headphones.

"Good morning to you," Aspirin said.

"You are up early," Alyona said.

She didn't look all that well—pale, thin, and haggard. When Aspirin found her on the street, the girl had looked decidedly healthier.

"You must be hungry again."

She blinked, and he realized she was about to cry.

"Hey," he said, regretting calling to her and getting out of bed in general. "What's wrong?"

She held it together for a few seconds; then she pressed her hands to her face, and her fingers immediately became wet.

"Hey, hey." He came over meaning to pat her on the back, but changed his mind. He went to the kitchen and made coffee. No sound came from the living room.

He drank his coffee, counted to one hundred, then again to one hundred, then he washed his cup and went back to the living room. He found the girl in the same pose, still sobbing in silent despair.

He lowered himself onto the floor next to her.

"What are you crying about? Are you sad? I am! I am very sad and miserable—because of you. But I am not crying, am I?"

"I want to g-go back," the girl said, choking on her tears.

"That's awesome." Aspirin brightened. "I will drive you. Where are we going?"

She howled louder.

"It's great that you are finally thinking straight." Aspirin had by now gathered enough courage to pat her on the back. He was almost surprised that his hand had connected with solid flesh, her words and actions so ethereal at times. "Are you scared? You shouldn't be. There are people out there whose job it is to help little girls in trouble. Do you understand? They get paid for helping you. Your sensei will go to prison, and you will go back to your parents. Or your grandmother. Whoever you have out there—you do have someone, don't you?"

"You sound like a broken record," the girl said, smearing her tears all over her cheeks. "Same thing over and over again. You have *seen* him. You *heard* what he said. And yet you keep saying the same thing over and over again. And here it's death everywhere, yellow leaves falling . . . dead. And dead people. And you speak as if you're dead yourself. I hate it!"

*I hate it too!*

Aspirin got up and went to the kitchen.

Today he had the twelve-to-six shift. And that night, a job at the Green Fairy. And people around him continued to exist, work, go for walks, sleep with women . . .

He nearly burned his teakettle, forgetting to fill it with water. He swore, then turned it off. He reached for something on the shelf and spilled a bag of ground coffee, took out two eggs and dropped one. He decided it was time to pull himself together.

"Alyona," he called in the most ordinary voice he could muster. "Breakfast is ready."

He didn't think she was going to respond and was very surprised when she stood at the threshold, face flushed and wet, the bear pressed to her chest, her eyes empty and withdrawn.

"Put on some pants," Aspirin advised. "Do you even realize that it's bad manners to show up at breakfast dressed like that? And wash your face and brush your hair."

Calmly, like a good host, he made some eggs sunny-side up, cut up two tomatoes and an onion, and set the table. Alyona returned, washed up and a little less red in the face, the bear still under her arm.

"So," Aspirin said when the breakfast moved into the tea-drinking phase, "I am going to listen, and you are going to tell me everything. Where did you come from? Why? What don't you like here? What can I do to help you? You are going to tell me everything because I must—finally—understand you. Does that sound good?"

Smiling, he switched on the recorder nestled in his lap.

The girl was silent.

"You said there is no death where you come from," Aspirin prompted her softly. "Is that true?"

"Everything is different there," the girl said, stirring her tea. "There is no fear."

"How can there be no fear?"

She thought about it for a second. Then, "Take your music—you like it because it carries a little spark, right? You all can feel it—even if you don't understand it. That's why you like music in which there is a spark, a reflection. Well, that spark is a reflection of the world I came from—and only just barely at that."

"Not everyone likes this sort of music," Aspirin said, surprised. "But where you're from, they not only like it, but revere it?"

"We don't revere it. We live it. We are it."

Aspirin tried to grasp what she was saying. "You keep saying that you came from another place. What other place? Pervomaysk?"

A tomcat, meeting a rival underneath the window, yowled.

She shook her head.

"Then where? Where do you want to go back to?"

"It doesn't matter," the girl mumbled. "I can't go back there."

"Why not?"

"I ran away."

"Why did you run away if it's so much better there than here?"

"Because I have to find someone." Alyona stared through Aspirin as if calculating dates on the calendar behind his back. "My brother. He fell."

"Where?"

"You won't understand," she said, suddenly irritated. "My brother . . . he's lost. He can be led back, though. They gave me strings to lead him. But now I have to learn how to play. I have to learn to play the violin. And then I will be able to find my brother. And I will be able to lead him out of here."

"That place you came from," Aspirin said, suddenly enlightened. "Is it Paradise by any chance?"

The girl looked at him strangely. "I never said that."

"But is that what you meant? And your brother—is he a fallen angel?"

Alyona stared into her cup.

"Very well," Aspirin said, very pleased with himself. "Tell me about your bear. What happened when those bad people showed up? The robbers, I mean."

He thought he saw reproach in Alyona's eyes.

"Mishutka attacked them. And they didn't steal anything from you. You could have said thank you."

"Thank you, Mishutka!" Aspirin's mood was improving by the minute. "And who do you know in Pervomaysk? Have you ever been there?"

Alyona stared into her cup.

"Tell me," Aspirin prompted.

Alyona said nothing.

"Fine, last question. That man who came here, the barefoot one. How do you know him?"

"He's not a man."

"What is he?"

"He is . . . you won't understand."

"Are you afraid of him?"

"Here—yes, I am. And there—there I am not afraid of anything. I told you, there is no fear where I come from. And there is no hunger," she added, rubbing her stomach. "Yesterday I was so hungry . . ."

Aspirin turned off the recorder quickly. The clock showed five minutes after eight, and he had a few hours before his shift. He had to find out whether psychiatric hospitals in the area had pediatrics wings. He was almost sure they did.

"Wonderful," he said and got up from the table. "Why don't you wash the dishes? I must make a few phone calls."

He shut the bedroom door and turned on the recorder. This wonderful gadget, the size of a lipstick tube, never failed him—powerful memory, excellent sound quality. He never had trouble deciphering even the softest whisper.

"You said there is no death where you come from," the recorder said in Aspirin's voice. "Is that true?"

61

Silence. Aspirin could not hear anything no matter how much he strained his ear.

"Not everyone likes this sort of music," Aspirin's voice again. "But where you're from, they not only like it, but revere it?"

He lifted the recorder to his face, stopped it, then clicked it on again.

"You said there is no death where you come from. Is that true?"

A pause. Silence. The sound of wind outside.

"Not everyone likes this sort of music. But where you're from, they not only like it, but revere it?"

A pause. Silence. A tomcat yowling.

"You keep saying that you came from another place. What other place? Pervomaysk?"

A pause.

"Then where? Where do you want to go back to?"

Aspirin stopped the recording. There was still the possibility of the focused recording function (Aspirin could have accidentally turned it on). But then what about the noise outside the window? The yowling cat?

Alyona was cleaning the table. Actually, she was simply pushing the rag back and forth—the table was already clean.

"Please say: one, two, three," Aspirin pushed the recorder in her direction.

"One, two, three," the girl repeated obediently. Aspirin pressed Play. He heard his voice, then Alyona's: "One, two, three."

"Thank you," he said, before returning to his bedroom.

**That night at the Green Fairy he was approached by the editor of** *Macho* **magazine.**

"Your article went over pretty well. No, not the one about the female orgasm, don't flatter yourself. The one about functionality."

"Uh-huh," Aspirin said. A month ago, riding the wave of sudden inspiration, he'd written an article for *Macho* entitled simply and candidly, "Woman: Basic and Supporting Functionality."

"Now we need to follow up with letters from the readers," the editor said. "From different chicks. One philosophical, with Baudelaire and Nietzsche, and the author should be a total dork, and she should call the author a chauvinistic pig. And another one, from a blonde, and that one should be talking about her 'functionality.' And one more letter—from a housewife, the kind you called 'the vacuum cleaner,' and she should be offering the author a nice blow job . . ."

"You have such terrific ideas," Aspirin said. "Go ahead and write 'em up."

The editor stared at him in mute shock.

"Don't you need any extra dough?" he asked finally.

Aspirin gazed at him through the screen of a thick, viscous, wretched drunken stupor. By then he'd been drinking for three hours, and yet oblivion never came; instead he felt heavy and nauseated, like in a bad dream.

"I thought you'd want to write it," the editor said. "Five thousand characters per letter, the blonde one can be eight."

"I'll do it," Aspirin said. "You twisted my arm."

The editor walked away, with a parting glance tinged with surprise. His was not the only questioning glance that night: it was obvious to everyone that Aspirin had not been himself. He didn't step onto the dance floor, he ignored girls and avoided his buddies; instead, he sat alone in the corner and drank one shot of vodka after another—and it was anybody's guess why he'd bothered to come in at all.

Eventually he got up to leave the dark room, decorated to resemble the jungle, and at that moment Dasha, his girlfriend of the moment, teetered in on sharp five-inch heels.

She'd come in from another party and was already rather cheerful. Smelling sweet and illegal, she pulled Aspirin into a corner, jumped into his arms and without preamble bit his lip. For the next ten minutes they slobbered all over each other, getting more and more worked up, and finally Dasha murmured, her tongue still in his mouth, "I hate everyone here—let's go to your place."

"You twisted my arm," he said.

They left the club and hailed a cab. Aspirin felt marginally better: for the first time in the last few long hours he knew exactly what he wanted. The backseat of the cab was soft but cramped; one of

Dasha's stilettos scratched the driver's ear, and the man got upset, but Aspirin promised to pay above the meter.

When they entered his building, he suddenly froze.

"Good evening, Alexey dear," Sveta the concierge said kindly.

Aspirin swallowed.

"What?" Dasha asked, looking between the two.

Aspirin pulled her into the elevator.

"My daughter is there," he said, choking on nervous laughter.

"Huh?"

"My daughter is in my apartment right now. Alyona from Pervomaysk. Hold me."

"Too much pot?" Dasha inquired.

"No, seriously, like my daughter for real. I have never seen her before though."

"Cut it out." Dasha frowned. "Why is your rug sitting in the hallway?"

The rolled-up rug was still where it had been left the night before—leaning against the door frame like a sentinel.

"It has blood all over it." Aspirin couldn't stop giggling. "I can't even tell you . . . there was blood everywhere . . ."

Dasha let go of his hand and looked inquisitively into his face: "Aspirin, have you totally lost it?"

Aspirin pressed the doorbell, for the first time in the ten years since he'd bought the apartment. After a minute of nonstop ringing, an anxious child's voice asked, "Who is it?"

"Open up, daughter darling, it's your daddy, and I brought mommy over." Aspirin's laughter turned into hysterical squealing. "Come on, open up!"

The key turned, and Alyona stepped back into the hallway; she was wrapped in a blanket, from head to toe.

"I thought you were lying," Dasha said. The corners of her mouth turned down, and she studied Alyona with curiosity and disgust, as if staring at a tarantula. "You know what, Aspirin, darling, I'm just going to step away, to the bathroom."

She sauntered down the hall.

"Who's that?" Alyona asked softly.

"None of your business," Aspirin said. By then he'd stopped laughing, but his throat still smarted a bit from the unnatural laughter. "Guess what, my darling. Get your blanket, your pillow, grab a chair—and get the hell out of the apartment."

"Where?"

"Just sit outside the door for half an hour. You won't die." Aspirin grabbed a stool with one hand, the girl with the other, and dragged both outside the door. "Sit here, and I'll come get you. Don't touch the doorbell. You touch it—you die. Is that clear?"

Alyona bit her lips and nodded.

"Excellent." Aspirin giggled again. "I'll buy you some ice cream later."

He closed the door, first the top lock, then the bottom one.

Dasha peeked out of the bathroom: "Have you solved our little problem?"

"Problem has been solved," Aspirin murmured, struggling out of his pants. "And what problem—there is no problem whatsoever."

He took the desirable, pliable woman in his arms and carried her into the bedroom, toward the pile of crumpled sheets.

# THURSDAY

He woke up with a start, as if from a slap.

The clock chimed seven. Dasha snored softly, her lips slightly opened.

Aspirin got up and took a walk around the apartment. Biting his lip, he looked into the spy hole, then unlocked the front door.

Alyona was sleeping on the floor, wrapped up in her blanket like a little ball. Tears had dried on her face, making random grooves on her cheeks.

**"Do you want to try on this dress?"** Aspirin's voice cracked under the weight of his own generosity.

"No, thank you. I don't need another one."

They had been getting quite a few curious looks from the saleswomen in the children's clothes department. The middle-aged one with the dark hair clearly longed for melodrama—the way she looked at Alyona was triggering within her thoughts of a new Cinderella. From provincial poverty to city riches, from orphanage into the arms of a loving father, and everything the child deserved would be hers: a fancy apartment, a handsome groom, a law degree. The young bleached blonde preferred a true crime scenario: she glared at Aspirin as if he were a demon seducer, purchasing a child's soul with a few cheap dresses. Fortunately, the blond clerk was called to the cash register, and they no longer had to deal with her unwanted attention.

Alyona spent some time choosing tights, socks, and underwear, while Aspirin continued to suffer. Then it was time for larger purchases; a life-size mannequin stood by the entrance, clad in a ballroom gown complete with a crinoline. Aspirin glanced at the price tag and decided it was high enough to soften the pangs of his guilty conscience.

"Why?" Alyona said. "Where would I ever wear something like this?"

"You can take it with you to Pervomaysk." Aspirin was getting more comfortable with his role. "You can show your mom. Or you can wear it to school, for the New Year's Eve ball or something."

The dark-haired clerk almost swooned.

Alyona lifted a corner of her mouth. "No, thank you. I would rather have a warm jacket. Because it's almost fall, and I get cold in just a T-shirt."

Trying not to look at the clerk, Aspirin followed Alyona into the depths of the stuffy store smelling of new clothes. They bought her a warm jacket and a tracksuit.

"Let's find a new bag," Aspirin said.

"What for?"

"To pack all this stuff in. How are you going to take it all to Pervomaysk?" He had been saying the town's name a lot, as if invoking it would make it where she was truly from.

Alyona said nothing. Aspirin chose a backpack with an image of Winnie-the-Pooh and stuffed all the purchases inside. Still saying nothing, Alyona strapped the backpack to her back.

"By the way," Aspirin said casually as they passed the school supplies department, "do you need anything for school? There are only a couple of weeks left until September—first day of school and all that. Notebooks? Daily planner? Pencil case?"

"I am not going to school," Alyona said.

"Meaning?"

"I am going to start music school." Alyona stared past him. "I told you—I need to learn how to play the violin. I don't need anything else."

"That's not going to happen," Aspirin said, discovering fatherly, almost sadistic notes in his voice. "Children have to go to school. Every day. At half past eight. Didn't you go to school in your Pervomaysk?"

Alyona said nothing. Aspirin noticed the cashier listening to their conversation. He grabbed Alyona's hand and led her toward the exit.

Her hand was soft and limp. Aspirin realized this was the first time he'd ever held her by the hand—the first time since he brought her to his home. It was hard to believe only three days had passed.

"If I am to be your father," he said, making his way through the thin crowd, "I must be responsible for you. Right? I must check your homework. Attend school conferences. Discipline you, if the need arises. This is my parental responsibility. So you should think about it—wouldn't it be better for you to return to Pervomaysk today?"

Alyona climbed into the backseat without a word.

"Because we're pretty close to the train station." Aspirin started the engine. "I can buy you a ticket. Give you some money for dinner, et cetera. What do you think?"

"Wouldn't hurt to have lunch first," Alyona muttered.

Aspirin sighed, paid for parking, and started driving.

# FRIDAY

Late at night, when the crowds at Kuklabuck cooled off, Aspirin was approached by Whiskas. "Are you still alive, buddy?"

At that point Aspirin was nothing but a burial ground for used-up adrenaline. His resources for today had been spent fully; he had no ability to converse with Whiskas. Aspirin opened his mouth to inform Whiskas about this, but didn't quite make it.

"Who is this homicidal maniac in your apartment?" Whiskas asked softly. "How did he do so much damage to two serious dudes?"

Aspirin was about to ask, "How did you know?" but held his tongue. Whiskas had a complicated biography: before Kuklabuck, he'd worked as a bouncer at a fancy casino, and before that he was somewhere else, and before somewhere else he was allegedly working for the government, but how and in what capacity, Aspirin didn't really want to know. So any of those past lives could be the source of Whiskas's information, and all of them were less frightening than the other possibilities flitting around in Aspirin's imagination.

"I was on the air," he said in a sleepy, bored voice. "The apartment was locked."

"But you didn't set the alarm," Whiskas specified.

"I forgot," Aspirin mumbled. "I've got so much going on right now—it's easy to forget your own mother."

He described the events of Tuesday in minute, painstaking detail. It was almost morning, and the club was nearly empty. Whiskas smoked, nodding and frowning.

"The two guys are now in the crazy house," he said after a particularly long drag of his cigarette. "That might actually help them get a shorter deal . . . although I doubt it. Both have priors."

"A monster," Aspirin said with a chuckle. "With paws and claws. With fur. Those two *belong* in a crazy house."

"This is a shitty situation," Whiskas said anxiously. "And I have no idea where this shit is coming from. How much would your place go for right now, do you know?"

"Ummm," Aspirin stammered, "in what sense?"

"It just doesn't compute." Whiskas stubbed out his cigarette in the ashtray. The filter end squirmed like a worm. "Two rooms, seven hundred square feet, a nice building, but a crappy area. It's not enough for serious people to make any effort. No, that's not it. This is very strange. Mystical."

"It is mystical," Aspirin confirmed. "Victor, listen to me. If you get rid of this girl for me, along with everything she has—"

"I saw you yesterday," Whiskas said, lighting another cigarette. "At McDonald's."

Aspirin stopped talking.

"It's interesting." Whiskas waved away the smoke. "One moment you want to choke her to death. Another moment you take care of her, take her to McDonald's, make her tea . . ."

"I feel sorry for her," Aspirin mumbled. "It's obvious the child has been taken advantage of, forced to do this. And she's not that bad. She's pretty smart. I'd say way too smart for her age. And she loves music."

"You should feel sorry for yourself," Whiskas said coldly. "Make a copy of her birth certificate and give it to me. I'll check my channels."

Watching Victor Somov move through the room—like a master of the ring, a predator on a savannah—Aspirin suddenly thought of his words: "One of these days I am going to send a couple of thugs over just to teach you a lesson."

Maybe he already had.

# MONDAY

**M**onday morning started with a telephone call from Mom. There was no reason for the call. Perhaps, it proved that such a device as a "mother's heart" truly existed, and that it was activated by the offspring's troubles.

"Everything is fine," Aspirin lied, watching Alyona, headphones on her head, sprawl on the freshly cleaned sofa. "How about you?"

For the past ten years his parents had lived in London. Both worked for the BBC. In the beginning, they tried very hard to get Aspirin to join them, but he refused. At that time he had an insanely awesome girlfriend, a girl of nineteen, with nineteen rings in different parts of her body. She subsisted on eggs and raw carrots, wore a nun's veil all year, and slept only on the naked floor and only with her head toward the east. Instead of a watch, she wore a tiny compass on her wrist. She and Aspirin fell in lust at first sight and made love like wild cats—on a park bench, on the beach, on the hood of someone else's car. They were as happy as they could be, and Aspirin never even considered moving away.

Three weeks later they had broken up, but still—he hadn't thought about going to London.

"Everything is fine," Aspirin made sure his voice sounded upbeat. "Mom . . . I was thinking. I have been so f . . . so busy lately. It would be nice to get away for a bit. What if I come for a visit?"

"What about your visa?" Mom asked after a short pause.

Aspirin couldn't remember if he had a visa, but he had good friends at the consulate.

"I will figure it out," he said confidently. "Go ahead and send me all the visa paperwork just in case, will you?"

"Are you sure everything's all right?" Mom asked for the third time.

Alyona lay on her stomach, eyes shut, head moving from left to right. Sounds of Wagner streamed from the stereo: *Lohengrin*, the prelude to Act III.

Aspirin perched on the arm of a chair. The girl's eyes remained closed; his presence seemed to be unnoticed. Her face did not look relaxed—it looked as if Alyona was in the middle of an intense mental effort.

How could a child be so well-versed in classical music? Alyona's relationship with music seemed almost unnatural. Aspirin thought of how she found a melody on his piano that first morning that nearly made him lose his mind. He recalled the strings that she did not dare to accept, and how the camouflage-clad guest simply dropped them on the floor.

The corner of the package with the strings poked out of Alyona's jacket. Aspirin tiptoed over and reached for the package.

Alyona opened her eyes. Her hand already held Aspirin's wrist, and her grip was strong—far stronger than a little girl's should be—and painful.

"Let go," he barked.

She let go of his hand, placed her palm over the strings, stuffed them deeper into her pocket, and removed her headphones. "Why did you do this?"

"What?"

"Why did you touch my jacket?"

"I wanted to make sure you're still alive," Aspirin said, as if it was the most natural action in the world. "Lying here like a stoned zombie. Want me to switch to some pop?"

"I don't want pop." Alyona clapped her headphones back on. "Would you mind leaving me alone now?"

"Oh really? Am I bothering you as you listen to *my* CDs in *my* apartment?"

Aspirin turned off the stereo, and stood in front of the sofa, hands on his hips. "Seriously—how else can I be of service? Sink's full of dirty dishes, there is nothing to eat here, bread's all moldy! Get your ass to the store!"

Silently, Alyona got up and went to the door. Aspirin followed her. "Three days you spent on this couch. Three days! All you do is sit around listening to music. What are you—a bloody young Mozart-in-training? You love it here, don't you? Freeloading, no cares in the world. So convenient to hang around daddy's neck, isn't it?"

"What do you want me to buy?" Alyona inquired calmly, tying her sneakers.

"You're the lady of the house, you figure it out! Meat, vegetables, whatever else normal people should have in the fridge. Here is the money, bring the change back."

He locked the door behind her and exhaled. Apparently, it was acceptable to treat her this way. Interesting. There we go. That is another way. We shall see.

In the kitchen the first thing he saw was Mishutka nestled in the chair. The toy's plastic eyes stared above Aspirin's head.

Aspirin swore, which made no impression on the teddy bear. Aspirin reached for the toy, wishing to study it more closely, but at the last moment pulled away. *What are you*, he thought, *a chicken?* He reached for it again . . . but was saved by a telephone call.

It was Whiskas, and Whiskas was in an extremely good mood. "Luba Kalchenko does reside in the city of Pervomaysk, and she happens to be married. So your little darling must have run away from her stepfather, or just wanted to have a nice vacation. My advice—give her some money, put her on the train, and bid her good-bye."

"What if she doesn't want to leave?"

"What do you mean—she doesn't want to? Send her away, and stop bugging me."

Like it was that easy.

Aspirin forced a feeble thanks to Whiskas. Victor Somov would much rather have believed in a stuffed teddy bear killing people than in the simple fact that Aspirin had never slept with anyone named Luba. However, now even Aspirin himself wasn't entirely sure. More than ten years had passed; he had been young, had always been game for just about anything, and it was quite possible that he took a quick trip to Crimea, pitched a tent, ate fish and clams, and watched clusters of cheerful girls with endless tanned legs stroll by . . .

Aspirin sighed, suddenly overcome with the weight of his years. His youth remained far behind; you couldn't pay him enough to live in a tent now—he preferred five-star hotels. Perhaps Whiskas was right—maybe there was a Luba. Aspirin once read somewhere about a surge of children conceived during the summer months, born in early April. They were called snowdrops.

And like snowdrops, it was just as likely he had forgotten about a random one ten years ago.

He wondered about Alyona's birthday.

He reached for his desk and pulled out the laminated birth certificate. March fifteenth. Interesting.

Rain came down harder, and the apartment grew darker. Aspirin sat on the sofa, smiling. *Let it all go to hell,* he thought. Enough puzzles, enough mystery. Let's assume there was a certain Luba. Let's assume a trip to Crimea did happen. Let's assume he had an illegitimate daughter—fine, I'll accept that. And that would mean the barefoot man was her stepfather, of Albanian descent.

Why Albanian? he wondered. Aspirin wasn't sure.

The recorder? It broke or had a technical glitch.

Mishutka the bear? Aspirin giggled. Bears love honey. But really, he didn't have an answer for that.

No, let Whiskas be right—that Alyona is his illegitimate daughter, she had a difficult family situation, and she wanted to have a nice vacation. He decided all the rest—the bear, the shoeless stranger, the deaths, the frightening song and frigid apartment, the fact that her "stepfather" had been okay leaving her with him—had explanations that he didn't need to contemplate. He had enough to process for now.

So, new daddy, what are you to do now?

He'd taken her to McDonald's, tomorrow he would take her to the zoo. After that, he'd take her to the train station. If anyone mentions child support—not a big deal, he'd send some money to her mother (å percentage of his official salary, of course). He was no deadbeat. He would send her presents on major holidays. Someday he'd buy her a trip somewhere. Luba was married, so he didn't have to worry about taking care of her . . . whoever she was.

Still smiling, he went back to the kitchen; a cigarette called for a cup of coffee. He reached for the teakettle and froze.

Mishutka's chair was empty.

Aspirin bent down expecting—hoping—to see the bear on the floor, under the chair. But there was nothing, aside from a few bread crumbs.

*Dammit,* Aspirin said to himself. *No one came into the apartment. Or . . .*

He ran through the rooms, peeked into the bathroom, glanced at the balcony. Cursing everything under the moon, he looked under the bed, opened the closet in the hall. He saw no signs of intrusion, but neither did he see any signs of the bear, and there was no way Aspirin would have missed Alyona's return from his position in the living room . . .

Plus, Alyona didn't have a key.

Rain was coming down harder. It was so dark that Aspirin had to turn on the lights.

*I saw him,* Aspirin said to himself for the hundredth time. *I wanted to pick him up . . . and then Whiskas called.*

Aspirin searched the entire kitchen, peeking into every single drawer. There was no bear. A window rattled in the bedroom, making Aspirin jump.

"Who's there?"

He thought he heard footsteps in the living room, but it was only a plastic bag rustled by the draft.

He went to the closet. Standing on tiptoes, he reached for his gun. Instead, his fingers touched something soft and fuzzy, and he screamed and jerked his hand away. Moving back, he saw that the teddy bear lay on the top shelf, his chunky plush body blocking access to the gun. How, goddammit, could the bear turn up in that particular place?

With tremendous difficulty, Aspirin pulled himself together. He used a vacuum cleaner nozzle to nudge the bear and push it to the floor. The teddy bear landed softly, as befitted a plush toy. Eyes fixed on the bear, Aspirin felt about on top of the dresser. Yes! At least the gun was in the expected spot. Aspirin caught a glimpse of himself in the mirror: a whey-faced unshaven thug pointing a gun at a plush teddy bear.

He swore. Clutching the gun, he went into the kitchen and made coffee. The smoke from his cigarette refused to draw out of the window and twirled above the table in a bluish cloud.

*Just wait until you get back home,* Aspirin thought. *I will not let you off the hook. Either you make your bear settle down*—in the heat of emotion, Aspirin was not thinking of Mishutka the way most adults think of stuffed animals—*or you both get the hell out of here. Go to hell, into the devil's clutches, to Pervomaysk—I don't care!*

The rain slowed down. Alyona had not returned.

About fifty minutes had passed since she'd left. The grocery store and market were nearby, and at this hour there wouldn't be any lines; she should have been back a while ago.

Was she waiting for the rain to stop completely? Raindrops no longer banged on the tin roofs, slow circles melted in the puddles, and the sun was about to peek through the clouds. She should have been back by now.

Another half an hour later Aspirin put on his jacket and threw a nervous glance at the teddy bear still sprawled in the hallway. A vision came to Aspirin: he comes back home, unlocks the door with his key, and is greeted by . . .

He shook his head and found in himself the irresistible urge to kick the bear hard enough to send him flying into the bedroom, under the bed. Would he have the guts to do it?

Aspirin took a deep breath . . . and kicked.

The bear turned a cartwheel in the air, flew into the open door, slammed into the foot of the bed and remained still, facedown on the bedroom floor.

He walked out of his apartment feeling more like a man than he had in the last week.

**Vasya the concierge had seen Alyona leaving the building an hour and** a half ago.

The rain had stopped, but outside it was still cold and raw. Aspirin shuffled around the market, went into the store, but Alyona was nowhere to be found.

Could she have taken the money and gone to the movies? Or to the park? Or back to McDonald's where she had such a good time on Thursday?

Of course. Aspirin had hurt her feelings—imagine that, he would not let her listen to *Lohengrin*, and now she was mad at him. She was probably just walking around, pouting.

Aspirin peeked into the lobby of a nearby building, an old property with a bad reputation. The security lock had been broken a while ago, and no one bothered to fix it. Mailboxes yawned, showing their iron insides, multicolored ads were strewn around, all the lightbulbs were broken, and the dark lobby smelled of old urine. Aspirin shuddered and thought that Whiskas was right—this *was* a particularly bad area of town.

He walked out, waited for a bit, sighed and went home. On the way back he shrugged, turned back, and—just in case—checked the other entrance of the old building.

He found Alyona crouching in the corner, with her back to the wall and her head hanging low, to her knees.

"What's wrong?"

She jumped up as if trying to fly into his arms, but at the last moment became self-conscious and only held his hand: "They took everything. Forgive me. I didn't get a chance to buy what you wanted."

Then she wept.

**She had hid from the rain in the lobby, and that's where she encoun-** tered three fourteen-year-old boys. The teenagers first asked her for a cigarette, then demanded money, and then, drunk on her fear and their own impunity, began "frisking" the victim. It was a regular workday, the lobby was empty, with all the retirees staying inside afraid of the rain. The boys took all her money before they found the violin strings in her pocket; that was when Alyona came to and began struggling for dear life. A door opened a floor above; the boys took off, ordering her to sit still and make no sudden moves, or else . . .

"You should have fought them from the very beginning!" Aspirin paced around the kitchen, dropping cigarette ashes on the table and windowsill. "You should have screamed—these jerks are afraid of attracting attention!"

"At first I lost my voice. And then they covered my mouth." Alyona gagged but kept it down. "With their hands."

"If I see them, I will kill them," Aspirin promised, clenching his fists. His early accusations had—as so often happens when men are confronted with victimized women—turned into righteous anger. "If you recognize any of them, if you see them anywhere and recognize them—tell me right away. Do you understand?"

Alyona nodded.

Mishutka sat in her lap. She passed her hand fitfully over his head, his face, over his plastic eyes. Aspirin suddenly wondered what would have happened if the teddy bear had been with her inside that old building?

His imagination obediently served up images of mailboxes splattered in blood up to the ceiling. Aspirin squeezed his eyes shut and shook his head. "Listen, I thought you were tough. I thought you were afraid of nothing . . . except that barefoot goon of yours."

"I am scared," Alyona admitted softly. "Every day I feel more afraid. I didn't think it would be as scary as he told me. And he never lies, but still . . .

"I guess when you grow up without fear, you can't possibly realize how much of it there is in this world."

Aspirin drowned his cigarette in a half-finished cup of tea, absorbing her words. Finally he said, "My advice to you: go back home before it's too late. If you get scared by every jerk in every dark corner, you will not fare well around here. You encounter a roach like that—you slam your fist in his face, you kick him in the balls, you scream at the top of your lungs. And then you run."

Aspirin stopped short. Out of the blue, he wondered—if he really had a daughter, would he have offered the same advice? Or would he walk her to and from school, shaking with fear and never letting her out of his sight?

How did modern parents keep themselves sane?

# TUESDAY

**G**ood morning, my little darlings! And it is Tuesday again, and nothing can be done, it always follows Monday and brings hope for imminent Wednesday . . . But *Radio Sweetheart* is here with you! We have long, soft arms, and with our long arms we have gathered in one wave all the easiest, lightest, the most comforting, carefree music we could think of, and that means you can curl up in your cozy office chairs, forget about your troubles, open up your ears and listen, listen, and that's all, and if you suddenly feel the urge to share, call us or text us, because from ten to ten thirty we have our special segment, 'Public Confession,' and that means you can admit anything—stealing your friend's candy when you were a child, or being afraid of mice . . . you can declare your love for your one and only, or for not so much yours and not the only, or your neighbor, your classmate, your gym teacher, your biology professor, anyone at all, as long as you remember—life is beautiful, and you are loved . . . *Radio Sweetheart* loves you . . . Listen to our program and dial that number, you may get lucky!"

Aspirin took a deep breath, leaned back in his chair, and wiped his mouth with a tissue. Speaking passionately for a long period of time always made him spray saliva, and there was nothing he could do about it. His spraying problem was part of why his attempt at hosting a morning program on a music television channel had failed so spectacularly. Although, no, that wasn't it. The management hated his progressive style of livening up the broadcast with an expletive or two. That said, the management had also voiced its displeasure in expressions that even Aspirin himself had never heard of, so he was pretty sure the spitting had played a role in his ousting.

Radio, though—he had a mouth for radio. A mind too. In all his years on the radio he had developed a few audio tracks in his head: One played a common, average tune, the equivalent of white noise, designed to block one's ears from perceiving anything outside the norm. The other track, the one Aspirin considered his base, presented absolute, sterile silence, of the sort that can only be achieved in a soundproofed space. Some nights in the country could be that quiet, but it had been a while since Aspirin woke up in his family's country house in the middle of the night.

Right now that played in his mind, and he did not want to move—he wanted to sit there, think of nothing, listen to the silence, process last night's dream, come up with more new details: *he and Alyona are boarding a plane going overseas, to the States or Canada, and just a minute before takeoff Aspirin gets out and tells the flight attendant that he changed his mind . . . but would not take her with him.*

That wouldn't really be possible. The flight would be delayed, the crew would have to check the luggage, Aspirin himself would have to be checked, and the element of surprise would be gone. They'd realize he'd come aboard with her, and then he'd be in even more trouble. Aspirin didn't think he could climb out of a plane taking off through a chassis opening, like Stallone . . . or was it Schwarzenegger?

He wasn't either of them.

Behind the glass window, Julia, the show's producer, took a call from a listener. Aspirin could read lips a bit, and now he saw Julia say: "Stay on the line." She nodded to Aspirin: yes, we have a caller, which meant they had someone they thought was interesting enough to put on the air.

. . . he could put Alyona on the train, just as Whiskas had recommended. The problem was that she wouldn't go voluntarily. If she really came from Pervomaysk, he could force her to go back home. But what if she hadn't? This nice little father-daughter game that Victor Somov bought hook, line, and sinker was being performed only for strangers. With Aspirin, Alyona was perfectly blunt: *I came from another world, I am looking for my brother, and until I find him, I am not leaving you. Period.*

He could escape to London. That would mean financial loss though, and, worse, damage to his reputation. Aspirin was everyone's sweetheart, established and successful and all that, but the fickle public forgot far more successful favorites within a month. Plus, how would he explain it to himself, about just who exactly was forcing him to leave, quit his job, and change his lifestyle so drastically?

A little girl and her teddy bear.

It was laughable . . .

"Aspirin," Julia said on the speaker, "are you still awake? Twenty seconds to go."

"Uh-huh," he said distractedly.

. . . to rent a flat in London would be too expensive for him, at least until he got a job. That meant a certain amount of time living with his parents, who refused to remember that he was thirty-four, not fourteen. Not having a place of his own where he could bring a woman would be quite humiliating. Almost as much as running away from Alyona . . .

"Aspirin . . . ," Julia hissed.

"And so, my darlings, we have our first caller. What is your name? Nina? Hello, Nina—Ninochka, a student, an athlete . . . What would you like to confess, Nina?"

. . . or should he go to Pervomaysk? Find that woman, Luba Kalchenko, and find out for himself—had it ever happened? She was clearly a real person, at least according to Whiskas. So maybe Alyona was lying about where she came from and actually was from that city?

"Very good, Luba. I mean Nina. Your alma mater is surely touched by your declaration of love. Incidentally, have you ever been to Pervomaysk? No? Shame. It's such a lovely town . . . And now we're going to listen to Cher and relax, thinking warm thoughts . . ."

His head swelled up with bits of nonsense. Random puzzle pieces still refused to fall into a complete picture. Mishutka the bear killing the dog and maiming the hapless thugs, if one were to believe Alyona's words. And yet, what other explanation was there that made any more sense? But that meant the thing was a transformer. Teddy-X.

To hell with the bear. But what about that tune Alyona played on the very first day? When the china doll shattered all over the keys? When Aspirin wanted so desperately to embrace the girl?

Relax and think warm thoughts.

Of course he could always drop everything and go to Pervomaysk, but it was bound to be a complete failure. He was positive he'd find nothing there worth his time—nothing that explained what was going on. Because this was beyond blackmail, beyond housing fraud. Whiskas was right, albeit grossly understating the situation: This was not good. This was absolute misery. This carried all the signs of a psychological assault—a classic case of delirium and fantasy and conspiracy rolled into a mess and stuffed inside him. I am being chased by aliens, the CIA is torturing me with electromagnetic radiation, they are modifying my subconscious mind, they have planted hallucinations on my subcortex . . .

"Aspirin, you seem a little out of it today," the speakers said with concern. "You're on!"

He waved off the booth, took a sip of coffee, wiped his lips, and fixed his headphones:

"The working day is gathering speed, some of us are driving, some are walking, some simply sit in their offices, curing their boredom with social media . . . Life goes on, everywhere, even inside mental institutions . . . That was a joke, in case someone missed it. *Radio Sweetheart* presents a half-hour segment of public confessions, only eighteen minutes are left, and we have our next caller . . ."

**He got to his car and called Dasha. Almost a week had passed since he** saw her last; they did not part well that day—Alyona had slept on the floor in the hallway, Aspirin had a splitting headache, and he thought he and Dasha may have quarreled a bit.

"It's you," Dasha said on the phone, and the tone of her voice told Aspirin that the stars would not align tonight.

"What are you doing tonight?" he asked out of inertia, knowing what the answer was going to be.

"Going to the sauna." Dasha laughed a little. "Girls' night. Why?"

"I miss you," Aspirin said.

"Don't." Dasha yawned loudly. "And you know what? Why don't you do me a favor? Get lost."

She hung up.

Aspirin sat in his car for a long time, elbows planted on the steering wheel, head hung low. He'd enjoyed the last six months of the carefree, no strings attached relationship with Dasha. It had to end at some point—everything must end, as the song goes. But not this abruptly, not in this way . . .

This little monster, whoever she was, had needed only one week to ruin Aspirin's personal life. And now he sat in his car feeling violated, yet also pissed off—and not at Alyona. Dasha had told him to get lost. *Who the hell did she think she was?*

It didn't dawn on him to ask the same question of himself.

Dark as a storm cloud, Aspirin started the car. His next step was the Housing Management Office. There, in the basement, he found the cement walls of the juvenile delinquents' room.

"This is not our jurisdiction," the uniformed woman said. "We are not authorized to deal with a child who has not committed any misdemeanors."

"So are we to wait until the child stabs someone?" Aspirin inquired grimly.

The previously indifferent youth liaison officer now glared at him with obvious distaste. "We do what we can. Do you know how many homeless kids we deal with? And in your case, as I understand it, no one had kicked the girl out on the street."

"You could at least check whether the girl is on the missing kids list. Her parents may be going crazy with worry, while she got on a train and rode away . . ."

As he spoke, Aspirin thought of those clean socks with the red stripes that he saw when Alyona first took off her shoes in his hall. Her new freshly ironed shirt. And no money whatsoever. Alyona definitely did not come by train.

The youth liaison officer turned to her monitor. Aspirin waited.

"Grimalsky, Alyona Alexeyevna, is not on the missing persons list," the officer said.

"She may have made up that name. She may be called something else entirely."

The officer sighed. She deeply disliked Aspirin. The feeling was mutual.

"What would you like me to do, then? I can only go by the information you give me. In the hallway we have photos of all the missing persons—have you checked them for yours? If you don't find her there, we can't help you."

"What if I give you a statement that she . . ." Aspirin hesitated. "That she stole something from me? That she's a juvenile delinquent? Then what?"

Aspirin was reminded of Alyona's teddy bear: the inspector's eyes had the same expression as Mishutka's plastic ones.

# THURSDAY

The day was cloudy, and by eight o'clock he had to turn on the headlights.

"This is *Radio Sweetheart*," Tanya Polishuk purred through the speakers; Aspirin had slept with her once a while ago, and they had—unsurprisingly—not repeated the liaison. "We are with you, you are with us, we are together on this nice summer evening, and evening is the best time to relax and dream, so let's dream together about what we expect in these last days of the summer, because August is the evening of the summer, and September is the morning of the fall, evening follows morning, and this is how it's always going to be . . ."

Aspirin turned off the highway onto a dirt road. The evening grew darker and he turned on the brights. The rain made the road slippery; potholes were filled with standing water, and the drive was making him nervous and uncomfortable.

The gun holster also made him nervous and uncomfortable.

After all, he was a modern man, not a cowboy, and a thick wallet or a credit card gave him infinitely more confidence than a dubious weapon under his arm. Unfortunately, the issue that led Aspirin into the woods on a dark evening could not be helped by a wallet or a credit card.

"From here we're on foot," he said to Alyona. "You see the condition of this road, right? We can't drive anymore, we'll get stuck."

"Are we going to just leave the car here?" Alyona asked incredulously. "And all our stuff?"

"Of course not," Aspirin said, improvising. "We need to get to the lodge. My friend is a ranger. He can use his tractor to tow our car to the cabin. Meanwhile, we're going to wait for him in the cabin, drinking tea and listening to music."

He mentioned music to make sure Alyona complied. Any other kid would probably have to be promised television or video games or candy—or all three.

"It's dark," Alyona said. "And it's about to rain."

"It's not far."

"I need to get Mishutka. Pop the trunk."

"Don't," Aspirin said, a tad too quickly. "If it rains, he's going to get soaked."

Strangely enough, the argument worked. Alyona never asked whether she and Aspirin would get wet, and what about raincoats or umbrellas—she simply followed him down the road, and the car with its lights turned off soon disappeared from view.

Aspirin used the flashlight to show the way. The road was terrible—they had to stick to the side and walk on the wet grass, pushing branches out of their way and making throngs of mosquitoes very happy.

"They can't bite through jeans," Aspirin murmured. "Do mosquitoes like you? What's your blood type?"

"I don't know."

"That's not good, you should know that."

"Is it far?"

Not far enough.

Ahead of them was darkness, and behind them was darkness, and nothing could be heard aside from rustling branches and creaking tree trunks.

"We are here," Aspirin said and turned to look at her. Alyona was hunched over, hands stuffed deeply into the pockets of her jacket.

Aspirin directed the flashlight at her and the reflective stripes on her sleeves lit up in white. *Just like that night in the street archway . . .*

"Listen, my friend," he said, trying to keep his voice from trembling. "You are going to tell me the truth. Who you are, where you come from, and what you want from me. And if you don't tell me, I am going to tie you to a tree and leave you here. This place is remote enough."

Alyona was silent. Aspirin moved the flashlight directly into her eyes, and she shut them and covered her face with her hand. *Those guys in the old building had scared her a lot more*, Aspirin realized; the thought made him angry.

"I have a gun." He reached for the holster. "The hunting season started already, so if anyone hears shots, they won't think much of it. I am going to cover you up with leaves and walk away. And if anyone asks about you, I will tell them you went home to Pervomaysk. And they will believe me."

Alyona was silent. Her scornful composure would drive a saint crazy.

"No one would look for you!" Aspirin shouted. "Or will they? If so, then who?"

The girl stared at him through her fingers. He couldn't quite read the expression in her eyes, but knew one thing for sure: It was not fear. She wasn't scared of him in the least. She held him in brazen disregard. She thought of him as a loudmouth, a coward . . . what did she say that day, "a coward and a traitor"?

He grabbed her collar and pulled her closer: "You are not from Pervomaysk. Tell me!"

"Let go of me."

He shook her so violently that her jacket ripped. He forbade himself to think of the teenagers manhandling Alyona in the lobby of the old building, quite the opposite: he forced himself to remember all the terrible things she had done. Her threats . . . her "he made me walk around naked." The fake photograph that disoriented Whiskas . . .

"Will you speak?"

Silence. For one deranged moment Aspirin seriously considered leaving her there under a pile of leaves, forever.

"I will make you speak," he growled, pushing the flashlight into her face. "Who are you?"

"I told you."

"You lied!"

"No."

"You lied!" He shook her with all his might. "Don't pretend to be an idiot—you are plenty smart! Who sent you?"

"No one! You brought me home yourself! You, of your own accord!"

She was right. Aspirin wanted to slam the flashlight into that arrogant mug.

"And you didn't want to give me back," she continued. "You, yourself!"

Aspirin was mistaken—she was not calm in the least. She was shouting, and she clearly wanted to kill him too.

"Yes, I did. Because I felt sorry for you." But he didn't feel that way now. He pushed her against the trunk of the closest tree. "And now I feel sorry for myself! Goddamn my altruism! Am I expected to pay for that for the rest of my life?"

"Let go of me, you are hurting me, you idiot!"

He grabbed her thin throat with his left hand, and with his right he held the flashlight next to her face.

"So," he said in a near whisper, "tell me how I can get rid of you. What am I supposed to do to make you go away? What should I do to make you disappear, you little bitch?"

"You are a coward and a traitor," she whispered, no longer shutting her eyes against the light, staring into his eyes. "Coward and traitor. You are lying when you say you felt sorry for me. You've never been kind. You—"

She fell silent. Aspirin saw her pupils widen. A second later he heard the sound of snapping branches; the sound was getting closer and louder. The earth shuddered rhythmically.

He let go of the girl and pulled out his gun. His hands trembled; the shaking flashlight illuminated tree trunks on both sides of the road, the low-hanging branches . . . and a dark, indistinct shadow hurtling toward Aspirin like an express train.

He screamed and pulled the trigger. Again. Then again.

**His eyes opened to absolute darkness.**

He thought his right ear was missing.

He struggled to reach his head. The ear was still there, but it appeared much too big and was coated in thick, sticky goo.

The gun!

He fidgeted, slapping his hands on the ground, trying to get up; he was reminded of a beetle turned on its back.

A white circle blinded him. Aspirin squeezed his eyes shut, but the circle only changed its color to dark red, like a cooling star.

"Get up," a thin, quivering voice said. "Get up! Now!"

The gun was nowhere to be found. In vain, Aspirin moved his hands over the wet grass.

"Get up, or I will shoot you! As you said, the hunting season started already . . . They won't think much of it."

The intense hatred in the girl's voice made Aspirin shudder.

He pushed himself up on all fours. He was dizzy and nearly blind. Red spots swam in front of his eyes. He assumed the girl was standing close, pointing the flashlight into his eyes.

"You shot Mishutka."

Groaning, Aspirin leaned on a tree trunk. His ear burned, his shoulder ached, and he had no idea whether he would be able to stand.

"Stand up!"

He remembered the shadow hurtling through the trees. It was at this point that he knew everything had been lost. No more trying to fool himself with stories of Pervomaysk and simple vacations, odd coincidences and serendipitous oddities; no more pouring brandy into the abyss that had just formed between Aspirin and the rest of the normal world. The world ruled by common sense.

That world was gone. He was in Alyona's world now.

"Get up," she said. "Let's go find the car."

He managed to stand up, holding on to the tree.

"If you take one side step, Mishutka will kill you."

He turned and walked down the path following his own black, limping shadow. Alyona walked behind him, flashlight pointed at his back. Aspirin's shadow stretched its neck forward, blocking the sides of the road; thickly entwined branches framed their way.

Occasionally he would turn his head to the sound of a snapping twig. He was afraid of seeing a light brown shadow gliding along the path. He never saw anything, though—the forest was empty and quiet, and only light rain rustled among the leaves. Every now and then raindrops sparkled under the flashlight like tiny meteorites.

The car was exactly where they'd left it. At first, Aspirin saw the hood and the left-side door with the broken glass and thought that was bad enough. He took a few steps closer and nearly collapsed again.

The trunk was ripped open from the inside, like a tin can, the edges jagged and crumpled.

For two or three minutes Aspirin simply stared at the car. The rain grew stronger.

"Let me go," Aspirin said finally.

"You shot Mishutka, and I will never forgive you."

He turned his head and saw the plush teddy bear in her arms, stuffing poked out in a few places.

"I haven't done anything to hurt you," Aspirin said. "I only felt sorry for you . . . once. By accident."

"By accident," Alyona sounded cold and indifferent. "There is no turning back. Now you will do what I tell you, or you will die."

"My life is over. I'm already dead."

"Don't be such a baby. Drive us home."

"My home?"

"*Our* home."

And he wasn't quite sure if she meant his and hers, or hers and Mishutka's.

They got home at half past midnight. Aspirin left the car unattended, which he never, ever allowed himself to do. However, the car—with a ripped-up trunk—held no significant value anymore.

Sveta the concierge opened the door and gasped, flinching. "An accident? An accident, Alexcy?"

"Yes," Aspirin said, covering his face.

"We skidded and smashed into a light pole," Alyona explained in a clear calm voice.

Once back in the apartment, she placed the gun on the kitchen table.

"Put it away," she said with disgust.

Aspirin put it in the closet, then locked himself in the bathroom and stared at his reflection for a long time. Four long scratches on his left cheek were bleeding slightly. Another one was on his neck—long, but shallow. The ear was swollen. He had a black eye and a bruise on his shoulder. All this was child's play compared to the fate of those two thieves.

A voice carried from across the apartment.

"Don't cry. I know it hurts. But I am with you. Everything is going to be all right."

He opened the bathroom door.

In the kitchen, Alyona held a needle and thread, the bear nestled in her lap. Alyona concentrated on the stitches like a surgeon, all the while cooing gently, "Just a little while longer. I am doing a good job. You won't be able to see a thing."

Aspirin shuddered. He locked the bathroom door again and sat on the edge of the tub.

It didn't matter who she was, a witch or an alien. It didn't matter what the bear was—a lycanthrope or a cyborg-transformer. Aspirin had to run, and as fast as he possibly could. But how far he could get—that remained to be seen.

Fifteen minutes later she knocked on the door, and he nearly fell off the tub at the sharp sound.

"What?" Aspirin asked.

"I need to wash up," Alyona said. "Let me in, please."

"And if I don't? Is he going to break down the door?"

"If you don't let me in, I will have to wash up in the kitchen sink," Alyona said after a pause. "I don't need that much from you. Stop flipping out."

"*Am I flipping out?*"

Yet he opened the door anyway. Alyona stood in front of him—

soaked to the bone, covered with stains, pitiful-looking . . . except for the steely, unforgiving blue eyes. Cradled in her arms, Mishutka stared at Aspirin with plastic eyes. They too seemed unforgiving.

"Wash away," Aspirin managed through clenched teeth.

Alyona did not respond.

Aspirin found a bottle of Armenian brandy in his bar—a crazy-expensive bottle he had been saving for a special occasion. He opened the bottle and took a big gulp. It did not seem to be enough; he lay down, staining the sheets with the blood that kept oozing from his scratches, and took another sip.

*I could take a handful of sleeping pills, chase them down with brandy, and dive into a warm bed,* he thought. But he wasn't yet ready to sleep.

"I hope you get washed away, straight into the gutter," Aspirin said, listening to the sound of running water. "Just you wait, I might burn the whole place down along with your friend. My apartment is insured, and he is not!"

This thought pleased him, and he laughed, imagining how he would pour gasoline all over his place, flick a lit match and walk away, locking the reinforced door from the outside . . .

. . . and how this door would burst open—from the inside. No, this would never work. He would have to arrange for a single powerful explosion.

The dead dog on the street corner came to mind. Just like that— ripped in two.

He got up and found his passport in the desk drawer. His visa had expired, unfortunately, so London wasn't an immediate option until he got a new one.

But maybe he didn't need to go across the globe. He just needed to destroy the bear outside this apartment. This wretched thing wouldn't attack him in public. And if it did, Aspirin would have witnesses. And then Aspirin would not end up in a mental institution, even if he told the whole truth.

The whole truth?

Cringing, groaning in pain, he sat behind the desk and turned on his laptop.

# FRIDAY

He had no idea whether Alyona had slept at all that night. At half past three, craving coffee, he found the kitchen empty. This made Aspirin happy since he had absolutely no desire to be in the same room with the two unpleasant creatures.

He filled up a thermos and carried it over to his room so he wouldn't have to get up to make more. He poured coffee into his mug, added brandy, took a sip and added more brandy, took another sip and added more brandy, and repeated until the liquid in his mug held practically no trace of coffee. At this point Aspirin would add coffee from the thermos, take sips and add coffee, until the percentage of brandy in his mug would go down to zero and Aspirin would start shivering. His whole body trembled—from too much coffee, or brandy, or stress, or, perhaps, inspiration. By six in the morning the text was finished; it was a long—almost eight thousand words—personal account of a certain Alexey G., chased by an infernal little girl and a murderous teddy bear. Assuming no one would believe his story, the desperate man chose not to disclose his name to the editors, worried that his neighbors would recognize him and think him insane.

Aspirin reread the article, made some minor edits, and congratulated himself; his own professionalism pleased him no end. He gulped down the rest of the coffee and felt nauseated. He lay down, pulled the blanket over his head, and closed his eyes for a moment. When he woke up, it was already eleven in the morning.

From the kitchen came the distant sound of clinking dishes.

Aspirin remembered everything; not even for a second would he allow himself to wonder whether it was just a dream anymore. And if he wanted to, his body wouldn't let him. His ear hurt more than it did last night. His head seemed heavier than the rest of him, and he felt out of balance. Aspirin reached for the phone and called the editor of *Forbidden Truth*.

His name carried a certain weight, and Aspirin was immediately connected to the editor in chief.

"Bring it over," the man said.

"In an hour," Aspirin said. "I can't make it earlier."

He hung up the phone and tried to get up. It took three tries, but he finally managed. His reflection in the mirror made him sigh heavily.

He wasn't hungry, just very thirsty. He craved water, and definitely no more coffee. He also craved a cigarette, but the crumpled pack was empty, and the ashtray stank unbearably.

He printed out his "confession" and stepped out of his room feeling like an astronaut exploring an unfamiliar planet. Alyona was in the kitchen; he heard her steps, a soft rustle of a newspaper, a fork clinking against a plate. The kitchen smelled of fried eggs.

Aspirin peeked into the living room. A blanket was neatly folded on the sofa, compact discs were arranged on the floor like stacks of coins in front of a money changer. The stereo system was on, which meant Alyona was wearing headphones.

Mishutka was nowhere to be seen. *She probably kept him with her at all times now*, Aspirin thought. She'd be smarter, carrying her bodyguard everywhere and wouldn't let him out of her sight.

And that was fine with him.

He shaved, cringing with pain, got dressed, made sure the disc was in his pocket and the printed document in his case, then reached for the car keys. A sudden realization of what his car now looked like almost made him cry.

He wondered whether the insurance would cover any of the damages. Any reasonable mechanic, upon a closer look, would wonder how one would achieve such bizarre damage.

"Where are you going?" Alyona asked.

The question reached him when he was about to step outside.

"I am going to work," he said grimly. "To the editor's office. Do you think the food you eat just falls down from the sky?"

She didn't respond; he shut the door.

"Not bad," the editor said. "Not bad at all. Have you ever tried your hand at sci-fi?"

"I have," Aspirin said. "When I was a kid. It was about astronauts."

"Astronauts aren't today's trend," the editor said.

"Depends on the astronaut," Aspirin objected sensibly.

"What happened to your face?" the editor said, changing the topic. "Did you get slapped around by some chicks again? Those scratches look just like nails!"

"I ran into a streetlight," Aspirin said. "Went mushroom picking last night."

The editor howled with laughter, clearly believing his version was the correct version.

Let him.

Fifteen minutes later Aspirin stepped outside, pleasantly burdened by a stack of bills. Sunglasses protected his eyes, one of which was so swollen it wouldn't even open, and his ear still ached, and yet Aspirin felt a hell of a lot better. His fable would have a large audience, perhaps pushing a million copies. Let people read it, let them be amazed, or let them laugh—that was fine with him—but the next time they saw a barefoot man in camouflage pants and with a leather pouch around his neck, let them pause and wonder. The modern world was insane, that much was obvious; in this world truth could turn into delirious nonsense, and delirious nonsense into truth, and everyone sensed it on some level.

Truth was what everyone believed in, but what truth was was always up for debate. Fact and fiction were blurred, and what mattered was often how loud and how often you could say something. As a journalist—or, at least connected to the journalistic establishment—he was a part of the worldwide mechanism churning the truth out of a vacuum.

And that meant what he got out to the wider populace could be very loud, indeed.

A group of boys loitered around his car.

"Hey, Alexey," his thirteen-year-old neighbor from the seventh floor said, "what happened here, anyway?"

"Well, I had this teddy bear, and I locked him in the trunk," Aspirin said. "But he got mad and climbed out."

The boys giggled, exchanging amused glances.

"'Telling the truth is easy and pleasant,'" Aspirin murmured, walking away.

**The apartment was empty—no sign of Alyona or her bear. The head-**phones and discs were strewn over the sofa. For all that mess, though, the dishes sparkled and the kitchen table was buffed to a shine.

Maybe she'd left for good? Aspirin wondered. He immediately chastised himself for such hopeful thoughts—yeah, sure she had. She must have been in such a hurry, she even cleaned the kitchen first, idiot.

He mused at the girl's confidence. He could always bolt the doors from the inside. Let her complain to the concierge, let her bother the neighbors—he was the master of his own domain after all. He had a right to kick guests out if he wanted to. Except, of course, people would view *him* as the monster. "But she's just a sweet little girl," they'd say.

Sweet my ass.

Also, even if they didn't put up a fuss, how long would he have to hide behind the bolted door? He would have to come out at some point.

He still wasn't hungry, but the thirst that had bothered him since that morning persisted. He'd gulped a bottle of mineral water and started making tea when the front door opened.

Alyona entered. Despite the sunny, warm weather, she wore a coat buttoned up to the top, and a beret pulled over one ear.

"I went to the music school," she said as soon as she saw Aspirin. "Here is an application form for you. There are no auditions—for violin they have open enrollment, because it's not very popular. There is a fee. But it's not expensive, it won't bankrupt you."

She coughed, covering her mouth. Aspirin noticed how pale she was—even paler than she'd looked when her barefoot friend came for a visit.

She took off her coat and placed the bear on the footstool by the door.

"Also, I need to buy a violin. For my height, I need a half. I talked to one of the mothers there. Her daughter is switching to a three-quarters. Her old violin is not very good—it's just a wooden case with a neck—but it'll be just fine for practicing. Are you listening to me?"

"I am listening," Aspirin said after a pause. "What else do you need?"

"Nothing. Here is the application form."

With the tips of two fingers, Aspirin held the paper she placed in the middle of the kitchen table. "I . . . request to enroll my child . . ."

He shuddered.

"Fill it out yourself," he said dully. "I will sign."

She didn't argue.


By the time he made it to the club, he felt like a squashed fly and was beginning to question the fate of this evening. He hid behind a pair of sunglasses and plastered a thick layer of makeup all over his face. His shoulder ached, and his neck pulsated painfully, but eventually he felt a surge of adrenaline, recovered his courage, and the world went almost back to normal.

Music could have that effect on him.

"Man, you were on fire tonight," Whiskas said with a great deal of respect. Under his breath, he added, "Any problems? Need any help?"

Aspirin fixed his glasses:

"Actually, Victor . . ."

Whiskas waited.

Aspirin took a deep breath. "Victor . . . can you get me a cab."

If Whiskas was offended, he said nothing. Five minutes later Aspirin lowered himself gingerly onto a leather seat, and half an hour later he was walking into his apartment—cautiously, like a reconnaissance scout entering enemy territory.

Lights were on in the hall and in the kitchen. Aspirin pulled off his shoes. In the living room, a table lamp was switched on.

"Do you have anything to break a fever?" Alyona asked, her voice sounding strange, rasping.

"In the medicine cabinet in the kitchen," he said, hanging up his jacket.

"I looked. There is only disinfectant and condoms."

"You are welcome to the condoms," Aspirin almost said, but bit his tongue. Instead, he went to his room.

Maybe she'll die, and he'd finally be rid of her.

A little guilty at the thought—but not too much—he closed the bedroom door behind him and fell onto the bed in his street clothes. The pain and exhaustion came back with a vengeance, multiplied by the punishing set he had put himself through at the club. It would have been prudent to shower and change, but Aspirin stayed in bed, staring at the dark ceiling. More than anything in the world he wanted to disappear. Simply close his eyes—and adieu.

He heard Alyona cough in the other room. Through the walls, through closed doors, Aspirin heard something gurgle and sort of rip inside her chest. He raised his head: was she doing it on purpose—to attract his attention?

A coughing fit. A pause. Another fit. That cough sounded terrifying—could she possibly have tuberculosis? It was one thing for her to die, but he had no desire to contract whatever disease she'd brought with her.

Hissing in pain, he got up and peeked into the living room. The desk lamp was on; Alyona half sat, half lay on the sofa, hunched up, wrapped in a thin blanket, coughing and shivering.

"How are you sick? You shouldn't ever be sick, right? You're a being from another plane of existence."

He was only partially joking, but she didn't respond, didn't even look at him. Her face looked jaundiced, brightened only by two red spots on her cheeks. Her nose looked sharper. *What if she does actually die?* Aspirin thought. *Will I be pleased?*

He glanced at Mishutka sitting right there by Alyona's arm. The plush toy looked perfectly indifferent.

Aspirin went back to his bedroom and lay down staring at the ceiling. Behind the wall Alyona continued coughing, but the sound was dull, stifled—she was coughing into her pillow. Or perhaps into Mishutka.

The clock was ticking. A dog barked outside, and someone's alarm system switched on and off. Aspirin thought of his mutilated car—he'd dropped it off at the mechanic's earlier, but had no energy to discuss the damage.

Alyona kept coughing.

Swearing, he got up once more, went into the kitchen, and emptied his medicine cabinet. Despite a heap of nasty habits, Aspirin happened to be a surprisingly healthy individual, and his medicine cabinet held nothing but the condoms that Alyona had mentioned, a tin of breath mints, a pack of BandAids, and an unopened bottle of sleeping pills.

Just in case, Aspirin put away the sleeping pills. He wasn't sure why. It was nothing but intuition.

The clock showed a few minutes past two. Aspirin had no idea where the closest twenty-four-hour drugstore was located. He remembered that it was Sveta the concierge's shift; she lived next door, and would certainly have the right medicine at home.

The entire building was asleep, and the noise of the elevator seemed very loud; it made Aspirin jump. What if he got stuck—would he have to stay inside the elevator until morning?

He took the stairs.

Sveta was not there. A note on the little window announced, "Back in a moment." Aspirin looked around. It would make a great headline: "Dr. Aspirin Looking for Pharmaceuticals." Although, no, the word was too long, and the rhythm was all wrong, it should be "Dr. Aspirin in search of a cure."

The front door banged open. In reality, it opened and closed very softly, but in the silence of a sleeping house, every sound made an impression. Aspirin looked: a woman walked in, an umbrella under her arm—his neighbor. They had exchanged greetings for the last few years, but he didn't know her name and didn't even remember whether she lived on the third floor or on the fourth.

At the sight of Aspirin, the woman tensed almost imperceptibly, then relaxed in recognition.

"Good evening."

"Good evening," Aspirin mumbled, seeing himself through her eyes: a crumpled, banged-up, not-quite-adequate thing. "Do you happen to know where a twenty-four-hour pharmacy is around here?"

"On the corner by the subway station," the woman said. "But it's closed tonight."

"So much for it being open twenty-four hours," he muttered.

She laughed politely. After a pause, she asked, "Why?"

"I need something for a fever. For a high fever. Something to break it with."

"Are you sick?"

"It's not for me."

"Would ibuprofen work?"

"Yes, of course. Is it safe for children?"

Something in the woman's eyes changed.

"How old?"

"About eleven," Aspirin said and immediately regretted his answer. "I mean, eleven."

"Yes, it is safe. What's your apartment number? I will drop it off."

"Fifty-four." Aspirin felt a great deal of relief.

Five minutes later she rang the doorbell.

"Excuse me, Aspi . . . Aspirin?"

"Alexey," he said.

102

"Sorry. Here is the ibuprofen. I also have this cold medicine—you need to mix it with a glass of warm water."

Alyona had a coughing fit in the living room.

"Impressive," the neighbor said. "Have you called the doctor yet?"

"No," Aspirin said.

The woman frowned. Her thick blond bangs could not conceal the two deep vertical lines on her forehead.

"Have you given her an expectorant?"

"Huh?"

The woman glanced into the living room. Alyona did not react—she still sat on the sofa, hunched over, eyes half-closed.

"How could you let the child get to this condition?" the woman asked sharply. "What's her temperature?"

Aspirin did not reply. The woman gave him a cold, measuring stare and walked into the living room without an invitation. She wore slippers, and they slapped against the floor in accusation at his parenting.

"Hello." She sat down by Alyona's side. The girl finally turned her head. "How are you feeling?"

"Lousy," Alyona said, and her voice matched her answer. "It'll be fine. It's just a cold. It'll pass. It's nothing serious."

"Of course it will pass," the woman said. "But we should try to break your fever. And I am going to bring you an expectorant. I have *Dr. Mom*, and it actually tastes pretty good. Is that your teddy bear?"

Shuddering inside, Aspirin watched his neighbor cradle the monster in her arms.

"He's very cute," the woman said. "What's his name?"

"Mishutka."

"Hold him tight, he'll help you get well."

The woman turned to Aspirin, all of the warmth in her voice when talking to Alyona gone.

"Give her the ibuprofen, now. Take her temperature. If anything happens, call the ambulance—this is no joke!"

The door closed behind her. Aspirin looked at the pouch in his hand, turned it over, read the directions. He understood nothing, even though the steps were as simple as they come.

"How is this not a joke?" he asked the ceiling. "I don't understand. Because you and I know your friend is going to come over, wave his hand over you, heal you, make you whole—after all, he made your birth certificate right in his bag, one wave of his hand, yes? So what's the point of this whole coughing drama? Am I supposed to feel sorry for you?"

Alyona almost choked from coughing; she opened her cloudy, sick eyes. "To feel sorry? You think too much of yourself, Aspirin."

"Of course." He was far too tired to feel irritated. "You are in my house, you eat here, sleep here, bait me with your bear, and yet I am not worthy of your attention. I am a tool for you, that's about it. Why are you shivering like that?"

"Because I'm sick, you idiot."

He came closer, watching Mishutka out of the corner of his eye. The teddy bear lay on the sofa, spreading its soft paws over the blanket, staring beyond Aspirin.

"I will never tell him about that night," the girl said, and at first Aspirin thought she was talking about the bear. "I will tell him everything . . . but this. I will find an intersection. I will play a song. My brother will hear it and he will respond. I will go and find him . . . even if he's dead. The gates will open for us. I can see how they open, and beyond the gates I can see the sun. And there is no death. We will live for many days, and life will be everywhere. Their eyes shine like the stars, they laugh, and they float. And there is no fear, even though they know of fear. And there is no pain, even though they know of pain. But I will never tell him about that night. Never."

She lay there, staring through Aspirin, hugging the bear to her chest, continuing to speak deliriously, every now and then breaking into a language Aspirin had never heard before, only broken up by coughing.

Someone knocked lightly on the door.

"Be quiet," Aspirin demanded. "Be quiet, or she will know what's going on!"

The door creaked.

"It's me," his neighbor said. "I brought *Dr. Mom*, and some herbal tea. Have you made her a warm drink yet?"

"Are you a doctor?" Aspirin asked.

"No, I am an engineer," she said, pushing her bangs to the side, and the two vertical lines became more obvious. "And you are a DJ, I know. I listen to you every now and then. In a cab, or on a bus, you know, they always have music . . ."

"I will get her a warm drink," Aspirin said. "Right away."

"Is she your daughter?" the woman asked softly when he was in the kitchen making the drink under her supervision.

Aspirin sighed. "Actually . . . she was a complete surprise. She came from Pervomaysk. She lives there with her mother. She told me she was my daughter. And I had never seen her before, I never even thought . . ."

"Such melodrama," the woman said. "Does it even happen like this?"

"I don't know," Aspirin admitted. "With me—I guess so. I mean, obviously it did," he said, pointing to the living room. "And did you see what happened to my car?"

"Yes," the woman was silent for a moment. "Very strange. As if a grenade blew up in your trunk."

"You have never seen a grenade." Aspirin stirred warm, lemony liquid with a spoon. "The grenade damage is quite different."

"So then what happened to your car?"

It was Aspirin's turn to be silent.

"An accident," he said finally. "You know—an accident in the global sense of the word. A hole in the universe. In the macrocosm. Or micro—in my own, individual—cosm."

"You don't look great yourself," she said and suddenly placed a hand on his forehead. She had a cool touch, peaceful, calming; Aspirin wanted her to keep her hand on his forehead for a long time.

But she took her hand away. "And what happened to you?"

He looked away. She stared at the four scratches on his cheek. "So—serious troubles?"

"Could be worse, I suppose," Aspirin mumbled, then added after a pause, "But not much."

"A car is just a thing," the woman said carefully.

"Of course."

"And you don't have much of a connection to the girl?"

"Other than being my secret daughter? Put yourself in my shoes—what if, out of the blue, a child came to you and told you she was yours?"

"Hard to imagine." The woman glanced at the cup Aspirin held in his hand, automatically stirring the cooling liquid. "You should give it to her, she needs to drink a lot."

Walking into the living room, Aspirin hesitated before approaching the sofa and Mishutka lying in its center. With the woman watching him, though, he finally handed the cup to Alyona. "Here, drink this."

Alyona drank, noisily, greedily, almost choking.

"Were you thirsty?" Aspirin asked, puzzled.

"She needs to drink warm liquid, lots of it, nonstop," the woman called from the door. "And milk with baking soda . . . I'm going to go now. Good night. Call the doctor in the morning."

The door closed behind her. He looked at it for a while, wondering if the woman had even been real.

"Thank you," Alyona said, handing him back the cup.

"Here is your medicine." He gave her a green bottle and a spoon.

"Thank you."

"*Can* you die?" he said, looking into her eyes.

"No," she said, but she didn't sound very confident. "For me to leave this place, this special music must be played. *He* must play it. No one else can do it."

"Then what are we worried about?" Aspirin wondered. "You told me so many times that you are not afraid of death!"

"I am not," Alyona whispered. "I am afraid of something different. I am afraid of people who appear to be alive . . . and then it turns out that they are not just dead—they are all rotten inside."

"Real nice," Aspirin said spitefully. "Here I am taking care of you, and you take a jab at me. You enjoy making those nasty hints, don't you."

Alyona coughed again.

"I do have milk," Aspirin managed through grim lips. "And baking soda."

"Can I have some, please?" Alyona asked. "And could you give me another blanket? I can't stop shivering."

*Real* nice.

**Half an hour later the medicine finally kicked in.** Sweat formed on Alyona's pale forehead; she relaxed and stretched out, Mishutka nestled by her side.

"When I saw you for the first time," she said, closing her eyes and shifting as if trying to work out a body ache, "I was sure you were dead. Just like everyone else here. Frightening. You passed me, and that was fine. But you came back. And it turned out you were alive after all. I was mistaken."

"You are delirious," Aspirin said coldly.

"Yes," Alyona said drowsily. "Can you play the piano?"

"I did, when I was a kid."

"Whose instrument is this, then?"

"My parents'. And I used it to practice. Children's songs, you know."

She tossed the blanket to the side. Rivulets of sweat glistened on her temples, her forehead, her neck; the same T-shirt she wore to the music school was soaked through.

"You need to change your clothes," Aspirin said.

"I don't have anything to change into." She kept her eyes closed. "Let me sleep."

He found an old white T-shirt in a stack of clean laundry, fresh out of the laundromat.

"Here, put this on."

She struggled to open her eyes. "Thank you. Don't look."

**Once Alyona fell asleep in the arms of her bear,** Aspirin went to the kitchen and made himself a cup of tea. For over a week he'd been living in an inside-out world, and somehow life went on—he walked around, talked with people, even made a little money . . .

He felt tired now, though. And because of that, he stared into his mug thinking simple thoughts: *But maybe that was just how things ought to be. Maybe what she needed wasn't that bad. She could live here for a bit. I would buy her a violin . . . let her enroll in her music school. And one of these days she will disappear just as suddenly as she showed up. The barefoot guy in the camouflage pants will come, play a song. (What would he play it on? It doesn't matter.) And Alyona would go back to where she came from. Where there is no death and everyone is happy.*

Humans adjust, otherwise they wouldn't survive. The scratches would heal, the thugs who robbed his apartment would plead temporary insanity and be transferred to a mental institution. Aspirin would survive, as long as he didn't bother that strange little girl, didn't threaten her, and didn't touch the bear. And eventually he'd think of something. Or, if worse came to worst, he would drop everything and move to London; the girl and her bear would never get a visa. Or it would all be moot.

Outside the night was black, as dark and grim as it gets in the fall. The clock showed half past three. Alone, Aspirin sat in the kitchen desperately trying not to howl—from the dull ache in his damaged ear, from the utter despair, from fear—*What if he was losing his mind? What if he'd already lost it?*—when the black phone on the white table (like a dead seal on a sheet of ice, he thought) suddenly rang. Aspirin jumped up.

"I am sorry," a woman's voice said on the other end of the line. "Are you still awake?"

"Yes," Aspirin said, rubbing his eyes, parsing together who this voice belonged to.

"Is she feeling better?"

Ah, right—his neighbor. "Yes . . . she's asleep."

"That's good. I forgot to tell you about rubbing her down with vinegar. If the fever does not break, you take one part of vinegar and two parts of . . ."

"Yes, I know," Aspirin said. For a second a childhood memory flashed in front of him—the smell of vinegar and a wet rag on his head.

"Very good," his neighbor repeated and fell silent, as if expecting him to say something else. As if there was nothing more normal than calling a stranger at three thirty in the morning. Aspirin did not reply.

"Shall I drop off some vinegar?" the woman asked.

**He poured her a snifter of the Armenian brandy. She didn't refuse, but** drank very little; cradling the snifter in her hands, she studied the "legs" of the liquid on the glass.

"Do you have children?" Aspirin asked.

She shook her head. "No, just nephews."

"You must be a very kind person."

"What makes you think so?"

"Well," Aspirin chuckled, "you've come to my aid. Armed with vinegar. And that, whatever it's called. In the middle of the night. Of your own volition."

"It's not a big deal," she smiled. "I never sleep after my shift."

"I don't sleep either," he said, and poured a little more brandy into her nearly full glass. "Second night in a row. And I have to be on the air at nine in the morning."

"I read somewhere," the woman touched her lips to the surface of the amber liquid, "that occasionally . . . in some cases . . . sleep deficit and an intense workload may have a therapeutic effect. I mean, when psychological trauma is present."

"Are you a psychologist?"

"No, I am an engineer."

"Right. You said that earlier."

"Yes. I'm a techie. I work at a power plant and had a late shift tonight."

"You don't like *Radio Sweetheart*, do you?" Aspirin guessed.

"Why do you say that?"

"It's just something that's come to me."

"I am quite open-minded." She spoke calmly, but her eyes sparkled with a hint of sarcasm. "If someone listens to something like that—that means it's needed."

"It is needed," Aspirin said. "Kids from vocational schools, and truck drivers, and office drones . . . And there is no reason to be condescending."

She inclined her head. "Alexey, I'm not asking what happened to you. But perhaps you should sleep for a few hours, and then you'd be in a better position to decide—"

"There is nothing to decide," Aspirin said quickly. "Everything is going to resolve on its own . . . or not. Whatever I do to try to fix things only makes them worse."

She studied his face; tactful, she didn't ask what sort of violence one had to endure to have a trail of four claws on one's face.

"Have you tried contacting the police?"

Aspirin groaned.

"You should take a time-out," the woman said touching her lips to the brandy. "Just go to bed."

"I will try."

Walking her out, he suddenly remembered. "I am sorry . . . what is your name?"

# SATURDAY

My darlings, today is a special holiday for all sensible mankind. The work is finished, Saturday is again upon us, and we're anxious, we're willing, but not all of us are able. . . . It's a glorious Saturday morning at *Radio Sweetheart*, the last weekend of the dying summer, and it's sunny outside . . . What a silly heavenly body—in the morning it rises, and in the evening it sets, and if only it were the other way around . . . But we digress, and my producer tells me we have a caller. We have a lovely caller. Hello, we're listening! Tell us who you are and what you desire in this life! Oh no, I suspect our girl is shy—she hung up. But no fear; at least now we can listen to our next performer, and what will she sing for us, I wonder . . ."

Aspirin spoke with his eyes closed.

A minute, then another. Commercial. Weather report. A minute, then another, minutes following minutes. Aspirin's measured, upbeat, occasionally even stylish mumbling filled the interiors of cars and apartments, whispered in headphones, and roared from speakers. *If I am mad,* Aspirin thought, lifting his eyelids for a split second, *then you are certainly insane. I am pulling your leg, babbling in your ears, lulling you to sleep, I bleed nonsense, and I can right now, without changing the tone of my voice, share my entire story,*

*and nothing will change, nothing will happen. Another idiot will*
*call in with a song request . . .*

In the morning a doctor from a local clinic made a house call, listened to Alyona's chest, and diagnosed bronchitis. She took a long time writing a prescription, even longer to explain to Aspirin how to use mustard plasters, and why cupping therapy was barbaric and belonged to the previous century. She threatened him with the possibility of pneumonia, which would definitely happen if he didn't take certain measures, and told him about a few cases in her own practice, in which children would have to be hospitalized even though everything started with a simple cold.

Aspirin pulled the doctor into the kitchen.

"Would it be best to hospitalize her right now?" he asked, expressing a great deal of trust in modern medicine. "Because, you understand—my work keeps me very busy, and she may be better off . . ."

The doctor looked at him as if he practiced cannibalism. "You know, this is the first time in my practice someone has asked me this. Usually parents are strictly against hospitalization . . . it gets downright ridiculous! But in this case, I strongly recommend that you keep her at home, she'll be much more comfortable."

When the door closed behind the doctor, Aspirin felt relieved.

Still burning up, Alyona continued to cough, but she had antibiotics, and they should kick in soon. The doctor promised improvement by the next day—quite possibly in the morning, but definitely by nighttime. Before he left, Aspirin put a thermos filled with hot tea by the sofa. The bear lay on Alyona's pillow; Aspirin did his best to look the other way.

The cab got stuck in traffic, and Aspirin made it to work just in time. He put on headphones sideways to avoid touching his injured ear while everyone in the studio glared at him through the glass. He closed his eyes to shut everyone out, longing to see nothing; he began muttering like a voodoo man: "Just recently we sang praises to summertime, and all our worries were postponed until September. And here comes September, it's almost here, but we don't care—all our worries will happen next September, next year, or maybe they happened last September, and now we can all forget them as stories from our past . . . Children are getting ready for school, but keep your chin up, this too shall pass, and someday your school years will emerge in your memory as a fondly remembered holiday or a long-forgotten nightmare. Here is the top of a new hour, and we greet it by playing our favorite game—Finish with *Radio Sweetheart*! And when I say 'finish,' I, of course, mean finish a sentence, and forgive me for an inadvertent vulgarity . . ."

He shouldn't have fallen apart the night before. He shouldn't have offered brandy to his neighbor. She may have thought it was an invitation to continue. But she *had* helped, bringing that medicine for Alyona. And those chats with her helped too, even though he hated to admit it. He was so close to telling her the truth—he almost spilled the whole story. He wondered what she would have done. Calling an ambulance seemed kind of unlikely, because what would she have said? "My neighbor is suffering from acute psychosis . . . or acute hypnosis, more likely."

It would have made a great headline: "DJ Aspirin in the Hands of a Band of Hypnotists." He considered printing that, just for his own public relations' sake.

"Alla? Greetings, Alla, here is your task. Are you listening? You are to finish this sentence, but very quickly, no time to waste: The day was dry and rather sunny. I spent the day with my pet . . . All right, Alla, that's your cue—with my pet . . . ?"

"Rabbit," the headphones suggested.

Aspirin opened his eyes and blinked.

"I appreciate your sense of humor, Alla. I truly do. Well, the five percent discount for any merchandise at *The Tech Station* store is yours. Stay on the line, don't hang up . . ."

Somewhere in the untidy living room, Alyona lay on the sofa, sipping tea from a thermos.

*Everything passes,* Aspirin reminded himself.

That meant this too shall pass.

# PART II

# SEPTEMBER

On September 2, still pale and weak, Alyona went to her first class at the music school. She returned an hour and a half later carrying a small violin in a shabby black case and a cardboard binder for sheet music. Mishutka's head stuck out of her backpack.

"I need more money," she informed Aspirin. "I have to pay for the rest pad, and buy music notebooks and pencils."

"What rest pad?" Aspirin snarled. "Where are you planning to rest?"

Alyona rolled her eyes and pulled out a black cushion with strings used by violinists. "I understand your pain. We've already spent so much money, and now there are notebooks, pencils—all these *huge* expenses . . ."

Her sarcasm was very adult in nature, without a hint of a smile. Aspirin pulled a wad of bills from his pocket. "Here. Get whatever you need to buy."

She went to the living room. Aspirin anticipated a revolting screech of tortured strings, but his fear had been premature. Twenty minutes later Alyona reappeared in the kitchen pressing the violin to her shoulder with her chin, without using her hands. She walked back and forth, deep in thought, looking so bizarre that Aspirin couldn't help but think of a statue with missing arms.

He bit his tongue and said nothing.

"Your girl must've settled down," Vasya mused. "To tell you the truth, I thought you were going to ship her back to mommy. Yet here she is, and with a violin too. What grade is she in?"

"Fifth."

"Oh yeah? I thought she was in fourth."

The damn elevator was taking a long time.

"And looks like she's quite a helper to you," Vasya continued. "I see her carrying bags from the market. You couldn't get my grand-daughter to do that . . ."

"I don't force her," Aspirin said. "It's her decision."

"Sure, sure. But, listen—what is up with that bear of hers? I see her going to school—and that bear is in her backpack. I said to her, you are a big girl, other kids carry books in their backpacks, and you have a toy . . ."

The elevator finally arrived.

"Good night," Aspirin said with relief.

He was perfectly happy with Alyona taking her bear anywhere she went. He would never agree to stay alone with that "toy."

Groaning at every floor, the elevator finally crawled up to the fifth floor. Aspirin stepped out; the entrance to his apartment had been swept and the rug looked clean. Alyona was indeed excellent at housekeeping, especially considering she was only eleven.

There were little caveats to everything she did though. So, for example, she always washed the dishes, but only her own, touching nothing Aspirin may have left in the sink. Once, as an experiment, Aspirin behaved like a total pig for a few days in a row: every single plate and cup he owned eventually made it into the sink, bits of food stuck to the surface. And only when Alyona had nothing to eat her oatmeal from did she pick up one plate with the tips of her fingers, wash and dry it—that single dirty plate.

Since then she kept that plate in her room, on the shelf with the musical CDs. She ate, washed the plate, dried it, and carried it away. Aspirin's blood boiled.

And yes, she went to the store and to the market, she knew what to buy and how much to pay, she could make soup and fry meat. Yet she never even pretended to please Aspirin with her cooking. Everything she did at home—and her responsibilities included wishing Aspirin a good morning and good night—she did frugally and rationally, making sure everything was done well, but never wasting even a single extra drop of her energy. She needed her energy for practicing her music—from the very first lesson. Every minute that Alyona did not spend on household chores she spent practicing her violin.

For hours she moved her bow over her bent left elbow. She read, rested, listened to the music standing up, the violin pressed against her chin. Endlessly, she pinched the same sequences of sounds; thankfully, she didn't make too much noise. After a week of practicing, she developed a bloody blister on her chin and unflinchingly treated it with iodine. Aspirin shuddered at that level of fanaticism.

He tried to stay out as much as he could. He went to parties, drank a lot, hooked up with girls—young, silly ones; older, desperate ones. He brought them home (the trunk of his car was finally repaired). On those nights Alyona did not come out, and for a few blissful hours, it was as if she didn't exist; the girls walked about naked.

Occasionally he enjoyed making his roommate uncomfortable and behaving as if his apartment still belonged to him alone and no one else. He threw dirty laundry on top of the washing machine; turned on the television, preventing her from practicing; left his stuff all over the apartment; banged on the door if Alyona stayed in the bathroom longer than five minutes. Alyona endured his impudence stoically, and that angered him even more.

He considered renting a different apartment. Or moving in with a friend. Even today, he would have gone to the club directly from the studio, but, having a snack at a coffee shop, he spilled some food on his shirt. Rubbing at the spot with his napkin, he felt annoyed, and that annoyance was directed at Alyona. Why the hell couldn't he just go home, take a shower, and change?

The key turned in the lock, and the door opened without a sound. Aspirin held it ajar and listened.

Alyona was playing piano. In Aspirin's presence she never even dared (or never wanted?) to touch the instrument.

The same musical phrase was played again and again, in a fast tempo. The combination and sequence of sounds was definitely music and definitely harmonious. Aspirin had no idea how this could be played on such an old piano, especially within two octaves.

The phrase repeated, and Aspirin suddenly realized it was a request. It was a request for something unknown, directed at an unknown someone, and it was played over and over again, with different intonations, but its meaning remained unchanged . . .

He came inside and slammed the door. The musical sentence ended abruptly. The lid was lowered immediately. Alyona stood with her back to the instrument as if she'd never touched it. As if she didn't even care.

"Who asked you to touch stuff that doesn't belong to you?"

She sat on the sofa and crossed her legs. She glanced at Aspirin as if he were nothing but a mosquito. Mishutka sat on the sofa by her side, his paws crossed, his eyes indifferent.

As he did every time they had such a confrontation, Aspirin gave up and went to his room. He made some tea, took a shower, and changed. He had a few hours to kill before his next shift, and he could spend them at some cozy pub. However, Aspirin would have greatly preferred taking a nap for an hour or so, or just lying down with a book, but there was no rest to be found in his own home.

A few soft "pinching" sounds came from behind the closed door; then the violin came in in full force. Aspirin had never heard Alyona use her bow, and got up to look. She probably practiced when he wasn't home. The sound, slightly screechy at times, every now and then grew clear and expressive, surprisingly confident and sonorous. Alyona played an étude.

She saw him in the door and stopped playing. "What?"

A second ago he wanted to speak with her. Now, under that contemptuous stare, he only mumbled, "We are out of bread. The butter is almost gone too."

Without a word, she untied her rest pad and returned the violin to its case. Full of anger, Aspirin left the room.

The front door closed.

He put on his shoes and jacket, hoping the little bitch forgot her keys. When he went down the stairs, though, he saw that Alyona hadn't left the building. She stood by the entrance to the lobby, clutching Mishutka to her chest.

"What's wrong?"

Alyona stared at the floor. "It's them."

"Who?"

"Them."

Aspirin followed her eyes. Two boys, around fourteen or so, stood by the garage, smoking and spitting. At first Aspirin had no idea what the issue was, and only a minute later did it connect for him.

*"At first I lost my voice. And then they covered my mouth . . . with their hands."*

These guys had truly lousy timing.

Alyona clutched the bear to her chest. Aspirin wondered whether she would be able to set Mishutka off. Would it work if there was no immediate threat to the bear's owner, but rather an order?

"Are you actually afraid of them?" Aspirin asked brightly. "With *that* by your side?"

Alyona did not respond.

"Or have you made a mistake? And it's not them?"

Alyona said nothing. Aspirin tried to look into her eyes, but she turned away. Her fingers, worn out with work, hangnails on each tip, dug into the bear's chocolate fur.

She was scared and she was disgusted. She was trying to overcome her revulsion, but—right in front of Aspirin—she kept failing. And as much as he loathed her, she was still just a little girl, and the pity—and outrage—welled up inside him.

He glanced at the teenage smokers again, then back at Alyona. He winced inwardly, then crossed the yard.

The boys noticed him; they exchanged surprised glances, but didn't try to run. There was no reason for them to run.

In the time it took him to cross the yard, he came up with

absolutely nothing. No words came to mind. He simply approached the boys and grabbed them by the scruff of their necks.

One of them managed to pull away, but Aspirin grabbed the other with both hands.

"What? What the hell, man?"

"I will tell you what the hell," he said, the words appearing by themselves, tinged with ice. His internal stupor gave way to the excitement of retribution. "We're going to the police station. Robbery and an attempted rape. Are you fourteen yet? Jail time."

"Who the hell are you . . . ?"

The one who broke away now ran over to the side, just as the one held by Aspirin started fighting for real, but Aspirin pulled the boy's elbow behind his back. The act of violence felt unexpectedly good; perhaps that was how the cuddliest, most domesticated predator goes wild at the scent of its victim.

"Dude, what are you talking about? What robbery? What rape?"

"In the front entrance. A month ago. The girl recognized you. And someone else will recognize you eventually, you little bastard."

The one who'd broken free jumped away a few more steps and picked up a rock. "Let him go!"

"You are looking at jail time yourself," Aspirin promised, maneuvering the other kid so that he would most likely take the rock to the face if his friend threw it. "They'll be coming for you. Will bang down your parents' door and haul you away. So go ahead, throw the rock, add to your term."

The kid dropped the rock and disappeared. Aspirin pushed his prisoner against the wall. He considered taking the kid to the police station, but his outburst of passion was dwindling. And the closest police station was two whole blocks away . . .

"Tell me your name and your address, or I'll cut your balls off."

"What did I do?" the kid whined.

"You know what you've done. You can't get away. I will find you. And your friend. Talk!"

He slammed the boy's forehead into the garage wall, not too violently, but the wall echoed anyway.

"Take your money," the boy screeched. "What if I got nothing to eat! Take it, choke on it, bastard!" And then he started crying, in bitter, heaving, slobbery sobs, and Aspirin became aware of his complete power over this pitiful, nasty, cowardly, and cruel creature, who was bound to spoil everything he touched, bound to stomp on, break, and ruin everything in his way, bound to kill if he could muster up the courage to do so.

Aspirin wanted to hit him again. He wanted to throw the boy on the ground and kick him with his boots. He wanted to teach this vermin a lesson once and for all. He wanted to destroy the boy, to tar and feather him, to drag him through the mud.

But as the boy wept, sticky with snot, Aspirin saw himself from a distance: a grown man twisting a teenager's arms.

He shuddered, pushed the boy toward the garage wall, and walked away toward his building, wiping his palms on his pants in disgust. "You're a nasty piece of shit. If you ever come near her again—or if I hear about you coming near any little girl, I *will* kill you." Even as he said it the taste of iron slowly dissipated from his lips. His five minutes of courage were used up.

He found Alyona in the same spot where he'd left her. She was still clutching Mishutka to her chest. Aspirin wanted to take his anger out on her, and he came closer and stood by her side.

She stood there in silence, shoulders pulled down in her usual manner. She was so small. Thin to the point of transparency. She looked pale and miserable.

He swallowed. "Let's go."

She followed him into the elevator, then into the apartment. Aspirin rushed to the bathroom; he recalled that night when he hit her, and how long it took for him to feel clean again.

"It's not like I could kill him," he mumbled, desperate to justify his own actions. "And dragging him to the police station would be perfectly useless. No one would deal with him until he grows up and gets caught in a real crime."

Alyona was in the living room, and he could hear her uncovering the piano's keyboard. At the first notes, Aspirin perked up, and for good reason: A new musical phrase hung in the air. It contained a hidden meaning. Aspirin sensed it, but could not understand.

He went to the living room. "Are you . . . speaking?" he asked.

She looked up from the keys. "Do you understand me?"

"No," Aspirin admitted after a long pause.

Alyona closed the lid. "And you cannot."

"Clearly, I am not worthy," Aspirin agreed. "Listen . . ."

They hadn't spoken for several weeks, unless one counted a few functional words such as "Come over," "Go get it," or "Good morning."

Aspirin hesitated. Alyona stared at the floor, and it was a good thing: had she bestowed her usual look full of disdain upon him, he would have left without asking any questions.

"Who are you talking to, if I can't understand anything?"

She said nothing for a while, then admitted, "To myself, really. You know, I should have simply kept walking, as if I didn't even see them. I should have kept walking."

Aspirin looked at Mishutka.

Anger returned to Alyona's eyes. "What are you staring at him for, like he's a butcher! He's not a killer . . . if you don't provoke him."

"Fine," he said placatingly. "I just can't understand how you can be afraid of those little jerks with a bodyguard like him."

"You can't understand anything at all," she said bitterly. "One of them, if you must know, could be my brother. Any one of them. He may not remember who he is. He may have lost his mind in this world, become part of it—probably even the most heinous part. I think about this all the time, I can't stop thinking about it . . . he may have drowned in hatred like in a pile of shit, or become a chunk of hatred himself . . . hatred and fear. He may have turned into this, and if I end up killing him, it would be all my fault and I'm trying to find him—so hard to find him—and my fingers, these goddamn fingers, don't want to obey!"

With all her might, she slapped the fingers on her left hand with her right, then attempted to do it again, but Aspirin grabbed her hands. "Stop that! Don't be such a drama queen!"

She twisted and pulled, but Aspirin was stronger. She gave up, sighed, and pushed him away. "It's over. Let me go."

He let go of her hands. She crossed the room and sat down on the sofa next to Mishutka. Belatedly, Aspirin shook with fear: what if that creature had thought of his actions as an act of aggression?

"Nothing happens overnight," he said, taking a step back toward the door. "No one can learn how to play a musical instrument in one day. Even a recorder."

"Yes. I have to practice," Alyona said grimly. Aspirin remembered he had a shift at Kuklabuck.

When he returned—at half past two in the morning—Alyona was still practicing. A very soft, quiet pizzicato.

"Alexey," Vasya said, "can I talk to you for a minute?"

Aspirin approached the glass window framed by announcements and reminders and leaned on the narrow ledge. "Yes?"

The concierge was in a foul mood.

"That daughter of yours was very rude to me today. I only meant to be nice to her and asked how school was going! You know, why she's not in school in the morning, why she's always out with that violin of hers at night . . . I asked, does your father know you're skipping school? And she . . . honestly, if my granddaughter ever said this to me, I'd kill her!"

"Did she swear at you?" Aspirin asked.

Vasya frowned. "Well, no. If only she had. She uses these words . . . worse than swearing, I am telling you. And the way she looks at me—like I am dirt. Worse than dirt!"

"I will deal with it," Aspirin promised.

But Alyona was not home. In the fridge he found a pot of chicken stew, put some in a bowl, and warmed it up in the microwave. He wondered if Vasya could be Alyona's brother. Purely theoretically. Could he, metaphorically speaking, be a fallen angel who didn't remember himself?

*And the way she looks at me—like I am dirt. Worse than dirt!*

Aspirin knew from personal experience the way Alyona looked at the concierge. She'd looked at Aspirin this way many times.

He was chewing the last piece of chicken when the phone rang.

"Hello?"

"Good afternoon." He didn't recognize the voice. "May I speak with Alexey Igorevich?"

"Yes, this is him."

"Hello again. I am Alyona's teacher from the music school. My name is Svetlana Nikolaevna. I would like to speak with you. Preferably in person, but if you are busy . . ."

"I am very busy."

"We can do it over the phone, then," the voice said. "I have fifteen years of experience as a music teacher, and I have never, ever had a student like your daughter. Of course, she started rather late, but she's extremely talented. And more important, she is devoted to music. She undoubtedly has an enormous future ahead of her, enormous—"

"How may I help you?" Aspirin cut her off.

The voice continued, undisturbed by the interruption. "Here is what I wanted to tell you: you will receive various offers."

"What sort of offers?"

"For the ten-year professional program, of course. You may be given all sorts of promises, and you will be pushed to change teachers. It is your decision, obviously, but I would strongly suggest taking your time. Four of my students graduated from the music institute with honors. One girl was admitted into the conservatory. But the ten-year professional program is a conveyor, where children are frequently abused, psychologically crippled . . . I wouldn't want someone with Alyona's gift to . . . to serve as a tool for someone's ambitions."

"I see," Aspirin said with relief. "But it's not my decision. She applied to your school, she decides where she is going to study. Talk to her, not me."

"But surely as her father, you have the final say."

"You'd be surprised."

"Just think about it, please. I insist."

"I will think about it. Good-bye."

The key turned in the lock. Alyona stood at the door, grim and red-faced.

"Another fight with Vasya?" Aspirin asked.

"What's he bothering me for?" Alyona shook her head. "There are no laws to make me go to his stupid school, are there?"

"I don't know," Aspirin admitted. "The laws probably do exist, but to implement them is a different matter."

"To hell with that." Alyona made a surprisingly morose, grown-up face. She pulled off her old sneakers (the striped socks no longer looked clean) and walked toward her room in bare feet.

"Your teacher called me," Aspirin said.

Alyona turned to look at him. "What did she want?"

"She's afraid someone will steal you from under her nose. You're such a treasure, apparently." Aspirin giggled.

Alyona stared at him coldly, and he stopped laughing.

The door closed behind her.

**"Hello," Aspirin's mom said, her voice sounding strangely tense.** "Alexey dear?"

"Hey, Mom."

"How are you? Are you feeling well?"

"Perfectly well."

"And how's your job?"

"Just fine, as usual."

"Alexey"—Mom's voice grew stern—"who is that child living with you now? Whose child is that?"

Aspirin had expected this phone call for days. Way too many people wanting to know about his business, and someone had clearly—and finally—contacted his mother.

There was no point in denying it—at least, not when the truth would upset his mother even more when she discovered he'd gone mad. "She's my daughter. From Pervomaysk."

A pause. Aspirin imagined his mother sitting in silence, in London, on the other end of the line. He nearly choked.

"It just happened," he said apologetically. "She's going back to her mother soon. It just happened this way."

"You are going to be the death of me," Mom said, and her voice did sound like it came from beyond the grave.

"What's the big deal, Mom? She's a good girl. She's not spoiled. And she's leaving soon."

"How old is she?"

"El . . . eleven."

"Alexey." Mom must have pressed her lips together sternly. "Are you lying to me?"

"No," he said as beatifically as he could manage.

As in most cases during his life, Mom did not buy it.

**The end of September turned cold.** Leaning against the kitchen window, Aspirin watched Alyona leave for music lessons: the collar of her jacket raised against the chill, head pulled into her shoulders, violin case pressed against her chest like a weapon of retaliation, Mishutka packed into her backpack.

He imagined Sveta kvetching over the girl: "Where is your hat, Alyona dear? Where is your scarf? It's going to rain, and you don't even have an umbrella!"

It wasn't the money—everything could be purchased easily. A hat, a scarf, a cheap kid's umbrella. Even a coat. But what was one supposed to do about a kid choosing not to attend goddamned middle school? It wasn't like he lived in a village where everyone knew each other, but still—yesterday he got a visit from a cop.

When Aspirin went to the juvenile detention center, they treated him like a vile idiot. But as soon as Alyona had gained a certain, albeit shaky, status, their cohabitation sparked an immediate interest from the law enforcement agents. A local police inspector, a middle-aged man in plainclothes (a rather elegant trench coat, which conflicted with Aspirin's concept of a modern police inspector), came by another day to inquire as to whether an eleven-year-old girl lived in his apartment, and if she did, how she was related to Aspirin.

With a crooked smile, Aspirin presented Alyona's birth certificate. Yes, his daughter. Yes, from Pervomaysk. No, she will not need to be registered. She's registered in her home, in Pervomaysk. She's a gifted violinist, she came in search of a bright future. Why wasn't she at school? Because she was applying for the ten-year professional music school for gifted children. She was preparing for auditions. Any more questions?

There were no further questions. Much more relaxed at this point, the inspector wished Alyona success and good luck, suggested she got her musical talent from her father, admitted his love for *Radio Sweetheart,* and finally departed.

Aspirin locked the door behind him and for some reason felt for the gun on the top shelf. The gun was exactly where he'd left it—within reach. Aspirin moved it under the shoe stand.

Lies were a curious thing—they were so easy to believe in, especially for someone used to lying. Aspirin wondered what would happen if Alyona was actually accepted to the ten-year professional school. He wondered if it was a boarding school.

Then she wouldn't need Aspirin any longer.

A month ago he'd be pleased with the idea. Now he felt a touch of sadness, but mostly fear—what if, upon leaving, she'd seek retribution?

**They made their way to the closest store and bought a jacket for** Alyona—a warm one, with a hood, and the first one that fit. Alyona had no interest in fashion, and Aspirin could care less about looking through the rows of cheap rags. They found one, they bought it. The hood eliminated the need for a hat. On the way back they picked up a blue scarf and a blue flowery umbrella.

Aspirin insisted that Alyona put on all her new things, allegedly to prevent a cold. In reality, he wanted to ensure that his fatherly duties had been observed by the general public as represented by Sveta the concierge.

In the lobby they ran into Irina, the downstairs neighbor who had been so helpful during Alyona's sickness. They had seen each other a few times since their last conversation in Aspirin's kitchen, and exchanged hellos here and there, but nothing further. It had taken Aspirin a moment to even remember her name.

And now she stood by the entrance, visibly upset. The usual

calm of her pale narrow face looked like a mask, about to melt off at any second.

A man stood next to her; he was tall, corpulent, clad in a long unbuttoned coat over a business suit. *The man smiled and said something, adding another point,* Aspirin thought. The last straw, so to speak.

Irina saw Aspirin and Alyona and smiled with exaggerated joy; she seemed rushed, almost fidgety.

"Hello," Alyona said politely and looked at the man in the overcoat.

Her eyes went cold.

Aspirin could have sworn she had seen that man before, and under rather complicated circumstances.

"Good afternoon," Aspirin said, instinctively drawing Irina's (and the man's) attention to himself. "We are just coming back from the market. We bought this warm jacket for Alyona."

He had no idea how this sudden chatty behavior would fly with Irina, a near stranger, but these few seconds of babbling were enough for Alyona to get her bearings and stop staring. Like a nice, well-mannered child, she looked down and nodded. "I really like it."

"Please forgive us," Aspirin said sincerely. "Have a fabulous day!"

He closed the door; out of the corner of his eye, he caught the man in the long coat wave good-bye and get behind the wheel of a large black BMW.

Luckily, the elevator was already down on the first floor, otherwise, they would have to talk to Irina, which was something he wasn't in the mood for at the moment. Slipping by Sveta ("Oh, a new jacket! So pretty!"), Aspirin pulled the compliant, obedient Alyona by the hand into the elevator and jabbed his finger into the fifth-floor button.

When the door closed, he asked, "Where have you seen him before? Do you know each other?"

"No."

"You're lying."

"You love arguing, don't you." She sounded like an exhausted adult. "I swear in my brother's name that I have never seen this man before. And he's never seen me."

Aspirin took a while to process the information.

"Why did you stare at him then?"

He unlocked the door into his apartment and let the girl in.

"I wasn't staring at him."

"Then who? Tell me!"

He turned her to face the light. He had to admit to himself that the child looked neither happy, nor healthy. Pale face, sunken cheeks, dark circles under her eyes. And her eyes . . . they were sad. Sad and old.

"What's wrong?" he asked, letting go of her shoulders.

"Nothing. Do *you* know him?"

"No." He was confused. "Why?"

"He is going to die."

"We are all going to die." Aspirin reacted automatically, knowing beforehand what Alyona was about to say, that knowledge making his blood chill in his veins.

"Yes, but he will die before all of us. Before the sunset."

Aspirin glanced at his watch. Five minutes after five. When does the sun set in September?

"Are you pulling my leg?" Aspirin asked hopelessly.

With deliberate care, she hung up her new jacket, folded her scarf on the shelf, and placed her umbrella in the corner.

"Thank you. I really was very cold."

She couldn't have been nearly as cold as he was right now.

Aspirin went into the kitchen—he wanted tea. No, what he really wanted was a drink. He reached for a bottle of brandy, and then froze—should he tell Irina? He realized that he didn't know her phone number, though, or her apartment number—or even her floor. Was it three or four?

A single musical phrase floated from the living room. A fragment of a melody. Another cold shiver went down Aspirin's spine, perhaps from the music, perhaps from this new sensation of "*a hole in the universe*." As if a thin film quivered slightly, and beyond that thin film was absolute chaos.

"Do you know where Irina lives? The neighbor? The one with the medicine, you know? That one?"

"Fourth floor. I remember taking the elevator with her."

"What's her apartment number?"

"Ask Sveta. She knows."

"But how do I explain why I need it?"

"Why would you need to explain? You are such a child."

Alyona was right, of course.

Not bothering with the elevator, he ran down the stairs. A moment later, he ran up the same stairs to the fourth floor. He reached for the doorbell, then paused, holding his breath, and lowered his hand. He ran back to his apartment, grabbed his jacket, ran down the street to the drugstore. He bought cough syrup, and a handful of the most expensive pills and supplements, then tossed the receipt. A few minutes later, he was back at Irina's door.

He rang the doorbell.

"Who is it?"

"It's me, Alexey. Your neighbor."

"One minute . . ."

She must have taken a moment to compose herself. At least, when she opened the door—only an actual minute later—her face looked calm and even peaceful, and only her inflamed, bloodshot eyes spoiled the overall impression somewhat.

"I brought you some pills," Aspirin babbled. "Because I have been such a jerk—you helped us, probably emptied all your stash, and now it's flu season, and you should always have something available at home just in case." He almost added: "My dear listeners, we need to take care of ourselves, as no one loves us more than we do, so let us all march down to the nearest drugstore, replenish our medicine cabinet, the Department of Public Health wants you to . . ." But he bit his tongue just in time.

"Thank you," Irina said. "But you shouldn't have. I didn't lend it to you."

An awkward pause hung in the air. Aspirin stepped from foot to foot.

"Would you like to come in?" Irina said without a hint of hospitality.

"No, thank you. I am only here for a second. That very nice man you were talking to . . . I feel like I've seen him somewhere. Is he a local official, by any chance?"

"No," Irina sighed. "It was my husband. An ex-husband. A never-has-been, really."

"It's her husband. An ex-husband. A never-has-been, really. I am not sure I understood it."

"Does she love him?"

"Who the hell knows. I have no idea," Aspirin admitted.

The sun went down.

"Tell me you made it all up, please?"

"I made it all up." Alyona dangled her legs under the table. Steam from a cup of tea in front of her pretended to be a tiny tornado.

Aspirin, not believing her, took a sip from his cup and burned his mouth.

As soon as the burning subsided, he demanded: "Tell me what you saw."

Alyona said nothing.

"Was it the Grim Reaper over his left shoulder? Was that it?"

"What do you think," Alyona asked, very businesslike, as if she'd never heard his question. "Will they tell her right away? Or later?"

"How do I know? I've never had an ex-husband. Or a never-has-been one for that matter."

Alyona carried her cup to the sink, washed it, and placed it carefully on the dish tray.

"I have to practice," she said sternly.

"How much are you going to practice? You've got violin marks on your face, like someone busted your jaw. I wonder what the neighbors will think of me . . ."

"Do you really care what the neighbors will think of you?"

Alyona left the kitchen and once more picked up her violin. Aspirin listened: she played scales, the sounds coming fast and clean, then an étude, then another one, repeating it over and over again, aiming for absolute perfection. A pause hung in the air; quickly, as if afraid of changing her mind, she played a sequence of notes, the beginning of a melody that made Aspirin's entire body break out in shivers.

He forced himself to finish his tea.

**Alyona went to bed at half past ten, Mishutka nestled by her side.** Aspirin stayed at the kitchen table. The neighbors above turned on their stereo, and Aspirin cringed for ten minutes, listening to the cacophony (it was a shallow sound, with an arrogant bass that drowned out the vocals), then banged on the ceiling. The neighbors stalled for three minutes, then all went quiet.

Aspirin made more tea.

At half past twelve he put on his jacket and went outside. A couple of dog owners shared a late smoke, while their pets—a bulldog and a rottweiler—circled both sides of a playground demonstratively ignoring each other. Aspirin patted his pockets—he'd left his cigarettes on the kitchen table.

Irina's window, right below Aspirin's kitchen window, was still lit. Aspirin went home.

At half past one he went outside again. Vasya the concierge had dozed off in his booth, but at the sound of the door he jumped up and forced his sleepy face into a mask of true vigilance.

"Alexey! Coming from the club?"

Aspirin was wearing a plaid shirt and pajama pants.

"Nah. Just a walk."

Vasya looked surprised.

Aspirin stopped at the entrance and threw his head back, staring at the sleepy façade of his building. It was nearly all dark, with a few dim lights here and there, and only Irina's apartment—Aspirin shivered—was fully illuminated.

He walked up to the fourth floor and rang the doorbell.

**"I don't even have anything to drink in his memory. No wine, no vodka."**

"I could bring some brandy."

"No, Alexey. Wait. Let's just sit here."

She looked as white as a sheet, yet very focused.

"What did you call it? A hole in the universe?"

Aspirin was taken aback. "You remember?"

She forced the corners of her mouth into a smile. "Of course I do." She looked off into the distance, then quietly said, "He flew head-on into the opposite traffic lane half an hour after our conversation."

Aspirin was silent. He hated listening to the outpouring of other people's emotions; even when on long journeys, he avoided talking to strangers at all costs. He realized that Irina had to get a lot off her chest, that it would be long and painful, and that tomorrow she would try to avoid his eyes in shame and embarrassment. He knew all that—but was ready to fulfill his mission to the end anyway. To pay her back what he owed? No, he didn't really feel like he owed her anything. He just knew he was supposed to be here, with her.

"I didn't bear him any ill will," Irina said. "Honestly. And look what happened—'If I can't have you, no one else will,'" she said, quoting the great Ostrovsky.

"It's not your fault," Aspirin said.

"I know. Yet . . . it still feels that way. Strange, no?" The wrinkle between her eyebrows softened a little. "How is your girl? I see her with her violin . . . Looks like you found common ground?"

"More or less."

"And you fixed your car. See, at least the hole in your universe has healed."

"I wish," Aspirin almost said, but he was fighting hard to control his big mouth. It wasn't easy, and he longed to blurt out something clever and yet almost certainly insensitive. He had come here to listen, though, and that's what he would do.

"Hasn't it?" Irina gazed into his eyes. "Hasn't it healed?"

"It grew wider," Aspirin said heavily. "But I've gotten used to it."

Alyona slept on her side, one arm under her head, the other by her side, clutching her teddy bear. Aspirin stopped in the middle of the room.

It was five in the morning. He felt dizzy.

"Hey."

He decided: If she doesn't wake up, he is not going to try. He will turn around and leave. He will wait until morning, although it would be tough.

But she woke up. No turning from side to side, no stretching—she simply opened her eyes. A professional intelligence officer rather than a little girl.

"Listen," Aspirin said. "I have . . . When am I going to die? Do you know?"

"Not today." She rubbed her eyes. "Is that why you woke me up?"

"You don't think it's a valid reason?"

"Perhaps." She turned on her back. "Depends on one's point of view."

He swallowed a glob of saliva.

"Umm . . . listen," he said again. "How long am I going to live?"

"How would I know?"

"How do I know what you do know and what you don't know?"

Alyona sat up and wrapped the blanket around her shoulders.

"Was she crying?"

"No. She'd actually broken up with him for good. And then he went ahead and got himself smashed into pieces. She's afraid it's her fault . . . like she cursed him or something."

"Childish nonsense," Alyona said. "Cursed . . . that's ridiculous. Please tell me you calmed her down?"

"As well as I could. In this case, being calm is somewhat subjective."

"At least she wasn't alone." Alyona picked her nose. "Why did they break up?"

"Well, supposedly he was going to marry her, but he already had a family, and he lied about it. When it was discovered, they still stayed together for a while because she couldn't let him go even though he was a total asshole. And then she decided to end this bullshit, but he was sure she would still crawl to him on her knees, because what else would she do without him . . . something like that. Or maybe not—I am not an idiot, I'm not going to press a woman for such details. Especially on a night like this."

"That might be the smartest thing you've ever done."

"Very nice." Something came to him then. "What about your-self? Do you know when you're going to die?"

Alyona gave him a reproachful look and lay back down, pulling the blanket up to her nose.

"You said"—Aspirin was still standing in the middle of the room, weary of getting too close to the sofa and Mishutka—"that you will never die. Is that a figure of speech?"

"No, it's not a figure of speech. I will live, and live . . . and you will get old. You may have children, then grandchildren. And then you'll die. And I will live and not get old. I will never become an adult. I will never have children. I will have nothing aside from one single goal—to find my brother and lead him out of here. I will roam this world for a thousand years if I have to . . ."

"I see," Aspirin's voice suddenly became hoarse. "It's mankind's dream—eternal life without old age. Perhaps even eternal childhood like Peter Pan's."

"A dream?" Alyona repeated bitterly. "That's because you're all so stupid."

She pulled the blanket over her head.

# OCTOBER

The phone rang. The voice was dry, businesslike.

"Alexey Igorevich? This is Svetlana Nikolaevna, Alyona's teacher. I need to speak with you urgently."

"I'm sorry, but I am very busy—"

"I am in your neighborhood, very close to your house. Don't you have fifteen minutes to discuss your daughter's future?"

"What's going on with my daughter?"

"Could you just come over to the café on the corner near the subway station? I am not going to insist that you come to school . . . but this is of the utmost importance."

Aspirin rolled his eyes. He considered telling her to go to hell— that would probably prevent her from calling again. But how would Alyona react?

Besides, he had to admit he was now curious.

"Fine," he said. "But I only have fifteen minutes. Not a second more."

The café on the corner was new, opened only a month ago. Aspirin immediately saw the teacher: she sat in the far corner, a cup of tea in front of her. Another empty cup was placed on the edge of the table along with a dessert plate.

The teacher was rail thin, dry, and fidgety.

"Alexey Igorevich? Good afternoon."

He sat down. A girl in an apron ran over and pointed her pencil at a notepad, as if expecting Aspirin to order dinner for twelve.

"Coffee," Aspirin said.

"Turkish? Espresso? Cappuccino?"

"Espresso."

"Pastry? An appetizer?"

"No. Just coffee."

The girl fluttered away. While Aspirin ordered, the fidgety woman studied him. She almost sniffed him—at least, her nostrils definitely quivered.

"Alexey Igorevich"—she didn't wait until he got his coffee—no small talk for this one—"Alyona has some serious issues."

That piqued his interest. Of *course* Alyona had issues. He wondered what she'd done to make that clear to her teacher.

"What kind of issues?"

"She apparently knows what she needs. She chooses her études. We start learning one piece in class—and she prepares a totally different piece at home. But that's not even the most important thing. We have an annual recital, a tradition. The first years don't normally play at this recital—they are usually not ready at this time. But Alyona is different. I wanted to show her off. Do you understand? She's a unique case—such tremendous results after only two months of lessons. But she refused! She said she doesn't want to waste time on preparing for the recital. Do you know what she said to me? 'I take lessons to learn how to play one single piece. I need to master second and third positions, and vibrato.' Vibrato! After six weeks!"

"She sets challenging goals for herself," Aspirin said carefully. "What exactly is the problem?"

The teacher stared at him, her eyes burning with disdain.

"Her head is getting too big," she said finally. "She started missing chorus and solfège. If she continues in this manner, her enormous talent is going to be wasted. She is not going to succeed. Ever."

Aspirin glanced at his watch. The teacher noticed, and her nostrils flared even further.

"I will speak with Alyona," Aspirin said placatingly. "But you shouldn't pressure her. She is having a difficult childhood."

He paid for his coffee and left without drinking it.

**It rained. Uncharacteristically, Alyona took a break from practicing;** she stood by the window, tracing the path of the raindrops on the glass.

"Why wouldn't you perform at this recital?" Aspirin asked as soon as he entered.

"I knew she was going to complain to you," Alyona said without turning her head. "Called for the heavy artillery. Asking Daddy for help."

"It's not an unreasonable request. You are her pride and joy. She wants to show you off. What do you have to lose?"

He bit his tongue. If an outsider heard their conversation, it would sound like a perfectly normal conversation between a father and a daughter on a perfectly normal topic of important school issues . . . and that scared him. Had they settled into their parts? Was it easier for them to function this way?

"Sometimes I think I will never learn it." Alyona continued to gaze at the rain. "I practice and practice . . . Everything hurts. And still, I am as far away from his song as I am from the sky. No, more like from . . . It doesn't matter."

"You've got all the time in the world. Within a thousand years you'll definitely get the hang of it."

She turned to look at him, and he instantly felt guilty about his joke. He flinched at her glare. "Why are you looking at me like that? Anyone standing over my shoulder?"

"I am tired of you. If you only knew how tired of you I am."

"Oh—*you're* tired of *me*? Do you think I feel any differently?"

She made a face. "Good morning, my loves, DJ Aspirin is here with you, you can relax, we have many wonderful cozy hours in the soft cuddly arms of *Radio Sweetheart* . . ."

"Such an excellent impression of me. I'm entirely wounded." Having heard such sarcasm from her, he was positive she caught it from him this time.

He went to his room.

He had an article due at *Macho* last Friday—today was Monday. Aspirin turned on his laptop meaning to get some work done, but instead he surfed the Web for an hour and a half.

Alyona spent that time practicing. Aspirin listened to the endless, exhausting repetitions of the same measures. By the end of the second hour, the piece sounded perfect; Aspirin had to admit that, aside from a light, easy touch, there was expression in Alyona's style. She played a simple dance melody with as much temperament as if it were the "Ride of the Valkyries." He went to the living room.

"Nice job."

She looked at him askance.

"I am sure you will get really good sooner than a thousand years," he said, trying to ingratiate himself. "I give you a couple of weeks—you'll probably play it then. Is it complicated, that song?"

"Not really. It does take people outside the limits of this world. Occasionally, it raises the dead. Otherwise, it's nothing special. Just a simple tune."

Yes—quite simple.

**"Good morning, my doves! And now Tuesday is finally here, and DJ** Aspirin is here again to spend a few cozy hours with you in the soft arms of . . ."

He nearly choked on his words, as if a bone was stuck in his throat, preventing him from pushing the words out.

". . . of *Radio Sweetheart*," he managed. "Some of you listen to us at home, and some of you listen to us at work. There is even a very stubborn little girl who listens to us—and thinks that easy music is a bad thing. We know that people sang at work since the birth of time; they cut grass and sang . . . milked cows and sang . . . what did they sing about? Simple songs, about love and about their heavy fate . . . or perhaps about their lucky stars. And why wouldn't we do the same? Open your ears—today with us we have a special guest, Valeria!"

He couldn't shake off the thought that Alyona was sitting in the kitchen in front of the radio, an expression of disdain on her face.

He'd never told her where he worked, which station and how to find it. She'd found it on her own. She needed to, for some reason.

("**And at the club—do you do the same thing?**" she asked casually, her face demonstrating how little she cared about his answer.

"At the club," Aspirin declared, "I exercise my creativity."

"Slap someone else's tracks together—that's what you call creativity?"

Aspirin silently counted to ten.)

". . . And what is our life, my darlings? No, not a game. And not a dame either. Our life is the constant struggle between our predestination, determined by the forces beyond our existence, and the necessity for daily bread . . . preferably with a pat of butter. We love to live! Why should we be ashamed of it? We want to enjoy things, we want to eat well, we want to follow fashion, we want to love! For those of us who are in love—half an hour of love on *Radio Sweetheart!*"

He imagined Alyona turning off the radio and felt better.

**Wednesday was the day of the Hat Party.** Aspirin had forgotten all about it, but his current girl, Zhenya, took care of him and unearthed a plaid Arab keffiyeh. Hanging around cowboy hats, Korean caps, feathered and deplumed toppers, Aspirin felt bored and awkward. A crisp young reporter turned up, aiming an old mic at Aspirin; had she been homely, he'd have allowed himself to be rude. However, the girl was fresh-faced and curvy, with not a single red spot marring the perfectly clear whites of her naive eyes; Zhenya, who'd found the plaid head covering for Aspirin in the first place, acted jealous.

The dance floor buzzed under dozens of feet. The lights flickered. Aspirin thought the Phantom Club had a bit of a problem with its style—the atmosphere reeked of a village dance. So at an opportune time, Aspirin slipped away, avoiding both Zhenya and the other one, whatever her name was. His desire to finish the evening in bed with one—or both—women was replaced by a simple wish for peace and quiet.

It was raining.

Leaving the club, Aspirin remembered that Alyona was at the philharmonic, which happened to be a hop, skip, and a jump from Phantom. The concert was supposed to end five or ten minutes ago, and so he drove over to see if she was just getting out.

He was right.

The dignified audience was just leaving; black umbrellas sparkled, spreading wet membranes like Dracula's wings. A girl in a cheap jacket stood under an awning by the entrance, clutching Mishutka to her chest.

He'd forgotten about Mishutka. How could he forget? He just did. But he couldn't turn around and leave.

He drove up to the entrance.

"Get in. Quickly. It's a tow zone."

She dived into the backseat.

"Thank you." She sounded sincere. "This rain . . . and it's late."

In silence they drove through the brightly lit center, still alive with crowds. The closer to their house, the darker the streets grew, and the duller the shop windows looked.

"How was the Schnittke?"

She was silent, and Aspirin didn't think she was going to respond.

"You know," the girl said when he stopped under the blinking yellow light, "when I listen to the music written by humans . . . mankind seems so beautiful. Noble. Why is that?"

Aspirin passed the intersection and gained some speed.

"Maybe it *is* beautiful and noble."

As if illustrating his words, a red Ford cut them off. Aspirin slammed on the brakes. Alyona was thrown backward, while Aspirin sucked in his breath from the crushing safety belt.

Three doors on the Ford opened at once.

"Go!" Alyona shouted. "Drive!"

The other car blocked their path. Aspirin looked behind him, only to see an old BMW skid up to his bumper.

The driver's-side window cracked. Sharp fragments flew all over the car, landing on the floor and on the seats. Aspirin's door was jerked open. He was pulled out of the car.

"Get out!"

He punched a hard, hairy mug. He didn't have a chance to land the second punch.

"Asshole!"

A fist in his own face made everything unbearably bright, but he couldn't see anything anyway. Alyona shrieked.

"Bastards! She's a child!"

But she wasn't really a child.

And she wasn't alone.

He heard a low, almost at the audible limit, roar of an enormous beast.

Shadows flew in the mirror. A man shrieked—a high, piercing sound, like a wounded hare. Something scraped on the asphalt, and though Aspirin couldn't see clearly, he could feel a presence straightening to its full height, and the silhouette was gigantic. Something was thrown up like a rag doll, flew about thirty feet in the air, and slammed into the ground with the sound of a rotten melon smashing into a brick wall.

Feet running away in a panic echoed in Aspirin's ears. Tires screeched, attempting to move faster than the earthly laws of physics would allow. His vision clearing, he noticed the road was now clear as well—as if the red Ford had never been there.

Aspirin found himself lying on his belly, head down, half in the car, half out of the car. Broken glass crunched under his palms.

A dozen steps away from him a very large man lay very still. He looked like a dead hippopotamus or a sumo wrestler down for the count. Above was the yellow streetlight, and below a dark puddle grew under him.

The BMW backed up quickly.

"Go!" someone screamed into Aspirin's ear. "What are you lying here for—get up, let's go, now!"

He pulled himself back into the car and slammed the door, forcing shards of broken glass to rain down. He attempted to turn the key with his shaking hand; the third time was the charm. Rare streetlights and dimly lit windows swam backward.

Aspirin shook violently, nearly bouncing in his seat. Glancing in the rearview mirror, he met Alyona's bright eyes; a second later a velvety face stared back with plastic buttons.

Wind and rain blew into the hole in the window. The steering wheel grew sticky with blood from his injured hands. Still shaking and glancing in the mirror—were they followed, was the plush monster contemplating killing anyone else—Aspirin made it to the garage and even found enough energy to greet the guard and make small talk about his bad luck with the trunk and the broken window . . .

He unlocked the garage. The familiar action calmed him down, but to get back into his normal mental state would require unlocking a hundred garages.

"Is he alive? That man who . . ."

"I don't know," Alyona admitted.

Aspirin drove the car into the garage, aiming the lights at the opposite wall, where he left an old vacuum cleaner and an ancient suitcase with brass caps, stuffed with papers of the sort that take up too much space but cannot be thrown away.

The engine rumbled.

"Does it hurt?" Alyona asked softly.

Aspirin realized the right side of his face was significantly larger than the left.

"He . . . that one. Did he kill him? Did he break his neck?"

Alyona scowled. "Why, would you rather he kissed him? Would you rather we were thrown out of the car, beaten, robbed, the car hijacked? Would that be better?"

"No, of course not. But there is no better—everything is worse! What are we supposed to do now? Do you have any idea?"

"Nothing," Alyona said carelessly. "And don't worry, your hands are clean. It's just a few cuts—you should put some hydrogen peroxide on them, but you'll be fine."

Aspirin found her eyes in the mirror. "And my soul? How fine is that?"

"You need to have a soul to care about one."

He sat, fuming. Finally, "Listen. You don't like our world, do you? It's dirty, isn't it? And you—you came from there, you brought that thing . . . And now you get to decide who lives and who lies there with his neck broken?"

"Well, I'm very sorry," Alyona said after a pause. "I spent so long hunting down that two-hundred-and-fifty-pound carjacker. I followed him. I cut off his car, and broke his window, and started beating up his friend. Then I attacked him, and things just got out of hand. So so *so* sorry."

"Your sarcasm is noted. But what if it was your brother?" Aspirin asked darkly. "That precious sibling of yours? The one you're looking for? Hmm?"

Her eyes changed. They looked almost plastic, just like Mishutka's.

"Yes. Maybe. Maybe it was my brother. Then it's all been a waste."

She hunched over, hiding her face in Mishutka's fur.

Aspirin took a deep breath. He had to get up, lock the garage, and walk home, and home was about ten minutes away through dark streets. He had to do something with his battered face and his injured hands, as well—he was still in too much shock to feel pain, but what would tomorrow be like? And yet he didn't move.

"Don't you remember your brother?" he asked. "Could he possibly be . . . like this?"

"He could be anyone," she said from behind her velvety barricade. "Young, old. He crossed the border between . . . Anyway, he could change his appearance entirely. He could change his skin. And he could forget everything. He is likely to forget himself."

"Could he turn into a thug?"

"Yes." She finally moved the bear away from her face. Her eyes, despite Aspirin's fears, were dry. "It would be quite easy. Natural. Because when you—come here—from there—and the first shock passes . . . you want to become even worse than this world. It's like revenge. You want to overcome it. To make it even more horrible than before, to become the worst of the worst. It's like a form of protest."

"It's a child's protest," Aspirin murmured. "The world's shit, and we've got to make it even shittier than before."

"Perhaps," Alyona agreed. "And yet . . . it also happens against one's will. Or maybe it's the other way around—maybe it's this world that wants revenge. It turns white into black, black as night, the blackest in the world."

"And you?" Aspirin asked tensely. "Are you going to start following pedestrians down dark streets? Your bear at your hip and revenge in your heart?"

"No. I am not going to fight or compete with this world. I have a goal. I need to get my brother out of here. And he . . ."

She fell silent.

"He what? What about him? And by the way, could you please tell me what your brother is even doing here? Why did he leave?"

"He came . . ." She struggled to find words. "He wants . . . He is actually a composer, if you can understand that. In the general sense of the word. He is a creator, a maker. Something like that."

"A 'maker' is quite a word."

"Don't pick on words."

"I'm not. I know the importance of words." It bothered him more than he wanted to admit, the fact that she didn't respect what he did as a writer or as a DJ. It wasn't easy, his extemporaneous explosions, yet she clearly didn't care. But he was too tired to fight. "I just want to understand."

"A maker in the sense of someone who does creative stuff. He simply writes . . . he composes."

"Composes music?"

"Yes, music too. Or more like first music, and then . . ."

"Then what?"

"You won't understand."

"Uh-huh." Aspirin was exhausted, both from the events tonight and his entire relationship with Alyona. "How could I. And what does he need here? In our imperfect world?"

Suddenly he saw Alyona smiling at him in the rearview mirror.

"Imperfect world. That's right. Creativity is only possible in an imperfect world. In a perfect, complete world it is not possible at all."

She hadn't answered his question.

They sat in silence for a while, the stinging in Aspirin's hand almost a beat that he could keep time to as he counted the seconds. After a few minutes, Alyona spoke.

Apparently, her brother had run away from paradise.

Alyona argued against such wording. When Aspirin mentioned "paradise," she yelled and scolded him, insisting he just didn't get it. Aspirin did not fight back; it was more important to him to get at least a general idea of what had brought Alyona and her bear into his house and she was finally talking.

Alyona and her brother (and a bunch of other people) lived in a wonderful place where they were happy and free, where there was no death and no evil. Her brother knew all the melodies by heart (Aspirin never quite understood what Alyona meant by "melodies"— the way she said the word made the concept seem quite abstract). However, her brother wanted more—he longed for new songs.

He ran away into an imperfect world, the only place where, according to Alyona, creativity was an option.

But the underage idiot (Aspirin assumed Alyona's brother was her age, maybe a couple of years older) did not consider one thing: an imperfect world was impossibly different from a green valley where one could play a pipe under the delicate rays of the gentle sun. In other words, wanting to learn how to swim, the boy jumped overboard during a violent storm.

And, of course, he immediately drowned.

The adults (and Alyona's world did have adults) decided that the boy's freedom and self-actualization was more important than their micromanagement, and so they left everything as it was. And her brother continued to drown and drown.

Alyona was the only one who had not agreed. So she ran away, following in her brother's footsteps. She also had no idea what to expect.

At the last moment she decided she'd be lonely without Mishutka.

**"And who busted up your face this time?"** Whiskas asked.

"I ran into a wall." Aspirin adjusted his sunglasses.

Whiskas did not bother to smile.

Listening to the beat, watching shadows bouncing in the violet, blue, and yellow lights, Aspirin felt like a snake charmer.

The people on the dance floor, they were in his power. In just a moment, he would boost them up, speed up their pulse, make every one of them feel like the winner of a world race: like thousands of sperm that die on the way, and only one makes it to the end—that's what each one of them would feel, like a winner. The chosen one! Me! And when they got tired, Aspirin would add a hint of eroticism: let them soften and flow in each other's arms, let them long for pleasure, and then Aspirin would boost them up again, and finally—for once— "there will be happiness, for everyone, and let no one be forgotten."

They would never get an Oscar, never stand on top of Mount Elbrus; in all likelihood, they would never even go skydiving. But thanks to Aspirin, they experienced emotions that were not that far from the ecstasy of an artist drowning in a standing ovation. Right at this moment, he created—constructed—a new reality for them, not just entertainment, not just an evening, but another, wondrous, and extraordinary, existence.

He felt like the shaman of a large tribe. He had this honorable position. He sacralized nighttime dances. And he was a creator, because goddamnit, the world was imperfect, and that meant change was possible!

Courage swept over him—not the common, professional kind actors experienced every time they stepped on the stage. No; what he felt was akin to the feeling gladiators must have felt when the door of the cage slid to the side and the first lion sauntered out onto the white sand of the arena, squinting in the bright sun.

Sweat dried on his temples, making his skin taut and itchy. The bruise he had covered with makeup throbbed. People on the dance floor screeched and embraced and danced and lived.

And from a far corner, Whiskas stared at Aspirin, alert and focused like a cobra.

The next day, around noon, when Aspirin was still lounging in bed and Alyona tortured her violin, his phone rang.

"Hey," Whiskas said. "Mind if I stop by?"

"Umm," Aspirin did not like this turn of events. "I am not quite dressed yet. I am still sleeping."

"And what about your daughter?"

"She's practicing. Why do you want to know about her?"

"Listen," Whiskas said, "we need to meet up. Are you out tonight?"

"I am in tonight. I cannot be out with my face."

"Then I will swing by."

"Sorry, man," Aspirin said. "But seriously. I am not exactly in a welcoming mood today."

"Not at all?" Aspirin detected a harsh, unpleasant note in Whiskas's voice.

"Umm," Aspirin was rattled. "Why?"

**Whiskas leaned forward to make his point.**

"Listen, man, I am on your side here. At first you had those thugs chopped up into pieces in your apartment. Those guys are now in a crazy house. Now . . . how are your car windows?"

"Victor, I am not sure I understand. What does it have to do with my car windows?"

Whiskas winced and scratched behind his ear, like a dog. "You can tell me. You know I like you. You are a good guy. And you're talented to boot. And if I see that you're having trouble . . . I can't just sit back and watch it happen."

"Why do you think I am having trouble?"

"Because it already happened twice. Once—all right, could be a coincidence, two guys losing their marbles simultaneously. But the second time? Fine, a few idiots wanted your car. They were wrong, that's for sure. But one of them was thrown in the air like a basketball, and his neck was broken. How? Who did it? No one seems to know. There is talk of shadows, monsters . . . demons. It's a good thing I read this just in time." Whiskas slapped a month-and-a-half-old issue of *Forbidden Truth* on the table in front of Aspirin.

"'Dear editors, my name is Alexey G. I know no one will believe me. You will probably think I am insane, and that's why I am not telling you my last name . . .'"

Aspirin's head swam.

"Wait a moment, Victor," he said slowly. "How do you know about the idiots who wanted my car? Who was thrown up in the air like a basketball? Who told you?"

Whiskas shook his head as if to say: here you go again, paying attention to little things and ignoring the important issues.

"Listen, I am trying to protect your interests here. I've almost convinced someone up there not to hold it against you personally, that you have nothing to do with this. You don't, do you?"

Aspirin glanced at the paper. There was an illustration right above the letter to the editors—a frame from a third-rate horror film.

"Victor. That's how I earn money," Aspirin said softly. "The next letter is about cloned monkeys who raped an old lady. It's a story, and we just pretend it's a real letter. You don't believe all this, do you?"

Whiskas sighed. Sounds of harsh, measured scales came from the slightly ajar door to the living room.

"Is she still living with you? Why didn't you send her back to Pervomaysk?"

"I have my reasons."

"One could imagine that suddenly you got all super tough and took up ripping people into shreds with your bare hands. But it's not you."

Aspirin picked up his story and pretended to be reading it. "Then is it the teddy bear?" he said, tapping the magazine.

"This isn't funny, Aspirin. You should listen to someone who actually cares about you," Whiskas said sadly. "If I'm the one asking you, you can always make a joke. But what happens when serious people start questioning you? Who is this girl, they may wonder, and what is all this stuff happening around her?"

Aspirin felt a combination of fear and anger.

"Victor," he said in a low whisper, trying not to look toward the living room. "A teddy bear that transforms into a man killer? That's a topic for a psychiatrist. Your 'serious people' are going to send you to one right away if you keep thinking this way. And if someone else tries to hustle me—sorry, but you will need to think through your own defense."

Whiskas frowned. "Excuse me?"

"You heard me." Aspirin looked away, already regretting his words, but not backing down. "If those idiots punched me and took my car, I guess I would be in the clear. But when . . . in any case, if anyone else hustles me or Alyona—I am not responsible for the outcome."

The scale in the living room ended abruptly.

"You're an idiot, Alexey," Whiskas said coldly. "How is your girl going to protect you? From whom? Street thugs, maybe? What if the revenue services become interested? What if the cops find dope in your bag? What if you are arrested? Then what?"

Aspirin forced himself to look Whiskas in the eye.

"You should see who's behind this girl," he said in a whisper. "Revenue services . . . planted drugs . . . these things do not concern me. What concerns me is *your* well-being.

"I'd be careful if I were you."

Whiskas blinked, and something changed in his impenetrable eyes.


**"Can he actually cause you harm?"**

Whiskas had left. Aspirin stayed in the kitchen, twirling an empty glass in his hands and listening to Alyona's exercises. An outsider would never have believed a girl who picked up a violin only two months ago could manage such complex passages so skillfully.

Eventually Alyona stopped playing. She came into the kitchen, sat down across the table, and took the initiative of speaking to Aspirin—a previously unheard of occurrence.

Recovering from the shock of this new experience, he replied, "A while ago he offered me protection services. Personal safety, things like that. But now he thinks I know something important and am hiding it from him. And people like him don't like even a hint of disloyalty."

"Can he cause you harm?" she asked. "Serious harm?"

"I don't know," Aspirin said after a pause. "But it's a possibility. No, not a possibility. Yes, he can hurt me. Why do you care?"

"Are you afraid of him?" she pressed.

"I suppose I am," Aspirin said unwillingly and thought that some things in his life—some recent things—were much scarier than Victor "Whiskas" Somov.

"Is it because of Mishutka and me?"

Aspirin glanced at her in surprise. Alyona was not kidding.

"What can he do?" she asked again. "Attack you, try to kill you? Mishutka will protect you."

"Me?" Aspirin snorted.

"You," Alyona said softly. "You are not a very nice person, obviously. But if we are causing you some distress, we owe you that much . . ."

"You don't need to worry about me. I am leaving," Aspirin said wearily, going back to his room. "You can have the apartment. You can do whatever you want."

**On Thursday he submitted his documents to the embassy. He was told** to come back for his visa on Monday.

He had lunch at a café. He felt more comfortable in open, crowded, public spaces. His cell phone made him nervous; Aspirin now jumped at every call, which made him angry, but he couldn't help it.

Zhenya called and tried to ask him on a date, but Aspirin gently discouraged her. His mother called—she now called daily, ignoring the outrageous international rates. As if some relief could be found in the series of tense questions: "How are you? What are you doing? What's going on with you?"

Aspirin ended up turning off his phone.

*Do I even have time to get away to England, or were they going to get me before I escape?*

*And if I do get away, what will I do in London? My savings will not last long. And as strong as my English is, it isn't going to translate into radio work.*

*What would Whiskas do? What about his "serious people"?*

*With me gone, would that allow them to pay serious attention to Alyona without my interference?*

*And then would Mishutka step in . . .*

In frustration, Aspirin pushed away an overflowing ashtray. The waitress pretended not to see it; she continued fluttering amidst the tables, imitating busy service, clearly avoiding his bruised and scowling face.

*Could Mishutka be killed? I managed to shoot him once. It cost Mishutka a clump of stuffing. What if I used an automatic weapon instead? That would lead to a stuffing explosion. Could Alyona fix that?*

It also led to another thought:

*What would happen to Alyona if Mishutka was killed?*

*For God's sake, now I'm thinking of Mishutka as something actually alive . . .*

He called the waitress over, paid the bill, and walked out the door into a thin October rain. He shivered, pulled on his hood, and opened the umbrella.

A black car pulled over to the curb. Aspirin recoiled, but it was only a businessman who climbed out of the car and ran into the office building. *This sucks*, Aspirin thought. *If I jump from every passing shadow . . .*

*This is no way to live.*

It was already getting dark at four in the afternoon. Aspirin had been awake since early morning; he should have been heading home, but he was scared. *What if someone rang the doorbell and showed him a badge? Sveta the concierge would be asked to come up as a witness, a plastic bag with unknown powder would be dug up from a sofa cushion, his gun would be found on the shelf, and it would be announced that the gun was used only a month ago. An appropriate body with a hole caused by this very gun would be found quickly and efficiently. And then Aspirin (who from his infancy had his own room and from his youth his own apartment), a spoiled, privileged Aspirin, would find himself in prison for years.*

*Could they kill Mishutka? Even though the bear was a monster,*

*Aspirin's amateur shots caused some damage.* Aspirin wondered how many of his three shots had found their mark.

He turned on his phone and called home. For a long time no one picked up. Just as he was about to hang up, a voice answered.

"Hello?"

"Hey," Aspirin said, hiding a sigh of relief. "What are you up to?"

"Practicing."

"Has anyone called or stopped by?"

A pause. Aspirin felt a chill.

"No."

"If anyone rings the doorbell, don't open it. Don't make a sound, pretend no one is home. I have my keys."

"That's fine." She hung up.

If he had surprised Alyona, she hadn't let on.

**He unlocked the door soundlessly. Well, almost soundlessly, the lock** did click, but softly.

Alyona was playing the piano. Aspirin sneaked into the living room without taking his shoes off, leaving a wet trail.

Alyona perched on the edge of the bench. Her left hand hovered over the small octave, her fingers forcing a heavy, powerful, unkind mechanism to revolve (or at least that was how Aspirin perceived it), and her right hand wanted to survive and fought for the right to live. A melody fought through the hum of invisible cogwheels, sliding along the slick walls of a well. For a moment Aspirin thought he recognized Grieg's *Concerto in A Minor,* but it was only a fleeting impression; Aspirin had never heard this music before. Moreover, he wasn't even sure it was music at all.

The sounds that Alyona's hands—small, with bitten nails— extracted out of an ordinary piano should not have been possible from an eleven-year-old girl. Aspirin listened, chills running up and down his spine, his umbrella dripping on the hardwood floor. In her music, Alyona seemed to portray the world the way she saw it; Aspirin's heart seized and his lips cracked when that image revealed itself.

The iron clockwork of the music turned one more time and

slowed down. Alyona's right hand dropped on the keys, then slid off, as if having lost its last strength. The girl sighed and hunched over, still staring directly ahead.

Without a word, Aspirin turned and went into the kitchen. He boiled some water, forgot about the teakettle, and had to boil the water again. He took some salami out of the refrigerator and put it back again. He made tea and only then realized he was still wearing his wet raincoat and dirty shoes.

Alyona came out of the living room and stood in the doorway.

"So what are we going to do?" Aspirin asked out loud.

"Did you get your visa?"

Aspirin shook his head. "Monday. Alyona, how old are you?"

She shrugged. "Eleven."

The kitchen was quiet. Aspirin wanted to say something, but words that usually poured out of him in a stream now dried up and hardened, blocking his throat.

"Take off your raincoat," Alyona said. "You are making a mess."

Getting up to hang his coat, Aspirin saw a strange expression on Alyona's face.

"Are you telling me you *saw* what I was playing?"

"I didn't see it," he admitted. "I think I sensed it."

"You don't say," Alyona said, and again Aspirin missed something in the way she said it.

"Listen," he said. "The guy who gave you the strings. If anything happens, will he protect you?"

"If what happens?"

"If . . . if an enemy attacks."

"If an enemy attacks, Mishutka will protect me," she explained to Aspirin in the same way parents calm their children's fears.

**"And here we are, my darlings, and how unlucky we are with this** weather! Alas, October is not May, not in the least! *October is here at last; the grove has shaken off its last reluctant leaf* . . . I saw a grove today, and it had shaken off everything, just as Aleksandr Pushkin described it, it had shaken it all off. Seeing things so bare, we crave warmth, simple human warmth, and now our warm and soft *Radio Sweetheart* is enveloping you in super-comfortable, super-autumnal music!"

On Friday he worked a long, dull shift at the club, pulling a set through like pulling a car along a wet dirt road. He then worked a radio shift on Saturday morning; time stretched, medieval, dusty time. He chose a saccharine song next, knowing quite well that it was going to make someone young and impressionable lose any sense of nuance and halftones. He didn't care.

The day after tomorrow he would get his visa. They couldn't deny him. And the day after tomorrow—on Tuesday at the latest—he would get out of here. For a long time. Probably forever. The god-damn girl with her bear had managed to destroy his life, and she was welcome to what remained.

He was recalling her playing the piano when he missed his cue. The song had ended, and now the sound engineer was swearing like a sailor behind the soundproof glass, and Aspirin just stared at nothing, trying to figure out—who was he? What was happening to him?

"My dearest listeners . . . today is Saturday. *Radio Sweetheart* is here with you. For the next half hour we have everyone's favorite texting game. The first person who sends us a text . . . wait, wait. It's too early to grab your phones . . . you have yet to find out what we want from you. And all you need to do is to think and tell us—what does a shark have in its middle? Think of an answer and text us, and the winner receives—what will the winner receive? Ah, the winner will receive two tickets to the *Shark* movie theater. And while you are thinking—please listen to our next song!"

When he got home, he was frazzled and cranky. He only barely noticed how pale and strangely focused Alyona looked, but it didn't register fully.

In the afternoon the clouds parted and eventually gave way to a decent sunset. When the last of the sunlight seeped into the kitchen, Alyona picked up her violin and left with a sparse "I'll be back" in Aspirin's direction.

He waved her away, lost in his own thoughts. But it dawned on him then:

She didn't have lessons on Saturday.

Out of the kitchen window, he watched her walk down the street—with an exaggerated spring in her step, as if trying to overcome suppressed fear. Not exactly knowing why, he rushed to get dressed.

**He caught up with her at the intersection near the subway.** Alyona looked ahead and did not notice him.

She entered the subway station, and Aspirin followed. The situation was getting really stupid, and Aspirin had no idea what he would say if Alyona noticed him in the crowd; however, she probably wouldn't notice if a hand grenade exploded right under her nose.

Aspirin hadn't taken the subway in a really long time. He'd forgotten how stuffy it was, how harsh and grim the faces of the passengers—his daily listeners. After seeing this, who would ever blame Aspirin for all his inane babbling, for trying to make their lives just a little bit livelier, just a tad brighter?

Alyona leaned against the door on which white letters clearly stated DO NOT LEAN AGAINST THE DOOR. When Aspirin was a child, he liked to entertain himself during long rides by making up new words out of the white letters, coming up with "rod," "stain," and once even "tandoori."

Alyona did not look entertained. She stood in the corner, hunched over, pressing the violin case to her chest. Aspirin suddenly realized that Mishutka wasn't with her. For the first time in many days Alyona left the house without her plush friend and bodyguard, and he suddenly felt nervous for her.

He looked around. All the faces on the train seemed suspicious and unkind.

Where was she going?

Could Whiskas have scheduled a meeting with her, to get her out alone? Or someone other than Whiskas? While Aspirin babbled on air . . .

Aspirin felt hot and sweaty. It was not too late to approach

Alyona, confess to his creepy tactics, and squeeze the truth out of her. If she complied, of course. If not, he could simply stop her from going, he could scare her, physically force her to return home.

Or he could follow her and find out who was after her this time . . . and then decide if he cared enough to rescue her or was truly ready to be rid of her.

At the next stop the train filled almost to bursting with people. Aspirin had to stand on tiptoes to see Alyona. She remained hunched over in the corner, staring straight ahead, visibly nervous. The doors opened again, the human vortex twirled, and Aspirin almost missed Alyona leaving.

She made a dash for the door, and Aspirin followed. A girl in stilettos swore at his back, her voice unexpectedly jarring to his ear. Aspirin squeezed between the closing doors onto the platform; Alyona was far ahead of him, carried by a throng of people.

In turn slowing down or rushing through the crowds, Aspirin caught up to her and positioned himself about ten paces behind. All Alyona had to do to discover him was to turn her head, but—again—she never did.

They left the station and found themselves in a long, underground walkway. Alyona's gait was growing less and less determined. Aspirin was pretty sure she was about to change her mind and turn back from wherever it was she was going, but Alyona shook her head as if ordering herself to shape up and marched on, passing a small pharmacy, an entrance to a café, and a round-cheeked seller of wind-up toys (his assortment of mechanical kitten monsters with glowing green eyes shrieked incessantly, while camouflage-clad soldiers crawled and shot each other). Alyona reached an intersection where two underground human streams collided, and stopped by a soda machine.

Aspirin paused a few paces behind. Was the meeting supposed to happen at this intersection? In this dark, crowded place, in the middle of an underground walkway?

Alyona crouched down and placed the violin case on the pavement. She unzipped her jacket, opened the case, picked up the rest pad, and tied it onto her neck in a smooth, practiced movement.

She then took out her instrument. Passersby walked on, occasionally glancing in Alyona's direction, but Aspirin soon saw the backs of their heads.

He kept watching her though, already knowing what she was going to do and somehow experiencing simultaneous relief, aggravation, and anger. There was no meeting scheduled. The girl was simply going to panhandle with her violin.

Alyona lifted the violin to her chin and picked up the bow. Aspirin noticed for the first time how lightly and delicately her fingers touched the instrument.

She waited a few seconds, then started playing. Aspirin expected to hear anything but the clearly false, harsh sound that came from her bow.

Commuters continued on, paying no attention. Alyona dropped her arms and stood for a minute or maybe longer. Aspirin saw—or rather felt—how she tried to calm her trembling hands and how (not right away, but eventually) she succeeded.

She took a deep breath, picked up the violin, and moved the bow once more. Maybe she couldn't quite control her fingers, or perhaps the piece she chose was too complex, but the sounds that flew under the damp underground arches elicited nothing but bewilderment in him; it seemed the child had picked up the instrument for the very first time.

Passersby walked on.

Aspirin took a few steps around the corner. He could hear the distant meowing of the monster kittens and the racket of the toy soldiers' automatic rifles. Hundreds of shoes shuffled along the pavement. Alyona led her bow over the strings, repeating the same sequence of sounds, and suddenly a melody broke out of the grating of a beginner's exercise.

It lasted five seconds, maybe ten at the most. The roar of the child's violin was intense and terrifying. Both human streams around Alyona lost their rhythm. Someone stopped, someone broke off a conversation, someone dropped a bottle of beer on the ground and it broke in what seemed like absolute silence. All the faces turned to the girl with the violin, and she continued playing, her face focused, eyes narrowed, like a skier on the Olympic trail.

And then a woman of about forty, well dressed, holding a long, elegant umbrella, threw herself at Alyona and brought the umbrella down on Alyona's head.

The melody stopped. The crowds began moving again, most people walking away briskly, emphatically gesticulating and showing how busy they were. Others rushed over to Alyona—to see what was happening. A man in a black jacket caught Alyona; she struggled to remain on her feet, holding on to her violin, even though a thin stream of blood ran down her face.

"What are you doing?" the man in the black jacket barked at the woman who had assaulted Alyona. "What's wrong with you? I am going to call the cops . . ."

The woman with the umbrella scowled like a character from a horror movie.

"The cops? For me? This bitch—this stinking bitch needs to be put away! This human trash doesn't belong here!"

The man gaped at the language, unsure of what to say. Fearful the woman would attack Alyona once more, Aspirin ran over to the young girl. She stood in the middle of the intersection, very pale, with a blood-stained forehead, but she was perfectly calm and even smiling a little. Aspirin tried to take her violin, but it would have been simpler to remove a rabbit from an alligator's jaws.

The woman screamed again, hissing and suffocating in her hatred, and it looked as if she was going to strike Alyona again—then suddenly, as if recalling something important, she ran. Someone near the scene tried to grab her by the sleeve, but she shook off the champions of justice like an old wolf shakes the hunter's dogs off its hide, and disappeared in the crowd.

The man in the black jacket turned to Aspirin. "Did you see that?"

Aspirin said nothing; he picked up the violin case and handed it to Alyona. She placed the violin and the bow inside, and Aspirin pushed down the locks. Alyona hugged the case like her favorite doll. Aspirin grabbed the girl by the collar and dragged her outside, aboveground.

He didn't have to think very hard. Everything happened as if following a script: he stopped at a pharmacy to get some first aid supplies, then grabbed a cab (good thing he'd brought his wallet), and told the driver to go to the nearest trauma center. There was no line. A middle-aged surgeon examined Alyona (a black satin pad still dangling around her neck) and said there was no concussion, just a laceration. He put in a couple of stitches ("purely cosmetic") under local anesthesia and gave her a tetanus shot. Alyona seemed to feel no pain.

"You are quite a little soldier," the surgeon said with a great deal of respect.

"I wish," Alyona said softly.

Pale, with her bandaged head, she looked pathetic.

**"Why did you follow me?"**

Aspirin sighed.

"I thought Whiskas wanted to meet with you."

"Who?"

"That guy who was interested in you, in Mishutka, and all the bloody mess."

"Ah," Alyona said, smiling faintly. "That's silly."

They sat in the kitchen, with the opened violin case on a chair between them. Aspirin looked closer—the strings were . . . perfectly ordinary at first sight, metal, with a dull silvery glow.

"Yes," Alyona closed her eyes. "I put on *his* strings. I was afraid . . . in any case, I succeeded a little."

"You succeeded?" Aspirin asked. "Your goal was stitches?"

"You heard it," Alyona said softly.

Aspirin shuddered.

"What was it?"

"His song. The first few measures."

"And that crazy broad?"

"She is not crazy. It got to her."

"I think it got to everyone there," Aspirin offered.

Alyona shook her head.

"Not all. You see, this song—if you play it properly—it's like light for a blind person. And all blind people suddenly realize that they have never seen light—and never will, and the most terrifying thing is that it's no one's fault but their own. It's a horrible, revolting feeling, and they hate it—it feels foreign and wrong. That woman, she . . . It was physically uncomfortable and painful for her to realize that she could have, but didn't, or was too scared, or just didn't have enough willpower . . . Do you understand?"

"No."

"That song is perfection," Alyona said softly, "playing in the world where perfection does not exist."

The clock was ticking. It was pretty late; somewhere at the club Zhenya waited for him, angry and confused—he was supposed to meet her tonight. She called his home number and his cell, but he had turned everything off—*the person you are trying to reach is unavailable at this time*—and that was it.

He'd had enough of crowds and other people today. Maybe forever.

"Why did she hit you? To punish you for the perfection?"

"In a way. She wanted to shut me up. No one likes seeing their lives—and lies—exposed."

"She could have used other methods."

"She could not. And now she has no idea what came over her. She's in pain."

"Mm-hmm."

"What?"

"It's just . . . why don't you feel sorry for her?"

"Why should I? Tomorrow she will decide it was the right thing to do. She gets so tired at work, her nerves are frayed, and her environment is unhealthy, furthering a weak immune system, and these people keep coming—human trash, these bare-assed hazards, pretending to be . . . *something*."

Alyona spoke in one fluid breath, smiling slightly, but Aspirin felt a sudden jolt of fear.

"How do you know? How do you know all that?"

She smiled even wider, but gave him no answer.

Aspirin tried to recall the feeling that had washed over him at the first sounds of Alyona's violin. It was probably fear. An instant fear, like a dream of a precipice. But, unlike that woman, he felt no revulsion or hatred blinding his senses—he experienced nothing of that sort. He wondered what would have happened if Alyona kept playing.

"Want a drop of brandy?"

Alyona shook her head. "I can't. But you should offer Mishutka some honey."

Aspirin winced, meaning to say something, but stopped short—something else struck him. "Did you know you were going to be harmed?"

"Why do you say that?"

"You didn't bring Mishutka!"

Alyona sighed.

"Well, I didn't know exactly that something like that would happen. But I thought someone might yell at me, or grab my hand . . . and you can't explain that to Mishutka."

She touched the top of her bandaged head gingerly.

"Does it hurt?"

"The anesthesia is wearing off. It's not too bad though."

"You should take a painkiller or something. How will you sleep?"

"I still have to practice." It was as if she'd never heard him. "My hands feel wooden. But if even two measures come out right . . ."

"And if you . . . I mean, when you play everything correctly, then what happens? Everyone who hears you will attack and kick you, or beat you with their umbrellas, or lead pipes, or whatever else they find lying around? Is that what is going to happen?"

Alyona smiled. It was always that: a cold stare or a condescending smile. "You have quite a vivid imagination."

"But if only two measures caused this woman to hit you—"

"Bad luck." Alyona rubbed her cheek. "It's fine, Alexey. I just need to play it well. All I care about is to play that song from the beginning to the end and not make any mistakes."

Aspirin sat down facing her, then got up again.

"And there's no other way to find your brother? If someone comes from out of nowhere, like you—people must notice, shouldn't they? Maybe we should look at some police logs, or even just the newspapers for those months when he left, like accident logs, something like that. Maybe he is in a hospital, or a mental institution. Or even an orphanage. You said he could be any age? Maybe he's a baby, like a foundling or something. If that's the case, then why wouldn't you at least try looking for him in some other way, without those strings of yours?"

"Those are not my strings."

"Fine. *His* strings. But that brings up another point—how did *he* find you so easily, but you can't find your brother."

Alyona touched the top of her head again and winced, biting her lip.

"I already told you everything, Alexey. I told you the truth. You just don't understand it. My brother—here he could be an old man, and it's not like he appeared from out of nowhere—he'd have been here all his life, and he would remember all of it. And his children, his grandchildren, his wife—they would all remember. He'd have memories of the war, his family hiding from the bombs in the basement . . . he'd remember everything but who he really was and what he was doing in this world. Your newspapers would tell us nothing."

*Could this be real?* Aspirin thought. *Am I really sitting in my own kitchen, chatting with Alyona about this world and that world, about passages from here to there, and the temporal paradoxes caused by these passages?*

"I am going to get some painkillers," he said hopelessly. If nothing else, maybe they'd help with *his* headache.

"He will remember who he is when he hears that song," Alyona said, lost in her thoughts.

"Will he? What if he's not anywhere near you? What if he's a thousand miles away?"

"He's here." Alyona was no longer smiling. "I took the same route. He's here, he must be nearby."

"Do you think the entire city walks through that intersection? And even if that were the case . . . You'd have to play this song day and night for him to hear it!"

"No. If I play it well—just once, but with no mistakes—he will show up, no matter where he is."

Aspirin splashed some cold water from the kitchen faucet onto his face, then froze, shocked by a sudden suspicion.

"How long is that song? From the beginning to the end?"

Alyona was silent.

"How long is it?" Aspirin said. He couldn't hear his own voice.

"One hundred and seventy-three minutes, in good tempo," Alyona said dejectedly. "I told you I have to practice so much more, and you, with your 'how long are you going to torture that instrument . . .'"

"I am sorry," Aspirin mumbled.

It might as well have been one hundred and seventy-three years.

**"Good evening," Irina said. She must have just returned from a run,** judging by her warm jogging suit and slippers. Her wet, dirty sneakers stood in the corner.

"I'm sorry," Aspirin began. "This is turning into a nice tradition . . . more like a dumb tradition, but Alyona needs a painkiller, and I don't have any."

Irina sighed. She probably wanted to tell him how irresponsible this was, raising a child and having no first aid supplies in the house. Thankfully, she restrained herself; she simply went into the kitchen and came back with a small pharmacy container.

"Thank you," Aspirin said. "I will bring it back, I promise. And I will buy some for myself. It's just that I needed it so suddenly."

"What happened to Alyona?"

"A head trauma."

"What?"

Aspirin hesitated: "Umm, you know. Happens to children. We already went to see the doctor, there is no concussion, so . . ."

"Alyona is a very unusual child," Irina murmured.

"You noticed."

They stared into each other's eyes for a few seconds.

"How are you, anyway?" Aspirin asked awkwardly. "How are things?"

"Fine. As usual. I work a lot."

"Do you still run?" Aspirin nodded toward her sneakers.

"Yes," Irina said vaguely. "I need to stay in shape. So I run. But you should go back to Alyona, give her the medicine."

"I am going," Aspirin stepped outside the door. "Thank you again. You should . . . call me if anything comes up."

"If what comes up?" she asked.

"I don't know," Aspirin said. "But you should call."

**Alyona had been winding** *his* **strings.** Two were already coiled inside a plastic bag, the third one writhed in Alyona's fingers. The fourth one waited for its turn on the now empty violin.

"Here." He handed her a pill and a glass of water.

Alyona swallowed the pill and took a sip.

"How is she doing?" she asked, coiling the third string.

"Irina? She runs."

"That's not good."

"It is good," Aspirin objected, albeit without much conviction. "It's healthy, and it helps to stay in shape and all that."

"At ten in the evening? In the dark, in the rain?"

"How do you know she runs in the dark, in the rain?" Aspirin had run out of the energy to be surprised.

"I saw her last night." Alyona twisted the peg, freeing the last string. "And she did the same thing the night before last. She only runs at night, several laps around the building."

"Maybe she has no other time—"

"No," Alyona cut him off. "It's because evenings are especially hard for her."

**On Monday he received his visa.**

He stuck the passport into his pocket and went outside; the first snow, white and soggy, had replaced the rain. All he needed to do was to get to the airport on time. Or at the very least he should buy a ticket for tomorrow's flight.

On the way home he considered asking Irina to watch over Alyona. Or was it a bad idea? Of course, his neighbor would ask for an explanation: how could a father leave his eleven-year-old daughter behind?

He decided against it. If Alyona needed anything, she'd ask Irina for help—Irina would never refuse her.

Or she wouldn't say anything. He was abandoning her—what did he care?

But the idea that Irina would be around—this made him feel better, because in some sense Irina was more reliable than Aspirin himself. He was never home, he had no concept of girls' clothes or girls' needs, he didn't even have a basic first aid kit in the house. He'd leave Alyona some money; she was good at budgeting.

What if she lost her keys?

She'd never lost them before.

What if the pipes burst?

So they burst. Alyona will call a plumber. And Aspirin would call her every now and then, just to see how things were going. And after all, Irina lives alone, why wouldn't she care for a girl who also lives alone?

That wound on her head . . . Alyona said it was nothing, she was stubborn as a mule and proud as a granite monument. But Aspirin made a lousy nurse. He wouldn't know how to treat himself, how could he help the girl? Irina, on the other hand . . .

Greeting Vasya, Aspirin knew he would be taking tomorrow's flight. He'd do his morning shift, but say no to Kuklabuck, head to the airport, and let Whiskas and his "serious people" deal with the disappointment.

Although why would Whiskas or his people have to deal with the disappointment? No one would be there to stop them from going to Aspirin's apartment and taking Alyona and Mishutka with them. This would not be exactly a black op, this task of capturing a little girl and her teddy bear.

A dozen chopped-up bodies, and that's that. The stuffed toy would be eliminated.

And who would look for Alyona if she disappeared? No one. They would assume she went back to her mother, to Pervomaysk.

He shook his head. A vivid imagination was a curse for a modern individual.

The apartment was empty. On Mondays Alyona had lessons, and such a minor thing as a head wound would never stop her. Still in his raincoat and street shoes, Aspirin sat on the piano bench and opened the lid.

He had taken music lessons for four years. After that, no matter how much his parents pleaded with him, he fought vehemently for his independence. Occasionally, when the mood struck him, he would sit at the piano and pick out a tune or two; a year later he joined the school orchestra as a drummer. And that was how his path toward becoming a DJ started.

He played a couple of chords now, dull and lifeless. If he'd had Alyona's willpower, could he have become a musician?

It wasn't out of the question. But what would have been the point?

He tried to recall a piece that had stuck in his memory since preschool: "In the Garden." He couldn't remember the composer or the notes. Muscle memory extracted a few cheerful measures out of the piano. Aspirin cringed at the sound and pulled his hands off the keys.

What if he, Alexey Grimalsky, was Alyona's lost brother? What if he'd forgotten himself, forgotten creativity, what if it was him, her spoiled, unanticipated bro?

He couldn't stop giggling.

The key turned in the lock. Alyona walked in, holding her violin case and her music binder, the bear in the backpack, the edge of her bandage peeking out of her hat, her face pale, her eyes as stubborn as ever. She was surprised to see Aspirin by the piano.

"What?"

"Hey," Aspirin said.

"Hey. Did you get your visa?"

"Yup."

"Congratulations," Alyona said after a second and started taking off her coat.

"Alyona," he giggled.

"What?" She stopped in the doorway.

"Could I be your brother?"

"You could. Just like anyone else." She answered immediately, without a hint of surprise. "I have thought about it."

"So maybe it is me. And you and I will go into the sunset, holding hands?"

"I doubt it." Alyona hung her binder on the door handle. "When is your flight?"

"Tomorrow. Wait, did you say 'I could be'? And now I can't?"

"You can't. I've analyzed a few things," Alyona spoke drily, very much like an adult, "and I realized that no, it is not you."

"Why, because I don't look like a fallen angel?"

"Not in the least." Alyona put on her slippers. "But I told you many times that my brother is not a fallen angel."

"That's a shame," Aspirin said.

Alyona sat down on the sofa and looked at him expectantly. With a heavy sigh, Aspirin got up and went into the kitchen.

The day, already quite short, was lost in the gray fog. There was no promise of snow: rain kept tumbling down in long gray ribbons. A streetlight switched on, making raindrops sparkle on their way down through its halo of diffused glow.

Aspirin looked down.

A woman in an athletic jacket with a hood pulled down low ran by the streetlight, her sneakers cutting through the puddles. Keeping her pace, she followed the road around the corner of the building, where he could no longer see her.

He remembered Alyona saying "Evenings are especially hard for her." But it was still daytime, around four in the afternoon, no later than that. He could hear the sounds of a firm, steady, particularly harsh, mechanical-sounding musical scale from the living room.

**"This is enough for about three months,"** Alyona said after carefully counting the money.

"If you try hard enough." Aspirin was unpleasantly surprised. "You could blow it in one day. Right?"

"And what about paying bills?" Alyona stacked up the money. "The apartment fee, the phone bill, the electricity bill . . . Of course, I could always buy candles, but the refrigerator requires energy, doesn't it?"

"You are so practical," Aspirin mumbled. "How do you do this? If you came from another world, your head should be in the clouds!"

Alyona looked at him. Aspirin knew that smirk of hers quite well, that unpleasant, grown-up, full-of-bile grimace.

"I don't have any more cash on me," he said, restraining himself. "I will send it to you later."

"And I suppose I should use my birth certificate to receive it, shouldn't I."

"Then don't pay the apartment fee!" Aspirin exploded. "And let them turn off the phone—you don't need it anyway."

"So I shouldn't expect daily calls?"

He walked off, exasperated.

It was just after eight o'clock. The neighbors' water pipes hummed noisily. Irina was doing laps around the building, her wet hood pushed down low on her face. She took breaks, then came back out and ran another couple of laps. Aspirin was amazed by her tenacity; he'd drop after four laps (and that is if he was being generous).

A pair of new socks, still in their packaging, lay on the bottom of a small suitcase. Aspirin shuffled around the apartment, moving clothes from place to place, losing things he needed, finding them, then immediately losing them again. Alyona played her scales: for the fifth hour in a row, she made them sound harsh, then soft, then smooth, then violent. The extraordinary force that lived in that flimsy-looking girl terrified Aspirin, and yet it fascinated him more and more.

The phone rang. Aspirin flinched.

"Alyona! Get the phone! Tell them I am not here, I am away on business."

The scale stopped.

"Hello. Good evening. No, he's not here, he's away on business. I don't know. I don't know. May I take a message? I will. Good-bye."

"Who was that?" Aspirin said, taking a deep breath.

"Zhenya." Alyona picked up her violin.

His cell phone chirped. Aspirin found the phone in his pocket, glanced at Zhenya's number and declined the call.

"If you don't want to talk to anyone, please turn off your phone," Alyona said. "It's distracting."

Just as Aspirin pulled out his phone again to comply, another call came in on the landline. He felt like an unlucky soldier on a minefield.

"Will you—please?"

Alyona rolled her eyes, but didn't argue.

"Hello. Good evening. Unfortunately, he is not home. He's away on business. I don't know. May I take a message? I will. Good-bye."

"And who was that?" Aspirin took his phone back and turned it off.

"The editor of the *Lolly-Lady* magazine."

Aspirin had completely forgotten about an article assignment for which he'd already gotten the advance payment. Deep in thought, he pulled his business suit out of the closet, threw it on top of his suitcase, and sat down on the edge of the bed.

Alyona started playing again. Aspirin admitted to himself that the endless scales and études that had aggravated him so much in the past now had a calming effect. The more she played, the better his brain functioned. Could it be that he'd simply gotten used to it?

He had to pack and consider tomorrow's plan, but, as Aspirin's head grew clearer, he simply sat on the bed, hunched over, thinking of his classmate Olga who had kissed him in the school lab. Olga now lived in America, and all was well with her.

And all was well with Aspirin. Except for the fact that he was a jerk and a coward, his life was a mess, and it was not clear how this crisis would resolve itself. His parents, of course, would support him; first, they would push his nose into his own mess, like a puppy, and then they would find him a job. Luckily, Aspirin's English had always been pretty good.

He picked up his shaving kit in a leather case, a birthday gift from his father, and placed it on top of his suit.

It was at that moment that he decided not to go to London.

Was he guilty of anything? Did he owe money to anyone? Did he have a fight with anyone? And what gave Whiskas the right to scare DJ Aspirin, a popular figure, much loved by thousands?

He was not going anywhere. He simply decided not to go, that was all.

A heavy load tumbled off his shoulders. Aspirin imagined how Alyona's eyes would light up when he told her about his decision. He rose to talk to her and make her happy, but at that moment the doorbell burst into sound, and Aspirin's hair stood on end.

Could it be Irina? Or Sveta the concierge? Or the postman? Or Whiskas?

Why didn't he opt for today's flight? He could have, it was absolutely in his power. And there was a crack in the mousetrap, but he didn't slip out. Instead he'd hesitated, and because of that, he'd lost!

Alyona kept playing. The doorbell rang again, a long, demanding sound.

Aspirin got up, went to the door, and peered into the spyhole.

An official-looking identification document nearly blocked the door.

"Get the bear," Aspirin croaked. "Hold him. Tell him no! Do it."

The violin went silent.

**A dozen people pushed through the door, all clad in bulletproof vests** and black masks, as if Aspirin was not a DJ, but a notorious drug dealer. They brought no witnesses; the protocols for searching residences of alleged criminals must have changed since the police procedurals Aspirin loved as a child.

"Grimalsky? You are under arrest."

"What's the charge?"

"You will be informed later."

Handcuffs snapped shut on his wrists.

A wave of strangers' sweat and cigarette smoke rolled through the apartment. Men with automatic weapons spread throughout the rooms, taking over as if setting up a perimeter defense. The owner of the identification papers, the only one who did not hide his face, stopped by the opened suitcase.

"Going far, Alexey Igorevich?"

The door shut. Aspirin had no idea how much time had passed since the start of the "operation": three minutes? Thirty?

"Alyona," he said hoarsely. "Hold the . . ."

Mishutka sat on the sofa staring, with the empty plastic buttons, at the armed men and making no attempt at resistance. None whatsoever. Just a fluffy stuffed toy.

Alyona sat by Mishutka's side, her bandaged head hung low. She paid no attention to the nightmare around her. It took Aspirin a few moments to realize that she was changing the strings on her violin.

Had she planned to lead the black-clad brutes to the land of kindness and love with her magical song? Right at that minute?

"Alyona. Call Irina. Let her . . . tell her . . ." His voice broke.

Alyona seemed not to have heard him. She was having trouble pushing the string through the peg hole.

"Let's go, Grimalsky. Put on your coat."

"Wait! I have a sick child, I have to . . ."

He was poked in the stomach—not hard, but enough. The pain made him freeze, then bend double; as he was dragged through the doors, he watched the tiles of his own hallway floor, those familiar tiles that had been part of his home, part of the normal life that he had so carelessly wasted and had probably lost forever.

"You have no right," he managed with his remaining breath.

Alyona was tuning up her violin. The sounds were familiar to Aspirin; he'd heard them many times since he was a little boy. When his parents took him to see *Swan Lake*, and in the orchestra pit before the ballet . . .

He held on to the door frame with his shackled hands: "Wait!"

They hit him on the fingers, and at that moment the melody began.

This was a very different music, not the same one Aspirin heard in the underground walkway. It was neither loud nor strong; instead, it was deliberately constrained and, because of that, ominous. Aspirin slid down to the floor, but no one hit him again.

The fingers that clutched the collar of his shirt let go.

Still playing, Alyona walked out of the living room into the hallway. Aspirin saw her face: narrowed eyes enraged. Tightly pressed lips. Two bright blotches on white cheeks.

A wave of primal fear washed over him. He shrieked like a rabbit, tore away from his captors, and, no longer caring, rushed into his bedroom and dived under the bed.

Darkness covered him.


**"Alexey?"**

Aspirin propped himself up on his elbows. His wrists still handcuffed, he lay under the bed in the farthest corner.

"Alexey? Are you all right?"

Aspirin took a deep breath, exhaled, and had a coughing fit. His head felt full of iron, too heavy for him to hold up. Every time he coughed, white stars flashed in front of his eyes.

"They left," Alyona said. "How are you feeling?"

Using his elbows for leverage, he climbed from underneath the bed. Alyona sat in front of him on the floor, looking even paler than usual.

"I played for them," she said, proud of herself and smiling. "I did it. And you got affected along with the rest of them—sorry about that."

"*What* did you play for them?" Aspirin whispered, feeling his lips crack.

"Fear. Fear is the easiest emotion to play."

Aspirin shut his eyes. *A hole in the universe?* There was no longer such a thing as a hole in the universe. He was on the other side of the hole, having fallen out, like from a ripped pocket, into an alternate reality. There was nothing unusual about that. It was a perfectly ordinary matter.

"And what did they do?"

"They ran. Who were they, anyway?"

"I don't know," Aspirin admitted. He glanced at his shackled wrists. "Do you happen to know any songs that unlock handcuffs?"

**"Good morning, my darling compatriots, brothers and sisters of *Radio Sweetheart*!** DJ Aspirin is here with you once again, have you missed me yet?"

He showed up at the station no later than usual and got into his seat still wearing a coat. Putting on his headphones, he pulled up his sleeves, making everyone on the other side of the glass stare at his wrists, on which two halves of handcuffs dangled like bracelets.

"Aspirin," Julia said when the next song started. "What the hell?"

"I hung out at a BDSM party," Aspirin said without batting an eyelash. "This idiot girl lost the keys. Wouldn't be a good reason to miss my shift, now would it?"

"Are you serious?"

He bared his teeth in a smile and went back on the air.

"And yes, my dearest, I know that there are some of you who did not expect to hear my voice on air today. Indeed, some of you were not prepared to hear your aerial, ethereal Aspirin. But I am with you to ensure that your day is light and pleasant. It is a nice and pleasant thought that there is danger in sticking your paw into a wasp nest. Terrible things could happen to a bear. I am here with you, my dears, so let's think of our lives, let's decide how to lead our existence from now on—let's think and, while we're thinking, here is a new hit song from our favorite artist!"

**It had taken Alyona half the night to saw apart the handcuffs.** Her hands, tireless when it came to her violin, turned out to be too delicate and gentle for dealing with chains.

Playing *fear* was easy, she'd said, whether her audience was a human being or an animal. In a rush, Alyona didn't get a chance to change all the strings on her violin and that made her nervous, but it turned out that only two of *his* strings had been enough.

By now, Alyona had already learned most of the melodies that were the same for humans and dogs. Why didn't she say so before?

he'd asked. She had no reason to. It would be weird to play *fear* to someone out of the blue, no?

"And if you played it at that intersection? In that walkway?"

"Why would I?"

"But it's possible—in principle?"

"Why not? But it wouldn't be a good idea."

Nothing about her music seemed like a good idea.

Alyona had rested for a bit, then wrapped her arm in a kitchen towel to avoid blisters, then started cutting again. The unpleasant screeching noise of the hacksaw made Aspirin feel like a prisoner stuck inside forever and ever.

His idea of dumping the apartment and running away—such a natural response after being extracted from underneath his own bed, not to mention exactly what he'd been prepared to do not more than an hour before his last epiphany—was immediately rejected by Alyona.

Alyona dismissed the suggestion of another visit from the masked thugs. She was convinced that they had absolutely no reason to fear them anymore. The men would have to figure out what happened, change their soiled pants, look into each other's eyes . . . Then they would need to figure out what to report to their superiors. Or perhaps they would chicken out of reporting, and the superiors would demand to know what happened and threaten them with repercussions, to no avail. No matter what, any or all of these things would have to happen before any new raid would be attempted.

"Why bother with a raid though?"

"Because it isn't worth blowing up the entire building."

That possibility hadn't dawned on him, and he had looked toward the windows, wondering if there could be snipers ready to take him out. He looked back at her.

"How do you know?" Aspirin asked grimly. "How do you know anything about them at all? I, for instance, have no idea which organization they are from, who their superiors may be, and what they can possibly have on me."

"Forget it," Alyona dismissed his worries. "They won't touch you again."

"But how do you know?" he insisted. "You have no idea about the rules of this game. Right now would be the perfect time—"

"Are you sure?"

"I am not sure about anything at all!"

"Exactly."

The hacksaw had screeched once more, and delicate metal powder flew around the kitchen.

"Are you telling me you can easily play *fear* to anyone at all? And have you always known how to do that?"

"Not always. But I've learned. I'm learning."

"And what else can you play, you magical little girl?"

"Joy. Sadness. Strong emotions, but straightforward ones, without any nuance. Flat ones, like an animal's."

She moved her head in time with the hacksaw. A ponytail in serious need of a cut stuck out from underneath the bandage on her head.

"Let's switch places," Aspirin said hoarsely. "You hold the saw, and I will move my wrists over it, back and forth. Sorry . . . that came out kind of dirty."

"There is nothing dirty about it," Alyona said, glancing at him. "It's just that you are used to seeing things as dirty everywhere you look. Occupational hazard."

Aspirin swallowed the insult. He had no energy for a fight, not when he was still shackled, and not after everything that had happened.

A long pause ensued.

"So you are omnipotent," Aspirin muttered. "And you are not afraid of anything."

Alyona looked down.

"That woman who hit you with her umbrella . . . could you have played her a bout of repentance? Or at least a violent case of diarrhea?"

"I can't play repentance," Alyona said indifferently. "I don't know how. Apologies are so much harder than fear."

Aspirin stopped moving his hands over the saw and hunched over in his seat.

"Plus," Alyona added in the silence that settled in the room, "it's a little difficult to play when someone hits you over the head. It's uncomfortable."

Aspirin swallowed.

"Let me move the saw again," Alyona said. "Otherwise, we're getting nowhere."

He nodded, and the saw screeched again, back and forth.

"What else can you play?"

"Let's rephrase your question," Alyona said as she continued working. "What is possible to play with *his* strings, and what can *I* play? Because every day I can do more and more. Because *his* song, the one I need to find my brother, is the hardest of all. It is almost as complex as playing a person. You, for example."

"What?"

"Yes. It is possible to play an entire person. But it would require a large orchestra, and of course, there is no way I'd ever learn how to play a person, even the simplest one."

"You won't learn how to play a person, but that song, all hundred and seventy-three minutes of it, that you will learn?"

"I will," Alyona said very softly and very stubbornly. Aspirin's chest hurt without warning.

"Can you play *love*?"

"Lust—yes, I can. Easily."

"Not lust. Love, Alyona. Do you know what that is?"

She continued sawing, eyes downcast. "What you mean is a book concept. The love they write about in *Lolly-Lady* cannot be played. Because it's not an emotion. It's nothing—a candy wrapper, an empty word."

Aspirin had still been looking for the proper response when the hacksaw screeched for the last time and the handcuff chain broke off.

"**. . . And so, my dear listeners, here is what I wanted to tell you. All of** us are at work right now, all want idleness and comfort and dream of vacation, and none of us realize this: music can be a hell of a lot more of an escape than we think. More powerful. Imagine this: you get home from your office, your refrigerator is empty . . . and what do you do? You pick up a violin, or maybe a harmonica, and you play yourself a pizza. That is, if you don't have a music degree, and no musical ear whatsoever. And if you have a good ear, you can play yourself a bit of poached fish in white sauce, or mushroom julienne, or a wild parrot baked with cacti, whatever you want! And if you are a really good musician, you can play yourself a woman, and oh what a woman you can play for yourself! One to take your breath away! Can you imagine? And now let's imagine what the next singer could sing to us? What sort of, shall we say, *material* results would her singing bring us? Is your imagination vivid enough? No? Then simply listen."

He wiped his saliva off the mic with a tissue.

Love, an empty candy wrapper . . .

**"You, young magician, can you play *death*?"** he'd asked her the night before, poking a screwdriver at the handcuffs.

"Leave me alone," she said. "I am going to bed." Alyona got up to go to the living room. Before she left the kitchen, she turned around to look at him. "Do you know what my scariest dream is? It's about a string breaking. Ding—and that's it."

**"And now, my dear friends, we have a phone call! Tamara is on the** line, good morning, Tamara! What are you going to share with our listeners?"

"I want to share how much I love my boyfriend," a shaky young voice mumbled. "His name is Slava. And I want us not to fight so much . . ."

Aspirin's cell phone buzzed in his pocket. It quivered like a fish on a hook.

"Not to fight so much—what a splendid idea, dearest Tamara! All the philosophy of love in five words. If you didn't fight at all, I would certainly doubt the true nature of your feelings, because lovers' quarrels are essential for a good relationship, and as the old Russian saying goes, if he doesn't beat you he doesn't love you!"

Behind the glass, Julia winced and rolled her eyes.

Babbling away, Aspirin pulled out his phone and saw Whiskas's number.

The familiar shiver ran down his spine. Leaving for work, Aspirin had to fight the urge to ask Alyona—with Mishutka and her violin—to accompany him to the studio. As bodyguards.

He had overcome the urge and gathered enough courage to leave on his own, utterly defenseless.

And now, at least electronically, they'd found him.

"This song is for you, Tamara, and for your wonderful Slava!"

His phone kept jerking and buzzing. Bracing himself, Aspirin pressed Answer.

"Hello."

"Alexey, we need to meet," his old friend said solemnly.

Aspirin said nothing.

"Untwist your knickers," Whiskas said in an unexpectedly friendly manner. "You are very lucky. You don't even understand how lucky you are, Aspirin."

**"This girl of yours is a hypnotist—a regular Franz Mesmer."**

They sat in a dark, smoky café. A connoisseur of expensive cigars and an expert on smoking pipes, in moments of trouble Victor Somov always reached for a pack of cheap unfiltered cigarettes.

"Gypsies have nothing on her, Count Cagliostro is turning in his grave, Anatoly Kashpirovsky is shitting bricks. She could be a millionaire, a billionaire, actually. Maybe she already is."

Aspirin was shaking his head. "Hold on. When that guy was thrown up in the air and smashed against the pavement—was that hypnosis? Come on . . . when I myself was smacked against the tree hard enough for me to pass out—was that hypnosis, too?"

"*Yes*, Alexey. And wounds open up, and blood flows, and there are voices . . . the girl herself has no idea what she is doing—her medical file mentions a light form of mental retardation."

Aspirin choked: "What?"

Whiskas waved his hand: "We went to Pervomaysk. Her mother, Luba Kalchenko, has been in Portugal for the past two years, maintaining no contact. The stepfather is there as well, and they took their youngest daughter with them. Alyona has been left in the care of her great-grandmother, a blind, deaf, eighty-two-year-old woman. Of course, the great-grandmother failed to take care of her great-granddaughter, obviously, especially since the girl has had a disability and went to an institution for children with intellectual deficiencies."

"Alyona?"

"Grimalsky, Alyona Alexeyevna."

Aspirin shook his head. "That's bullshit. There is no intellectual deficiency."

"Intellectual deficiency has a wide range."

"She's a mature, developed child."

"Who doesn't part with her teddy bear," Whiskas said gently. "I have a niece of the same age, and she's all into dances, and lipstick, and boys." To Aspirin, that seemed a bit much for an eleven-year-old, but he said nothing. Whiskas continued. "And all those stories she fed you? Was that normal?"

Aspirin said nothing.

"She was reported as missing by the institution at the end of May," Whiskas went on. "She was still missing as of September first. The great-grandmother had no answers, but what could they have asked of an old woman? And when did the girl show up at your place?"

"In August. August thirteenth."

"Mm-hmm. So, for two and a half months she had been roaming around somewhere. In the summer, vagrants like to be outside."

"Victor, she came to me in a clean T-shirt and very clean socks. She's a bit obsessed with personal hygiene. What vagrants are we talking about here?"

Whiskas blew out a cloud of malodorous smoke, just like a small chemical plant.

"Let me play along for a second. What kind of hypnosis are we talking about?" Aspirin spoke louder than he meant to; it was a good thing the café was nearly empty. "Who ripped that dog in half? Or did someone hypnotize the dog to the point where it just cracked in two all by itself?"

"The dog was not hypnotized," Whiskas said softly. "*You* were. *You* saw it being ripped in half. Or did you? Because, in reality, those juvenile delinquents simply called it away. Or there were no teenagers at all."

"Abel," Aspirin said.

"What?"

"The dog's name was Abel. I remember that."

"Good for you," Whiskas said. "You know, I owe you an apology. When you called me that first time, I believed her, not you. Even though I've known you for a long time, and have never met her before. That girl is damn good."

Aspirin wasn't to be deterred, though. "Who cut up the thugs in my apartment? I saw it with my own—"

"They were made to believe that a monster attacked them. They may have wounded each other trying to defend themselves. Or maybe . . . Have you heard of those cases when a cold iron was placed against someone's skin and, believing the iron was hot, the person would get a burn? And those cases when under the influence of a hypnotist, people's scars disappeared, and their gray hair went dark again?"

Aspirin held his head in his hands. The ends of the chain from the handcuffs swung in front of his face.

"Jesus," Whiskas said. "You still have those on?"

"Of course I do. Apparently you can't hypnotize handcuffs off, I guess."

"You're so dramatic—"

"What about hypnotizing a whole crowd in literally one second, to attract the attention of an entire throng of people who don't care for you . . . enough to make a normal, decent woman attack you? Why would she do that? Hypnotize a stranger to attack her, hmm?"

Whiskas frowned. "When was that?"

Aspirin told him. Whiskas lit another cigarette, shaking his head sorrowfully.

"Wow, that girl is something. She could be doing sold-out shows, full stadiums. Have you ever seen a stadium full of zombies? I have."

"Why did you say I was lucky?" Aspirin asked hoarsely.

"Because your case is now closed."

"What? Was there a case?"

"Of course there was. The cops don't just arrest people for no reason," Whiskas said, smiling beatifically. "Tax evasion on a large scale, manslaughter, something else . . . I had nothing to do with it, don't look at me like that. On the contrary, I did everything I could to get you off."

"Off *manslaughter*? Why was I even accused of that?"

"I told you, it's been closed."

Aspirin fell silent, trying to process Whiskas's words.

"It may be for the best," Whiskas said thoughtfully. "That time underground—I think she was provoked to show her power in front of witnesses. To leave no doubt what she is capable of."

"A panic attack," Aspirin said, incredulous, "but where she's attacking with panic?"

Whiskas nodded: "Your Alyona is a walking psychotropic weapon. And the thing is—someone must have trained her in those two months between the time she ran away from the institution and showed up on your doorstep. It must have been that weirdo you wrote about in your article, *'whose stare made the mirrors frost over.'*"

Aspirin felt a pang of shame for writing that stupid article.

"When's the next time she's going to play at that intersection?" Whiskas was all business now.

"I don't know."

"Listen, Alexey. When you see her going somewhere without her bear, call me."

"Why would I do that? And wait . . . why without the bear? Do you actually believe that bear is a monster?"

"She believes it, that's the problem. We can't be an easy target. Her powers of hypnosis must be tremendous if it squeezed large adult males like kittens."

"And if those powers didn't squeeze them like kittens?" Aspirin asked. "What if they had gotten me? Speaking of which, where was I supposed to be taken?"

"Never mind," Whiskas inhaled. "Bygones."

Aspirin lowered his head. Whiskas's smug complacency annoyed him, and the news of an instant case against him—and the just as instant dismissal—did not elicit any trust. Was it a bluff? A fairy tale?

"She made up a fairy tale," Whiskas murmured. "About this world she's from, about her brother she must save . . . The kid wants a brother, that's all. She needs a good psychiatrist, and for what it's worth, this institution in Pervomaysk is quite a dump."

Aspirin met Whiskas's eyes; he saw sympathy and understanding.

"Wait a second," Aspirin said. "I still don't get it—is she my daughter or not?"


**The rain stopped. Aspirin shuffled along back roads.**

Here was that archway covered with graffiti. Here was where "Alyona Alexeyevna" stood when she was placed in Aspirin's way. Aspirin always took the same road from the garage to his building.

At least, that's what he used to do, before the dog incident.

He passed the archway, holding his breath (it stank of urine), then proceeded to the next corner. The trash barrel remained in the same spot; a mangy cat stood sentinel on its edge.

Aspirin walked toward the playground. At this hour it was empty; a puddle sat in the middle of a soggy sandpit, and a wet flyer was stuck to the bench.

Aspirin slowed down, then stopped. What did he expect? That they stayed here, months later, waiting to be interrogated?

A street cleaner, a middle-aged, exhausted-looking woman with henna-colored hair, gathered rotten leaves into a pile.

"Excuse me."

The woman turned.

"Does anyone in this building own a pit bull?"

"Did someone get hurt again?" the woman asked with interest. "It happens all the time. Twenty dogs in each building, and three or four pit bulls. Last month a little kid had to get stitches. Those bastards, the owners, they just do whatever they want. We've collected signatures, gone to the police, and every time the police show up, they are not home. They take the dogs to the country, then bring them back, and they tell the cops the dogs died . . ."

The woman droned on and on. The leaves under her rake looked like chocolate.

"If those dogs bit you, you should go to the cops right away. Every time I talk to the owner, she just cusses at me, that's all."

"Thank you," Aspirin said, walking away.

The front door opened behind him.

"Abel, halt!" the familiar voice said. Aspirin froze.

An animal resembling a pale stuffed sausage flew by Aspirin across the courtyard, paying him no attention. The cat on top of the trash barrel disappeared without a trace.

It must have melted into thin air.


**"What happened?"** Alyona asked.

She was practicing when he got home. The little cushion hung around her neck as usual.

"Nothing."

"Were you attacked? Threatened?"

"No."

"But you managed to get the handcuffs off?"

He glanced at his hands. By pure chance, Whiskas had the correct key in his pocket. He must have always carried it with him.

"She needs a good doctor," Whiskas had told him. "Whether she's your daughter or not, you can't just drop her like this, leaving things as they are. She needs a doctor, and with the correct treatment, she will relax and tell you who sent her and why. And maybe no one sent her; maybe her mother always told her that she had a father, Alexey Igorevich Grimalsky, and it was easy enough to find this Grimalsky in the phone book. After all, she is lonely, an orphan if you think about it, plus she's got issues. She is talented, she is phenomenal, really, no question about that, but what does it matter if she refuses to study? And that violin is not going to lead to anything serious—in a week she may decide she needs another way to look for her brother, singing mantras, or whatever. No, Alexey, she needs a specialist."

The hole in the universe was being repaired. It was being sewn shut, with white thread, with rough stitches, but an ugly seam was better than an endless void. He, Aspirin, was not crazy.

"I remember!" he yelled suddenly as he and Whiskas were saying a terse good-bye. "She predicted the death of this guy, a stranger, actually, but she predicted his death!"

He told Whiskas about the untimely demise of Irina's ex, or rather, might-have-been husband.

"Right," Whiskas said, nodding sagely. "I am telling you, she's a phenomenon. She must have felt something. Maybe the guy had a fight with that broad, got all discombobulated, got behind the wheel, wishing to be dead. Or maybe there is really such a thing as a damaged aura that a powerful psychic can see."

"What are you saying?" Aspirin was shocked. "If you believe in a damaged aura, why not believe that Alyona is a fallen angel who came down to our sinful earth to look for another angel, her brother?"

"Apples and oranges," Whiskas pointed out. "They study psychics in special institutes, you know. But angels and demons—that's bullshit. Are you coming to the club today?"

They said good-bye.

And now he stood in front of Alyona, studying his bruised wrists. Nothing was left of this morning's courage, glee, and healthy, devil-may-care attitude.

*Apples and oranges . . .*

"Something must have happened," Alyona said quietly.

"You know what—why don't you leave me alone."

He went into the kitchen, but there was no more brandy left in the cupboard.

Alyona was playing a scale, slowly, subtly, as if tasting every note, as if looking through the round notes like children looking at the sun through colored glass.

Aspirin made a cup of tea. What was happening right now—was it hypnosis?

He went into the living room.

"Listen."

She lowered the violin.

"Have you ever been at the Pervomaysk Institute for children with intellectual deficiencies?"

She frowned.

"I may have been. I've spent so long in this world that by now I am growing a history. Roots. A long train of sorts."

He perched on the arm of a chair. Alyona gazed at him, her eyes serious and calm.

"And the fact that you are my daughter—is that a train as well?"

"I have to be someone's daughter," she smiled. "But don't worry. When I find my brother and finally get him out of here, my local roots will pale, dissolve, and then disappear entirely. Like stitches," she touched the top of her head. "And then you will be absolutely sure you don't have—and have never had—a daughter."

The bandage on top of her head had darkened a little, but overall it remained relatively clean.

"Let's go to the clinic." Aspirin got up.

"What for?"

"They did tell us to get your wound looked at in a few days. The bandage may have to come off, plus you'll need ointment, and whatever else. Come on, hurry up."

The doctor at the clinic said Alyona's wound had healed perfectly; he insisted that she needed a medical file, which would require filling out a questionnaire. "Where are her immunization records? Where are *any* of her medical records? It's like the girl fell off the moon."

"Shall we take care of the questionnaire now?" Aspirin asked the girl.

"It's a waste of time," Alyona said indifferently. She did not seem to be affected by the doctor's presence. Unlike her, Aspirin remembered his childhood fear of white coats and still preferred suffering to being poked and prodded by doctors.

The doctor looked at him as if he was crazy to be asking his daughter for permission.

Aspirin shrugged.

Now they were on their way home. It was six o'clock, time to start getting ready for Kuklabuck, but at the thought of tonight's shift, Aspirin nearly threw up. Controlling the urge, he asked her, "How are you feeling, anyway?"

"I am fine."

When they reached an intersection, he held her hand. He wasn't sure why—she was perfectly independent—doing the shopping, going to school, taking the subway on a regular basis—and could probably walk across town all by herself. But he just felt the need to have physical contact with her at that moment.

"That dog is alive," Aspirin said. "The pit bull. Abel. Or maybe it was a different dog . . ."

"Maybe it was," Alyona said. "Why do you bring it up?"

Aspirin sighed. "You really think I am not a very nice person?"

She squeezed his fingers. "Why do you ask?"

"Because I care what my daughter thinks of me."

She laughed, cheerfully, and without a trace of sarcasm.

"Alyona," he forced the words to come out. "How did you get to that corner under the archway? Who brought you there?"

"I don't remember." She was no longer laughing. "I came over, and found myself in the alley, under the streetlight, with Mishutka. People passed me by, none were looking at me, they were all dead. I stood there, for about an hour, and just couldn't move—I thought I would get some sort of a sign, a hint, or that my brother would feel me and come get me right away. But nothing happened. And then I realized *he* came for me, and I decided to hide in the dark. And found a hiding place. That's what happened."

Aspirin thought how much better it would have been if she were an angel. It would have been so much better if everything she said always turned out to be the truth. On the other hand . . . if she was simply a crazy little psychic, a runaway resident of an institution for children with intellectual deficiencies . . . if she—whether by accident or forced by someone else's will—ran away from her previous life and came here, to live with her father . . .

With her father.

Aspirin stumbled.

"What's wrong?" Alyona asked.

He held her hand tighter.

# NOVEMBER

And now let us put our heads together. How can we help this child?"

Aspirin sat in a spacious, well-furnished room, strikingly different from the shabby offices of his local clinic. And yet, this elegant place had something to do with medicine, according to Whiskas.

"At this point we're trying to locate her mother. To be honest, that woman is not exactly a poster parent, but a mother is a mother, don't you agree?"

Aspirin nodded like a bobblehead. The man he was speaking to nodded back, adjusting the white lab coat he wore over a gray business suit.

"The search may take a while, since the girl's relatives are currently overseas. Of course, as a father, you feel responsible—it is your daughter, your parental duty, et cetera. But children with this sort of disability require supervision by a specialist, twenty-four seven."

"She doesn't have any disabilities," Aspirin said grimly.

The man in the white coat narrowed his eyes: "Is that a fact? Are you sure?"

Aspirin looked away.

"That's what I mean." The man sighed a little. "This is a very complex child, a very difficult case."

"But she wants to live with me. And she isn't causing any problems!"

"Again: are you sure? That aside, we *do* try to take the children's wishes into consideration. However, an eleven-year-old girl with a psychological disorder cannot decide her own fate, don't you agree?"

The man waited for an answer. Under his expectant gaze, Aspirin felt a sudden bout of despondence.

"What am I supposed to do?" he blurted out.

The man nodded with satisfaction: "Alexey Igorevich . . ."

Aspirin immediately thought of Alyona's barefoot mentor with his eyes resembling drill bits. He too called Aspirin by his full name.

"Alexey Igorevich, please make an appointment for a home visit."

"A home visit?"

"Yes. A doctor will come to your place, say, between nine and twelve to examine Alyona."

"She is perfectly healthy."

"Is she? Two months ago she had bronchitis, and just recently she suffered a head trauma. See, Alexey Igorevich—your attitude toward her health leaves a lot to be desired."

Aspirin had nothing to say to that.

**That night it snowed for the first time this year.**

Aspirin had been at his laptop, working on the story for *Lolly-Lady*. Many years of working for glossy magazines meant that he did not need to think much about what he was writing; it was as if a fully functioning robot inside him produced other people's confessions by request. On this occasion, he was writing the story of a forty-year-old woman who lost her husband to a younger woman; the deserted wife did not plunge into despair, but instead went to work on herself—esthetician, gym, sauna, solarium . . . (Aspirin sighed and scratched his nose). And very soon the woman met a guy, completely out of the blue, in the middle of the street, and this guy turned out to be the head of a large trading corporation. They fell in love. Meanwhile, her ex-husband became very ill, his young girlfriend dumped him, and he returned to his ex-wife. "I imagined this very scene so many times, when he would crawl back to me on his belly like a dog . . . And here he was, crawling back, begging me to forgive him, forgive his, as he put it, 'mistake.' And I watched him and couldn't help but feel pity for him—I loved this man for many years, I gave him my youth, he was the father of my . . ."

Aspirin stopped. The children would have to be introduced earlier in the story. The way they sobbed when daddy left home . . . No, not exactly: how the little girl sobbed, and her older brother remained stoic, drying her tears. They did not accept the new businessman right away, but later they treated him as their own father, and when their own biological father returned, ill and humble, they met him with indignation . . . No, not like that: the brother met him with indignation, and the little girl fell apart. Would that work?

Aspirin sighed and saved the file in the Drafts folder. The story was shaping up to be rather bland: too many tears, not enough passion. If someone had added a spoonful of poison to someone's coffee, splashed acid into someone's face, led someone to suicide . . . But then the story would have a criminal angle to it, and *Lolly-Lady* stayed away from criminal subjects.

Then what if . . . a woman loved a man for many years, accepting the fact that he wasn't in a rush to marry her. And then she found out that he already had a family, a wife, a couple of children, and that he never planned on leaving them. Upon finding out, she broke up with him but before he left, she cursed him: "If not for me, then not for anyone at all." No more than half an hour had passed after their conversation when the man died in a car accident, and now the woman herself was considering suicide.

This piece was dramatic enough, sentimental enough, had a hint of mysticism and absolutely no criminal angle. Aspirin leaned back on his chair and grabbed his hair with both hands.

Alyona was practicing. A cold, dreary melody drifted across the room like fog. Aspirin got up, drank some water, then opened the door to the living room; Alyona stood facing the opened piano, her eyes trained on the music score in front of her.

She glanced at Aspirin, who perched on the edge of the chair in the corner.

"What do you want?" Alyona asked, putting down the bow.

She wore a pair of sweatpants and the same threadbare T-shirt with the picture of two dragons. A small Band-Aid had replaced the bandage on her head. Tousled blond hair, a short ponytail held by a rubber band.

"Listen," he began tentatively. "Will you play me that song? You know—the one you talked about. Just a little bit. But with the regular strings, please, the plain ones."

He smiled pleadingly. Alyona thought about it for a moment, then picked up her rosin. A scent of pine swam in the air. A cloud of white dust rose, then settled. Alyona moved the rosin up and down the bow, visibly enjoying the process.

Aspirin moved to the sofa. Alyona stood in the middle of the room, and hoisted the violin to her chin with a smooth, proud gesture. She held up the bow and closed her eyes.

Aspirin placed both hands on his knees, ready to listen.

"I'll play the middle part," Alyona said with nervous uncertainty.

"Go ahead."

She played.

At first Aspirin simply listened, trying to understand how the melody affected him. Alyona played extraordinarily complex passages, the technical level of which should have been impossible for a young girl, and occasionally she would lose her place and make a mistake, but she delivered each note with such temperament and yet so naturally that Aspirin froze in his seat, afraid of spooking her.

At some point he felt as if he were floating around the chandelier, looking down at the girl with her violin and at himself from above. He truly believed that was what the melody was supposed to do to him—but only for a split second.

"Wait. That's Mozart!"

She put the violin down and smiled, openly pleased with herself.

"'Fool me once, shame on me . . .' Oh come on, are you offended? Don't be, I was just kidding."

But he did feel hurt, and he went to his bedroom, never gathering enough courage to speak with her. He felt helpless and hollow. A runaway from a mental institution, an angel falling from heaven—everything was topsy-turvy, nothing could be trusted, and only one thing was clear: if this continued, he, Aspirin, was going to lose his mind.

He opened the window, letting in one of two instantly melted snowflakes. Outside Irina ran laps around the building following her own footsteps.

**Lap after lap**—this measured pace reminded Aspirin of Alyona's zeal in music. Wet snow flew from under Irina's wet sneakers.

Aspirin ran by her side: "I can't handle more than a hundred laps. I maintain a sedentary lifestyle."

Irina turned her head, meaning to say something but then probably decided to save her breath.

"Have you ever done track and field?"

"When I was a young girl . . ."

"I thought so. You still have the professional athlete's approach to movement."

The road turned a corner and went uphill. Aspirin's breathing got heavier; they passed a parking lot, a bus stop, turned another corner, then went downhill. Aspirin sped up. Irina kept her pace. By the next turn Aspirin slowed down, got his breathing under control, and allowed Irina to catch up with him.

"I see you running every night."

"Not every night," she said evenly. "Sometimes I am on call."

"My work gets busy too. But I wouldn't pick up running in any case. Running is boring."

She said nothing. They ran across the courtyard, took another turn, and the road went uphill again; wet snow fell, threatening to glue their eyes shut. Puddles sprayed from underneath their feet.

"I don't even own sneakers," Aspirin said, his shoes thudding in the snow.

They passed a parking lot, a bus stop, turned a corner, then ran downhill. Another lap around the courtyard. He could see Irina's breath in the cold air.

The road went uphill. Aspirin fell a little behind, then leaped ahead to catch up with Irina. He stopped her, and she didn't protest. He held her shoulders and turned her to face him.

Snowflakes sparkled on her face. Brightly lit distant windows reflected in her eyes.

He held her, so thin, so tense, belonging to no one. Their mouths met, and her lips felt chapped, like cracked desert soil, and he licked them like a dog licks his master's wound.

Snow fell like down from a ripped pillow, refusing to melt.

**He woke up in the darkness and knew Irina was awake.**

It was morning. Water pipes grumbled, the elevator screeched. The front door slammed shut. Aspirin pulled his body back under the blanket like a snail back into its shell. He didn't want morning. He wanted rest.

Irina remained still. In the darkness he found her shoulder, goose bumps all over her skin.

"Are you cold?"

"No. It's time to get up."

"No, it's not," Aspirin murmured.

Irina pulled away. In the darkness she climbed from underneath the blanket, slipped from the room, and he caught a glimpse of her silhouette against the door frame. The door closed.

He was irreversibly awake.

**"Good morning," a tall woman of about forty said. "I am your doctor."**

She had on a uniform with an emblem sewn on her chest. Aspirin would never have believed that average clinics supplied their staff with such outfits.

"And you must be Alyona Grimalsky?" the woman asked, baring her teeth in a professional smile. "Hello."

Alyona was playing her scales, and the quick glance she threw at the woman over her bow did not bode well for the future. The woman wanted to come closer, but after taking a tiny step, changed her mind and sat down on a chair, pretending to listen to Alyona's exercises. Aspirin winced: he would have preferred that the doctor reprimand the girl, saying that an adult is addressing you, and you . . . But the doctor listened and smiled, behaving exactly how—in Aspirin's mind—specialists in pediatric intellectual disabilities were supposed to behave.

What if the girl moved from the scales to playing *fear?* Or (Aspirin's hair stood on end) *lust?*

He began to panic, but at that moment Alyona finished the scale and brought down the bow with a flourish. She placed her violin in its case, sat down on the sofa, and pressed Mishutka, the silent witness to the scene, to her chest.

"Is this your teddy bear?" the woman asked sweetly.

Aspirin flinched as if something flew over his head—he recalled Irina asking the same question in a similar situation. But Irina had come right over, Irina wasn't afraid of anything; she had to help a sick child, and she, unlike the uniformed woman, had no ulterior motives for asking that question.

Apropos of nothing he thought of how infinitely loving Irina was in bed. Thinking of the scent of her skin made his nostrils flare. His fingertips remembered her breasts—like a pianist remembering a melody; meanwhile, the uniformed woman beckoned Alyona to come closer: "Let's take a look at your stitches."

Alyona hesitated for a moment, then went over, leaving Mishutka on the sofa.

The woman examined the stitches on Alyona's head, nodded, murmuring something unintelligible, asked to see Alyona's throat, and listened to her lungs.

"You are not afraid of shots, are you?" she asked cheerfully.

Alyona raised an eyebrow. Aspirin stood very close to the woman as she rummaged through her doctor's bag; for a second their eyes met and the fingers of Aspirin's hands went numb with fear and revulsion.

"Why do I need a shot?" Alyona asked innocently.

"It won't hurt at all, it will just pinch for a second," the woman chirped, filling up a syringe. "Your stitches are not healing all that well, and there is a chance of infection. But I have this wonderful

Swiss medication—a quick injection, and by tomorrow you will forget anything ever hurt."

"It doesn't hurt right now," Alyona informed her. "And the surgeon at the clinic told me my wound was healing perfectly, didn't he, Daddy?"

She stared into Aspirin's eyes; this was the first time she'd ever called him Daddy. It was a signal, perhaps a threat, perhaps a reproach, or maybe it was a cry for help. Standing in the middle of the room, Aspirin had no idea what to do. Was he supposed to pick a physical fight with this woman?

"At the clinic," the woman said with contempt, "they simply didn't have this medication—it wasn't even delivered until yesterday. Are you really that scared? It doesn't hurt at all."

Alyona looked from Aspirin to the doctor and back.

"Excuse me," Aspirin said hoarsely. "May I speak with you for a moment?"

"Can this wait?" the uniformed woman asked with a hint of aggravation. "I have the syringe ready to go."

"And we're not going anywhere. I would like to hear a little more about this medication," Aspirin said. "Alyona has allergies to certain drugs."

"Really? Well, not this one. This medication does not cause allergies."

"May I see the label?"

Now visibly annoyed, the woman stared at him. "Are you a medical professional? What is the point of arguing?"

"I don't need any shots," Alyona said. "Who are you, and what do you want?"

The woman threw a quick glance at Aspirin. He shrugged as if saying—not much I can do here. The woman's eyes measured the space between her and Alyona. The syringe twitched in her hand like a stinger.

Aspirin held his breath.

Several things happened at once. The woman threw herself on Alyona like a cobra, Aspirin rushed to stop the hand with the syringe, the upstairs neighbors turned on their stereo system, and a low growl spread across the room like distant thunder.

The woman shook Aspirin off and jumped over to the door. Alyona sat on the sofa, her teddy bear pressed to her chest; Mishutka's button eyes stared directly at the doctor and no one else. Aspirin would have sworn on his right arm that that was the case.

The bass of the neighbors' stereo made the wall shake and the chandelier sway back and forth. The doctor breathed heavily. Aspirin imagined Mishutka leaping out of Alyona's arms and growing, becoming gigantic right in front of their eyes, his claws at the ready. He imagined sprays of blood marring the ceiling, the blue uniform turning brown, skin hanging in shreds, and the screams stopping abruptly . . .

The doctor caught his eye. Behind the walls, the stereo hummed—just like distant thunder. The doctor looked from Aspirin to Mishutka, then to Alyona . . .

She was in such a hurry to leave she almost forgot her bag.

**"So you have been planning to hand me over."**

Seemingly unaffected, Alyona had been sliding the rosin over the bow. Aspirin paced around the room, his hands shaking, his fingers still numb. He looked at her as if she hadn't just seen him defend her.

"Who was that woman? Did you ask her to come?"

"You would really ask me that? You really think that little of me? You know what?" Aspirin stopped in his tracks. "Get your violin. Go ahead, play for them. Play fear, scabies, diarrhea, anything at all. They will come, and you will give them concerts. Go ahead. They will arrest me over and over again, you will get me out over and over again, until some sharpshooter peeks into our window from a helicopter and shoots the hell out of both of us."

"Calm down." She looked at him over the bow, the same way she'd looked at the doctor. "No one really cares about you. No one is going to abduct, maim, or arrest you. And as for me, I can stand up for myself. Don't worry."

She began another scale.

"No!" he barked over the sound of the violin. "You *can't* stand up for yourself. Call your mentor, your guru, whoever that barefoot jerk was. If you don't, they will take you when you are asleep, or on the street, or during your music lessons. They will inject you with something and take you away, and I won't be able to do shit about it!"

But Alyona kept playing, paying him no attention. Like a kicked dog, Aspirin shuffled into his bedroom and spent the rest of the night on the Internet, drowning his anger, frustration, and fear in a muddy stream of useless information.

That night, unable to resist, he went one floor below and rang Irina's doorbell.

**The snowstorm continued for days.**

Located right above each other, their apartments had at some point been identical, but in the last ten years each apartment had been remodeled according to its owner's taste. And now Aspirin felt like he was living in two parallel realities, and the road between them consisted of only two sets of stairs, an Escher-like loop. Coming back to his own place, he sighed with relief and sadness.

Cars got stuck in snowdrifts, municipal services struggled with multiple issues, and the city overall suffered from blockage. Children shrieked with glee, jumping in the snow and having snowball fights, but they seemed the only ones to find any joy. Alyona continued attending music lessons, her boots squeaking in the fresh snow, a plush head dusted with snowflakes peeking over her shoulder.

For the first few days Aspirin felt extremely nervous. He was worried Alyona would not come back. However, she would return as usual, have a bite of supper, and pick up her violin. To all Aspirin's questions she would give the same answer: no. Nothing happened. No one approached her. No one asked her anything. Nothing was different.

The expectation of a catastrophe had been building up. Aspirin felt frozen in midair, like a mutant snowflake, as if he were floating in zero gravity, his stomach somewhere near his throat.

Irina had a habit of keeping her windows slightly open, letting warm air out into the cold. Every time he looked up at her window, Aspirin knew he had to make some decisions. He would attempt to do so, but enough time would pass, and he'd have to get ready to go to the club, or to see an editor, or some other place he absolutely had to go. And then he would leave his apartment and escape into some other reality, a noisy, cheerful one, where he, Aspirin, was loved and admired by all. He would become himself again, easygoing, sarcastic, indifferent. He would think it was forever.

But at midnight a light would switch on in her bedroom, a dull green light behind tightly shut curtains. Coming back from the club, as if returning from Mars, Aspirin would see that light and fly toward it like a happy butterfly, strangely emerging from the cocoon of his "regular" life into a being unrecognizable to the outside world.

No one knew when this strange snowy romance would end—until one day it did, on the first calendar day of winter. Aspirin had stayed late at the club. Upon his return home at five in the morning, he looked up and saw that all of Irina's windows on the fourth floor were completely dark.

For a while he stood under the falling snow watching the dark windows. That night all the babies and all the sick people slept well—no one got up to get some water, and no one feverishly composed poetry or stared at shadows. All were asleep except Aspirin, who stood under Irina's windows feeling the effects of alcohol wear off, thinking of nothing, regretting nothing at all. The snowfall slowed down, then stopped. The clouds parted quickly, and the winter sky revealed a multitude of stars.

# DECEMBER

My doves, winter is here! I mean, we have all noticed it before when we had to work our shovels, digging out our cars, but now it's here officially, proved by the calendar, and that, my dears, is no joke. Soon we'll hear the growl of a blizzard—are you frightened? You shouldn't be! Remember, *Radio Sweetheart* is here with you, with its soft paws, ready to protect you from the frost! Stay with us! Call us, text us, and we will play the warmest, coziest winter music for you, the music you deserve!"

Irina never called him. Aspirin never called her either. Thank God they no longer needed to figure out who dumped whom, like a couple of resentful teenagers.

"We have Vita on the line! Hello, Vita. Whom shall we make happy today? Who is going to receive your musical hello?"

The previous night Alyona had performed at a city-wide student winter recital. Aspirin drove her downtown, to the old Center for the Arts, where the flat stage still kept memories of past assemblies. The concert hall was nearly full—most of the audience was the teachers and parents of the performers. When the MC, a girl of about sixteen, announced that the first-year student Alyona Grimalsky would perform the Gluck "Melodie, Dance of the Blessed Spirits" from *Orfeo ed Euridice,* a slight murmur ran through the concert hall—the audience was surprised.

Alyona wore a white shirt and a black skirt, bought the day before without trying it on and without any fuss. She came out and squinted at the audience. Aspirin broke out in a cold sweat; he thought the girl managed to switch the strings and, instead of "Melodie," she would now play a song that raised the dead.

But that didn't happen. Alyona was simply looking for him, Aspirin, and when she saw him in the audience, she relaxed, lifted her violin and played. It wasn't pure emotion, in the way she talked about playing in the underground passage. But it was pure—pure music, and perhaps it was even more powerful.

The concert hall froze.

Alyona played the way people talked about beautiful memories. She spoke with the audience, without a trace of smugness or a hint of arrogance, restraint, or inhibition. At that moment everyone in the concert hall realized that if truly happy and free people existed, they looked exactly like that girl in a slightly wrinkled white shirt and a skirt that was a tad too long. And when she finished, the audience remained in shock for a minute, and then it exploded in a barrage of voices and applause. One of the children in the audience even whistled, but was quickly called to order.

Alyona took a bow, accepting the crowd without showing off or shying away, then left the stage without looking back.

The concert got off the rails a bit—the crowd simply could not settle. Someone rose from his seat, someone snapped at a neighbor, a chunky boy in a shiny shirt was sobbing for no reason. The MC had trouble announcing the next performer. A large crowd gathered backstage, their own children's performances forgotten.

Alyona still held on to her violin. Svetlana Nikolaevna, the teacher Aspirin had met before, stood by Alyona's side, ready to protect her treasure from a minute threat, and the two of them had been circled by a bald man and two women, like a family of sharks surrounding potential dinner.

"And I am telling you for the fifth time, she is not going to change teachers!"

"Please, there's no need for drama—I just want to talk."

"What is all this talk about being a first year—whom are you trying to trick? How long have you been studying violin, dear?"

". . . must discuss with the parents . . ."

"Quiet, please! A child is onstage!"

And it was true—onstage some hapless child had been trying to overcome the noise in the audience.

Svetlana Nikolaevna noticed Aspirin, and her eyes took on an impression of a goalie facing a penalty shot.

"Alexey Igorevich! Let me congratulate you—as you know, I gave Alyona extra lessons in the last few weeks . . ."

"Let's go," Alyona said quietly; Aspirin had no sooner understood her than he heard the actual words.

"Thank you very much to all," he said politely but firmly. "The child is not well. We have to go to the clinic—I'm sure you understand."

With one hand he grabbed Alyona's case, lying nearby on a rickety stool, took Alyona's elbow with the other, and cutting through the crowd, moved toward the wooden steps leading off the stage.

He felt their greedy stares on his back. At that moment every one of them had decided that Alyona could not go far—the school's address was listed, her phone number was recorded; to locate the young genius would be a piece of cake. What would they promise her? A competition in Vienna? A tour in France? Golden rivers, diamond shores?

Skidding in the dirty snow, Aspirin drove away from the Center for the Arts. Alyona stretched out on the backseat, a reflection of distant warm light on her face.

"Alyona," Aspirin said. "What if you take their advice? They have a point. It would be a shame to waste a talent like yours."

She did not respond. He misinterpreted her silence and continued enthusiastically:

"But seriously, you have quite a future ahead of you. Huge concert halls. Posters all over the world with your face and your name. 'Alyona Grimalsky everywhere . . .'"

"And *Radio Sweetheart* will have a new theme," she said. "Grimalsky Grimly."

Aspirin stopped short.

"Don't be offended." She sat up on the backseat. "If someone offered it to you—all these concert halls, posters, throngs of fans—would you have agreed?"

"When I was eleven—sure I would have."

"Have you ever been offered something like that?"

He put the brakes on in front of a set of lights. Wet snow squelched under his tires; the street crawled with the speed of a few miles per hour.

"I have never been a true wunderkind," Aspirin admitted.

"That's not the point." Alyona picked her nose, lost in thought. "Do you believe that the whole point of creativity is to get someone to applaud?"

"I said absolutely nothing on the subject of creativity," Aspirin said coldly.

Both were silent for a few minutes. Windshield wipers slid back and forth, whisking wet dirt away from the glass.

"I don't think I need to go back to music school," Alyona said suddenly. "It causes too many problems. I already know what I need to do."

Aspirin caught her eye in the rearview mirror and nearly collided with a passing Mercedes.

"Congratulations," Whiskas said. "How's your prodigy doing?"

"How do you know?" Aspirin mumbled.

"You seem to forget I am a man of the people," Whiskas said. He leaned back on his chair. "The whole city is talking about it."

Aspirin winced.

"I am not lying," Whiskas said. "Get this—my wife has a friend whose sister's daughter took violin lessons with Svetlana Nikolaevna. She graduated a couple of years ago, and they are still very close. That's how small our world is."

Aspirin said nothing.

"How are things going with her?" Whiskas asked in a very different, very businesslike tone. "How is she with you? Are you friends?"

"Bosom buddies," Aspirin said grimly.

"That's good. Try not to annoy her. Say yes to everything. Spoil her, keep her happy. I worry about you, Alexey."

"You *worry* about me? For what bloody reason?"

"For the sole reason that you are in her power. That bear of hers, and now the violin. Does she ever sleep? The girl, I mean?"

"I can only assure you the bear never sleeps. Ever. Trust me on that."

Whiskas bared his teeth. "Very funny. So why hasn't she been at the music school lately? She's missed two lessons already."

"So you've been staking out the school."

Whiskas shrugged. "Well?"

"She's done."

Whiskas frowned. "What do you mean?"

"She dropped it," Aspirin snapped. "Quit cold turkey. I am afraid she may never leave the house now."

Whiskas gazed at Aspirin as a chess player gazes at the board. Swirls of tobacco smoke floated between them like a dozen weary gray worms.

"Take care of yourself," Whiskas said finally. Aspirin caught a glimpse of nearly genuine compassion in his eyes.

Nearly.

**"Alyona!"**

He had just come back from his shift. The snow on his shoes melted like candle wax.

"Alyona! Can you get me a rag?"

Leaving the shoes by the threshold, he glanced into the kitchen. A single plate was left in the sink, a lonely petal of boiled onion stuck to its bottom. Lights were off in the bathroom; in the living room Mishutka sat on the sofa, staring at Aspirin with his plastic peepers.

Aspirin's knees buckled. How did they get her to come out? What promises had been made? How?

He collapsed in the chair. His apartment was empty, it had been de-Alyonaed. Hadn't he been dreaming about it for so long?

But hadn't those dreams turned into nightmares the last few weeks?

Stumbling, he went into the kitchen and took a sip of brandy. He opened his laptop and started a game of Miner. The simple game proved to be as effective as a drug. Aspirin managed to perish on the cartoon minefield before the brandy kicked in, and an outline of an article appeared through the fog in his leaden head.

It was about intelligence agencies abducting people. About an extremely talented girl violinist who becomes famous after a single performance at a single recital. Rushing through the first five thousand characters, he took a deep breath. The article was rather insipid, and he was too professional not to notice it. So a child was abducted. Big deal.

He fought the impulse of slamming his fist into the keys and pulled himself together. He should make the girl a genius of extrasensory perception and telekinesis, and her abductors should be not just any intelligence agency, but a worldwide web of deeply secretive experts on astral projection. Or aliens? No—aliens were so last year.

Mulling over the details, he slid closer and closer to the edge of his swivel chair, and when a key turned in the lock, the chair slid from under Aspirin and rolled backward, seemingly in jest.

Luckily, there had been no witnesses to the fall, and his tailbone—if not his dignity—remained intact.

Standing in the puddle provided by Aspirin's wet shoes, Alyona pulled off her snow-covered boots, a gigantic bruise under her right eye.

"Did they hit you?"

"Who?"

Alyona's voice was tired and perfectly calm. With an enormous effort, Aspirin pulled himself together again.

"Where have you been?"

"I fell." She could barely move her lips. "I slammed my face into that goddamn machine."

"What machine?"

"The automatic coffee machine." She smiled with one corner of her mouth. "What did you think I would say?"

**This time she nearly succeeded—she played for fifty-three minutes with** very few mistakes. However, Alyona admitted, the tempo was slower than it was supposed to be. Aspirin imagined Alyona standing at the intersection of two human streams, playing, playing, playing . . .

"And how did people react?"

"Differently. Because of my tempo being too slow, the melody became kind of vague. Some people swore. Some passed by without looking. An old woman screamed for half an hour, then got tired and left. And then . . ."

Alyona unlocked the case. Aspirin froze: a pile of wood chips lay where the violin was supposed to be.

"It's fine," Alyona said. "It's nothing. The strings are intact."

She pulled out the remains of the neck and began taking off the strings.

"How did it happen?" Aspirin asked.

"This old cop showed up," Alyona explained. "He couldn't handle it, and—"

"Did he hit you?"

"I told you already, no one hit me. We simply fought over the violin, I stumbled a little and went face-first into that stupid thing, the coffee machine."

"You fought a cop over your violin," Aspirin repeated.

"There was this other guy, in plainclothes. He protected me from the cop. But the cop still took my violin and then he threw it against the wall. At first I . . . well, there was a moment when I got really scared. But when I saw that the strings were still intact, I felt better. Everything was fine."

"A guy in plainclothes?"

She was indifferent to that detail. "Then I picked up all that was left, put it into the case, and came home." Alyona wiped her nose with the back of her hand. "I was afraid Mishutka would worry."

She plopped on the sofa, hugging Mishutka and gently stroking his ear. "Did you miss me, sweetheart? I told you I'd be back soon."

"They could have taken you! Without the bear, and without your violin, they could have stuffed you in the car, and that would be it!"

"You are obsessed with abduction." She allowed herself a dry smile and pressed Mishutka to her chest. "Don't worry, Alexey, it's not that easy to stuff me into a car. Did you buy any honey?"

"Honey?"

"I asked you to buy more honey for Mishutka! What is he supposed to eat tonight?"

Her voice was so full of accusatory scorn that the dejected Aspirin shuffled into the kitchen in search of options.

**"My child is no longer involved at your music school."**

Svetlana Nikolaevna stood on top of the staircase facing Aspirin. It was extremely rude of him not to invite her in, but wasn't she being incredibly rude herself showing up unannounced at a stranger's house, especially when he'd made it clear he had no interest in seeing her?

"Alexey Igorevich, you are wrong. We are talking about your child's future . . ."

"Svetlana Nikolaevna, one more word, and I will throw you down the stairs."

She took a step back. At that moment he looked like someone capable of going through with his threat.

"I insist you stop bothering me about this issue," he said, just to make sure she really got the message.

She turned and ran down the stairs, barely containing her tears. Aspirin remained standing; a second later he heard two women's voices scream in unison.

"Oh!"

"What are you . . ."

He leaned over the railing.

Irina stood on the staircase. The music teacher's steps resonated through the building as she ran down the stairs. Irina watched her, a horrified expression on her face. They'd run into each other, Aspirin realized. It was lucky the impulsive Svetlana Nikolaevna didn't knock his neighbor down.

Irina looked up and saw him.

A single second passed, a cold draft wafting through the building.

They went into their apartments without exchanging a single word.

**The time before New Year's always brought significant extra income.**
Office parties began in the middle of December, and Aspirin brought
holiday cheer to office workers, businessmen, particularly mature
high school kids, then office workers again, and so on without a
break. He was utterly exhausted, but the family budget grew healthy
and almost fat.

Aspirin bought a new violin to replace the murdered instrument.
This new violin was far superior to the old one—the difference in
sound was discernible even to an untrained ear. Alyona was pleased.

Catholic Christmas was fast approaching. Driving by a tree ba-
zaar, Aspirin slowed down. It had been years since he'd bothered with
a tree; he celebrated New Year's Eve anywhere but at home. He saw
an enormous dark green tree leaning over the fence (it must have
been used as an advertisement). Aspirin didn't bother asking where
it came from; the seller charged him an arm and a leg—the tree was
his pride and joy, there were still a few days remaining before the
holidays, and Aspirin did not look destitute. Despite this, Aspirin
pulled out his wallet and asked for the tree to be packaged and tied
to the top of his car.

Dragging the tree into the elevator, he cursed his ridiculous impulse. He was about to come out and pull the tree up the stairs when
the green top finally squeezed into the elevator. With a sigh of relief,
Aspirin pressed 5; at that very moment a woman jumped into the
space left empty by the tree.

Aspirin saw Irina's expression change from calm to panicky and
from panicky to decisive. The elevator crawled up. Irina fixed her
bangs; the vertical lines on her forehead became more pronounced.

"I thought we should talk."

The elevator stopped on the fifth floor. Before Aspirin had a
chance to move, Irina pressed 9.

"I thought we should talk. I thought it's normal for people to
speak."

Aspirin thought he was mistaken about her. In his relationships
with women, more than anything he appreciated the absence of

complications. He and Irina had a bit of fun together, and then they parted ways. By mutual consent, or so he thought. Was she going to make a scene?

The elevator arrived on the ninth floor. Hesitating for a second, Irina pressed 2. The elevator went down. Aspirin held on to the tree with both arms; his palms were sticky with sap, needles poked his cheek.

"I understand that in your circles this is how it's done. When people are like tomcats, when they don't care if they are together or . . ."

Her face was very red. Embarrassed by every word, she could no longer hold back. Locked within a tiny space, in the company of a gigantic prickly tree, they traveled up and down like the crew of a small, forgotten, doomed spaceship.

"I despise you, Alexey. I just wanted you to know that."

The elevator arrived on the second floor. Irina sniffled, pressed 9, then caught herself and put her arm between the doors to stop them from closing. Irina slipped out and ran up the stairs. Without thinking, Aspirin pressed 9 again.

A minute later, dragging the tree out of the elevator, he heard Sveta the concierge swear downstairs: "Who's playing with the elevator?"

**"What is that for?" Alyona asked.**

Aspirin placed the tree on the floor, immediately stumbled on it, and wanted to kick it in frustration, but held back at the last second.

"Has something happened again?"

"No, nothing happened."

"Oh come on, I can see something did. Why did you bring the tree?"

"If you don't like it, feel free to toss it out of the window," Aspirin said and shut himself in his bedroom.

For five minutes the apartment was quiet, then Alyona began playing again.

He lay down in his street clothes and closed his eyes. A few minutes later he fell into a parallel reality: he dreamed that he was lying in the bedroom with green curtains, and an old dusty lamp stood sentinel on the windowsill. Irina slept by his side.

He reached for her, happy that things had been resolved, and that those days when they considered each other strangers had never even happened. His hand fell into nothing, but Aspirin refused to wake up. Keeping his eyes closed, he tried to reach for her once again . . .

He came to.

The curtains were gray, the room—different, and there was no lamp on the windowsill. A stripe of light lay under his door.

Squinting, he stepped into the hallway. The entire apartment smelled of pine. The tree no longer lay on the floor tied with a rope. Its trunk nestled in a large pail in the middle of the living room, the tree was huge and moist, and took up almost half the room.

Mishutka sat on a rug in the corner of the room, staring at Aspirin.

"Where do you keep your ornaments?" For the first time in many days Alyona seemed happy. "I mean Christmas ornaments."

It was a good question, and it took a while before Aspirin dug up a cardboard box from the depths of his wardrobe. The box had migrated from his parents' apartment and hadn't been opened in ten years at least. Alyona wiped the dust off the cover and opened the box. One after another, the ornaments came out and Alyona's cheeks grew pink with pleasure. She gazed at the shiny bulbs and made faces at her funny reflection; when she came across a red sparkly hat, she put it on Mishutka's head. Aspirin recalled sitting in front of the same box many years ago, touching the treasures inside, anticipating the holiday joys. And next to him, on the floor, or on the sofa, his mother or father. Or both of them; Aspirin thought—one more second, and the sensation of childhood would reappear. One more second.

"Did you and Irina have a fight?" Alyona asked out of the blue, and the illusion dissipated, the memories melting away.

"Why would you think that?"

"I just did."

"We didn't have a fight. It's just that, you know, sometimes grown-ups have complicated grown-up problems, it has to do with relationships . . ."

"You slept with her," Alyona informed him with a patronizing smile. "And both of you enjoyed it. Why did you break up?"

Aspirin dropped an ornament, and it shattered into tiny pieces. Hissing and swearing, he shuffled to the kitchen for the broom.

Alyona reacted much faster by bringing out the vacuum cleaner. He watched her vacuum the carpet, then the sofa and the space under the stereo system.

"Irina and I are strangers," he said when the vacuum cleaner was finally turned off. "Besides . . ." He fell silent.

Alyona lifted the piano lid and played a chord. Aspirin flinched.

"And besides, you're perfectly happy with the status quo, aren't you, Alexey? You are cool, fun, popular, confident. You will have women chasing after you until you are old and decrepit—you will never lack money or women to spend it on. Why would you bother plowing, irrigating, weeding, or harvesting, when you can just show up at the carnival and sweet fruits would be handed to you, more than you can eat?"

Her hands flew over the keys. A melody escaped, like a squirrel—hop, and it's not there, only the branch swaying behind it.

"That was quite artistic," Aspirin managed.

"But in general, it's true, isn't it?"

"Why do you care?"

"I don't," she said and shrugged.

"Then why don't you shut up?"

He went to his room once more, boiling over with anger and bitter resentment, like a little boy. Alyona toyed with him, in turn pretending to be a real little girl and provoking his paternal instinct, then ripping off her mask and poking her finger into the most painful spots with a cynical smirk. Why had he ever thought of bringing home that tree . . .

He glanced at his watch and realized he was late for the club. Rushing out of the house, he promised himself that after his shift he would get absolutely hammered.

# JANUARY

Yes, Valentina, we are listening! Valentina, you are on the air!"

"Hello?"

"Yes, yes, everyone can hear you, and I want to remind you: we're playing Words, and our topic tonight—love on New Year's Eve! Valentina, have you met your boyfriend at a New Year's Eve party?"

"Yeah . . ."

"And what is his name?"

"Igor . . ."

"And you would like the holiday to continue, wouldn't you? You have a chance to win a night at the five-star hotel Flamingo, one night, the memories of which will surpass centuries! All you need to do to win that night for you and Igor is to answer one question, to be assigned a number, and to be entered into this lottery. Are you ready?"

After work on New Year's Eve he had returned home around nine in the morning, sober, gloomy, with a dull pain in the back of his head. The courtyard was littered with the burned tips of fireworks; dog owners smoked in the corner, while their charges, a bulldog and a rottweiler, ran circles in the snow like two perpetual-motion mobiles.

Irina's windows remained dark.

He unlocked the front door and peeked into the living room. Alyona slept with her arms around Mishutka. A plate with a half eaten slice of cake, a glass of juice, and the violin in its opened case nestled under the tree.

Aspirin took off his jacket and shoes. Moaning with pleasure, he slid his feet into a pair of slippers and went to the kitchen. He opened the refrigerator and took out a bottle of dark beer. Foam gushed over the edge of a faceted mug. Aspirin swallowed the liquid greedily, like a desert camel.

*Happy New Year,* he had said to himself when the mug was empty. *And many wishes for a wonderful new year.*

Later that day he was back at the station.

"Are you ready, Valentina?"

"Yeah . . ."

"Listen carefully. Listen carefully: Pentateuch is—a type of computer? A set of holy books? A pen that only writes in German? Your answer?"

When he had reentered the living room, she was already awake. She lay quietly, hugging her bear, gazing at Aspirin with inflamed blue eyes.

"Hey," he had whispered. "Happy new year."

"I was thinking," she said, skipping the polite banalities. "I am not going to have a chance to say good-bye to you."

"What do you mean?"

She smiled. "When I find my brother, and we leave . . . I won't have time to stop by and say good-bye."

"And are you going to find him soon?"

"Yes." She closed her eyes. "Last night I played the whole thing correctly. Everything, to the last note. On the regular strings, the normal ones. But that means I can do that with *his strings* too."

Keeping his eye on the bear, Aspirin came closer and cautiously sat down on the far edge of the sofa.

"Listen," Alyona had said. "That night you brought me to your place. Why? Why hadn't you just left me there on the street?"

He hadn't had an immediate answer.

"Valentina, your time is up. Your answer?"

"A computer?"

"Not quite. A computer would be Pentium; the Pentateuch is the first five books of the Old Testament. Sorry, Valentina, your answer is wrong, say hello to Igor, and better luck next time! And we have our next contestant, what is your name?"

"Lena!"

"Lena! Your voice sounds so cheerful—you are destined to answer my question! Listen: what is the original meaning of the word 'joystick'? A joystick is a control for commercial pilots, a gaming device, or a sexual term?"

"A sexual term!"

"But of course not! Originally, a joystick is a control used by pilots. Who would have thought? And thus the battle for the night of love in a five-star hotel with pools, garden, restaurants, and other pleasures continues, and while you, my friends, are gathering your thoughts for the next round, please do remember the love that descended upon you on New Year's Eve, and listen to Britney Spears!"

He had sat on the edge of the sofa with a glass of beer in his hand after her question, dripping foam on his pants, staring at the girl and her bear. Two pairs of eyes stared back demandingly: plastic and human.

"Are you trying to say that for an asshole like me, it would be more natural to leave a child alone in the street?"

Alyona said nothing.

Aspirin put the glass down on the floor. "Of course, if it weren't for certain circumstances, I would probably have walked by. I walk by every day. Everyone else does. And not because I am an asshole, or everyone else is. It's because that's how life is. Otherwise, people would have to go to a monastery. Or work at a hospice. If we were being honest."

Alyona said nothing.

"I can't love people in general," Aspirin said. "I can love a certain individual—for a certain amount of time. And I hate when my personal space is invaded, whether by adults, children, or women . . . This is my privacy. My ecological system. It's very fragile. I like to keep it safe. I like to keep myself safe, I suppose."

"Whom do you love now, Alexey?"

"Right now—no one," Aspirin said severely. "Love is not a cake of soap for everyday use."

She lowered her eyes and hugged Mishutka to her chest. He raised his glass and took a sip of cold thick beer, feeling a lot better. At least he hadn't lied to her.

". . . we are continuing our conversation about love, about love on New Year's Eve, and it's not a secret for anyone that it is quite common for the young and naive to get a taste of this magical ambrosia grown-ups call love on that special night, New Year's Eve . . . We have a caller, what is your name?"

"Alyona."

"Alyona, welcome, we're playing a word game . . . *Alyona*?"

A second of silence morphed into an abyss on the air, a softly humming cosmos.

"I have decided it will happen today," a familiar voice said softly. "I am taking him and leaving myself. Good-bye, Alexey."

"Hold on," he said, staring at the mic in horror. "Wait, hold on, listen to me—"

Short beeps. Julia the producer broke the connection and waved for Aspirin to continue.

"You are listening to *Radio Sweetheart*," Aspirin said hoarsely. "We are continuing . . . but we need to take a short break and listen to some music. Music!" He scowled at Julia, who was shaking her phone in the air. "The happiest, most cheerful, comforting and friendly music!

"Right now!"

The crowds flowed through the dark rectangular pipes of the underground walkway in the same manner as before; mechanical kittens still meowed in their boxes, and the toy soldiers kept shooting their rifles. Aspirin rushed through the throngs of people, bumping into passersby, apologizing (but not really meaning it), well aware that there was no Alyona at the intersection. Not a single sound broke the habitual atmosphere, and nothing could be heard aside from the rustling of steps, the electronic meowing, or the rattle of rifle fire. Perhaps she hadn't had a chance to start her song yet?

No one stood by the automatic coffee machine. Aspirin stopped (someone immediately ran into him from behind), but had no time to take a deeper breath: in the dark corner, leaning against the tin panel, was the familiar violin case.

He ran over. No footsteps were visible on the wet pavement; if it were not for the case, he would have believed that Alyona did not act according to her plan, or that she chose another location for her final concert. Or that she had been late. Or made a joke. Or never showed up.

The case was empty. Aspirin looked around helplessly. People passed him by, and no one paid him any attention.

He was too late.

At first he had to make a scene to get out of his shift on the air. Then he got stuck in traffic. Then he left his car in some courtyard and took the subway, and all trains had been full. Somehow Aspirin managed to miss his station. But *that* song was supposed to be played for three hours, so he should have been on time anyway!

He twirled the resin in his fingers imagining how Alyona would play her violin, and her brother would step out of the crowd . . . what would he look like? They would hold hands and step through the walls . . . or where would they go? And now they were back in their world that knew no fear or death. Alyona had achieved what she longed to do, she even had a chance to say good-bye, and he, Aspirin, could console himself and sigh a deep sigh of relief.

He closed the case and placed it by the coffee machine, then picked it up again. A horrible association slid into his mind: he thought that the case was like a heap of clothes a drowned man leaves on an empty beach. Hesitant to let the last vestige of Alyona's existence out of his hands, he walked toward a small pharmacy stand.

"Good afternoon, I am DJ Aspirin. Do you know what's happened here?"

"Lots of noise," the pharmacist shared with gusto. "A fistfight, or something like that. Or a protest. It was hard to see from here. Something always happens here—the gypsies, or boys with guitars, or some crazy girl with a violin."

"What about today? Did she play today?"

"I told you I have no idea. There were tons of people, tons of noise, and my entire stash of Valium was sold out."

"When was that?"

"Half an hour ago. Everyone had just left. You wanted aspirin, and what else?"

She handed him a pack of pills.

Holding his newly purchased pack of aspirin, he made it to the exit. An old woman selling roasted sunflower seeds demonstratively ignored two young cops, one tall and one short. The cops looked like winter pigeons, disheveled, grim, and confused.

"Hey guys," Aspirin said quickly. "Seen a chick with a violin around here?"

The tall cop's eyes were morose, the short one's—suspicious.

"Identification," the tall one said for some reason. Aspirin pulled out his passport.

"Grimalsky, Alexey. DJ Aspirin."

The cops exchanged glances.

"So, I take it you've seen the chick with the violin?"

"That girl is nuts," the short cop admitted.

"Where did she go after? Was she taken away? Who took her, what did they look like?"

"Try taking that one away." The short cop avoided Aspirin's eyes. "She's got some serious protection. Who are you?"

"I am her father," Aspirin said.

"What?"

"I am her father." Aspirin cleared his throat. "I have her birth certificate. She . . . she's not quite right in the head. Where did they take her? Where am I supposed to go, tell me!"

"She left," the tall cop said with a hint of hostility.

"Where?"

"Home. Where else would she go?"

"She is not home!"

"You should check again," the short cop said. "It's not summer anymore, it's not that easy to bum around the parks. She will get cold, hungry—then she'll come home. She has no choice. Hey, you, now, get your stuff!"

The last sentence was not directed at Aspirin, but rather at an old woman selling socks who was setting up her merchandise nearby. The short cop must have had some hypnotic skills of his own, because suddenly Aspirin clearly saw Alyona, tired, chilly, stepping into the apartment with her violin stuffed under her arm. Seriously—would she have any other choice?

He left the intersection and, leaning against a wet tree trunk, dialed his phone number.

No one answered.

**"Alyona!"**

Seeing the dark windows, he had hoped that she'd gone to bed and turned off the lights. But the sofa was empty, a blanket folded carefully on top of a pillow. The tree was drying up in the corner. Stacks of discs lay on top of the stereo, and sheet music, mostly xeroxed, on top of the piano.

He placed the case on the sofa and looked around again, suddenly aware of something very important.

Mishutka was nowhere to be seen.

Aspirin searched the apartment. He found the gun on the top shelf. Then he sat on a kitchen stool, put his elbows on the shiny table, and forced himself to think, like during a test.

She had left forever, taking Mishutka with her.

But before leaving forever, she had to play *his* song, from beginning to end. In that underground walkway. No matter what, that would have taken one hundred and seventy-three minutes.

And if Mishutka had been with her in the walkway, no one could have hurt her.

At least they wouldn't get away with it.

But there was no puddle of blood or police patrol in the walkway, which meant no one threw themselves at Alyona with umbrellas at the ready.

Or had she talked the bear into being patient?

Or maybe Mishutka wasn't there?

Aspirin paced around the apartment, then called Whiskas.

"Hello, Grimalsky," Victor Somov said, his voice unusually unkind. "So where is she?"

"I don't know where she is! I was going to ask you!"

"They failed," Whiskas said after a pause. "She's been announced as a missing person. Don't worry, they will find her."

"Don't hurt her."

Whiskas hung up.

**Aspirin stopped in front of the coffee machine once more, dug inside** his pockets, pushed the mochaccino button, and, while the machine hummed and winked, tried to find a barely formed thought that kept escaping him.

"'. . . we fought over the violin, I stumbled a little and went facefirst into that stupid thing, the coffee machine.'"

Forgetting about his mochaccino, Aspirin stepped forward and looked into the gap between the machine and the wall. He reached inside. A school bag was stuffed into the gap.

**He returned home around midnight. One of his windows was lit up,** and Aspirin nearly lost his mind. He couldn't wait for the elevator and ran upstairs; when he unlocked the door, he realized the apartment was still empty, and he himself had forgotten to turn off the light before he left.

**Alyona's bag got stuck on something inside the gap between the coffee** machine and the wall. Aspirin spent half an hour trying to get it out, in the process provoking the curious stares of the passersby. When he finally got it free, he regretted his actions because the school bag contained nothing but the folded-over and secured-inside Mishutka.

Aspirin's knees weakened. He stood next to Alyona's school bag with the toy bear stuffed inside, slowly, step by step, realizing that she hadn't gone into the beautiful beyond. The beautiful beyond did not happen and probably did not exist at all. Something else must have happened.

He left and came back. He didn't know what to do with the bag and the . . . monster? . . . stuck inside. But really, it was just a plush toy. Here, in this walkway, smelling of cigarettes, dampness, and that specific subway scent of urine, garbage, diesel, and ozone, Alyona and Aspirin's true story seemed a particularly insane type of hallucination. What lay ahead was not the beautiful beyond, but the Pervomaysk Institute for children with intellectual deficiencies, a distribution center for juvenile delinquents, and in the worst-case scenario—a pedophile den.

"How could you have left her alone?" Aspirin whispered to the bear. Of course, the bear did not answer.

Of course Alyona would not have left Mishutka of her own volition. That meant someone else had made the rules, someone powerful and unkind.

He remembered the barefoot man in a gray sweater and camouflage pants. Aspirin wondered if he walked around barefoot in the winter.

The crowds flowed by. Shoes rustled on the pavement. Aspirin stood frozen on a spot, feeling the time running out. Somewhere— and now he was sure of it—Alyona was in trouble.

He called Whiskas but heard nothing but cursing.

"They are searching for her!" Whiskas yelled. "Looking for her, do you understand?"

Aspirin picked up the bag. Mishutka did not weigh much. This time Aspirin did not give himself any time to think. He wanted to go home.

**He put the bag under the tree. Mishutka did not look at him. Mishutka** was a toy, fabric and stuffing, an inanimate object. Aspirin moved the bag closer to the wall with his foot.

The hands on the clock came together and stopped. The pendulum slowed down, swaying with shorter amplitude.

It was twelve o'clock. Midnight.

"Hello."

"Hello . . . good evening. It's Alexey."

A pause.

"What happened?"

"Alyona left. She . . . she's lost. Something has . . . she's nowhere to be found. I thought she might be with you."

A pause.

"No. I haven't seen her in a while. Wait. What could have happened to her? When did she leave?"

"This afternoon. She called *Radio Sweetheart* when I was on the air and said she was leaving for good and wanted to say good-bye. She left her violin case, school bag, and . . . Mishutka. She'd never parted with him before."

"Have you called the police?"

"I have! They told me to come over tomorrow morning, fill out an application, and bring a picture. Irina, I don't have any pictures of her! Not a single one!"

"Wait. I will be right over."

*"And here it's death everywhere, yellow leaves falling . . . dead . . ."*

What if she had lost her memory and no longer remembered Aspirin, or his address? What if she had once again appeared out of nowhere, fell out of the sky, and found herself on a street corner, but this time without Mishutka?

It was the longest, darkest, coldest night in his life.

What had happened before Alyona showed up at that street corner where he first met her? Where did her little socks come from, so clean, so new? Who gave her a T-shirt with the KRAKOW. LEARN TO FLY picture? He doubted a mental institution would outfit patients in this style.

Perhaps she had a family—not the fake one from Pervomaysk, with a fake mother called "Luba," but a family whose members had been looking for her for the last six months, calling hospitals and morgues, bothering the police, putting pictures into newspapers . . .

Assuming, of course, those people had been lucky and actually had some of Alyona's pictures in their possession, which he did not.

Was Alyona even her name?

"Here," Irina handed him a pill.

"What is that?"

"Valium."

"Thanks."

He took the pill, and his fingers touched her palm for a split second. He recalled a snowstorm, her window with the soft green light—recalled and immediately forgot it again.

It was past six in the morning, the fifth hour of his dispiriting search. Irina stuck by his side the entire time, accompanying him to the stuffy police station, a cold morgue, out on the snowy wet streets, to the hospital waiting rooms.

"What exactly did she say? Did you have a fight?"

"We didn't have a fight. She'd been planning on leaving for a while. I just didn't think she could."

"What didn't you believe? She was going to leave—wait, why?"

The words repeated over and over again, the conversation went in circles, and, strangely enough, Aspirin found some comfort in that. He needed Irina to sit by his side and ask him inherently idiotic questions.

That night was populated by doctors and nurses, their drunk, bloodied patients, cops, security guards, prostitutes, and the homeless— but no one had seen Alyona or knew where she was. It was probably for the best; Aspirin shuddered at the thought of Alyona meeting one of these people.

"Does she have any friends? Not a single one?"

"No. No one she mentioned, at least. She didn't even go to school— just went to her violin lessons. And she'd stopped that recently too."

"This is so terrible, Alexey. It's a disaster. Why did she leave?"

At nine in the morning Aspirin made a long-distance call from a hospital, but no one at the Pervomaysk Institute for children with intellectual deficiencies picked up the phone. He wasn't even sure it was a real number to a real place.

"You were going to tell me how she came to live with you," Irina reminded him gently.

He shook his head. "Not now. Later."

He called his apartment, but, as he expected, no one picked up the phone either.

"What if she'd lost her keys?" he wondered without much conviction when they got to the car and started driving. "She could be standing by the locked door . . ."

Irina shook her head. "I don't think so."

The sun came up slowly. It started to rain, mixed with wet snow. Aspirin turned on the windshield wipers.

"Should I take you home?"

"What about you?"

"I will keep searching. You know what could be helpful? Do you think you could stay in my apartment for a bit, just in case she calls? Or in case anyone calls my home number?"

Irina hesitated.

"You have to work, don't you," Aspirin realized.

"It's fine," Irina said. "Don't worry about it, I will figure it out. Let's go."


**The apartment remained in the same condition. The violin case, the** school bag under the tree, the head of a stuffed bear sticking out from under the top flap. Aspirin didn't get a chance to say anything before Irina bent down and picked up Mishutka. She fluffed up the fur on his face.

"You poor thing. Be patient. She will return."

Aspirin swallowed, worried for her safety. But the toy remained a toy.

"I'm going to go. If anyone calls, let me know—on my cell, all right?"

She nodded and then pressed Mishutka to her chest, just like Alyona.

Aspirin left. He smoked a cigarette sitting in his car and glancing at his own windows. Something bothered him, like a grain of sand in his eye, or a pebble in his shoe. Irina, Mishutka . . . Irina.

He smashed the cigarette in the ashtray and went back up to the fifth floor.

"Sorry. Let me take the bear."

Irina did not seem surprised.

"Here," she said solemnly. "For good luck."

**Awkwardly, he picked up the bear by its front paw.**

"No funny stuff," he whispered to Mishutka once they were inside the elevator. "No funny stuff, you . . ."

He winced at his own idiotic behavior.

**It was Thursday, a regular working day, but no one answered the** phone at the Pervomaysk Institute. Aspirin was about to assume that the number was wrong when someone finally picked up at half past eleven. The shrill woman on the other end of the line had trouble understanding what Aspirin wanted from her. She called someone else, couldn't find who she wanted, demanded he call back; she butchered Alyona's last name (Glimansky? Imansky?) and finally announced that only the director could answer Aspirin's question, and he wouldn't be in until Monday.

Hanging up, he no longer experienced disappointment, only exhaustion.

He went to McDonald's, as many locations as he could cover. He looked into the patrons' faces. He vaguely remembered Alyona liking McDonald's.

She didn't have any money . . .

But she had her violin! She could have earned some cash at least for a bread roll. On the other hand, Aspirin couldn't force himself to imagine Alyona wandering around the city, playing at intersections, eating at McDonald's, refusing to go home at least for Mishutka's sake . . .

Had she truly forgotten everything?

He went down the stairs into the underground walkway and almost immediately heard "Melodie" by Gluck.

He pushed through the crowd. He didn't know whether to hug her or hit her. Or pretend that nothing had happened?

He turned the corner and stopped. A girl of about twenty played indifferently and steadily. In front of her in an open violin case Aspirin saw a few coins and a stack of discs with a photo on the cover. For a few minutes Aspirin stood near her, trying to catch his breath. A curly-haired young man with a pleasant, slightly saccharine smile sauntered over.

"Would you like to purchase a CD?"

Aspirin said no.

Twenty-four hours had passed since Alyona called him on the air. It felt as if years had gone by. Aspirin had a cup of coffee at an underground café, ate a sandwich, and smoked a cigarette.

He tossed the empty cigarette pack into the trash.

Whiskas called after midnight.

"Good news—she is still alive. At least she's not among the dead bodies that had been found and accounted for in the last twenty-four hours. There had been no major accidents, and she hasn't been part of any criminal episodes. That bitch is hiding somewhere. Or she's on her way back to the institute. Let's hope she'll be located tomorrow."

"What should I do now?" Aspirin asked.

"Go home, get some sleep," Whiskas advised. "Your convulsions are not doing anyone any good."

**Aspirin parked the car in the courtyard. All the windows were dark,** in both his and Irina's apartments.

He unlocked the apartment door. Irina slept on the sofa, curled into a ball. She sat up and blinked, squinting at the hallway light.

"So?"

"Nothing."

"That's good," Irina yawned spasmodically. "No news is good news, isn't it?"

Aspirin had no energy to respond. He nodded.

"Have you eaten?"

"Yes. Has anyone called?"

"A lady named Zhenya who was shocked by the fact that I answered your phone. The editor of *Macho* magazine. That's it."

"Thanks." Aspirin leaned against the wall. "What if we never find her?"

"We will find her," Irina said without conviction. Then she repeated firmly, "We will keep looking until we find her."

**He woke up not quite aware of where he was** and what was happening. Then, remembering, he sat up in bed.

It was the middle of the night. The building and the courtyard were asleep, the moon, half hidden behind a cloud, hung outside. The door to his bedroom was open, and the kitchen lights were on. Aspirin looked at the clock: it was 3:30.

He had slept for only about forty minutes.

Why did he wake up? He had a very distinct feeling of something happening. Right this minute. Could it be something with Alyona?

He jerked the cord of the table lamp, squinted, turned his head; his eyes met Mishutka's plastic gaze. The toy bear sat on the nightstand by the bed, his head leaning to his shoulder, staring at Aspirin.

Aspirin swore. He rubbed his eyes and swore again: where did he . . . Oh God! He couldn't remember if he had brought Mishutka home, or left him on the backseat. He wasn't quite himself when he came home. But was it possible that he would bring the bear home and place him on the nightstand, a few inches away from his face? Seeing how much he hated the thing, it seemed unlikely.

He recalled locking the door behind Irina when she went back to her place. She'd had a rough night as well.

So who'd brought the bear into his bedroom?

"Alyona!" Aspirin yelled.

He ran into the kitchen, turned on the lights in the living room, peeked into the bathroom, knowing full well that it was empty. The front door was locked. Alyona hadn't come back.

The bear was still sitting on the nightstand. His eyes glimmered in the light of the lamp. Aspirin faced him. The bear stared back, dull as plastic.

"Where is she?" Aspirin whispered.

The bear did not answer.

"What kind of a beast are you? You," Aspirin reached for Mishutka. "Stuffing. Plush. A rag . . ."

He jerked the bear up by the front paw. Mishutka hung passively, making no attempt to free himself. Aspirin grunted and threw the toy against the wall with brute force. A soft impact; the toy fell on the floor. Aspirin looked down and only then saw by the foot of the bed a handful of discs, a cell phone charger, a recorder box, a newspaper—everything that lay on the nightstand before the bear made himself comfortable. As if someone had thrown everything on the floor to free up some space.

"Bloody hell," Aspirin murmured, realizing he'd never be able to fall asleep again.

**He drove through the city without a plan.**

It was four in the morning. The lights at intersections blinked yellow. At the last moment Aspirin worried about leaving Mishutka at home, so he'd brought the bear along for the ride. The bear sprawled on the front seat, his eyes reflecting the lights floating by.

They drove by locked stores, lowered window blinds, a random cab at an intersection, fir trees with leftover ornaments, the symbol of a lingering holiday. A thin layer of ice formed on the road, and Aspirin's car skidded a few times.

He made it to downtown, passed it, and realized that he was driving in a certain direction, as if led by an instinct. He had a clear notion of what was expected of him at the end of the road—a dark, sharply angled street and a nine-story building, number 2-14.

Why?

He hit the gas pedal only to immediately slow down. The icy street made the car practically unmanageable. The road went downhill. Aspirin crawled, maneuvering, braking gingerly, working the clutch. The descent was replaced by a climb, the tires squealed, the car skidded. Aspirin backed up, accelerated, and shot forward; the air filled with the stink of exhaust. The car crept forward like a fly on a glass surface. As soon as Aspirin reached the top, the lights on the other side of the street came into view. Aspirin took a deep breath and saw building number 2-14.

A wrought-iron lantern glowed above the front door. An old car with deflated tires, long unused, covered with snow up to its roof, blocked the entrance. The light of the lantern fell on the sign: a dormitory of a technical college, the official name of which was hidden by obscene graffiti.

Aspirin returned to his car. He raised his head: a few windows were lit; he heard distant laughter and sounds of music. The building was clearly inhabited—an ugly gray box, a parody of a normal human abode. What was Aspirin doing there? Why did he come to this place?

He was cold. He got back into the car, turned on the heat (the engine hadn't had time to cool), and smoked a cigarette. Mishutka lay on the front seat, spreading his paws in a demonstrative gesture of peace.

"What the hell?" Aspirin muttered.

He climbed out onto the dirty snow, stuck the bear under his arm, locked the car and turned on the alarm system.

The front door squeaked. Aspirin entered the lobby, empty and dismal, with the remains of a decrepit telephone booth stuck in the corner. A naked bulb hung on a long cord, throwing a dim light onto the deserted concierge booth with a broken window.

Adjusting the bear under his arm, Aspirin walked up to the second floor and found himself in a dark hallway among a row of identical wooden doors. He heard music and voices—the sounds of forced, almost hysterical, mirth.

Again he thought, *What am I doing here?*

Holding the bear tighter, he took a few steps down the corridor, following a strip of light oozing from a door left ajar.

An ancient refrigerator purred right behind the door. A guy with bleached dreads leaned against it, holding his head and swaying, exhibiting clear signs of an intense inner existence.

Aspirin passed him by.

He saw a multitude of them, and every one of them appeared busy; no one paid Aspirin any attention. They smoked, ate out of cans, drank beer and vodka, chopped onions on a wooden plank, talked about relationships. ("Where is my accordion?" a girl of about seventeen demanded of a pale, sleepy-looking guy who shook his head in denial.) Aspirin waded through, trying not to step on random arms and legs, looking around like a scuba diver in deep waters.

"Dude, who are you looking for?" a teenage girl with blue circles under her eyes asked him. "Are you looking for Svetlana?"

Aspirin made a vague gesture with his fingers.

"What have you got there, man? Is that a bear? Lemme hold 'im."

"In a minute," Aspirin said. "Have you seen a girl here? Her name is Alyona. Do you know where she is?"

The girl shrugged.

"The rugrat? No clue. Ask Dergach, I don't know anything. Listen, you're not a cop, are you?"

No longer listening, Aspirin stepped through the bodies sitting and lying on the floor (there were very few pieces of furniture and quite a few people) toward the door into the next room. He only just now noticed it as the door was nearly fully covered with fragments of old newspapers. He pushed it, but the door did not budge. He pulled; the room was dark, someone snored in the corner, someone breathed heavily right by Aspirin's side. Aspirin pulled the door open farther. The floor was covered with old mattresses, littered with random junk and sleeping bodies; in the far corner of the room he saw a little girl with her knees pulled up to her chin.

He couldn't quite believe his eyes. He approached the girl and looked into her face.

"Alyona!"

Her eyelashes, stuck together with dried-up tears, fluttered open.

"Alexey," she said, gazing into his face as if trying to recognize him. Slowly, apprehension dawned. "Oh, Alexey, is that really you?"

He stepped on someone's arm. Swearing replaced snoring, but Aspirin ignored it. He dragged the girl to the exit, fully expecting the door to slam in front of his nose. *It was a trap, there is no way they would let him escape, fate will not give Alyona back to him.*

And as he expected, a hand grabbed his shoulder.

"Hey, dude."

Not listening, Aspirin turned and punched the man in the jaw with surprisingly effective precision.

Something clattered on the floor and someone fell. Nearly taking the door off the hinges, Aspirin burst out of the room, Mishutka in one hand, Alyona in the other. Someone's shrieking followed him; he heard swearing and a nasty growl, "Let me get him! Let me get him!" Aspirin stopped in his tracks, handed the bear to Alyona, and pushed her behind his back. A man in a blue T-shirt faced him, a chef's knife in his hand, a slice of onion stuck to its blade.

The man's eyes appeared to be made out of tin, devoid of any thought. Aspirin stood in the middle of the corridor, staring into his eyes like a chief fireman gazing at a burning building.

"I'm gonna kill you!" the man barked (at least, that's what Aspirin assumed based on the unintelligible pronunciation) and took a step toward Aspirin. *Will she be smart enough to run?* Aspirin thought hopelessly. At that moment the man's eyes cleared.

He stared at something behind Aspirin's shoulder. Aspirin suppressed the desire to look back. He gritted his teeth and took a step forward, but his adversary was already gone. The man sprinted down the corridor, sliding on the slick linoleum. Only a slice of onion that fell off his blade remained behind.

Aspirin finally turned to look behind him. Alyona leaned against the wall, clutching Mishutka with all her might—an ordinary stuffed bear with plastic eyes.

**No one had abused her, raped her, or given her drugs. She'd simply sat** in the corner of the room by the radiator, trying to get warm. She was freezing and very thirsty.

"Who dragged you to this place? Were you kidnapped?"

"No. I came by myself. I don't remember how. Mishutka was upset with me. I left him behind. I locked him in my bag and left him behind so he wouldn't interfere, and then everything happened. And—and I didn't think about him at all."

"What happened?" Aspirin couldn't wait any longer. "What happened, why did you leave, where is your brother? Why didn't you come home?"

"Alexey," she smiled. "Thank you. You found me. I was lost. I was completely lost. I even forgot my name."

"How?" Chills ran down Aspirin's spine. His worst suspicions had come true—Alyona *did* have a psychological disorder, and it was progressing.

"No." She shook her head, as if reading his thoughts. "I am not crazy. My string broke. The E string. This music—this world can't handle it, so something had to break, either the world, or the string. This music is perfect. You see, playing it is the same as stopping the clock." She pulled a bag with coiled strings out of her pocket. "Here. Now I have only three left."

"Where is your violin?" Aspirin asked automatically.

"I don't remember. But it doesn't matter. I don't need the violin anymore, Alexey. I don't need anything at all. It's all lost. He's going to stay here forever. And me too. I will never be able to lead him out of here. My string broke."

She spoke slowly, smiling, and her smile made the skin on Aspirin's face stretch tighter.

"Nonsense," he said as calmly as possible. "Your . . . the guy who owns the strings should give you another one. That would be fair. It's a technical issue. That's fair, don't you think?"

Alyona shook her head; she said nothing, but Aspirin got the distinct impression that there would be no free passes. No breaks. The girl sat by his side, gazing into his face with dry, inflamed eyes, and Aspirin felt like an amateur standing by a surgical table. Here was a wounded patient, bleeding profusely, needing urgent help—but Aspirin had no knowledge of how to even start.

"Umm." He knew he had to say something quickly, and with great conviction, without any amorphous "calm down" and "it'll all work out." "Listen. They say Paganini could play on one string. You see, his strings broke too and he still played his *Caprices* on one string. If Paganini could do it, why can't you?"

"On one string," she said slowly, as if half asleep. "No, Alexey, that's not possible."

"Then," Aspirin said, feverishly searching for the right words, "then use a regular E string instead of the special one. You know, a normal one. It'll be like a crack in a clay pitcher. Like they did in the ancient times to prevent the Gods' envy. Remember, like when a potter made a particularly good pitcher, he'd leave a small crack in it, a flaw, to make sure he didn't anger the Gods. Then maybe you can play your song, and the world won't break."

She stopped smiling. Aspirin's heart jumped into his mouth: "Alyona?"

She threw herself at Aspirin, her arms tight around his neck, her face pressed against his cheek so hard that Aspirin felt a twinge of pain; Mishutka was squeezed between them so hard that the bear's hard plastic nose poked Aspirin's chest.

# PART III

# FEBRUARY

**W**hat's up?"

He'd woken up a minute ago. Irina lay with her eyes open, her cheek resting on her hand.

"Nothing," she smiled with her lips closed.

"Was I snoring?"

"No."

He glanced at the clock. It was half past six, a bit early, but he had the morning shift today.

Aspirin sat up in bed and lowered his feet to the floor. Lately their morning ritual of waking up in the same bed had developed a tiny crack, a hint of discomfort. A vague false note.

"Still sleepy," he complained. "But I need to get up. You should go back to sleep."

She didn't respond.

Aspirin reached for the bathrobe hanging on the back of the chair. The robe was soft and comfortable. Everything was good, calm, comfortable, easy. If only it weren't for that look and that silence.

"*If I ordered a general to change himself into a seabird, and if the general did not obey me, would that be my fault or the general's?*" he asked spontaneously.

"Is that from *The Little Prince*?" Irina asked after a pause.

"Yes. The answer is 'Yours, Your Majesty. Because you asked for the impossible.'"

"Am I asking for the impossible?"

Aspirin tensed up. Early morning was not the right time for this sort of discussion.

"You don't ask for anything." He touched her arm gently, conciliatory. "I am off."

"Go," she pulled the blanket to her chin. "Have a good show."

"You have a good day too."

Her door slammed behind his back. Still wearing his bathrobe, a cigarette in his mouth, he went up to his apartment. A neighbor carrying a full trash pail gave him a knowing look.

He sat in his kitchen, by the window, took a long drag on his cigarette and closed his eyes. He had to give Irina some credit—she was certainly perceptive. She was right. She did ask for the impossible. Her steep demands took a toll on their relationship, like a worm eating away at an apple, and no one could tell how long the second round of this neighborly idyll would last—a week? A month?

He was thirty-four years old. He liked his status. He valued his relationships with women on their own, without any additional expectations. Either she would understand that, or . . . that would be a pity. What a shame that would be. There were very few women like Irina out there.

Alyona was still asleep. He left a pack of defrosted ground beef on the counter for her to make meatballs.

As he was leaving the club, a young woman, fresh as a daisy, asked for an autograph. He drew a man behind a controller, signed "Aspirin," and the girl nearly melted in gratitude.

From the car he called his music guy, got a list of all the new stuff, and stopped at the store. He grabbed a cup of coffee with the sales guys and signed another flyer for the girl at the cash register. He spent all his cash on a stack of vinyl and discs, put the bag into the back of the car, and drove home.

Alyona was washing the floor, furiously wielding the mop, sharp shoulder blades sticking out from her T-shirt. Once again, Aspirin was startled by how thin she was.

"Take off your shoes," Alyona said instead of a greeting. "Am I wasting my time here?"

"Don't waste your time. Who asked you?"

Alyona straightened up and smoothed her hair back from her forehead.

"I don't like living in a pigsty," she said clearly, looking into Aspirin's eyes. She hesitated, then said, a little softer: "What are you so happy about? Good news?"

"Do I look happy?"

Aspirin glanced at the mirror. He looked exactly the same as before—although perhaps his eyes shined a little brighter than usual.

"Nothing special," he said, pulling off his shoes. "I may pick up the third night shift at Kuklabuck. That would be a bit of a stretch, especially if you count the Saturday morning air. But it is really a wonderful thing—to be paid for doing something you love!"

Alyona smiled, a sad, patronizing smirk. She picked up the pail and dragged it to the bathroom, dirty water cascading with deafening noises.

"You know, I should totally drop *Radio Sweetheart* . . . I may actually do that and switch to the club full-time."

"What's the difference?" Alyona asked from the bathroom.

"The difference is enormous," Aspirin slid his feet into his slippers. "A DJ at a club is simultaneously a creator and a performer. And the radio gig—it's not much more than being a clown, an entertainer, that's all."

"I don't understand." Alyona wiped her hands on a kitchen towel. "What exactly are you creating at your club?"

"A mood," Aspirin smiled. "You see. Here is the dance floor." He placed an empty plate in the middle of the table. "The dance floor has its own mood, its own goal, its own contents—age, social standing, interests . . ."

He took a cookie out of the jar, half a loaf of bread from the bread box, a day-old cooked carrot from the refrigerator. In a flash of inspiration, he added a few toothpicks.

"This is a complex object. And I am a master manipulator. I am not a villain, not a mass murderer, not a spin doctor. I don't want or need anything from them, I just want their world to be better. I want them to feel better and to be better, that's all."

Alyona sat down to examine the plate in the middle of the table. As Aspirin spoke, the boiled carrot danced on the plate, obeying his will; the cookie hopped. The bread and the toothpicks waited for their turn.

"Every composition is a mood," Aspirin continued, quite inspired by his monologue. "When we listen to music, we pick up on the mood . . . or we don't pick up on it, if the mood feels foreign to us. I feed them my compositions—and while I do that, I manipulate them."

"The people?"

"The people, and the music as well. When I speed up the rhythm, they get a shot of adrenaline. There are a lot of tricks, enough to talk until the wee hours in the morning, but the most important concept is that I respond to their mood, take control, and smoothly transfer it into something else. From calmness to ecstasy, from ecstasy to euphoria, from euphoria to nirvana . . . Do you see? I am a DJ. My professional talent is in sensing the mood music brings to my audience."

"So that makes you a professional manipulator?"

"I am a musician." Aspirin came to his senses and returned the bread to the bread box. "Every musician is a little bit of a manipulator. You should know."

"No," Alyona said softly. "A musician, especially a composer, he takes a piece of himself, a bloody piece, with the taste of life, love, and the fear of death. And he preserves it . . . no, that's not right, he translates the best—or the most terrifying—moments of his life into another semiotic system. Another code. And then he sends it into space. Or writes it down on paper using symbols. And he doesn't care whether the bar has sold enough alcohol, whether the people sitting down are tapping their feet in time with the music, or whether the dance floor is vibrating." She picked up the boiled carrot with the tips of her fingers and tossed it into the trash.

Aspirin had no idea how to respond. Ice-cold demeanor, ice-cold gaze—she had already forgotten sobbing on his shoulder, forgotten how he pulled her out of an incredibly shitty situation, how he bought her a new violin (a third one by now), how he provided psychotherapy sessions, day and night for weeks . . .

"Fine," he said as indifferently as he could manage. "I will take your opinion into consideration."

He got up and left.

**"I got into a hassle with my director,"** Kostya said. **"It was kind of a** big deal. I am up to my ears in debt, can't sell any discs. Everyone likes it, but when it comes to purchasing, they bail out."

"You know I work for wages, right?" Aspirin said carefully. "I just do what the boss tells me. I don't make decisions."

"But you are well respected. Can't you talk to someone?"

Aspirin shrugged. "I can try. But I am not making any promises, you understand."

"Fine, don't make any promises," Kostya said wistfully. He pulled out a disc with a half-naked Hindu woman on the cover. He opened the case, signed the insert, and handed it to Aspirin: "Here. That's my blood, sweat, and tears here. No one needs it, as it turns out."

"Take care of yourself." Aspirin twirled the disc in his fingers, not knowing where to put it.

People were trickling in. It was Saturday, the first Saturday after Kostya Foma, his competitor, was fired. Aspirin was slightly nervous.

"Well, here I go."

"Good luck," Kostya mumbled.

A waitress placed another shot of vodka in front of him. Aspirin thought: *Here is a talented man who dedicated his life to the arts. What will happen to him? What awaits him in the future?*

He greeted an unfamiliar crowd like a pilot greets the passengers before takeoff. Almost immediately he knew this was no sinecure. Various clerks exhausted by the long week wanted simple pop pleasures, the cutting-edge youths expected something extreme, more mature members of the audience desired having a gorgeous, stylish evening, and then there was a handful of teenagers who confused Kuklabuck with an acid disco club. Aspirin sat behind the controller feeling like the first man in space right before takeoff. *Let's go!*

He didn't own them right away, but eventually he got them all, from simple to complex. The atmosphere took its time, but eventually it submitted to his skillful hands and sensitive ear. The crowds migrated from the bar to the dance floor, from the dance floor to the tables, and back to the dance floor. The feet tapped in time with the music, the bartender worked tirelessly. Aspirin calmed down and was feeling pretty relaxed when a sweaty, corpulent man wearing a tie off-kilter stumbled into the DJ booth.

"Put on 'Vladimir Central'!"

Aspirin was mixing two complex tracks. He was happy with the mix; it was long, eight squares. Aspirin moved the crossfader, faded the first track, and only then looked at the visitor.

"'Vladimir Central'!" the corpulent man repeated meaningfully. "Did you hear me?"

"I am sorry, but we don't take requests here," Aspirin said politely.

"You bitch!"

A hand flew toward Aspirin's collar. In a split second one of Whiskas's guys appeared behind the man's shoulder; in another instant, the booth was empty, and only the reek of stale alcohol was left behind.

"My apologies," Whiskas said, appearing from out of nowhere. "We didn't catch him on the way out."

"No problem," Aspirin said, fixing his collar.

"Ah, the memories of old times, the good old nineties," Whiskas sighed nostalgically. "Fanned fingers, chains, 90s-style raspberry-colored sports jackets . . . Me and the guys . . . ah. You were young back then, you probably don't remember."

Aspirin smiled involuntarily. "Victor, how old do you think I am?"

Whiskas shook his head: "Much too young. So, are you happy about Foma being booted out?"

"Why would I be happy?" Aspirin asked. "He and I were . . . we got along. I subbed for him, he subbed for me, you know how it was."

"I know," Whiskas nodded absentmindedly. "How is your daughter?"

"She is fine."

Aspirin tensed up expecting the conversation to go further, but Whiskas nodded in understanding, slapped Aspirin's shoulder, and moved to the bar.

The rest of the evening went A-OK. Working with the tracks, mixing them, fading them, playing with special effects like a juggler with a handful of dinner plates, Aspirin thought of Alyona's words about real composers "preserving" selected slices of life and sending them into space. *A creative personality as a canning factory*, Aspirin thought, watching the dance floor swimming in euphoria. *And here I am wielding a can opener and feeding them all these cans of sardines. What if I could travel somewhere with all my equipment— would you get off the dance floor and follow me? In a long line? Tapping your feet in time with the music?*

Almost immediately he stopped thinking about it because a couple of girls, identical twins, jumped onto the low stage and, in one synchronized motion, ripped off their tops, showing off their tanned chests. The crowd roared and applauded, the happy girls danced, and Aspirin glanced at the clock—it was too early for a slow number. Let them enjoy the chaos a little longer.

He suddenly felt terrible. Irina's silence, the conversation with Alyona, Whiskas's knowing look, all this nagging and minor comments rolled up into a single poisonous lump, stuck in Aspirin's throat, and only now did he realize how tired he was of this life. He was exhausted. He felt like dying.

Moving like a fly in honey, he put on a slow number. He needed to last until morning. There was no need for Russian roulette, all he needed was to collapse on his controller and not move. And let someone else deal with his problems.

"Aspirin?"

He turned his head.

The girl was no more than twenty; she had bright green eyes, freckles, and was wearing a sailor's shirt. Her smile held a hint of danger. Aspirin could have sworn he'd never seen her before—he would have remembered.

"Who are you?" he asked, looking her up and down.

She thrust out her chest, catching his stare. "They call me Castor Oil."

"Be nice to yourself," he said, catching himself at the first spark of interest.

She laughed.

"Hey," Aspirin said. "Can you put this disc into your bag? It's a gift from Kostya."

"Wow!" The girl looked at the disc with appreciation. "Sure, I can, but I want one of those for myself. Where is Kostya?"

"He's sitting right over there. You can talk to him later, but I don't want to miss the slow dance."

He took her into his arms right inside the DJ booth.

**The night had passed, full of uncomplicated fun.** Aspirin woke up in her bed, kissed Nadya on the naked shoulder, and went into the bathroom, wrapped in a sheet. Nadya's parents were skiing in Switzerland, the apartment was clean and spacious, and standing under the hot streams of water, Aspirin smiled as if a load had fallen off his shoulders.

Coming out, he asked, "Got any food?"

"I don't know, look in the fridge."

They cooked a light breakfast. Nadya made some coffee.

"I am going to become a regular at Kuklabuck."

"Awesome."

"I listen to *Radio Sweetheart* too."

"That's dumb. Why would you ruin your taste?"

Nadya frowned. "You're a snob. This pop stuff feeds you, and you turn up your nose."

"Pop to you, bread and butter to me," Aspirin said. "Where is my disc, the one Kostya gave me?"

"Are you leaving already?" Nadya asked.

"I am on air at noon."

Nadya got up to take the dishes to the sink. Aspirin lightly slapped her ass.

"Hey!" Nadya jumped.

"There was a mosquito there," Aspirin said.

"A mosquito? In winter?"

"I know—lucky I got it."

She laughed, wiped her hands with a kitchen towel, then sat by Aspirin's side.

"Will you teach me how to mix tracks? I want to be a DJ too!"

"Sure thing," Aspirin said.

**He had half an hour to stop at home and change.** The slush on the road had frozen overnight, and Aspirin nearly wiped out right in front of his building. He unlocked the door; the apartment was unusually quiet. Alyona must have been asleep.

He changed his shirt and went into the kitchen for a beer. A fleeting thought passed through his head—how nice it would be if Alyona never existed, and if this long, difficult story had been nothing but a bad dream. Everything was working out for him right now: his work was going well, his personal life couldn't have been better, he had money in the bank, the beer was cold, and all he had to do was to live and enjoy living.

So, of course at that moment, the doorbell rang.

Swearing under his breath, Aspirin shuffled into the hallway. He opened the door and saw Irina.

"Hey," he said cheerfully. "Sorry, I am about to run to my shift."

"But it's Sunday," Irina said.

"Right, but someone asked me to take his shift, at noon. I have zero time to talk."

Irina remained standing, as if she had not heard a word he said. Her light brown hair was swept back and two vertical lines stood out against her forehead. Aspirin noticed that she had lost weight and looked pale and gaunt.

"I have been trying to reach you. I called last night, and the day before last, and today I saw you pull up."

"I am sorry. I will call when I get back from my shift, deal?"

She kept gazing up at him. Unnerved by her stare, Aspirin glanced in the mirror to make sure everything was in order. A trace of lipstick on his collar? But he'd just put on a fresh shirt.

She flared her nostrils. He could have sworn she could smell the scent of another woman, like a she wolf, even considering that Aspirin took a shower, changed his clothes, and was generally preoccupied by other things.

"Irina, did you want something? I seriously don't have even a minute . . ."

He saw her pupils dilate. It was like an explosion, the birth of two new black holes. He took a step back. "What's wrong?"

She opened her lips but said nothing; she turned and went down the stairs. The door on the fourth floor slammed shut. Everything went quiet again.

Aspirin swore through gritted teeth. He really did have very little time before his shift, and the roads were icy.

A sleepy, disheveled Alyona stood in the doorway of the living room, watching him with a great deal of interest.

**"And here is February, my friends, the shortest month of the year.** New Year's Eve and Christmas have already been forgotten, but St. Valentine's Day is coming up, hope everyone remembers that! We have discounts for lovers, tours for lovers, washing machines, Paris, Lake Baikal, new computers—everything is marked with a heart, everything is for lovers, and so is *Radio Sweetheart*! Today we are listening to songs about love. When do we ever listen to anything else, you may ask? Never! But now, if you have a free moment, if your boss has left the office, and your trusted coworkers won't sell you out to him, dial *Radio Sweetheart*'s number, guess a song about love, get a pass for a party at the Digger club, and listen to the song! Ooh, we have our first caller, that was quick! What is your name?"

"Igor."

"Attention, Igor, you must guess at least one song—where they take it away, where they let it go, and where they play! And the timer is on, where they take it away, where they let it go, and where they play! Which one can you guess?"

"Umm . . ."

"Let us all think about this. A song about love where they take it away—any ideas? Oh, short beeps, our Igor must have gotten scared, but we have another caller on the line—who is this?"

"Rita!"

"Rita, Rita, Margarita, so nice to hear your voice, so, any guesses?"

"Where they take it away—'Landslide'?"

"Bravo! Bravo, Rita, stay on the line, the pass to the Digger club is all yours, and we are listening to 'Landslide'—'I took my love, I took it down'!"

Aspirin took off his headphones. The studio felt stuffy.

"Jules, tell them to turn on the air-conditioning."

"Are you nuts? We are freezing our balls off in here."

"And I am suffocating, like a dragonfly in a vacuum chamber! What are you laughing at?"

"You crack me up, Aspirin. Will you sign a photo for my niece?"

"Sure, do you have an extra photo?"

He had forgotten—and then remembered again—Irina's widened pupils. She was more of a private investigator than a woman, for God's sake. How did she figure out he'd been with another girl? He imagined marrying someone like that and then spending the rest of his life apologizing.

It was abundantly clear that their relationship was finite. But couldn't they simply part as friends? Especially since they were neighbors.

Against his will he remembered that night back in January, the night when Alyona disappeared. The night he and Irina were closer than . . .

Than who?

Aspirin knew that Irina tried to get Alyona to trust her. Irina was worried that Alyona didn't go to school, worried about the violin that had to be replaced, and she worried about the most important thing: What happened on the day Alyona left? Where did she go? Alyona must have known that her father had been going crazy with worry for a full forty-eight hours!

Father—that's what Irina called Aspirin in her conversations with Alyona. He couldn't quite decide whether this upset him or not. Aside from the incident with the suspicious doctor's visit, Alyona never called him "Daddy," and that was just fine, it would sound fake anyway. But "father"—the head of the family, overworked, exhausted by all sorts of problems.

He would prefer that Irina did not poke her nose into their business.

He expected Alyona to behave as usual—to glance at Irina with her icy blue eyes and put the woman in her place, the way it had happened to Vasya the concierge, and the way it routinely happened to Aspirin himself. To his great surprise, the girl took pity on their neighbor. Patiently, she explained: she would start school next year, it didn't make sense to enroll now. As for why she had left—it was a stupid thing to do. She should not have done it. She was sorry.

Irina had bought her vitamins, gloves, and warm tights. Irina called her every day, and Aspirin knew that sometimes Alyona called her back. Irina brought her CDs even though Aspirin's collection was a hundred times richer. "She has the potential to be a phenomenal mother, practically perfect," he remembered Alyona saying. It was wonderful and quite lovely, but what did it have to do with Aspirin?

"*Radio Sweetheart* is with you, my dears, and we are continuing our game! You have three more love songs to guess: in one they lie to you, in another they kiss you, in the third, unfortunately, they upset you . . . but love is dangerous, love is cruel! And . . . we have a caller!"

Two more hours to go. Aspirin asked for coffee.

**Sounds of piano music woke him up. Still half asleep, he thought he** was sitting in a concert hall while the entire audience was giving an invisible performer a standing ovation. A second later he patted the blanket by his side: "Irina . . ."

He immediately sat up: there was no greater crime than calling a woman in one's bed by another woman's name.

But Nadya wasn't there either. Aspirin woke up fully and realized he was home, in his own bed, and that the deafening noise was coming from the piano on the other side of the wall—and it was truly deafening, like an entire enthusiastic orchestra.

"For God's sake," he mumbled, getting up.

Alyona looked radiant. Perched on the edge of her chair, head thrown back like a virtuoso pianist, she made the instrument shriek with happiness—it was not necessarily harmonious, but certainly quite emotional.

He wanted none of it.

"What do think you're doing? People are sleeping!"

"It's two in the afternoon." Alyona continued playing. "Good morning to you, Alexey."

"Enjoying yourself?" he asked in a calmer tone.

She held her hands over the keys, then took them off in a gorgeous, concert-appropriate gesture.

"Am I enjoying myself?" she asked innocently. "I am working my ass off while you gallivant around clubs pawing random women."

She attacked the keys again; failing to come up with a witty response, Aspirin went into the kitchen.

Nadya didn't come to the club that day—she called with a vague complaint about her parents, the weather, a bruised knee, and the fact that Aspirin had "behaved like a pig." Aspirin sent her love on the air and dedicated a saccharine-sweet composition to "the girl named Nadya."

**A fairly large spider ran across the hallways on jointed legs.**

*This place is going to seed*, Aspirin thought dejectedly. *Now there are spiderwebs in all the corners. You'd think it wouldn't be the case since it's wintertime—what, pray tell, do they eat when there is not a single fly in the house?*

In a great rush, the spider finally crossed the hallway and dived under the living room door. Aspirin turned to go into the kitchen, but at that moment another spider descended from the attic, grabbed the door handle, moved over the wall, and scampered in the same direction—toward the living room.

"Come on over, Spider dear, tea is served for you and yours . . . ," Aspirin muttered. "We have pie for Mrs. Fly."

He opened the door and looked for Alyona. She stood facing the window, her back to Aspirin; she played her violin, swaying with her entire body, and by her feet a couple of dozen spiders of different sizes gathered around her in the circle. They moved slowly, as if in a trance.

Aspirin rubbed his eyes and recoiled.

"What the hell!"

The melody stopped. A long second passed, then the spiders, as if coming to their senses, burst in different directions and hid in the tiny cracks in the walls.

"What was that?"

"What?" Alyona asked innocently, batting her eyelashes.

"Like you don't know?" Aspirin felt nauseated.

"No." Whether she was disagreeing with him, or simply denying him a response at all wasn't clear. She rubbed her chin—the spot where the bloody sore made by the violin in time turned into a hard callus.

Aspirin growled. Of course now he could have said he imagined things, plus what was the big deal anyway—it was just a handful of spiders. But he was absolutely sure that he did not imagine anything. And little girls shouldn't be having concerts for arachnids.

"Sit down." He nodded toward the sofa. Such an obedient girl, Alyona sat down, patting Mishutka's soft paw. Aspirin strolled around the room. The spiders disappeared without a trace.

"What were you playing?"

"Saint-Saëns," Alyona lied without batting an eye, "'The Swan.'"

"Do you really think I've never heard 'The Swan' before?"

"Why does it matter what I played?"

Aspirin steepled his fingers. "Listen, I am quite close to losing my cool."

"Scaring a porcupine with a naked ass again? All you do is lose your cool."

He made another circle around the room and recalled Whiskas's warning:

*"Do your best not to upset her. Try to agree with everything she says."*

"Fine," he said as meekly as he could manage. "Join me for an omelet?"

"Sure." Alyona rose and put the violin to her neck. "Please call me when it's ready."

He kept an eye out for spiders the rest of the night.

# MARCH

With the first days of spring, it seemed Alyona had been possessed by a demon. She made a terrible racket on the piano, listened to music without headphones, danced and jumped, stomping her feet so loudly that Aspirin wondered if paint came off Irina's ceiling.

Sometimes he wished Irina would call and say something like "Stop stomping your feet, my chandelier is about to crash." But Irina never called, not even when Alyona decided to jump off the sofa at half past eleven in the evening. Irina simply pretended her neighbors a floor above did not exist.

Alyona spent hours in the bathroom. She played her violin when Aspirin was trying to sleep, she disappeared somewhere and showed up out of nowhere—but he said nothing, recusing himself. Once, looking under the bed in search of a lost disc, he saw a tiny spider and shuddered so forcefully that the back of his head slammed into the bed frame. Every time Alyona began playing an unfamiliar, strange melody, Aspirin tensed up and looked around for some crawling creatures.

None had been detected, but that didn't mean they weren't there. He still had Nadya's complete adoration and devotion, but it no longer held any excitement. Her parents left again, this time for Egypt, and their apartment was at the disposal of the "young 'uns," as Nadya called herself and Aspirin, but the problem was that he no longer felt young. Next to Nadya's sailor outfit (he discovered that all her clothes were rather infantile, almost doll-like), he felt at best like a preschool teacher, at worst—like an old pervert.

Also, he tired easily these days. Previously, he always had enough energy for the club, for *Radio Sweetheart,* for parties, and for moonlighting. But now, with three nights a week at Kuklabuck added to the mix, it all absolutely exhausted him: he had a headache, his ears were itchy and sensitive, and the only treatment he had at his disposal was brandy. Having slept until midday, Aspirin looked at himself in the mirror and recoiled at the sight of a puffy, unwell, middle-aged monster.

"Vitamin deficiency," Nadya had said. "You should take some vitamin C."

He wasn't sure orange juice was going to cure whatever malady afflicted him.

Once on his way back from the garage, Aspirin saw Alyona.

She had gone for walks before, strolling around the building, kicking icicles with the tip of her shoe, occasionally stopping to stare at a rainbow oil slick on the wet pavement, or some broken furniture left by the side of the road, or a puddle. Aspirin had never seen her in the company of other children. Also, Alyona never took her violin outside. Today, for some reason, was different.

The sun was shining. Alyona walked without purpose, the violin squeezed between her shoulder and chin, and she played something very softly, pizzicato. She seemed to have been completely lost in her thoughts. But it wasn't Alyona who made Aspirin stop.

A boy followed Alyona, step by step, only a couple of dozen steps behind. The boy was about fourteen or fifteen, and Aspirin thought he looked familiar.

Could the boy simply be going about his business? Of course he could, and yet Aspirin had no doubt that the boy was following Alyona, and no one else. A second later, looking more closely at his face, Aspirin realized that it was one of those juvenile assholes who'd attacked Alyona inside the old building. One of those boys Aspirin had tried to intimidate behind the garage.

Aspirin tensed up, ready to run after them and grab the boy, but for some reason he didn't run. Maybe because of a strange expression on the boy's face: an expression of fear. The boy looked confused and scared—mostly scared—and with each step his wide face with its potato-shaped nose grew paler and paler, and his mouth opened wider, as if the boy wanted to scream.

But he didn't scream. He opened his mouth wider yet, like a fish, and continued following Alyona, step by step. Alyona went down the street toward the intersection. Aspirin followed the strange little procession. He didn't know what to expect, but had a terrible premonition.

The passersby looked at Alyona with curiosity. Some looked back, others smiled. Aspirin weaved in and out of the crowd, keeping Alyona in his sight.

She reached the intersection when the green light started blinking. She crossed the street, and Aspirin could have sworn all the drivers watched her with fascination. The light turned red for pedestrians, green for the cars, and a roaring stream of vehicles gushed into the intersection. The boy stopped at the edge of the sidewalk.

Alyona stopped and lowered the violin. She watched the boy across the busy street. Aspirin couldn't see the boy's face, but he had a clear view of Alyona's.

She was smiling.

With a sweeping concert gesture, she brought the violin to her shoulder, the bow suddenly appearing in her hand from out of nowhere, like a magician's wand.

Aspirin threw himself forward and bellowed over the din of the street: "Don't you dare!"

**"What if he was run over by a car and killed? Fine. I assume you consider murder a fair and just punishment for a terrible person. But what about that man, the driver, who would run the boy over—what about him? What had he done to you?"**

Alyona carefully wiped the violin with a dry cloth.

"Alexey, what does this have to do with me? What murder?"

"I saw it with my own eyes."

"What did you see? That I was playing, and the boy was following me?"

"Show me your violin," Aspirin demanded.

"Why? It's not like you'd be able to tell which strings are normal, and which—"

"Aha! Then you did use *his* strings?"

"Only two," Alyona admitted. "G and A."

"G and A," Aspirin muttered. He got up, went into the hallway, and unlocked the front door.

"Go."

"Where?" Alyona asked.

"To the intersection. To the square. Anywhere you want. Play your song, find your brother, and get the hell out of here—I don't want to see you ever again."

Alyona made herself more comfortable on the sofa.

"I can't. I am not ready yet."

"You are ready," Aspirin barked. "I saw what you can do! You led him, like on a string, like a rat—I saw it!"

"You don't understand what you are saying." Alyona's face darkened. "And I don't want to hear you say 'rat' ever again, it just sounds creepy."

"You are not leaving?"

"I am not leaving." Alyona crossed her legs. "I certainly have a lot to thank you for, Alexey. But you should watch your step."

The fourth-floor window glowed, a pale green light. Aspirin sat in his car, smoking and watching the dark silhouette occasionally appearing on the green background.

Like a movie theater. Like a shadow play. Like a dimly lit aquarium. On the fifth floor, his own apartment was brightly lit and *Carmina Burana* thundered through the open window.

Aspirin forced himself to come out of the car. He walked in the door and pressed the button. Sveta narrowed her eyes and said slyly:

"Alexey, did you hear that Irina from the fourth floor is selling her place? And she said it was urgent. The agent stopped by today, with prospective buyers. Do you know how high the prices are these days? Even if there is urgency—"

"What?" Aspirin frowned. "Which floor? Irina?"

"Irina, yes—I just said that! She got the apartment from her parents, they got a good deal—two one-bedroom apartments instead of one with two bedrooms, and they made some money out of it. The parents are dead now, and Irina's brother owns the second apartment. And now Irina says she wants to make some money too. She doesn't make much. In the old days, an engineer's salary—"

"Engineers never made a lot of money," Aspirin said, staring dully into the opened elevator doors. "There is even a song about it."

The elevator offered a slight reprieve, but eventually its doors closed and the button for the fourth floor went off again. Aspirin pressed it again almost to the wall, the elevator clanged and reopened the doors. Aspirin saw a cop in winter uniform and a woman in an old coat walking in through the front door. Only finding himself face-to-face with him in the tight space of the elevator, did Aspirin recognize the cop. They had already met, only that time the cop wore plainclothes.

The woman was that same youth liaison officer on whom Aspirin tried to palm Alyona off a while ago.

"The child does not attend a mainstream school. Moreover, she stopped attending the music school as well. She plays violin in underground intersections for money."

"That's not true," Aspirin blurted out.

The youth liaison officer pursed her lips. The cop glanced toward the window, at the bright blue March nightfall.

"Doesn't she play in underground intersections?" the officer clarified.

"Not anymore. And she didn't do it for money."

"What for then?"

"For fun," Aspirin said through his teeth, feeling like a complete idiot.

The cop and the liaison officer exchanged glances.

"Don't you have anything to do?" Aspirin said, brimming over with quiet fury. "So many homeless people, abandoned children, beggars, drug addicts . . . Do you have that much time on your hands that you can visit me and question why my daughter chooses to perform in the underground intersections? There is no law forbidding doing that!"

"Alexey Igorevich," the cop said, "we have an official statement from the children's services. They want to take away your custody, via legal proceedings."

"What?"

"If the court decides that you are not providing the child with the reasonable amount of care, such as nutrition, education, et cetera, or that you treat the child with cruelty—"

"Cruelty?"

"I have a statement signed by her violin teacher," the woman said. "You have stopped the child from attending the music school under the threat of physical punishment."

"That's a lie!"

The woman shrugged. "I have spoken with the teacher; she assures me that you threatened to throw her down the stairs and that she has witnesses."

"Dammit," Aspirin muttered. "It's total nonsense, do you understand? Alyona! Alyona, get over here!"

Nothing happened.

Swearing under his breath, Aspirin went to the living room. Alyona lay on the sofa, her feet propped up on the wall, her disheveled head with headphones almost on the floor. The entire floor in the room was covered by CDs, sheet music, candy wrappers, and some other paper trash. Mishutka lay on the piano keys in the same pose as his owner, feet propped up on the lid.

Irritated, Aspirin jerked the cord out of the socket, switching off the tiny lights on the stereo front panel. Alyona opened her blurry eyes and sat up on the sofa. A pair of wrinkled sweatpants. Pale, withdrawn face.

The cop and the liaison officer walked in from the kitchen without an invitation and stood behind Aspirin without speaking. He gritted his teeth and walked over to the girl to pull off her headphones: "We have guests. You should brush your hair."

"Why don't you leave me alone, father dear," Alyona suggested in a clear loud voice. "Turn everything back on and close the door behind you."

Aspirin controlled himself.

"Tell me please: have I forbidden you from attending music school?"

She glanced at the visitors over his shoulder: "Why?"

"Have I ever forbidden you, or not?"

She fell back on the sofa and jerked her feet up in the air: "You have, you have forbidden me! You have put me on a chain, put a muzzle on me, made me live in a doghouse, gave me raw bones to eat! Bowwowwow!"

He grabbed the collar of her sweatshirt and pulled so hard the seams crackled. "Oh really? Then get out of here. Here they are, ready to take you to a detention center, right now! Get the hell out of here!"

The cop and the liaison officer did not utter a sound. Alyona glanced at them again over Aspirin's shoulder.

"They are not taking me anywhere. You are my father, you are supposed to take care of me. Let me go, you are hurting me!"

With a soft dull sound, Mishutka slid from the piano keys to the floor.

Shuddering inside, Aspirin let go of the girl's collar. Without looking at Alyona, ignoring the visitors, he left the living room and closed the door behind him. A minute later *Carmina Burana* rumbled through the speakers at full volume.

He wasn't sure what happened with their guests.

**By midnight the slush on the street had frozen to resemble a mirror.** Aspirin walked on ice; his reflection walked upside down, pressing on the soles of his shoes and constantly glancing at its watch.

The entire city was filled with clocks. Clock faces, electronic tableaux, winking, measuring minutes until death: one in the morning . . . half past two . . . five minutes to four . . .

He slipped and fell, hitting his elbow and hip. He rose, hissing with rage more than with pain, and shook dirty, prickly snow off his pants with his burning palms.

It was five in the morning. Clubs were closing. Happy, tired, temporarily deaf people went home. Two or three cars with hopelessly tinted windows passed by Aspirin.

"What the hell?" he asked out loud.

No one answered.

**"Wake up. Come on, get up."**

If it weren't for Mishutka nestling under his owner's arm as usual, Aspirin wouldn't have hesitated to shake her by the shoulder. The clock showed half past five; it was still pitch-black outside the window.

"Alyona! Get up, do you hear me?"

"What happened?" she asked earnestly, without a hint of irritation.

"Nothing. I want to know why you despise me."

She sat up.

"Why I what?"

"Why you despise me. What for? After all I've . . ."

He wanted to say "After all I've done for you," but made himself stop just in time.

Alyona took a deep breath, rubbed her eyes, and blinked.

"Just don't pretend you don't understand what I am saying," Aspirin said.

"I understand," she said catching him off-guard. "You are right."

For a minute they gazed at each other without saying a word: Aspirin—cold, tired, wearing dirty boots and a heavy winter jacket with traces of whitewash on the shoulder, and Alyona—pale, sleepy, wearing wrinkled pajamas, with Mishutka in her lap.

"I do despise you," she finally said. "Because my brother left . . . he dropped everything. Things you have no idea about. He dropped everything just to be in your place, Alexey. Just to have a right to compose new songs. And you live in the world where creation is possible, and you could care less. You could give a fuck about it. You took this right, this privilege for which my brother . . ." Her voice broke. "You took this privilege and you wiped your ass with it. And then you threw it in the toilet and forgot all about it. How could I not despise you?"

Again the room was silent.

"But it's not true," Aspirin said.

"It is true." Alyona's eyes glistened. "You know it is."

Aspirin opened his mouth and closed it again, not knowing what to say. He turned and went to his bedroom. He lay down on the bed, then remembered that he should have taken off his jacket. And boots. Heavily, like an ailing bear, he went to the hallway, but instead of taking off his jacket, he opened the front door.

He went downstairs, and into the street.

The fourth-floor window glowed green.

"Irina, please open the door."

Silence. The doorbell sent a long echo into the depths of the quiet apartment.

"Irina, I really need to talk to you! I know you're home."

Silence. Aspirin moved his hands along the reinforced door. It was locked. Was he in prison, or was he the warden?

"Irina, open the door!"

A shadow moved behind one of her neighbors' spyholes. He must have looked pretty dumb standing in front of a locked door. Like "The Ant and the Grasshopper," for God's sake. And he was the grasshopper.

Aspirin turned and shuffled back to his place. He unlocked the door and went straight into the kitchen. He hesitated, then plugged the sink, taped the drain, and turned on the water, at full capacity.

He sat by the table, propped himself up on his elbows, and stared at the graying morning sky. The clock showed nearly nine.

Happily splashing, water filled the sink. Aspirin recalled a school trip to the pool, and the way sunlight played on the white ceramic walls.

The water rose to the top of the sink and poured over the edges. It flowed over the table to the floor, spread in a puddle, dived under the sink. The faucet kept pumping out a thick stream that cut into the warm, dancing surface. Aspirin sat by the table and stared out of the window. Minutes passed by.

Alyona appeared at the kitchen door, clutching Mishutka to her chest. Silently, she watched the water, stepping back when it reached her bare feet.

The doorbell rang with violent force, like retribution. Only then Aspirin rose, slowly approached the sink, walking on water like St. Peter, and turned off the faucet. The doorbell kept ringing shrilly. Aspirin opened the door.

She stood at the threshold, a vicious Fury in a long terry bathrobe.

"Idiot! What do you think you're doing? It's now down to the third floor! You are a crazy asshole!"

He watched her silently. Under his gaze, she grew quiet, swallowed, gasping for air.

"What are you—"

"I have insurance," Aspirin said. "I'll pay for the damage. And I will pay those people from the third floor too."

She took a step back and looked at him, from top to bottom, then at Alyona standing still behind his back with her bear at her side.

"Irina," Aspirin said, "please don't leave me."

She took another step back, hugging her shoulders as if she was cold. She left, the hem of her robe rising and falling around her legs, her slippers slapping the staircase.

The door creaked, swaying back and forth in the draft. Aspirin listened to the rasping noises of the key turning in the door a floor below. Irina either locked it tighter than usual, or was having trouble with her locks.

His wet feet suddenly felt extremely cold, nearly frozen. He locked the door and returned to the kitchen.

Alyona wielded a rag. She squeezed gritty torrents of water into a pail, wiped the puddle, then squeezed the rag again. The plug lay by the side of the sink, a grubby gray ribbon of used duct tape next to it.

Aspirin sat by the table, propped himself up on his elbows and lowered his head onto his laced fingers.

"That was cool," Alyona said, her head still lowered down to the floor, "but it is not enough, Alexey. It is not enough."

# APRIL

reetings, my dearest listeners, I have sad news for you today. The most comforting, most delicate and gentle *Radio Sweetheart* is on the verge of a human resources overhaul, and you will never again hear your darling Aspirin on the air. Time passes, the old medicine for the soul gets replaced by the new medicine—soulful Advil, sensitive Prozac, kind-hearted Imodium . . . You don't need Aspirin when you can listen to the others and forget all about him! No? You don't agree? You, sitting in your office, or behind the wheel, or in your own home—are you outraged? And you would be absolutely right! April first is April Fools' Day, and you should not believe anyone, especially today. This was a joke, for those of you who haven't been paying attention, I repeat— this was a cheerful April first joke. Aspirin is still with you, and to confirm, we will now listen to t.A.T.u.!"

He took a deep breath and pulled off his headphones. Last night Alyona left the house and didn't return for almost two hours. Waiting for her to come back, he was late for his shift at the club.

"Where have you been?"

Alyona had breathed heavily. In one hand she held a grocery bag, an outline of a baguette peeking through the plastic. With another, she pressed Mishutka to her chest as if someone meant to take him away.

"Don't come closer, Alexey."

She opened her fingers and the grocery bag fell on the floor. Gingerly, Alyona pulled Mishutka away from her chest. In the bright light of the hallway, Aspirin saw a spark of something in the bear's chocolate fur, as if a shard of glass was stuck in Mishutka's temple.

"What is—"

"Don't touch it! Step back!"

Fear filled her voice. Aspirin took a step back.

With the tips of two fingers, Alyona grabbed the shard and struggled to pull it from the bear's head. Aspirin saw a needle, long and hollow. The needle contained a single drop of dark liquid.

"What is that?"

"He shielded me," Alyona said dully. "Mishutka. He always protects me."

"Is that . . . what is that?" he repeated dumbly.

"Give me a plate," Alyona said. "Quickly."

The needle clinked when she placed it on a saucer.

"This is evidence," Aspirin said, reaching for the phone. "Whatever it is—"

"It's made of ice," Alyona informed him in a voice just as hollow as before. "It started melting while still in Mishutka's head."

"*What?*"

But she wasn't kidding—in front of his eyes, the needle had started melting into a tiny puddle. The dark liquid spread, changing its color.

"This is not evidence," Alyona muttered. "Why would I care about evidence anyway? Had I known who shot us and from where, I would force him out with a song. I'd pull him out of his hiding place, and that would be his trial. But I didn't even understand what happened right away. Nothing. If it weren't for Mishutka . . ."

"Would you collapse and fall asleep?"

"Sit down," Alyona said, hugging the bear to her chest. "Do you think this hurt him?"

"Who?"

"Mishutka."

"I don't think he came to any harm from this. He's made of plush. Also, I am sure they had calculated the dosage for a little girl, not a . . . bear."

"Calculated the dosage." Alyona smiled coldly. "I have very little time, Alexey. Less than I thought."

Aspirin glanced at the saucer. The needle had melted without a trace. The cloudy water on the white porcelain formed an almost perfect ellipse.

"We could send this to a lab."

Alyona screwed up her face. "Are you really that naive?"

"But to kidnap children like this, in broad daylight—"

"Alexey," the girl said, planting her fists on the table. "If they wanted to kidnap me, they would have done so a long time ago. No. They want me dead."

Aspirin was silent.

"Each side is worried the other side will get me. And that I will be used against . . . against one of those who developed me in the first place."

"What sides?" Aspirin asked blankly. "Who's on each side?"

Alyona shrugged. "I don't know. I don't know what you call people like them. They took a long time, waiting, considering the possibilities. But I am too dangerous, don't you see? This kind of weapon should not exist. It should not be in anyone's hands."

Aspirin looked at the bear; Mishutka sat on the kitchen table by Alyona's side, staring coldly at Aspirin, as if saying: *Yes, I shielded her with my own body. And what have you done?*

"It's poison," Alyona said. "And there would be no traces, just a scratch, and who knows where a child could get a scratch."

"I don't believe in things like that," Aspirin said.

"And yet new songs are composed," she smiled. "Words are folded into lyrics. New walls rise, new cities are built. What a terrible world. There is no harmony. That means there is a way. And it does lead somewhere. I am so tired . . ." She suddenly yawned. "I went downtown today, found this one spot. From there I can play everything, up to the last note, no one will be able to stop me and everyone will hear me. I have so little time. I am going to do it tomorrow. No, the day after tomorrow. No. I will let you know later when I am going to do it."

**Two days had passed since then.**

"And now it's time for our traditional contest—it's Guessing Time! The winner will get two tickets to the underground club Digger!"

He felt like a concrete mixer, inside which concrete thickened to an inexcusable degree thanks to the criminal neglect by the workers. For the first time in his life, the words didn't flow out of him; instead, he had to push them out like thick clots.

"What is your name? Irina? What a stroke of luck. How old are you? Sixteen. Irina dear. Of course you are about to ask if it's animate or inanimate."

He glanced at the clock.

Two more hours on the air. Two hours was more than enough time for Alyona to disappear forever.

**"Did you see it? Alexey, you should have seen what happened here! So much had happened . . ."**

Aspirin's knees buckled.

"What?"

Almost immediately he saw Alyona standing by the garage, leaning against the metal wall, violin stuck under her arms, the bow in her hand by her side. The courtyard was filled with people, some wearing coats over their bathrobes, others barely dressed at all—as if a powerful and sudden fire had chased them outside.

Aspirin looked at the building in alarm. There was no smoke. He looked back at Alyona, who casually waved to him.

A janitor rushed around armed with a broom, trying to gather moist, brownish trash into piles.

"Need to call environmental services . . ."

"No, emergency services! The building must have cracks in it, it might collapse!"

"Rats always desert a sinking ship . . ."

"But that's rats!"

"Has someone exterminated them that effectively?"

"All of them at the same time?"

Aspirin turned to Sveta the concierge. "What happened here?"

"Cockroaches," the concierge said with widened eyes. "It was quite a spectacle, Alexey dear. Out of the blue, all these cockroaches started coming out of every apartment. Every single one. And most of them from Paulina's place—I saw it! She never cleans, and she keeps her trash in the kitchen for weeks!"

"All of them at the same time?"

"Yes. Just like a river of roaches. They left the building, and marched together across the courtyard, only to stop when they got to the road. We all came out, and no one knew what to do. It was a lucky thing that a contractor was paving the road nearby, so he turned around and drove right over them with his paving truck. And now no one in the building has any cockroaches. It's a good thing, of course, but what kind of a natural phenomenon was this?"

Across the courtyard Aspirin looked at Alyona. The girl smiled.

**"I asked you not to leave the apartment!"**

Alyona stood by the window. It was raining, and tiny drops stuck to the glass, watching them from outside like clear fish eyes.

The violin lay on the clean kitchen table. Mishutka sat nearby, leaning back on the chair and watching Aspirin with his benevolent (malevolent?) plastic peepers.

"Didn't I ask you—"

"Here is what I think," Alyona said, as if continuing a previous business discussion. "What if it is his right? If a person decides to make a sacrifice for something he considers important, it is his choice, isn't it? And here I show up and tell him, no, let's go home, let's do it all differently . . . I came to save him, but he never asked to be saved, did he?"

She turned her head to him, expecting an answer. Aspirin hesitated.

"You know he's in pain," he said, the first thing that came to mind.

"I *don't* know. When my fingers hurt and bleed, I am also in pain, but I am happy when I can play the variations in the right tempo. If I do save him, that means he's lost. And there will be no new music."

"Then we will make do without new music," Aspirin said.

Alyona looked at him from beneath her eyelashes, and, petrified, he saw himself as a cockroach. A tiny brown critter crawling out of a crack in the garbage chute.

"Yes!" he said, doubling down. "Because there are more important things than new songs. Human lives, for instance! Including yours!"

"My life is worth nothing," she said haughtily. "I cannot be killed."

"You shed blood just like everyone else."

"Yes . . . And I feel pain like everyone else. But pain is not death. Death is when the music stops."

Passing Aspirin, she went to the cupboard and stood on tiptoes reaching for a half-empty jar of jam on the bottom shelf. She placed the jar on the table and put the bear in front of it, tying a clean towel under his chin.

"Eat, Mishutka. Eat, sweetheart. It's almost time to go."

Aspirin glanced out of the window; paying no attention to the rain, the neighbors continued their animated discussion of today's incident. In the epicenter Sveta the concierge waved her umbrella and he could imagine her saying to anyone who would listen, "What kind of a natural phenomenon was that?"

*They don't understand*, Aspirin thought. *Instead of cockroaches, the girl could have chased the residents themselves out of their homes. She could have played joy, then lechery, then—for dessert— terror. And they would dance, then copulate in the sandbox, then soil their pants and run away in fear. And no one would have escaped, not even Aspirin himself.*

That she hadn't done that didn't make it any less terrifying, and for a tiny moment, he wondered if the people who had tried to kill her were right.

He hated himself—more than usual—in that moment.

"Good job, Mishutka. You had such a good dinner."

Alyona put away the now empty jam jar and used a napkin to wipe the bear's already clean face. She inspected her own hands, licked a spot of jam off her finger, and reached for the violin.

With his back to the window, Aspirin watched her pinch a few strings, tighten up the peg, and pick up the bow.

"What are you staring at?" Alyona asked.

He grimaced.

"Are you really afraid?" She frowned. "I thought you were teasing me."

"Yes, it was a nice topic for jokes." He had forced the words out, avoiding her eyes.

Alyona glanced at him above the bow.

"Every now and then I feel sorry for you, Aspirin. And every now and then I don't."

He felt the same way about himself. "Why did you exterminate the cockroaches?" he asked, curious at her altruism.

"What if I wanted to leave a good memory of myself in this world? Do a good deed?"

"A good deed." Aspirin shuddered. "That guy probably threw up all over his truck."

"Do you think exterminating rats is a more pleasant activity?"

"I never said a single word about rats."

"Then just shut up."

She played. Standing in the middle of the kitchen, looking somewhere in the distance, she began a sweet, gentle melody. Aspirin thought he'd already heard it once before. He sat down, propped his head on his elbow, and recalled camping with his parents, making fish soup in a huge cauldron in the fire pit, right on the riverbank, and how the fire crackled, and how stars were reflected in the half-submerged old boat . . .

The melody stopped abruptly.

Aspirin raised his misty eyes and shook his head. Alyona gazed at him with a strange expression on her face.

"What?" he muttered, suddenly drenched in cold sweat.

"I am so sorry, Alexey," Alyona said softly. "Maybe you do need help, but I cannot help you. I don't know what to play for you, and even if I knew, I couldn't do it. I think it must be a very difficult song."

**The rain came down harder. The dusk thickened. Aspirin sauntered** around the room, then pulled his laptop out of the bag, sat down, and wrote down the title: "Cockroaches Have Left the Building. What to Expect?"

He immediately felt better, like after a sip of good brandy. He made himself more comfortable and started writing, dropping cigarette ashes on the floor.

As the file grew in size, Aspirin felt better and better. "It is well known that animals leave buildings just before the occurrence of natural disasters. But a mass exodus of cockroaches has never been described before. What had terrified our normally fearless hexapod neighbors? What forced them to leave their warm cracks in the wall, simultaneously, as if on command? Cockroaches are tenacious, undemanding, and yet quite sensitive to minute fluctuations of the neurobehavioral field . . ."

Inspired, he wrote quickly, with minimal fact checking. He offered and debunked hypotheses and esoteric conspiracy theories, from the basic and trite, such as alien invasion, to the elegant and elaborate, such as "Momi, the Vietnamese ceremonial pastry in the shape of female genitalia, are used in the fertility rituals. However, the recipe is so complex that an average housewife who wants to try to make this exotic dish in her average kitchen risks lowering her apartment into the depths of negative energy . . ."

He finished at eleven o'clock. He put a period at the end of the last sentence and took a deep breath.

Behind a thin wall, Alyona was practicing—always practicing—and her violin moaned as if it had a toothache.

**"She's completely brainwashed you," Whiskas said. "Delirium is contagious."**

Whiskas and Aspirin sat in the Kuklabuck office. Half an hour prior to their conversation a scandal took place: the administration was deeply disturbed by Aspirin's sudden request for time off, and the only person who supported Aspirin in that difficult moment was Victor Somov.

"Go visit your parents. Enjoy London sights. If she tries to stop you . . . we'll have to take decisive measures."

"Decisive is a nice way to put it," Aspirin mumbled, and, almost against his will, told Whiskas about the needle made out of ice.

Whiskas listened attentively, a malodorous cigarette in his fingers twitching slightly.

"This is utter nonsense, Alexey," he said gently when Aspirin stopped talking. "It's an awesome story for *Forbidden Truth*, or some other glossy tabloid that has you on the payroll. In real life there are no terrible secret service organizations that shoot little children with icicles. This is nothing but the twisted imagination of a sick little girl, and, unfortunately, she's managed to pass these fantasies on to you."

Aspirin said nothing.

"Should I reserve your tickets?" Whiskas asked gently.

"I am not leaving her. She might be crazy, but she's my daughter."

Whiskas sighed and crushed out his cigarette in the ashtray.

"Your daughter . . . For months you've been walking on tiptoes around her. And we still don't know who's behind her. You should think about it."

Aspirin said nothing.


"So the deal is off," Vasya the concierge informed him in a whisper. "The buyer asked for his deposit back, and she agreed, would you believe it?"

"Who?" Aspirin asked, perfectly aware of the answer.

"Irina, of course. The buyer read your article about the cockroaches and goes, I don't want to buy an apartment in this building! Watch out, Alexey, people are going to complain about you. You even mentioned the address! People from other buildings are asking questions. One of the residents took her kids and went to live with her parents. Her husband is an alcoholic, so it may not have anything to do with the cockroaches, but still."

"Nothing to do with the cockroaches," Aspirin confirmed

through gritted teeth, pushing 5 as hard as he could until the doors closed.

"Irina called," Alyona informed him as soon as he stepped through the door.

The key got stuck in the lock. Aspirin jerked it once, then again, almost breaking it.

"She wanted me to tell you that you are acting like an asshole," Alyona continued evenly. "You should not have written that nonsense about cockroaches."

"Thanks," Aspirin hissed.

"In other words, Irina—"

"I got it!"

He slammed the door behind him. Almost immediately the doorbell began to rattle. Aspirin realized the key was still in the lock on the outside.

The now-familiar-to-Aspirin local cop and a perfectly unfamiliar woman stood at the door.

For a few seconds the visitors and Aspirin stared at each other in silence. Then Aspirin reached for the treacherous key and jerked it out of the lock.

"Alexey Igorevich," the cop began officially, but at that moment the woman sniffled, looking past Aspirin into the depths of his apartment.

"My baby!" she shrieked and, pushing Aspirin out of the way, threw herself at Alyona, taking the girl into her arms. "My sweetheart!"

Alyona neither resisted nor welcomed the embrace. She stood like a statue, slightly recoiling when the crisp black curls touched her face.

Luba Kalchenko had returned from her business trip abroad and discovered that her daughter, Alyona Alexeyevna, had disappeared from her school for an undisclosed location.

The school's administration had followed the required process, including informing the girl's guardians and police, and that was when the searching efforts stalled temporarily: the institution where Alyona was registered as a student was not a detective agency, and looking for missing children was not in its line of business.

Very quickly it became known that Alyona Grimalsky left Pervomaysk and now lived with her father, a well-known, wealthy businessman. The school officials secretly rejoiced on the girl's behalf, but did not call off their missing person report. In any case, neither the police, nor the school had enough money to deport Alyona back to the institute.

Horrified, Luba postponed all her business and personal plans, bought a train ticket, and rushed to rescue her daughter. And now she sat at the table set by Alyona, and there was no end in sight to this unnatural, disturbingly false tea party.

Because none of it was—could be—true.

Right?

The cop had a lot of trouble deciphering the genre of what was happening in front of him: a melodrama? A crime thriller? A bit of science fiction?

Luba dyed her hair the deepest black one could have imagined. Large ringlets adorned her big head, falling to her shoulders. She wore a tight bright red sweater; matching lipstick accentuated her full lips, and her lashes, weighted by a thick layer of mascara, sharply curled up and down so that each eye resembled a Venus flytrap. Aspirin stared at her across the table trying to remember . . . *It wasn't that long ago after all! What was that woman like when they met? He couldn't have slept with a woman and then forgotten her forever, as if his memory had been erased?*

*Or could he?*

*He drank heavily back then . . . but he never drank himself into oblivion. He was easygoing, cheerful, girls followed him around, and he remembered Lena, Vita, Katya . . . But he did not remember Luba. For the life of him, he couldn't remember her.*

Alyona sliced a store-bought cake that happened to be in the bread box. Her face expressed neither joy nor disappointment nor surprise nor fear before her suddenly changing fate. Only concentration like during her violin practice.

*How was it even remotely possible,* Aspirin thought. *The arrival of that Luba put everything in its place. No one fell from the sky in search of one's errant brother. No one came from a perfect world only to long to return. But what about the bear? The violin? The people he'd seen mesmerized in the underground?*

*What about the special agents who had come to abduct him?*

*What about the cockroaches?*

He glanced at Mishutka, forgotten on the windowsill. The bear stared up at the ceiling with senseless button eyes. Aspirin rose, intending to call Whiskas.

"Wait," Alyona said softly. Something in her voice made Aspirin sit back down immediately.

Everyone went quiet. Luba looked at Aspirin. He choked on his tea.

It was obvious that she remembered him well, but her memories were neither warm nor pleasant.

"You've gained weight, Alexey. Clearly, you are well off."

Aspirin stared into kohl-lined eyes and struggled to remember anything at all. That was how people suffering from amnesia must feel.

"Oh well." Luba got up. "Alyona, pack your stuff, we have to make the train. Tonight we'll stay at my friend's, and tomorrow . . ."

"I am not going, Mom," Alyona said softly.

The cop winced. Luba didn't look surprised.

"You *are* going. Because of you, my ulcer is acting up again. I can barely walk. Come on, pack everything he bought you and get ready."

Alyona stepped toward the window and stuck her hands deeply into the pockets of her sweatshirt.

"I am not going. I am staying here."

Luba got up, and the table shook. Unhurriedly and confidently, like a rhinoceros, she moved toward Alyona and grabbed her by the shoulder.

"You little bitch, start thinking about what you're going to tell your father! He's going to beat you black and blue for sure, and I will not lift a finger to defend you, you little shit. Let's go."

She dragged Alyona into the hallway, just as unhurriedly and yet fiercely, like a real mother.

Aspirin turned to Mishutka, but the bear sat on the windowsill with the look of a perfectly ordinary toy, an old one, not particularly clean, and absolutely helpless. Avoiding Aspirin's eyes, the cop got up and pushed his untouched cup of tea away.

"Alexey Igorevich, we need to talk—"

"Later," Aspirin said.

In the hallway, Luba Kalchenko was roaring in anger.

"You little . . ."

"I am not going!"

"Yes, you are!"

The sound of a slap.

Aspirin felt as if someone threw a pot of boiling water in his face. He threw himself into the hallway, slipping and almost falling. Alyona writhed in her mother's arms; Luba repeatedly slapped her daughter on the cheeks, simultaneously trying to stuff her into a winter jacket.

"You little shit, look at how spoiled you've gotten. Spoiled rotten! Just you wait."

Aspirin grabbed Luba's hand and jerked it toward him. The woman gasped and let go of Alyona.

"Alexey Igorevich . . . ," the cop said warningly.

Luba narrowed her eyes.

"Get your hand off me. Look at you, playing the defender. Where were you when I sobbed over the baby carriage? Or when I bought stinky shoes in a secondhand store just to get her to day care? Where were you? In Paris?"

Alyona pressed her back against the mirror, shifting her gaze from her mother to Aspirin and back. Her cheeks burned, and she struggled to contain her tears.

"Please restrain your emotions," the cop said. "The law decides everything. By law, you, Luba Kalchenko, have full legal rights . . ."

"I am not going anywhere," Alyona whispered.

Luba took a step toward Alyona, but Aspirin was faster, jumping between them just at the moment when the woman's hand reached for the girl's ear.

"This is my house. If you don't leave, I will call the police."

"Really?" Luba looked at the cop standing in the hallway, who didn't seem to be quite so interested in intervening.

Aspirin threw the front door open.

"Get out."

Luba put her hands on her hips. "Or what?"

"Or I will throw you down the stairs," Aspirin promised, stealing a quick glance at the cop.

"This is quite second nature for you, isn't it," the cop said. "Ms. Kalchenko, may I speak with you for a minute?"

"I am not leaving without her!"

"Yes, you are," Aspirin said quietly.

She looked him up and down, and under her gaze the hardiest cactus would have withered in an instant. Aspirin was the first one to look away.

"I wish I had never met you," Luba from Pervomaysk said softly. "You're not a man, you're shit." She turned to the cop. "Well?"

"Well what, ma'am? The girl is old enough to make her own decision."

"Oh, shut up!"

She stormed out. The cop followed, turning to look back at Aspirin for a moment, then shrugging, left.


"Alexey?"

Sitting in front of his laptop, he stared out of the window where wet tree branches were pushed around by the wind and storm clouds pressed down on the roofs. A change in the weather was coming. A big change.

"Alexey, how about meatballs tonight?"

"Tell me the truth. Is she your mother?"

A pause.

"Yes."

"So then you have been lying to me? Have you lied about everything? And you don't have any brothers?"

She sat down by his side at the edge of the bed.

"Remember how I told you . . . This reality is digesting me. When I met you, I lied about being your daughter. But now it has become the truth."

"It has become the truth," Aspirin repeated dully. "That is what she is like then, Luba from Pervomaysk. Unbelievable. Astonishing. And does her husband really beat you?"

"Not yet," Alyona said. "So far he's only threatened me. But now that she's said it, it would almost certainly become true as well."

"I am such an idiot," Aspirin said quietly. "You are going to go back to Pervomaysk. And she will go to court to file for child support. All this was the scam I always thought it was."

Alyona smiled thinly. "You can always settle out of court."

"Obviously," he said, not recognizing his own voice. "Just keep in mind that my official income is not that high."

She shook her head. "Don't worry about all that."

"How can I not?"

"Will you come with me?" Alyona asked.

He turned his head, the question so disconnected from their current conversation he wondered if he'd missed part of it.

"Where?"

"It's time."

They walked along the streets shiny with rain. The warm wind reminded them that spring had finally arrived. Alyona carried her backpack, the bear's soft head sticking out of the opening. In her right hand Alyona held her violin. With her left, she clutched Aspirin's fingers.

It was getting darker. People walked along the sidewalk, and any one of them could have been concealing a needle filled with an opiate, or a poison, or anything else, up his sleeve. Every roof could be hiding a sniper armed with bullets made of ice. At first Aspirin kept looking over his shoulder, but eventually he stopped, telling himself it was nothing but paranoia. An obsessive, delusional fear of pursuit.

If nothing else, Mishutka would protect them . . . and that thought almost made him laugh out loud.

"If you see anything going wrong, or if you simply get too frightened, just drop everything and leave," Alyona advised him in a calm, even voice,

"Thousands of people play musical instruments in underground walkways," Aspirin said, matching her tone. "They sing and dance, and nothing happens to them."

"We're not going to the walkway," Alyona said. "Remember, I told you—I found a better spot."

They took the subway, and half an hour later emerged downtown. The sky was dark, but streetlights and neon ads made it as bright as day.

"Here." Alyona stopped in front of a restaurant.

Its summer terrace was empty, and inside, behind a glass door, the silhouettes of waitstaff swam in the dispersed light. Napkins were peaked in the shape of icebergs. A wide ledge with sides made of glass circled the balcony. In the middle of the balcony stood a long table set up for a banquet, waiting for guests.

"Are we having dinner here?" Aspirin asked inanely.

"I have one question." Alyona looked up. "Why did you come with me?"

"Meaning what?"

"Why are you here with me now, and not at home?"

"Because I worry about you," Aspirin admitted after a pause.

"But why?" She jerked her chin up, challenging him. "What can possibly happen to me?"

Aspirin looked around. There were many passersby, but no one paid any particular attention to a girl with a violin, and no one recognized the famous DJ Aspirin.

"I don't know," he said tiredly. "I wouldn't say you are . . . that nothing happens to you normally. Usually . . ."

She stopped listening, fixed her backpack, and moved toward the restaurant entrance. Aspirin followed.

They left their coats in the coatroom. The attendant masked his surprise behind exaggerated politeness: Alyona and Aspirin were rather a strange pair, and an even stranger trio if one counted Mishutka.

"We have to go upstairs," Alyona said, and Aspirin obediently turned to the staircase.

"My apologies, but upstairs has been reserved for a private function," the maître d' said.

Alyona kept walking without looking back. The usual rest pad hung around her throat.

"I am sorry, this will only take a minute," Aspirin said to the attendant. "Alyona! It's reserved."

"I know." She did not slow down. "Please help me open the window."

"What?"

"This one," she said when they reached the balcony. Alyona reached for the handle of a large windowpane in a plastic frame. Behind the glass, so very close, the streetlights glowed, illuminating the evening crowds. "Oh, wait, it's easy to open."

The windowpane did open, letting in a blast of cool spring air. Alyona opened her case, picked up the violin and the bow, and before Aspirin could stop her, slipped through the crack.

The backpack with Mishutka got stuck for a second. Alyona jerked her body to free herself and stepped onto the ledge.

"What the hell are you doing?"

She turned her head.

"Good-bye, Alexey. Now I either lead him away, or—"

She cut herself short and began taking side steps along the ledge. The backpack hindered her movements, its clasps scratching the glass.

"Get the child!"

"What's happening?"

"Stop it immediately!"

A group of waiters led by the maître d' gathered around Aspirin, speaking simultaneously, but not taking any action. The balcony's glass walls only opened at the ends, on both right and left sides; Aspirin was sure that Alyona knew about this in advance.

She had said this place was perfect.

Reaching the center of the balcony, Alyona stopped. The crowds were already gathered below, looking up at her, pointing fingers, unsure of whether it was a prank or a marketing ploy.

Alyona tuned up her violin. Still stuffed into the backpack, Mishutka stared at Aspirin through the window, and Aspirin had trouble deciphering the expression in the plastic eyes.

". . . are you the father?"

"Me?" he asked in surprise. "Yeah . . . Why?"

The maître d' let out a long and crass obscenity. Women in evening gowns coming up in a slow stream stared at him in confusion.

"What's going on here?"

"Get the child back inside immediately!" a man in a black suit and a gold tie screamed. "What's wrong with you? What if she falls?"

Aspirin looked at them in bemusement.

Then Alyona began to play.

Everyone fell silent. All of them, all at once. Those who stood by the balcony, and those who looked up from the street. The melody began with a soft, clear sound that locked the audience in an instant freeze-frame. A street in dusk, a girl on the ledge—a real live girl? A circus performer? A shadow? Wrought-iron lanterns to the right and left. A violin in the girl's hands and the street under her feet. And— just for Aspirin alone—the fuzzy face of a teddy bear with his nose pressed against the glass.

The sound gathered force. A quick movement ran through the crowd when everyone recoiled. Aspirin recoiled too, standing only a few steps behind Alyona, separated by the glass, surrounded by the pungent aroma of cooling appetizers rising from the banquet table.

Alyona continued playing. The violin growled in her hands like a prehistoric monster. This sound, simultaneously bewitching and terrifying, sent chills down the entire length of Aspirin's spine.

The girl led on with the melody—if the sounds made by the violin could be called a melody, assuming it had anything remotely in common with music as he knew it. Aspirin's eyes watered as if from a bright light. He saw his expression in the glass, a distorted, broken reflection. He saw shifting shadows, the midnight-black hair of Luba from Pervomaysk; the drunken face of alcoholic composer Kostya, replaced by the laughing Nadya in her sailor's outfit; Whiskas stared at something above Aspirin's head; Irina gazed back at him with silent reproach, and Aspirin longed for the violin to stop, but it kept on playing, playing as if nothing in the world could stop the goddamn girl.

The mass stupor exploded. The maître d' attempted to climb onto the ledge through the open window, but he was four times bigger than Alyona, and would have had the same success trying to squeeze through the eye of a needle. The spectators below screamed and threw empty bottles; one of them shattered on an iron streetlight pole. White, thrown-back faces glowed in the dim light; black mouths gaped open.

Alyona played.

Aspirin found himself in the middle of unthinkable chaos.

The man with the gold tie picked up a massive armchair (the effort made his jacket rip under his arms), swung it heavily, and made to throw it against the glass, aiming at Alyona. A split second before the chair could be tossed, Aspirin managed to throw his body at the man and push him off balance; he wasn't thinking, he simply acted on instinct. The heavy piece of oaken furniture broke the glass and crashed on the floor of the balcony.

But the girl maintained her pace.

A shard of glass scratched her cheek. Two red drops swelled up and slid down the pale cheek like raindrops on the glass. Alyona played on.

Screams came from below, some of pain, some of violent anger. Someone was being supported and led out of the crowd. Aspirin saw faces distorted by rage, faces curious and seemingly undisturbed, and faces touched by fear; a police siren howled around the corner.

"Get her out! Take her away!"

A man in an elegant beige sports jacket flung himself onto the ledge through the hole left by the armchair. He reached for Alyona, slipped and almost fell to the street, holding on to the ledge with his fingers. A woman shrieked and attempted to help him, but neither her screams nor the din of the crowds below could deafen the monstrous force of Alyona's violin.

The man opened his bloody fingers and plunged down from the

second floor. Alyona kept playing, looking at no one. Aspirin recalled her saying, "If you see anything going wrong, or if you simply get too frightened . . ."

A cold, raw draft flew in through the broken window.

The crowd downstairs grew in size and was getting restless. It split down the middle, and a fire engine with an extending ladder made its way down the narrow passage.

Alyona played.

Mishutka peered at Aspirin. Behind the broken glass, the balcony was nearly empty; the evening-gown-clad women stepped back, dragging their dinner partners along with them. The maître d' continued to struggle to free himself from the crack in the window. A portly, middle-aged fellow perched at the end of the table snacking on a piece of ham, a bottle of vodka in front of him already half empty.

Alyona played.

With a gnashing sound, the ladder moved up to the ledge. Aspirin saw a firefighter in a Kevlar suit; the firefighter regarded Alyona not as a child with a violin but rather as a chemical factory up in flames. Aspirin took a step forward having no idea of what he intended to do, but at that moment Alyona finished part one on the highest note. A tiny pause followed; the firefighter seemed confused. Alyona took a deep breath (her shoulders jerked up) and placed the bow back on the strings.

The next sound was deep and subtle; it made one's breath catch. The firefighter hung in the air a few feet away from Alyona. Aspirin could no longer see his eyes—a neon sign was reflected in the plastic protective shield on the firefighter's face.

Alyona played.

The maître d' finally made it out of his trap, sat down on the carpeted floor, and began to weep. Aspirin himself was on the verge of tears: the melody emitted by Alyona's violin worked on him the same way a sentimental romance works on delicate teenage girls. He pressed his hands to his cheeks and saw himself soaring above an endless, flower-filled meadow. He flew very low, level with the flowers, then ascended sharply toward the clouds, his spirit rising along in ecstasy . . .

A cold touch of the glass brought him to his senses. He still stood behind Alyona, his face squished against the clear barrier, watching her fingers with their usual hangnails run along the neck of the violin, while the resin dust glowed blue in the neon lights. The crowd below grew again; some people swayed like sleepwalkers visiting a psychic. Others stared without blinking. Dangling his legs off the edge of the extended ladder, the firefighter watched Alyona, his head propped up on his fist.

Alyona played standing on her tiptoes at the border of the ledge. The glass panels shook and rattled from the gently vibrating sounds of the violin. Aspirin pressed his body against the window, nearly pushing it out of the frame, longing to hear the music not only with his ears, but with his entire body, with his skin. At that moment Alyona allowed for a tiny pause, and when she started again, the melody was completely different.

Alyona played.

The crowds grew restless. They stomped their feet and seethed, and then suddenly everyone scattered. Almost no one was screaming, except for a few isolated strangled moans underneath the balcony. Aspirin himself felt an urge to run, like a cat before a major earthquake. The red fire engine let out a cloud of foul exhaust and, howling in terror, drove off with the firefighter still perched on top of the ladder.

Shots rang out in the distance. Fireworks exploded over the street in yellow, green, blue lights. *How much time has passed?* Aspirin wondered, breathing heavily through his mouth. *Ten minutes, an hour?*

The balcony emptied. Expensive wine bottles stood sentinel over the banquet table, corpulent brandy bottles showed off their glossy, honey-colored sides, a single shot glass lay on its side—the middle-aged ham eater had long ago left the battlefield. The maître d' had escaped as well. The street below was now empty; all that was left was broken glass in the cracks between the cobblestones, a pair of glasses, a lost purse, and the man who had fallen off the balcony, abandoned. Alyona played—for no one. Mishutka pressed his face against the glass, his eyes cruel and demanding.

Aspirin bit his lip, fighting panic. Fighting the urge to run as far as his legs could carry him.

"If you get too frightened . . ."

Alyona played.

He took one step back. Then another. Holding on to the railing, he walked down the stairs. Do not run. Just do not run. Slowly, slowly, slowly.

The coatroom was empty. Leather coats and pastel-colored spring furs hung without supervision, and so did a cheap child's jacket. The door was wide open.

Aspirin knew that sooner or later he would give in to the music. Grabbing the curtains, backs of chairs, door frames, he fought his panic not for victory, but for a dignified step, the one before the last. And one more.

He made it out to the street and looked up. Alyona stood straight as an arrow, her bow rising, then plummeting. Aspirin thought he saw lights on a controller, little green frequency indicators rising and falling.

He stepped back, stumbled, and fell into a mud puddle. Making no effort to get up, he looked at Alyona and thought she was looking back at him from the distant ledge.

The melody ended abruptly.

Aspirin groped the wet cobblestones, trying to get up, distinctly aware that he had lost his hearing. He was deaf!

Only a few seconds later he realized that the melody had continued, it was simply of a different quality. It had flown to another orbital, like an electron.

Everything had changed.

Alyona played.

The hidden meaning of music, the one that Aspirin had only guessed at before, now came to the surface. To be alive—that was what it meant. To fear death. To experience joy. To live.

*Death is when the music stops.*

Aspirin raised his head. He imagined an enormous orchestra standing behind Alyona's back, thousands of bows rising and falling—up to the horizon.

The street was no longer empty. People emerged from dark corners and brightly lit streets. They moved without fear or commotion, as if they had an appointment for that particular time, and they had waited patiently and now the time had finally came. They stood in silence, shoulder to shoulder, in tightly packed clusters, and only a spot by the entrance to the restaurant, right under Alyona's feet, remained empty, flooded by the sharp white glow of a streetlight.

Aspirin got up. The melody grew harsh. Aspirin read it like a written text. Alyona no longer called and cajoled, she *demanded* someone to appear that very second, to step out of the crowd, to enter the glowing circle. People stood mesmerized. No one had the guts to step toward Alyona, toward the strange white light.

Alyona played.

The violin sounded louder, the call grew sharper and more demanding. Aspirin gave in and looked around—where was he? Where was the person for whom it was all done? The runaway from paradise, the hapless creator?

People remained motionless. The crowd became denser, but no one entered the white circle.

The violin roared . . . only for the roar to snap in a sharp metal sound. A broken string curled around Alyona's pale face like a grapevine, but Alyona continued playing without stopping, carrying the melody forward, carrying it on three remaining strings, and Aspirin had no idea which strings were ordinary and which were *his*. Or if any of that mattered at all.

People listened silently, but still no one came to her call.

Aspirin looked back and forth, pushing people out of the way, getting closer and closer to the ledge. She was going to fall, she was going to fall.

Another sound of a broken string. Someone gasped.

Alyona went on playing on two strings. The song ripped, false notes wove into the melody. No one entered the circle. Alyona played, broken strings curling around her arm, and the melody was no longer mesmerizing; it was not even a melody, it was a challenge, a furious challenge . . .

The third and fourth strings broke almost at once. It became very quiet. The girl on the ledge stood for a second like a statue, then gently leaned forward, like a statue pushed off its pedestal.

Aspirin made it just in time.

**He carried her home in his arms. He took off her clothes and gave her** a sponge bath, adding some vinegar to the water just in case, and made her comfortable on the sofa. Mishutka sat on the floor with a vacant expression on his face. The violin was left on the cobblestones in front of the restaurant.

Alyona's hands hung lifelessly, but she did not seem lost or crushed. On the contrary, she was smiling.

"Do you want tea?"

"No, Alexey. There is no need."

"There is definitely a need—you must be thirsty."

"I am not. I am dying."

"Stop it! You yourself said you cannot die."

"I can now. He would have come, Alexey. I only needed two more minutes."

"I saw . . ."

"I know. I would have led him out, that was definite. The door had already opened . . . But he did not come. I failed."

"You didn't fail." Aspirin practically forced the tea down her throat. "You did it. You played two strings!"

Alyona laughed softly.

"This world . . . It's so fragile. I made a window, a window in its shell. A wound, really, if I'm being honest. And it fought back. It resisted, it broke my strings. Your world. It must have hurt. I knew I wasn't going to last very long."

Aspirin picked up the phone and put it back down. Whom would he call?

"You need to rest. And then you can try again."

"No, I can't. I lost. I did my best, but I lost, Alexey. I don't have any more strings."

"So what," he asked hesitantly, "now you will be simply—my daughter? Right?"

She closed her eyes.

"I am sorry. There is no point for me in living. I won't be anyone anymore."

He held her shoulders.

"Listen to me. I don't care. You *are* my daughter, the rest does not matter. Your stepfather will never hurt you again, and your crazy mother—"

The doorbell rang.

"I am going to throw her down the stairs," Aspirin said through gritted teeth. "And let her complain as much as she wants to whomever she wants."

He took a few wide, decisive steps toward the hallway and threw the door open, not bothering to check the spyhole.

"Good evening, Alexey Igorevich."

A whoosh of cold air. An icy, wintry chill. Aspirin froze on the spot, his mouth opened, staring into the corkscrew eyes, greenish-blue, serene and merciless.

Aspirin's Adam's apple jerked up and down; he lowered his gaze. His guest was barefoot, camouflage pants rolled up, long narrow feet clean and white, as if made of alabaster.

"I am here for Alyona."

"I didn't invite you," Aspirin said hoarsely, not moving.

The guest smiled thinly.

"Well, Alexey Igorevich, sometimes I show up without an invitation."

He stepped over the threshold. Aspirin took a step back. His knees weakened.

Not a single sound came from the living room.

"Wait," Aspirin said quickly. "One minute."

The guest turned his head.

"Yes?"

"I need to speak with you." Aspirin forced the words out. "Let's go into the kitchen, I have, um, some wonderful brandy . . ."

The guest smiled wider and shook his head.

"No, Alexey Igorevich. Not today."

He entered the living room.

Aspirin ran after him, moving along the walls of the living room, nearly toppling a case of CDs in the process, and finally inserting himself between Alyona and the guest.

"Hey there, little one," the barefoot man said, paying Aspirin no attention.

Slowly, Alyona opened her eyes, and, to Aspirin's horror and surprise, suddenly smiled.

"You came."

"But of course."

"You didn't desert me."

"Of course not."

"You were right," Alyona lowered her eyelashes. "I failed. I couldn't do it."

A pause hung in the air. Aspirin tensed up like a goalie. He expected the barefoot man to try to approach Alyona, and he wasn't sure he would be brave enough to try to stop him, but still waited, trying to control his shaking knees.

The barefoot man said something then, a short, sonorous sentence.

Alyona shuddered and opened her eyes.

"What did you say?"

The guest repeated his sentence. He paused and said it again, and this time Aspirin understood:

"You did it. He heard you. He regained consciousness. He remembered who he was."

It was very quiet. Alyona took a deep breath, and her pale greenish cheeks suddenly blushed, as if someone splashed her with pink paint.

"It is his choice," the barefoot man said softly.

Alyona exhaled and shook her head.

"I am tired."

"I know. Let's go."

The man reached in his pocket and pulled out a long leather case. When he opened it, white metal flashed in the light of the lamp, and Aspirin thought he saw shiny surgical instruments.

"No!" Aspirin took a step toward the sofa, shielding the girl.

"Alexey," Alyona said weakly.

"You cannot . . . get out!"

The guest took out two parts of a flute, put them together and inserted the mouthpiece.

"Give us a chance to talk," Alyona said quickly.

The barefoot man shrugged. "Whatever you want. Talk as much as you need."

"Alexey." Alyona's eyes were as clear as on the day they first met. "Give me Mishutka."

Aspirin hesitated, then reached for the bear, picked him up—so light and fluffy—and handed him to Alyona.

"You see," she said, pressing Mishutka to her chest. "I have to go."

"I don't see! Where?"

She smiled. "Home. I wanted to go back anyway. This is the right thing. This is good. Don't worry about me, I did everything I could. And I succeeded."

"Is your brother staying?" Aspirin said blankly.

She frowned this time. "Yes. See, the thing is . . . it turns out I didn't come to lead him out. At least, that wasn't the only reason. Remember I told you that my brother had forgotten who he was? He couldn't do anything at all."

"And now he remembers?"

"Yes."

"Then why didn't he come?"

Alyona smiled again.

"Because he . . . he is a creator. He needs to live in an imperfect world."

Aspirin shook his head trying to process her words. He looked back at the barefoot man. His guest sat on the arm of a chair, polishing the flute with a chamois cloth.

"Is *he* taking you?"

"Yes. But it's a good thing, don't worry!"

"What if I don't want him to? I don't want him to! Can I not let you go?"

Without interrupting his polishing, the barefoot man looked up at him with interest.

"There are some things that cannot be changed," Alyona said softly. "I am . . . I am guilty. I have hurt you. Forgive me."

The guest got up, gracefully and soundlessly, nearly reaching the ceiling with the top of his head.

"Alexey Igorevich, why don't you go into the kitchen for a bit?"

"No! What are you going to do with her?"

"I will take her back and then return for a few words. She will not be hurt—quite the opposite. I promise. Sound good?"

Aspirin looked at Alyona. The girl was smiling, but was also looking a little tense.

"No," Aspirin said feeling his lips tremble. "I don't trust you."

"Pity," the guest stepped forward, bending down to avoid hitting the chandelier. "It's a shame I didn't earn your trust."

"Alexey," Alyona whispered. "Forgive me, but I simply cannot stay."

She propped herself up on her elbow and reached for him with her right hand, the one that so recently had held a bow.

Her palm was so cold that Aspirin nearly burned himself.

"Thank you, Alexey. Thank you. Try to . . ."

She didn't finish. Her hand slid out of Aspirin's fingers like a thin, icy snake. Alyona leaned back on her pillow, clutching Mishutka to her chest.

"Go," the barefoot man ordered.

That word was a compulsion. Aspirin walked out backward.

The door to the living room closed behind him.


**Aspirin didn't remember how he got to the kitchen. He pulled a cork** out of a brandy bottle with his teeth and took a big gulp.

He found a loading clip in his secret drawer, pulled the gun from behind the shoe shelf, and loaded it.

The sounds of a flute came from the living room, barely audible, as if they were coming through a thick layer of foam. Chills ran down Aspirin's spine.

The flute went silent. Aspirin straightened up and took a step toward the living room.

The door opened before he could touch it. The barefoot man stepped back. Holding a gun by his side, Aspirin burst into the living room, knowing in advance what he was about to see.

He saw nothing.

A flattened pillow. A blanket. His piano. A case of CDs. There was no place to hide, but Alyona was not there. Not a trace.

Aspirin looked behind the sofa, threw off the blanket, then turned and pointed the gun.

The guest stood in front of him with his arms by his sides. The shaking barrel of the gun almost touched his high yellowish forehead.

"Where is she?" Aspirin asked hoarsely.

The barefoot man glanced at the gun.

"This gun was used in the year two thousand to kill a cop. Today . . . well, no, tomorrow, when it gets dark, tie a brick to it and drown it somewhere in some pond. Only an idiot would keep this kind of shit in his apartment."

Aspirin gritted his teeth. The gun kept dropping until the hand that held it hung weakly by Aspirin's side.

"Where is her birth certificate?" the barefoot man asked quietly.

Aspirin did not respond.

"In the desk drawer," the guest answered himself. "Bring it over."

Still holding the gun, Aspirin went to his office and pulled out a drawer. Alyona's birth certificate lay on top of the other papers, and when Aspirin picked it up, it suddenly broke in two.

Aspirin dropped the gun.

The laminated paper, hard, nearly invincible, melted in his hands. The two halves turned transparent, the sharp corners became smooth, dust flew. "Grima . . . ona . . . Alexe."

Aspirin stared at his hands. They were empty.

"You have nothing to worry about," the guest said behind his back. "Everyone who saw her will forget. By tomorrow no one will remember."

Aspirin turned:

"Her mother?"

"And her mother too, of course. Although the mother should be the least of your concerns. All the daily stuff, the concierges, neighbors, teachers . . . those stupid chasers of anomalies . . ."

"What about me?" Aspirin asked softly.

The barefoot man raised an eyebrow. Without answering, he turned and walked toward the door.

Aspirin remained standing, watching him leave.

The guest stopped, glancing over his shoulder:

"Alexey Igorevich, please come closer."

His knees buckling, Aspirin approached.

"You neighbor Irina is three months pregnant. It's yours. She hasn't told you yet—my apologies, but you were not ready to listen. She will have a girl. If you care."

Aspirin's jaw dropped.

"And don't be afraid of anything," his guest said softly. "There is nothing to be afraid of. Good-bye."

He turned and walked out, shutting the door behind him. Aspirin stood still for a while, pressing his forehead into the cool surface of the front door.

He left his apartment, walked one floor down, and rang her doorbell.

# ACKNOWLEDGMENTS

**From the Authors**

Our deepest thanks:

To our friends and family, for being with us always, in joy and in sorrow.

To Julia Meitov Hersey, our translator and friend; sometimes we think she understands our books better than we do ourselves.

To the magnificent Josh Getzler, who continues to pave our way into American literature.

To David Pomerico, a brilliant editor, a professional of the highest caliber, and his wonderful team at Harper Voyager, especially Vicky Leech, Natasha Bardon, and Mireya Chiriboga.

To our HSG family, especially Jonathan Cobb, Soumeya Roberts, Julia Kardon, and Ellen Goff.

To Marina Lvovna Lyubimova, for the gift of her friendship and for the authors' photo.

To the readers of our novel *Vita Nostra,* whose kind words and heartfelt reviews support and inspire us every day.

## From the Translator

I am immensely grateful:

To Marina and Sergey, for allowing me more artistic freedom with this book than a translator should have;

To David Pomerico, for his guidance and his contagious love for well-written stories;

To Josh Getzler, for being an advocate, a cheerleader, an advisor, a psychotherapist, a friend, and everything in between;

To Jon Cobb, for always having my back;

To Matthew Sciarappa, for the most brilliant book reviews and the best Twitter chats ever;

To Anatoly Belilovsky, Alex Shvartsman, and Max Hrabrov, for our regular brainstorming sessions, for their dazzling wit, and all their terrible puns;

To my friends, for all their support and for not getting mad when I cancel plans "because I have to finish this chapter";

To my family, for indulging my passion and not rolling their eyes too often;

To Malcolm, who reads every single word I write and makes me feel loved every single day.

# ABOUT THE AUTHORS

Marina and Sergey Dyachenko, a former actress and a former psychiatrist, are coauthors of thirty novels and numerous short stories and screenplays. They were born in Ukraine, lived in Russia, and now live in the United States. Their books have been translated into several foreign languages and awarded multiple literary and film prizes. Marina and Sergey are recipients of the Award for Best Authors (Eurocon 2005).

# ABOUT THE TRANSLATOR

Born in Moscow, Julia Meitov Hersey moved to Boston at the age of nineteen and has been straddling the two cultures ever since. She lives north of Boston with her husband, two daughters, and a hyperactive dog, juggling a full-time job and her beloved translation projects.